MASK
OF NIGHT

Other titles by the same author

Sleep of Death
Death of Kings
The Pale Companion
Alms for Oblivion

MASK
OF NIGHT

PHILIP GOODEN

CARROLL & GRAF PUBLISHERS
New York

WITHDRAWN

Carroll & Graf Publishers
An imprint of Avalon Publishing Group, Inc.
245 W. 17th Street
New York
NY 10011
www.carrollandgraf.com

First published in the UK by Constable,
an imprint of Constable & Robinson Ltd 2004

First Carroll & Graf edition 2004

ISBN 0-7867-1312-7

Printed and bound in the EU

3/04 DPL

Thou know'st the mask of night is on
my face

Romeo and Juliet, 2, ii

Wolf's Bane

To begin with, you put on the costume.

You put it on for practice, to see how it fits.

No, you put it on to see how you *fit – how you fit the part which you have chosen for yourself.*

But first you listen at the door. There is no sound from the passageway outside, no scurrying feet, no talk, no subdued laughter. It is that dead point in the middle of the afternoon when the morning's business is all done and the preparations for evening not yet started. Even so you take the precaution of sliding the bolt home. Then you walk towards the cedar chest in the corner. The lid creaks as you open it. The chest is full. You remove the sheets that are neatly piled on the top and reach for the garment that lies half-way down, in the place where you stowed it last night. You reach under the garment and raise it up like a body. With a touch of ceremony you carry it, cradled in your arms, towards the gate-leg table and deposit it there. Then you return to the chest and retrieve the other items and place those too on the table.

You listen at the door once more. Nothing, apart from the thudding of your own heart.

Quickly, before you can think better of it, you strip yourself of your outer clothes and throw them carelessly towards the open chest in the corner. Your senses must be heightened because, despite the sound of your heart, you hear the soft sigh your clothes give as they land on the rim of the chest.

1

You also hear someone laugh, a little low laugh, and for an instant you think that a person has been in the room with you all this time, watching you, spying on you. Your head spins with explanations and excuses before you understand that the laughter came out of your own mouth. Then you are standing in front of the table, looking down at the black coat.

The black coat goes straight over the undergarments. It's too thick to wear anything else. Even so, the coat feels heavier than you expected, heavier than when you were carrying it in your arms. The canvas material is waxed so as to repel water – and other liquid matter – and has a stiffness which makes you conscious of your limbs and produces a certain awkwardness in your movements at first. It is already warm inside here. In a few moments you will be hot. Hot but sheltered. As if you were wearing armour. Well, that's appropriate. After all, this black coat is intended to protect its possessor against a sudden attack, against the fatal stab or blow – although not from any human agency.

Then you proceed to don the headpiece. A mask, but rather more than a mask. A black hood made of coarse cotton, which encloses the head completely and which is secured with points and buttons at the back. The headpiece has a long bill-like protrusion, similar to a bird's beak. There are two eye-holes made of thick glass, but no aperture for the nostrils or the mouth. This does not matter since you will not be feeding. You will take shallow breaths. Because of the position of the eye-holes there is a black bar in the middle of your field of vision, but somehow the bar is not part of what you can see, it is closer than that, the bar seems to be inside your head. The glass windows distort the shape of objects out in the world. The legs of the table beside you, for example, seem to curve as they reach the floor. The window light is broken up into shafts and splinters of yellow. The eye-holes give you a sense of detachment from your surroundings.

You feel calmer than you did before. You have been pre-occupied with putting on your costume. The sound of breathing is magnified inside the hood and now the blood whispers in your ears. Is it trying to tell you something, your blood? The air within quickly grows thick, but it is easy enough to breathe because the rough weave of the cloth permits new air to penetrate from outside. Of course the wearer would not wish to receive too many vapours from the outside, you tell yourself. There is a hollow pouch at the end of the "beak" which could be filled with herbs – with bay and dried rosemary, perhaps – or with the dried rind of a lemon or a pomecitron. The cloth itself might be soaked in vinegar or fumigated with frankincense. Opinions differ on what is best.

Once you are wearing the coat and hood, you pull on the gloves. These are also black but made of a finer cotton than the hood. They allow the fingers to have free play. The gloves are slightly too large for your hands and you tug them down over the fingers, leaving soft little ridges of material at the base of each where finger joins finger.

There the costuming is almost complete. Only one item remains.

On the table lies a white cane fashioned from willow. You reach towards it. Your black hand, as it comes into view through the eyepieces, doesn't look like your hand but someone else's hand. Yet it is your own fingers which curl around the handle of the cane and lift it from the table-top. The willow cane, which you know to be thin, almost elegant, appears thicker through the distorting eye-cases. For a moment you stand with it poised in front of you like a sword or foil. Then you fall to, and poke and prod at the ground, imagining that there is a sick person down there. Or a dying person. Or a dead one. With a flourish of the cane you point out the signs, the infallible marks of his condition, to an imagined audience.

The cane is a badge of authority, it is a wand of office. This is why it is white, so that it stands out against the waxy blackness of your costume. But the cane serves a practical purpose too. It allows you to keep a distance between yourself and the dead.

It wasn't my idea to visit the old fool. It was Abel Glaze who was eager to meet Will Kemp. The first time the name of Kemp was mentioned in my friend's hearing his ears pricked up.

"Is that *the* Kemp, Nick? The clown? The fool? He of the nine days' wonder?"

"Yes, that's him, nine days Kemp."

"I saw him arrive in Norwich."

"I saw him depart from Whitechapel."

"In Norwich he looked as green and fresh as when he'd set off," said Abel Glaze. "Jigging and bobbing among the crowd he was, like a cork."

"He's a bobber all right."

"You don't like him?"

"Hardly know the man," I said.

"That's odd, because you sound as if you share the opinion of the rest of the Company when it comes to Kemp."

"Perhaps I do, if you'll tell me what that opinion is, Abel."

"Disapproval. A sort of schoolmaster's disapproval, frowning and pretending he never was a child."

I might be slightly irritated to be told what I thought but I had to admit that Abel Glaze was right. We players of the Chamberlain's Company did look down on the clown Will Kemp, even though Kemp had been one of the original shareholders. He'd quit the players, to be replaced by Robert Armin. Armin was a much more subtle fellow, a melancholy fool, a clown with feeling.

By contrast Kemp used to go in for the belly laughs. He swaggered and flailed around. When he jigged he stuck out his arse in the direction of the male groundlings or thrust his codpiece at the female ones. Nothing much wrong with that, but it didn't always fit the mood of the play he was appearing in. And he added bits of business of his own, usually dirty bits – and usually to the irritation of the writers, who don't like their words being upstaged by a clown's antics, to say nothing of the other players, who just don't like being upstaged. I hadn't seen any of this myself as it was shortly before I joined the Company but I'd heard all about Kemp's ribaldry. Finally the Chamberlain's had enough of him. Or he had enough of them. So Kemp sold his shares and jigged his way from London to Norwich in nine days. He picked up big crowds on his journey as well as forty shillings from the mayor of Norwich for his pains.

After my single glimpse of William Kemp starting off from Whitechapel on his Norwich jig, I'd come across the clown a couple of times in one of our Southwark ale-houses, either the Goat & Monkey or the Knight of the Carpet, I can't remember which. This was after his return and after the failure of one or two other enterprises. I believe he'd actually set out to jig his way across the Alps. But the inhabitants of those wild regions were not so well disposed towards his antics as the citizens of Ilford or Braintree and he returned a poorer man, as well as a wiser and more bitter one.

In the tavern the jovial, clowning mask slipped and a jeering manner was revealed, together with an unkind word to anyone who treated him to a pint. When Kemp discovered that I was a member of the Chamberlain's he enquired after the health of Master Shakerag and the Bumbag brothers. I must have looked slightly taken aback at this disrespect – it was during my early days with the Company and before I grew familiar with the robust style of the players' speech – because I saw a little smile creep across Kemp's face at my discomfiture. And then, casting his eyes up and down my form, he said something about new players these days not being old enough to wipe themselves.

So I wasn't altogether keen to renew my acquaintance with the clown. But Abel Glaze was very fresh to the Chamberlain's and still in awe of the legend of Will Kemp. And I'd heard that Kemp, mellowed now and perhaps lonely, was willing enough to receive members of his old Company. He was living on sufferance in the house of a widow somewhere either in Dow-gate or in Elbow Lane. She charged him no rent, perhaps because she was under some kind of obligation to him. Or perhaps she was simply glad to have the celebrated jig-maker under her roof. Though I think that Kemp was beyond jig-making by now, even if it was only three years since his Norwich excursion. Anyway one morning when Abel badgered me for the fiftieth time about calling on the clown, I agreed to take him to the widow's house there and then. I paused only to establish from Dick Burbage exactly where the widow lived.

Abel Glaze and I had first encountered each other on a road into Somerset. I was running away from a Southwark gaol, travelling under a false name, while he was going in the opposite direction, towards London. Or, to be more precise, he was going in no particular direction until he met me and decided to become a player. Meantime he was making a good living out of conning charitable persons in the guise of what's called a counterfeit crank. When he saw a likely mark or victim approaching, he would pretend to be afflicted by the falling-sickness and tumble down in the road, frothing at the mouth and displaying piteous bruises from his previous collisions with the Queen's highway. The froth was produced by a hastily mouthed sliver of soap while the bruising was mostly paint. All the instruments of Abel's trade were contained in a few little pots and pouches which he carried round with him. He travelled very light.

Now, there are plenty of coney-catchers who don't receive a quarter of the alms which young Glaze pocketed. How to explain his success? He had what is probably the most valuable attribute a con-man can possess – an innocent air, a wide-eyed what-am-I-doing-in-this-world? gaze. And this pose of unworldliness was helped by a high forehead which made him look like a contemplative man rather than a trickster.

Abel Glaze was adept at playing simpletons, bumpkins, clowns or theoreticians. He could even, and this was an odd thing, do a good turn as a murderer. When he arrived in

London he was almost immediately taken on by the Chamberlain's Company. William Shakespeare and Dick Burbage, who did most of the hiring, must have detected something actor-worthy in him. I'd said nothing to them about our earlier meeting or about Glaze's trickery, and I would continue to say nothing as long as he didn't reveal that he had encountered me when I was travelling under the name of William Topcourt. Each of us had a little secret that we possessed in relation to the other and this was one of the things that brought us together.

But more than that, we liked each other's company. He was cheerful and open – for all that he was a confidence-trickster turned actor – and besides he had a fund of good tales of his times on the road, when he was willing to talk about it. So I wasn't too unwilling that he insisted on my going with him to see Will Kemp. It was a good day for a walk. Although we were only in February, the day was bright and the sky was clear. Spring hovered in the air.

As we walked across to Dow-gate, which was where Burbage thought the widow's house was located, Abel kept up a stream of cheerful chatter which was welcome as an antidote to my rather dull spirits. Despite the good weather I couldn't help feeling gloomy. From the players' point of view there were reasons to be apprehensive in these early months of 1603.

Briefly, the inducements to gloom were, in mounting order of importance:

First, the approach of the Lent season. This is a thin time for men's stomachs and a thinner time for players' purses. Our performances are limited or often banned altogether.

Second, the imminent death of the Queen. This moment, like the end of a drawn-out play, had been long foreseen and now it was almost upon us. At best it couldn't be delayed by more than a few weeks. Queen Elizabeth was not our patron but she was a true friend to the theatre and to the Chamberlain's Company in particular. What effect her departure would have on us no one could say, but it was not likely to be helpful.

Third, the approach of something much more threatening than any lenten sanctions or than the death of one woman, however great. What was approaching was the pestilence. The plague. The numbers dying were still low, more rumour than certainty, and confined to the remote outskirts of the city, but any increase in the weekly mortality bills would be bad for the theatre business. It might be bad for all our lives as well.

Considering all these worries, Abel Glaze's good cheer was agreeable enough, although in another man it might have been tedious. Whatever he did he had the knack of making acceptable. Since it was already late in the morning and we were hungry, Abel bought some mince-pies from Mrs Holland's shop and we ate them on the way before we arrived at Dow-gate, which lies in a tumbledown corner of the river bank although there are grand houses and streets not too far away.

Dow-gate seemed to me an insalubrious sort of place to end up in. Glaze was fond of theatrical tit-bits and old stories so I told him that this was where a man called Robert Greene had died. Greene had once been famous as a writer – which is to say, not very famous at all – but he perished in obscurity shortly after he'd attacked a young playwright called William Shakespeare, calling the outsider from Warwickshire an upstart – an "upstart crow", in fact. People weren't much kinder about the memory of Robert Greene. Too much wine all during his life, too many pickled herrings near his end, was what they'd said about Greene. This broken-down area did not seem a propitious place for Will Kemp the clown or his prospects of recovery either, since Kemp too had fallen out with his old friends, the seniors in the Chamberlain's.

He might have crawled into this corner never to emerge again. To think that this man had once been one of the Globe shareholders!

We knocked at two or three wrong addresses before arriving at the widow's. She didn't seem surprised that we had come to call on Kemp, although I don't suppose he received many visitors. She jerked her thumb down a passage, at the same time yelling out his name. There was an answering croak. Directed by the sound, Abel and I entered a room that was even smaller than my own lodgings in Dead Man's Place.

It was dim in the room and at first I could make out nothing apart from a figure on a plain boarded bed. There was a patched, dirty window. As it turned out, even when my eyes got accustomed to the dimness, there wasn't much more to see than this: a bed with a man on it. Kemp was a little person, with a mobile face that was gnarled and dull brown like an old walnut. A ragged white beard fringed his chin.

"Master Kemp?"

"Who calls?"

"Nicholas Revill and Abel Glaze – of the Chamberlain's Company."

"The Chamberlain's?"

"Yes."

"Then you can shog off."

"We have come to pay our respects."

"You'll have to pay more than respects," he said without shifting his position, although he did turn his head to look at us. I didn't know what was the matter with him – whether it was age or sickness or melancholy or poverty. Perhaps all of these, though any single one might have been enough to account for his dull state.

"More than respects," he mumbled again.

So far this seemed standard for Kemp, or for what he had dwindled into. No sign of the supposed softening in his manner. I would have left it there and then but Abel was standing beside me and it was he, after all, who'd been so eager to see this relic. Now he spoke up.

"I am sorry to see fortune has played so many tricks on you, sir."

From any other man the comment might have been resented but Abel spoke with such feeling that Kemp did no more than grunt.

"I saw you dancing into Norwich. As if you had feathers at your heels."

"Better than having them in your head," said Kemp.

"And I saw you leave London," I said, throwing in my penny's-worth.

"I danced myself out of the world," said Kemp, raising himself slightly from the horizontal.

"I have brought you a pie."

Abel burrowed into his doublet and presented one of Mrs Holland's confections to the old clown with a little touch of ceremony, adding, "Seeing as it's dinner time."

Will Kemp sat up on his boarded bed and took the mince-pie without a word of thanks to Abel or a glance at the pie. He bit into it. I wondered when he'd last had anything to eat.

"That is to say," said Kemp, after he'd swallowed most of the pie, "you must understand that when I say I danced myself out of the world I mean I danced myself out of the Globe theatre."

"And I brought you this as well," said Abel Glaze. He produced from another part of his doublet a small corked bottle. I realized that he had come prepared with these little offerings. He was a walking pantry. He handed the bottle to Kemp, who was by now perched on the edge of his low bed. Kemp flipped the cork off with his thumb, threw back his head and glugged down about half the liquid. His Adam's apple jigged in his scrawny neck.

When he'd satisfied his immediate thirst he looked up at Glaze.

"Sack from Master Richardson," said Abel.

"Taylor's is better," said Kemp. "Go to Taylor's in Bright Street. Richardson puts lime in his sack."

Some phrase about beggars not being choosers entered my head but I said nothing. Let Will Kemp cling to his scraps of dignity since it didn't look as though he had much else left. Besides, it was plain that Abel Glaze had gone the right way to gain the old clown's attention and approval. Whatever the shortcomings of the white wine, the effects of it were almost immediately apparent. Kemp stayed sitting on the edge of his bed but he grew more upright while his face – always the most mobile aspect of a body that had once been constantly shifting – took on a new interest in his surroundings and his visitors.

"This is only temporary," he said, looking round at his mean quarters. "I have an opening with Worcester's Men."

I doubted this. I didn't think he would ever dance a jig or make a joke in public again. But Abel was more understanding.

"It would be a pity, sir, if the stage was deprived of your genius for too much longer."

"I am much of your mind, Master . . . what did you say your name was?"

"Abel Glaze."

"It is good to know that there are still one or two members of the Chamberlain's Company with their heads on straight and their organs of appreciation in working order."

"Dick Burbage sends his greetings," I said.

"Bumbag? How is the old bastard?" said Kemp, taking another swig from the bottle of sack.

As a matter of fact, this "bastard" comment was closer to Burbage's actual words before Abel and I set off for Dowgate, only he had been referring to Kemp.

"And Master Shakeshaft? And Thomas Pap and Master Sink-low and all the other turdy-faced rogues and fat old shareholders?"

"The Company is in working order, like their organs of appreciation," I said.

Picking up on the slight stiffness in my reply, Kemp turned his attention back to Abel. One admirer is enough in a little room. Kemp drained the last drop from the bottle and then held it upside down with a forlorn but somehow actor-ly expression. As if this was a cue, which perhaps it was, Abel produced yet another bottle from his doublet and handed it to Kemp, who swallowed some of the new gift, this time without commenting on the provenance of the sack.

"Sit down," said the clown then, "sit down."

There was nothing to sit down on but Abel promptly lowered himself to the filthy rush-covered floor and, after a moment, I followed suit.

"I can still cut a caper," said Kemp, waiting for us to be settled like an audience and then standing upright.

As we watched in that dingy room in Dow-gate, he raised his arms and kicked up his heels, thrust out his groin and waggled his hips. But he was a dancing shadow.

Pausing, he said, "There was a rhyme to go with all this . . . but I have forgot the words to it." Then he sat down once more on the bed and swigged at the second bottle.

"My buskins . . . you know where they are?" he said.

At first I thought Kemp had lost his shoes – or perhaps had sold them for food or drink – since he'd been dancing before us in his stockinged feet, but Abel was quicker than I to grasp his meaning.

"Your famous dancing shoes, sir?"

"They are in the Guild Hall at Norwich, that's where my buskins are, the ones I wore to dance from London in. There they stand displayed side by side, nailed to the wall."

"You are the master of morris-dancers," said Abel. "The king of capers."

The clown, accepting the compliment as no more than his due, looked at us as we sat leaning against the rough-cast wall, only a few feet from him. His eyes glittered in the gloom.

"There were the women. The nut-brown lass with the large

legs . . . I put bells on those legs so that she could join me in a jig. I fitted them myself, low down and *high up*."

His hands shaped themselves round thick imagined hams.

" . . . and then there was the other girl whose petticoats I tore off – accidentally, you understand, quite accidentally as I fetched a leap and landed on her skirts and broke her points and ties – so there she was stood only in her underthings and turning scarlet in front of the people . . . who were not displeased . . . and then . . . "

Will Kemp paused to see how we were taking in all this suggestive talk. Speaking for myself, I was interested enough and could have done with more of it, though not too much more. But, good showman that he still was, Kemp understood that he'd caught his audience's attention. He stopped reminiscing at this point and, reaching under his low bed, produced a small clutch of pamphlets.

"Here's the full story," he said. "*Kemp's Nine Days' Wonder*, it is called. Perhaps you have heard of it. My little tale is contained in here where you may read it at your leisure."

He held up a copy. On the front was the title as he'd announced it and a picture of our friend jigging away, with his drum player in the background. Abel reached forward to take hold of a pamphlet but Kemp held it out of his grasp.

"Only a shilling," he said. "Or seeing as you are members of my old Company, nine pence. You may purchase my account of this epic journey from London to Norwich for a mere nine pence. Or – further – seeing as you are young*ish* members of the Chamberlain's and therefore without the resources of those fat old shareholders, a mere six pence. Sixpence. My final offer."

I waited for Abel to reach for his purse but he mimed regret with upturned palms, a downturned mouth and raised shoulders. So, somewhat grudgingly, I took out sixpence of my own, half a day's pay. I handed it over to Kemp, who passed across his *Nine Days' Wonder* in exchange. As he leaned forward he exhaled fumes of sack in my direction. I carefully folded the booklet and put it inside my doublet. My sixpence vanished into Kemp's thin, veiny hand.

"Thank you, Master . . . Neville?"

"Revill, Nick Revill."

"Tell me truly how we are doing."

"We?"

"Oh, the Chamberlain's."

The mocking, almost sneering tone had gone. No more references to Bumbag or Shakeshaft. Just "we". In his heart, Kemp remained one of the Chamberlain's. He'd spent the best years of his life with the troupe. I felt what I had not experienced since entering this dingy room: a dash of pity.

Still squatting on Kemp's filthy floor, I shrugged. I could not give the impression that we were pining for Kemp's return – we weren't, and anyway Robert Armin was a clown who was better suited to our later, more subtle times – but I did not want to hurt the old man's feelings by saying that we had never looked back since his departure.

"You above all are familiar with the playhouse, Master Kemp. Even at the best of times our fortunes hang by a pin," I said, voicing some of the thoughts that had occurred to me on the way over to Dow-gate. "And Lent is coming."

Perhaps I sounded more mournful than I intended because Kemp said, "You have a powerful patron in Lord Hunsdon . . . "

"The Lord Chamberlain is sick," I said.

" . . . and an ally in the Queen?"

"She is worse than sick as you must know. All London knows it."

"All London may be sick soon enough," said Kemp. "I have heard the stories. This is just the beginning."

I guessed that he was talking about the plague. Or perhaps it was merely an old man's belief that, since he was sinking, everything else must surely be sinking with him.

"But we shall survive," I said.

"No doubt you will," said Kemp, lying back once more on his thin bed. The momentary life he'd shown when cutting a caper or trying to sell us his little pamphlet had disappeared again.

The audience was obviously at an end. I clambered to my feet. Abel Glaze, who'd stayed quiet during these last exchanges, got up too. Then he did a strange thing – a thing which I should not have thought of doing or been capable of doing. He leaned forward and kissed Will Kemp as he was stretched out on his boarded bed, kissed his wrinkled brown brow. Kemp said nothing more but when we quit the room I looked back and saw the clown's eyes brimming, like an overfilled cup. The water in them reflected the small quantity of light coming through the bandaged window.

When we were safely outside in the street I was about to speak but, glancing at Abel's preoccupied expression, thought better of it. We said nothing for a long time but walked back towards Southwark, crossing the bridge rather than taking a ferry and then walking straight on down Long Lane. The afternoon remained clear. The sun shone from a blue sky. Even the dust in the road had a fresh spring sheen to it. Eventually, as we turned the corner by St George's church, I remarked to Abel, "Well, they always say that tears lie under the clown's paint."

"That's what they say, is it?" said Abel. "Next you'll be telling me that comedy and tragedy are the opposite sides of the same coin."

This sharpness was unusual, for Abel. Plainly something in Kemp's predicament had struck a chord with him. I would catch him in a more cheerful mood and ask him about it later. Normally I would have turned off at this point towards my own lodgings but instead I accompanied Abel in the direction of his. Fellowship perhaps. Also it was a pleasant afternoon, and I wanted to walk off the effects of Kemp's dim room. But then both our attentions were diverted. Or rather everything to do with Kemp – everything to do with every-thing (except for one subject) – was swept away.

Abel lived near the edge of Southwark, where town meets open country in a raggedy fringe. I don't think it was because he could not afford better lodgings closer to the Globe play-house ("better" is a relative term south of the river, you understand). In fact I'm pretty certain he could have afforded them. He'd hinted at a store of cash salted away somewhere, the fruits of his coney-catching days around the country. He might have abandoned his old dishonest ways but he still retained some of the tools of his trade – salves and other preparations – in a large wallet which he carried everywhere with him, as if at any moment he might set out on the open road once more. For there was still something of the open road about Abel. That may be the reason why he liked to be within sight and smell of the trees and fields, liked to keep a gap between himself and the worst stinks and vapours of the town. Anyway he was accommodated in Kentish Street, so called because once it had untangled itself from the city's vicious grip it ran off in the direction of that county as fast as its muddy heels could carry it.

Although there was plenty of space in this part of town, the houses tended to huddle together as if for protection from some malign force. These houses were crammed with mean, dirty rooms which made my own lodgings in Dead Man's Place appear generous. The individuals inside these rooms were frequently mean and dirty too. If you're looking for real spaciousness – for grand chambers and fine gardens – then it is the mansions and palaces in the heart of our city that you must visit.

When the plague attacks it often strikes at London's dirty skirts first, although, if unchecked, it may eventually creep its way into those same grand chambers and fine gardens. But the fringes and skirts of London are the earliest to fall. There'd already been rumours of cases, as Will Kemp had suggested, but nothing very definite. Now, however, the clown's predictions and forebodings took shape before our very eyes.

We hadn't yet reached Abel's lodging-house when we came across a row of squat single-storey dwellings. A group of official looking people was gathered before a single doorway in the middle of the row. Beyond them, and at a distance of a few yards on the opposite side of the street, stood a small, gawping crowd. Men, women and children, a couple of dozen in all. Some babies cradled at the breast. Naturally we joined the crowd. It would have been difficult to squeeze past them. No one was saying anything. Their eyes were aimed at the group in front of the door. I identified a constable and a beadle by their dress and badges. There was also a short man who appeared to be in charge of the scene, as well as a pair of shrouded, hag-like females. I knew what was up. So did the rest of the crowd. I felt goose-flesh break out over my body, and yet I would not, could not, have moved away. I suppose that everybody in the crowd — men and women and those children who were old enough to understand what was happening – must have been in the same frozen state.

A dispute was in progress by the door. Every word was audible. The short man was saying to the beadle, "And I tell you, Master Arnet, that this will *not* do. This – this is too quickly defaced or removed altogether. Like this."

So saying, he ripped down a paper bill from where it had been pinned to the door. LORD HAVE MERCY UPON US was printed on it in big black type (and the largest word by far was LORD), together with some other prayers and injunctions in smaller lettering. The short man held out the bill, crumpled and torn, in front of the beadle's evasive gaze.

I had the impression that the speaker intended his words to be heard not just by the beadle and the constable but by the rest of us. The beadle shifted uncomfortably and muttered something about "orders".

"I am giving you fresh orders, Arnet," said the small man, whom I took to be a councillor or alderman. Judging from his high-handed manner, which was in inverse proportion to his inches, he probably came from across the river. A fine white horse was tethered to a tree at the London-ward end of the row of hovels. Presumably it belonged to this important gent. He continued to address the beadle: "You are to return here with red paint and a brush and you are to set the mark upon this door. It is to be the prescribed fourteen inches in length. You will do it in oil so that it may not be easily rubbed off. These are the new orders from the Council."

"Well, Master Farnaby . . . " said the beadle but his voice tailed off as the other man stared at him. Arnet gazed across the road at the little crowd, as if he expected some help from that quarter. I guessed that the beadle was local, drawn from the parish like the constable.

"While you are obtaining the red paint," continued the alderman called Farnaby, "and the brush and a measure – remember that the mark is to be fourteen inches in length, that is prescribed – while you are obtaining the necessary items, this gentleman remains here to secure the premises. You understand?"

He was referring to the constable. The constable nodded energetically. The alderman turned back to the beadle.

"Well, what are you waiting for, man? Go get your brush, your paint, your measure."

The beadle scuttered off up the street. As Farnaby was issuing these instructions in a not-to-be-controverted tone, a flickering movement caught my eye. To one side of the doorway there was a low ragged window, more of a hole than a proper opening, covered with cloth sacking. Someone was looking out at the street through a gap between the sacking and the wall. All I could see was the white of a single eye. I find it hard to describe the thrill – of horror, of terror, somehow mixed up with fellow feeling – which shot through me at the sight of that single eye. It must have belonged to a child or to an adult who was crouching down low so as to see out into the street. The house was occupied!

I don't know why I should have been shocked at this. The dwelling, more of a hovel than a house, was much likelier to be full than empty. And this could explain why the beadle had put up a bill which was no more than a flimsy sheet of paper. It might have been that Arnet had been bribed by the occupants of the house to keep quiet about the infection, or that he was hoping to be bribed. Sticking up a bit of paper to warn of the plague was the equivalent of doing nothing since, as the alderman had demonstrated, it was easily torn down. Or it might have been that the beadle was moved to pity for the inhabitants of the hovel. With the painting of an indelible red cross on their door, and other restrictions, they were being condemned to a prison of sickness from which none could expect to emerge alive.

As if to confirm that the place was occupied, Alderman Farnaby turned to the constable and, motioning with his head in the direction of the door, said, "Their name?"

"Turnbull, sir."

"Number?" Then, realizing that he hadn't been understood, "How many Turnbulls altogether?"

The constable counted off on his fingers.

"Five, six . . . no . . . seven. And then there is a person called Watkins."

"There are eight Turnbulls," said a woman standing on the far side of Abel Glaze. She was clutching a small boy by the hand.

Farnaby looked across the street to the speaker.

"She had another at Candlemas."

"It perished," said someone else, a man this time.

"That was two doors away," said the woman.

"No matter where it was or what the baby did," said Farnaby. "In the matter of this dwelling now, constable: secure the door in the prescribed form with padlocks. After forty days you may remove the locks. All this to be at the charge of the parish."

I looked at the slit between sacking and wall. No sign of

an eye. But there were surely ears pricked up inside that dark room, listening to their fate. Now Alderman Farnaby directed his fire at the pair of hag-like women who were standing to one side, cowled and expectant.

"I don't have to tell you your duties, do I?"

"We know them," a voice came quavering from one of the scarfed heads.

"Are you honest and discreet?"

"We are, sir," said the second scarfed head.

"Vigilant and skilful?"

"Now, sir," said the first, "I should say we are that too, though we should be the last to claim it – but if you were to ask these good neighbours standing here – "

Alderman Farnaby wasn't interested in the old woman's meanderings and cut her off with a wave of his hand. He took one last look at the constable and the old women before sweeping his eyes across the group on the other side of the street. He paused as he glimpsed Abel and me. Perhaps we appeared out of place among the usual inhabitants of Kentish Street. His look seemed to say to all of us, "You've had your entertainment."

What he actually said was, "The keeper has just called you 'good neighbours' . . . well, you will show yourselves good neighbours to these unfortunate Turnbulls and, er, the person called Watkins in the following manner. This house remains undisturbed for the prescribed forty days. These two honest and discreet women will act as nurse-keepers. There is to be no intercourse with the occupants except through them. A warder will be appointed at the charge of the parish to ensure that no one leaves this place. The mark on the door will not be touched. Anyone who tries to wipe the mark off the door, or who enters the house, or who aids the unfortunate occupants to depart before the end of forty days will find himself – or herself – clapped into the stocks or the House of Correction."

Then, without waiting to see the effect of his words, he strode off, unhitched the white palfrey and mounted it. He turned the horse's head towards London and rode off at an even pace.

"A fig for you too, Farnaby," said the woman who'd given the number of occupants in the Turnbull household as eight. The words were almost shouted, and accompanied with the appropriate thumb-through-fingers gesture, although not until the alderman was at a safe distance. The small crowd nodded or murmured approval. One or two laughed. Seeing this, the little boy whose hand she was holding glanced up at her and laughed too.

"Now, now," said the constable, no doubt feeling the pull of his office, "the gentleman is doing no more than what is prescribed."

"The bugger should be prescribed himself," said the woman. "Him and his prescribes. Laying down the law."

"He's not the only one who likes doing that," said one of the two crones who'd been appointed nurse-keepers. She crossed the street to stand in front of the woman with the boy. The crone was less ancient that I'd taken her for at first. The quaver had gone from her voice. I wondered whether she'd assumed an older, more feeble manner for the benefit of the alderman.

"We all know what you're going to get out of it, Mistress Johnson," said the woman with the child. "You and your sister. Alderman Farnaby should've asked me. I'd've told him. You know why you are called keepers? Because whatever you get your griping paws on, you'll never let go of. I'd rather have rats at my linen or moths in my cupboard than let *you* inside my house."

There was a stir in the crowd. The plight of the unfortunate Turnbulls – as well as the person called Watkins – in the plague-house had been forgotten (not that anyone had shown much concern about them in the first place). The crone's sister now crossed the street to face their accuser who, sensing that more was expected from her, went on with vigour. The boy glanced at his mother with a confused expression.

21

"And nurse, call yourself a nurse? A nurse with a pillow to smother the head or fingers to pinch shut the nostrils, that's your kind of nursing."

It's one thing to accuse these crones of being light-fingered with the household goods of dying people, but it's quite another to accuse them of helping the dying on their way. I wondered if the occupants of the house were listening. As if the plague wasn't enough to contend with, they had these harpies on their doorstep as well!

I think that a fight might have broken out among the women – and was about to indicate to Abel Glaze that we should quit the scene – when Arnet the beadle returned bearing a pot and brush. Everyone's attention was distracted by the welcome prospect of watching a man apply red paint to a piece of wood. At the same moment the constable, seeing that the danger of a scrap had diminished, stepped between the two quarrelling women.

As Abel and I walked away the crowd regrouped in front of the plague-house, doubtless ready to give conflicting advice on where the cross should be postioned on the Turnbulls' door. I hoped that Arnet had returned with a measure. I wouldn't like to be in his shoes if Farnaby found that he was a couple of inches out in his dimensions.

I said as much to Abel.

"The alderman will discover that the plague is not so easily prescribed as a cross on a door," said my friend.

"Or kept in by padlocks."

"But they must do something," he said.

"There is nothing to be done by them or by anyone else," I said. "If the plague is set on causing havoc then there is nothing to be done."

"Why so hopeless, Nick?"

It wasn't just my comment, although what I said was true enough – how could one fight against the plague? It was rather the note of resignation in my voice. I'd never told Abel Glaze the story of how the plague came to my Somerset village of Miching while I was absent, of how it had struck down many of those I knew best, including my father the parson and my mother his wife. Of how I had returned to Miching one fine spring morning to see bodies being forked higgledy-piggledy into a burial pit. Of how I had witnessed all this, as well as the red cross on my parents' door, and of how I had run from the place where I was born until I was exhausted and could run no further.

I'd never told Abel any of this but I told him now as we were walking towards his lodgings further down Kentish Street.

He said nothing for a moment after I'd finished, then, "You ran away all those years ago. But you would not run now?"

He waved his arm around. He meant, run from this part of Southwark, perhaps from London itself.

"What would be the point?" I said.

"To save one's life. To get away from King Pest."

"Would you run?"

"This is my first glimpse of the thing," he said, not answering my question, as I hadn't really answered his. "Although of course I am familiar with the signs and symptoms of the plague. I studied diseases when I was on the road since being sick was a good living for me."

"When I came to this city," I said, "I grew to realize that the *thing* is always with us, grumbling away in the background, sometimes declining but never dying out altogether. People here seem hardened to it somehow. They believe that if you're going to catch it, well then, you're going to catch it. It's all in the stars. You saw that group outside the house of those unfortunates. You saw how they were . . . I don't know . . . "

"Stirred up? Excited?"

"Yes, for all that they were so quiet at first . . . yes, excited . . . and if I examine my own reactions I was a little excited too."

"I felt the same in the wars, Nick. There was death all around us and the risk of it for me was the same as for everyone else but I too was stirred up."

23

Abel Glaze had served as a young boy in the Netherlands campaign against the Spaniards in the '80s. He'd taken part in the battle of Zutphen in which Sir Philip Sidney had died so gallantly. Abel was lucky to have come off unscathed but, when he grew tired of pretending to have the falling-sickness, he could still show off a convincing limp and some good wounds (created with unslaked lime and a smear of iron rust). He regarded his "wounds" as a tax on those who'd stayed comfortably in their beds while English soldiers and sailors were fighting abroad, just as his "sickness" was a test of people's charity, an opportunity for them to show benevolence. He'd put such sophistry behind him though. Those days were over for he was an honest actor now.

It's an odd fact that, for all the horror of the discovery of the tainted house, there was also this excitement. And this despite the fact that I had the most personal reasons to detest the plague, quite apart from any threat it represented to the skin, blood and bones of Nicholas Revill. Still, it was so. I merely report what I felt and what Abel, by his own account, felt also.

When, Abel and I having parted, I retraced my steps towards central Southwark and my own lodgings in Dead Man's Place, I observed that the Turnbulls' door was marked by a neatly painted red cross. Arnet the beadle had done his job. A diminutive warder was standing on duty, clutching at a bill or halberd which was almost twice his height. When he saw me drawing near he struggled to put on a fierce expression which vanished when he realized I wasn't going to stop and gawp at the door, unlike the three or four idlers who were still hanging about.

There was no sign of the hag-like women. Presumably they were inside the sick-house tending to their charges. That is, seeing what pickings were to be had – pretty thin round these parts, I imagined – or plotting how to hasten the passage of the victims from sick-bed to grave. (Unless, of course, Mistress Johnson and her sister were genuinely honest women, ones who would look after the dying with care and compassion.) It's another odd fact, by the way, that these old nurse-keepers rarely contract the disease themselves. Which only goes to show that if you're going to catch it, then you're going to catch it. And if not, not. It's in the stars.

These last few hours had driven from my mind the visit to Will Kemp and I did not remember the melancholy clown until, that night, I retrieved from my doublet his *Nine Days' Wonder*. It was the account of his jig from London to Norwich. I tucked it back into my doublet to read on some later occasion, perhaps between rehearsals.

During the next couple of weeks the numbers of reported plague victims and infected dwellings increased, although only slowly. This was no longer mere gossip and rumour, however, but fact. The authorities had stepped in, as Abel and I had seen in the case of the officious Alderman Farnaby. And when the authorities put in an appearance, then bills, orders and constraints cannot be far behind.

All of this had its effect on the Chamberlain's Company and the Globe playhouse sooner than I expected. Our shareholders, being prudent men and sensing the way things were going, decided to make a virtue of necessity. We would leave London straightaway, without waiting for the inevitable notice from the Privy Council. The Council would order the restraint of stage plays either on account of Lent or on account of the plague or both. However, while you can get round some of the lenten laws, there's no way you can evade the plague. For one thing, your audiences tend to drop away rather quickly. I hadn't experienced this for myself but there were still enough veterans of the last bad outbreaks in '92 and '93 for the memory to be kept fresh among the players.

It was our good fortune that we had playing business to perform away from London. No, that's wrong, it wasn't our "good fortune" but the result of the prudence and foresight of our shareholders. The shareholders, that same band of middle-aged men whom Kemp the jig-maker had been so rude about. Will Shakeshaft and Dick Bumbag, Thomas Pap and Richard Sink-low and the others. These were the ones who – in addition to acting, dancing, singing, directing, writing, book-keeping and head-counting – kept the Globe spinning round on its axis.

Of course it wasn't such a simple matter to quit London. Most of my fellow players had wives and children. The families might be used enough to their men being absent on tour. It happens once or twice a year. But there's a difference between leaving your loved ones when the worst they've got to face is the stink of a London summer and leaving them when the plague is rampaging round the city's outskirts. Then it looks a bit like running away. Two or three of the husbands elected to stay behind, and one or two of the bachelors remained in London for reasons of their own. We would be a slightly reduced group, but still travelling in larger numbers than on the usual summer tour.

Speaking for myself, I didn't mind the appearance of running away. I had no wife and children, no one (more or less) to leave behind, no one whose good opinion I had to be concerned about. And, although the first glimpse of what Abel Glaze had termed King Pest in the house in Kentish Street had been exciting in its way, that sensation was quickly succeeded by a dull, distant fear as the death toll started to climb in different parts of London. So, when it was an-nounced that we were going on tour, I was glad enough.

We didn't know exactly what pieces we were due to to play, although various titles were thrown about. The final decisions were left in the hands of the seniors, to be sorted out on arrival. Anyway, requirements might be changed by the circumstances at our destination. So we would travel with some all-purpose costumes (from king to peasant), a few effects and an assortment of play scripts, jolted together in the property wagon and all pulled along by our trusty old horse, known as Flem and an older member of the Company than many of us players.

Nor did we know when we would return to London. All being well – that is, if the numbers dying of the plague didn't grow unmanageably – we ought to be back in town after the end of Lent. But there was no certainty to this. Instead there was an odd feeling among the members of the Company that we were destined for a long campaign, like an army marching into alien territory.

I made arrangements with my landlord Samuel Benwell to keep my room in Dead Man's Place available, agreeing unwillingly to reimburse him at the half-rate of sixpence a week, the first four instalments to be paid in advance. If I hadn't come back by the beginning of June he was at liberty to lease my room. I was aware however that, if the pestilence really took hold of the city, Benwell would have difficulty in letting my mouldy room to anyone, and so I should most likely be able to bargain him down and recoup some of my losses.

Small beer perhaps, all these calculations, but there was a kind of comfort during such difficult times in looking three months ahead and making arrangements for one's life as if everything was going to continue as usual. Strange how, as we walk towards the mouth of hell, we can divert ourselves with thoughts of the next meal or of saving a few pennies.

Apart from my landlord there was only one other person to whom I had to say farewell.

The previous autumn I'd met Richard Milford's young widow, Lucy. She was not a widow when we first met but a married woman. Shortly afterwards, however, her husband was murdered and for a period I was suspected of being the murderer and clapped up in gaol. Richard Milford was a playwright, an ambitious one who'd written for our Company several times. He was always in quest of success but before he'd had a proper chance to show himself, he'd been cut down on his own doorstep. I had suffered a loss of my own at about the same time when my precious Nell was brutally murdered by the same hand that disposed of Richard Milford. I suffered nightmares from that death, and from the other events which followed, suffered them for months afterwards. Inevitably, the two of us, widow and player, ran parallel in our grief. Then, not so inevitably, we turned towards each other for consolation.

So Lucy Milford and I had enjoyed a warm winter. She continued to wear her widow's weeds of course, and there were still many occasions when the memory of Nell would make me pause during the day, and more painful times when the image of my friend would slip unbidden into my head at night. But what they say about life going on is right enough in its way . . . although you must be careful about how you acknowledge this truth, in case people should think you indifferent or hard-hearted.

But everyone is entitled to consolation, and I don't think I was anything more than this to Lucy, consolation and comfort. I offered her these things together with a warm body on cold nights. She was shy, inward and secretive, although less so than at our first meetings. She did not see a future husband in me, nor did I discover a wife in her. I don't think I was looking for one, while she most likely had her sights set on someone a bit more elevated than a common player.

The day before the Chamberlain's departure, I went to say good-bye to her in her lodgings in Thames Street, an address which was average for north London but several cuts above most places south of the river. We talked for a time of the Chamberlain's Company and of where we were travelling to and what plays we were likely to stage there. We talked a little about her husband, and his last play, *The World's Diseas'd*, posthumously performed. Ironically it had been his greatest success, partly because of the quality of the piece (William Shakespeare had made some small changes to the text, unknown to most) but more because the audiences had been drawn to the play out of curiosity. It was a drama of revenge from a man whose bloody death might have been created by his own pen.

As I went to kiss her farewell – neither of us was in the mood for anything more celebratory – Lucy began to weep and I was touched until she told me that she was weeping not for herself or even for the both of us, but weeping on account of London.

"What is it, Lucy?"

I had a pretty good idea of what was troubling her. We had not mentioned the outbreak of the disease nor had I described the scene which Abel and I witnessed in Kentish Street. But the subject of plague could not be far from the mind of every Londoner.

Lucy's were not ordinary fears, however. Richard Milford's widow possessed the gift of second sight (even if this is more of a curse than a blessing in my view). In her case, the visions were fitful and fragmentary. She had had intimations of her husband's death, for example. Afterwards she had been certain that I was not guilty of his murder although she could not say who had committed the crime.

Now she said, "I can see things darkly. When I was walking by St Peter's yesterday I glimpsed an empty street with grass growing in it and a riderless horse, its nostrils stuffed with rue. I heard a low moan coming from the houses on either side. Yet the street was full of people going about their business, and they were laughing and chattering as if they could not see what I saw."

"Perhaps they were more comfortable like that," I said.

"They were as good as ghosts."

I grew cold. I knew better than to try to contradict her visions. Instead I said, "You must get out of London too."

"I'm not concerned for myself," she said, and I believed her. "I have cousins in Bromsgrove and an uncle in Middlesex. I will find shelter with one of them when the time comes."

"The time may not come," I said.

"Then why is the Chamberlain's Company leaving London?" she said, unarguably.

"Well, we shall survive," I said, falling back on the words I'd used to Will Kemp in Dow-gate. I struggled to keep any note of questioning out of my voice. Probably like the citizens near St Peter's, I did not want to know whether I was going to survive – or rather, if I wasn't, I did not want to know that I was imminently destined to die. Nor did I wish Lucy to come out with some prevision of her own death.

"We shall survive," I repeated.

"Oh, Nicholas, I am not thinking of myself or even of you."

"Nor was I. I meant that whatever happens here, this is a great city. Almost a complete world. It cannot come to an end altogether."

"Why not?" she said.

I had no answer to this. Like so much about Lucy, the remark was unsettling. I attempted to be cheerful.

"Why, in a few months' time you'll be attending the Globe playhouse and laughing at our clowns and sighing with our lovers once more. And so will our fellow Londoners, in droves."

"I hope so," she said doubtfully.

"Well then."

We kissed more thoughtfully and exchanged a few sweet nothings for form's sake.

Later as I made my way back towards the river, I was unable to shake off the sadness of my departure from the widow. This melancholy might be pleasant enough – parting is such sweet sorrow, as WS has someone say in one of his plays. But neither could I rid myself of my mistress's fears. I deliberately avoided the area of the city by St Peter's, in case I should be overcome by the same vision of grassy streets and horses without riders.

No vision was necessary, however, to make me feel uncomfortable. I would have welcomed anywhere some of the laughing, chattering folk whom Lucy had glimpsed the day before. But in every place I looked I seemed to see a gloomy confirmation of her imaginings of decay and emptiness. Not in precise terms but in the general feel of the town.

It was late afternoon and the sky was overcast. The promise of spring which had been hovering in the air for the last few days was withdrawn. Instead there was a dead, spiritless chill which quickened the stride of the few passers-by in the street and kept their shoulders hunched and their collars turned up.

I was walking behind a couple of tripe-women wheeling a tub of filth and offal on a creaky hand-cart. They alone did not seem to feel the cold, but grasped the cart handles and steadied the tub with great chapped hands. These women were most likely heading towards the Thames to deposit their cargo of discarded paunches and entrails. But they did not bother about the slimy red water and the bits of gut which slopped out of the tub and deposited a trail down the street or, no doubt, down the front of their bibs. I wondered whether at this rate there would be any rubbish left for them to throw into our mighty watercourse.

We came to a more open section of the roadway and I watched a kite glide past overhead and then slip abruptly sideways, seeming to lose its balance and fall from the air as it scooped up a bloody gobbet in its talons before soaring skywards again. Something about the bird – the skeletal tips of its great wings, its indifference to human presence – made me shiver.

I didn't know why the tripe-women were bothering to go as far as the Thames anyway since, as I passed over the Fleet Bridge, I looked down and noticed that the tributary contained more than its usual quota of animal corpses, dogs mostly. If Alderman Farnaby was looking for a place to enforce the city regulations he might begin here by cleaning up this filthy stream.

So it was in this flat, apprehensive mood that I returned to my lodgings. If there was any cause of cheerfulness it was that we were leaving this place the next morning. I did not realize that we were travelling towards greater dangers than those that were stirring in London. Why should I have done? I am not like Lucy Milford, able to glimpse the future in fragments.

Devil's Herb

This is by way of an experiment.

It is a test, like trying on the costume to see how it fits.

But now you are going on to the next stage.

You have already had a taste of success with the death of the dog. A little rat-like creature which annoyed you by yapping round your feet one day, although you had never been bothered with it before. It eagerly took the meat tainted with the preparation. Poor dog! The mixture was, from one point of view, too effective, for within moments the small thing had twitched its last. You wrapped the tiny body in a strip of cloth and waited until after dark before throwing it on to a neighbouring midden. A lesser dose would probably have been enough, would have given a clearer idea of the quantities and proportions required. A human being, now, would require – how much? – twenty times as much? Even a sick human being, even an old human being?

It happens that there is a sick old woman living nearby. Dying nearby. Old mother Morrison. You've never liked her. Used, in fact, to fear and hate her. Still hate and fear her – although now the hate comes first.

You cannot forget how she hit you with a stick when she caught you in her orchard, stealing the fruit. The other children were too quick for her and ran away. You stumbled over an apple-tree root, and she snatched you up and dragged you indoors. There she broke a stick across your buttocks and the back of your legs, cursing all the time. Your screams drowned her curses. She seemed old even then, all those many years ago, with her skin like a withered apple and her hands hooked like claws, grasping that stick. She had some strength in those claws! She haunted you while you were asleep, haunted you for years afterwards so that you feared her for a witch even if others said that she was merely a yeoman's wife. There was a broom in the corner of the room so you knew that she was witch, though.

Sometimes she visits you in dreams even now, dreams in which you are still little and helpless while she, old as she is, retains all her strength. When you heard that she had fallen sick, you were glad. Then you realized how her sickness might be put to some purpose.

You have intercepted some sweetmeats, added a contribution of your own and sent them on their way to her, taking care (and care is most important from this moment forward in all your dealings!) that it should appear as though the sweetmeats come from someone else. From time to time enquiry is made as to mother Morrison's welfare, and you are gratified to hear that she is rather worse. It is time she died anyway.

However, reports are not enough – and you cannot make too many enquiries about a poor old woman without rousing suspicion. It is necessary that you ascertain how matters stand for yourself.

Accordingly you have spied on the house where she lives (and is dying) to discover those periods of the day when it is unattended, when the men, her sons and grandsons, have gone out to the fields. It is spring. There is much to be done in the fields. The women of the house will have gone to market, it being a Thursday morning. You know that there is an old servant about but she is nearly as ancient as her mistress, and herself stooped and half-blind.

It is still early in the day when you step out from the shelter of the abandoned hovel where you have been changing into your costume. In contrast to your purposes, the day is calm, clear, bright. You have become accustomed to the distorted view through the eyepieces and find it easy enough to move at some speed. For an instant you wonder what kind of figure you cut as you glide through the trees and across the grass, still muddy and scrubby from the winter. Anyone looking from a distance would surely be struck dumb to see a shape clad in a great black coat, carrying a white cane and sur-mounted by a headpiece with a beak. They might believe that the devil himself was walking abroad on this fine spring morning in the country.

But you will not be seen, you are as good as invisible. The costume confers invisibility.

As you near the house of the old woman your heart beats even faster. This is the first time you have approached the place since that occasion, many years ago, when you were hauled indoors struggling and screaming. The apple trees are still there, the branches knotty and twisty. The cottage is a comfortable-looking place, fit for comfortable yeomen. You push open the door – it is ajar anyway – and listen to the silence within. Once more you hear the blood rustling in your ears and, beyond that, those little tapping and sighing sounds which every place makes even when empty, especially when empty perhaps.

Except that the house isn't empty. Old mother Morrison lies a-dying somewhere within. You raise your beak as if to snuff the air and scent out death. Sure enough – and it must be that your senses are heightened by all this bustle and activity – you know that the old woman is in a room on the next floor. You mount the uneven stairs rapidly but careless of any noise. Who is there to hear you or, hearing you, stand in your way?

There is a choice of three doors up here but, by instinct, you make for just one of them and listen outside. After a moment you are rewarded by a wheezing sound from within. You know that she will be alone. Since she is sick she will be allowed a room to herself. Perhaps for the first time in her life she is sleeping alone in a bed. You lift the latch of the door and enter the room.

The window faces east and the light is good and strong on this fine spring morning. There is a pinched-looking bed in one corner containing a woman lying on her back. She is breathing heavily, with her eyes open but unseeing and her arms outstretched. Her hands are clenched on the quilt. Her nose, hooked, is the most prominent feature of her face. The rest of her flesh seems to have fallen away from it.

You stand in the doorway. The wheezing stops. Then, after an age, it resumes, although nothing else about the supine woman changes.

You waver in your purpose. What is that object lying there before you in the corner? A mortal woman who once beat you until her stick broke and who then lived on in your dreams. Look at her now, helpless and alone, wheezing her way out of this world. You wonder whether it was necessary to send her the poisoned sweetmeats since she could plainly have managed the business of dying all by herself. She cannot have more than a few days left . . . a week at most.

You have seen enough and are about to turn round and exit the room when old mother Morrison, sensing the presence of someone, shifts her head on the bolster and stares at you. The eyes which were gazing blankly at the rough ceiling suddenly spark with life. These eyes are overtaken by horror at what they see but there is a moment before that horror when they are filled with an expression which you remember well. An expression of rage and contempt. Jolted, you are dragged back to childhood. You hear your own screams echoing through the walls of this solid yeoman house.

A sudden desire seizes you, a wild desire, to raise your thin cane and bring it down on her head, on her exposed arms and her tight fists, on her entire shrunken frame, and to dole out to her the punishment she meted out to you all those years before. You step closer to the bed and the eyes of old mother Morrison, like black pits on either side of her sharp nose ridge, enlarge in terror. So acute are your own senses now that, despite the distorting effect of the glassy eyepieces, you are able to see yourself in miniature reflected in her own optics.

You are a great black bird with a beak.

You wield a stick in place of talons.

You are about to swoop.

But, all at once, there is nothing to be done.

The terrified widow Morrison, confronted by the image of death, utters a screeching cry as if she were the giant bird not you. She makes a supreme effort to heave herself out of bed. She even manages to lift her head from the bolster and to raise her shoulders, but the strain is too much and she falls back with a great sigh and after that a rattling spasm which is succeeded by stillness. It is over. A spasm seizes your own throat, and you do not know whether to cry out – in grief or in triumph – but all that emerges is a croak which sounds strange even to your own ears.

You glide out of the bedroom and down the crooked stairs. From the far end of the cottage comes a stirring and shuffling but, not even glancing in that direction, you slip through the door and across the balding grass and back to the hovel where you have left your everyday clothing. Now you swiftly divest yourself of your costume . . . your protection . . . your armour. It is odd how you are one person when you are wearing it and quite another when you don your everyday garb.

You stand there regarding the black waxed coat, the mask with its bird-like protuberance, the white cane fashioned from willow. Your costume, like a player's. It was not a simple matter to obtain the garment. You consulted books. You discovered how they did things in foreign cities. Then, you had the items made up to your own specifications, pretending they were meant for another.

Now you fold up this precious gear inside a cap-case before you go on your way, clutching your bag, capering over the meadows.

A little dog . . . an old witch.

Life picked up when we left London. For one thing the weather brightened and we travelled in sunny spirits. Indeed, the moment that the plaguey city dropped behind us over the horizon – together with its smoke, smut and smells – there was a general lifting of the Company's mood. True, some of those who'd abandoned wives and children were a little thoughtful during the first night's stop but even they, I noticed, forgot their worries as we covered more miles or, if they didn't forget their worries, they concealed them better. We travelled on foot, juniors and seniors alike, while the property wagon was pulled by our good old Flanders draught horse, named Flem either on account of his breed or the wheezing sounds he made, or both.

I suppose this lighter mood was because we of the Chamberlain's were going about our lawful trade once more, while the only thing that London had to offer us at present was a constraint on that trade or its complete cessation. We had the prospect of gainful employment, of appreciative audiences and new surroundings. What player wouldn't be glad and excited?

The city of Oxford was our destination and we reached it after five overnight stops, coming up from the south through Wallingford and Abingdon and averaging twelve or so miles a day. I've walked faster as well as further in a single day but we were in no great hurry to arrive, and the journey had a touch of holiday about it.

Oxford! This great city of learning was unknown to me, but several of my fellows were familiar with it and talked of its fine old buildings and quick-witted young inhabitants. Although there was a tradition of playing, at least among the students, no playhouse had yet been erected. In fact, some ancient regulation actually forbade students to attend public performances of plays, although I imagined they would pay as much attention to that as young people pay to most regulations.

Anyway we were due to perform a medley of dramatic pieces – titles to be announced – in the yard of a tavern situated in the town centre. The Golden Cross was a handsome inn approached via a large courtyard with a gallery running round it. This would certainly do as a makeshift theatre. Temporary seats for the gentry were easily installed in the gallery and the penny-payers could stand on the cobblestones in the yard. We would play on an elaborate dais at the inner end, while a handful of small storage rooms could be used for dressing areas and places to stow the effects, & cetera.

There were other benefits in our change of place. The Oxford authorities may have regarded players as vagabonds but they were reputedly less concerned about the lenten laws than their London counterparts, perhaps because the Puritans were not so powerful in the university city. In addition there would be no Privy Council breathing down our necks, on the lookout for seditious material.

However, apart from performing in front of the good citizens of Oxford, we had another commission to carry out, as I discovered after our arrival there. The only other time I'd been on tour was in the midsummer of 1601, almost two years before. Then a group from the Chamberlain's had journeyed to Instede House in Wiltshire to stage *A Midsummer Night's Dream* in celebration of a noble wedding. The play had come off well enough but the wedding had not come off at all. Murder and other tragedies intervened and everyone was caught up in the affair, like it or not.*

Now, our current business in Oxfordshire also had to do with a prospective marriage but the circumstances of this one were very different from those surrounding the Instede match (or non-match).

A mile or so beyond the northern boundary of the city lies the village of Whittingham, and between the village and

*see *The Pale Companion*

the old city walls live two families, almost side by side. They are neighbours without being particularly neighbourly. The Constants and the Sadlers are not grand people – or not very grand anyway – but they are proud and prickly. They are proud of their name and their possessions. They are prickly over any attempt to diminish either. As with many neighbours there has been a falling-out over land. Or, more precisely, over a useless strip of marsh which is too sodden to graze on, too brackish to drink from and not deep enough to keep fish in. This patch of land doesn't even lie between their two houses but at some distance, to the south-east of the city in Cowley Marsh. The dispute over the title to this bit of bog goes back generations.

This quarrel has never flared into real violence although each side has taken the other to law again and again. To no one's benefit except the lawyers' since the families have spent a hundred times more in court than the patch of land is worth. Generally an uneasy peace exists between the Constants and the Sadlers but they have never quite been on comfortable terms. In the bad old days there was nearly a duel between the heads of the two families, the winner to take possession of the bog (with the loser probably left to rot in it – those were the bad old days, after all). But good sense prevailed or cowardice or fear of the law, and the dispute has grumbled on ever since although with periods of truce.

The oldest son in the Sadler household is a student called William. Among the Constants there is a daughter called Sarah. They hadn't seen each other for many years, William Sadler and Sarah Constant, not since they played together as children during one of the truces between the two families. Well, when the oldest son and the oldest daughter met for the first time since childhood on neutral ground, the almost inevitable happened. Whatever the coolness between their elders, William and Sarah had been drawn to one another; had apparently continued to meet as often as they could although in secret, knowing that their parents might be displeased; had liked, loved, & cetera; had determined to marry; had even thought of elopement; but had finally confessed their mutual feelings to their mothers and fathers.

Now, this story of old feuding families and young lovers, one from each side, may sound familiar to you. It's probably happened often enough in history, and William Shakespeare used it in his tragical story of *Romeo and Juliet*, one of the Chamberlain's Company's most successful pieces. Our audiences can't get enough of attractive youth just as they can't get enough of doom and destruction. When you put both together you're guaranteed a crowd-pleaser. But they say that life imitates art, and it was in the attempt to avert a real tragedy, if only in potential, that we were preparing to don our costumes and put on a private performance of the tale of the young lovers.

I heard all of this – the story of the Constants and Sadlers – from an authoritative source. It was told to me by William Shakespeare himself soon after the Chamberlain's Company had arrived in Oxford.

We junior and middling players had installed ourselves in the Golden Cross Inn, where we were to perform and where we were also being accommodated at half-rates for the duration. Our lodgings were nothing special, being a couple of large chambers at the rear of the inn, set aside for groups. But the welcome was warm. The landlord, a man called Owen Meredith, had greeted us in person. Some of the more senior members of the Company had made their own arrangements, having friends in the town and even in the colleges.

It was early evening. Dusk was thickening. I had wandered out into the town for a brief look around this great centre of scholarship, this famous Athens of England – without, to be honest, seeing any marks of higher intelligence or nobler thought in the faces of people than I was used to seeing in London (that is, not much) – when I ran across Master Shakespeare, looking all trim in a silk doublet. He had not accompanied us from London to Oxford but had travelled down instead from Stratford-on-Avon where he lives, or rather where his family does.

WS invited me to join him for a drink as night fell. So now we, William Shakespeare and Nicholas Revill, were sitting and drinking together in a tavern, not the Golden Cross Inn but another one on the same side of the wide street known as Cornmarket, in fact bang next door to the Golden Cross. Shakespeare told me he was lodging in this place, which was called simply the Tavern, as if the man who'd baptized it had simply run out of invention. The Tavern, a solid house on two floors with twin gables, wasn't so different from other similar establishments on Cornmarket and seemed to me to have nothing much to recommend it over the Golden Cross (where we might at least have got cheaper drinks). I wasn't sure why Shakespeare had chosen to drink here, let alone to sleep in one of their beds. However, when your company is requested by a man who is both your employer and a senior shareholder in your work-place, you usually fall in with his wishes.

While we sipped at our pint pots – WS being as deliberate, as careful a drinker as yours truly – he told me about the Constant and Sadler families, and about the young lovers, Sarah and William. Since his tone implied personal knowledge, I asked how he had come across them.

"We have a friend in common, Hugh Fern, who is a physician in this town. He was brought up in Warwick but he moved to Oxford about the same time as I quit Stratford for London. Once he wanted to act but he turned doctor instead. It was in his house that William Sadler and Sarah Constant first met, that is met for the first time since they were children. You could say that Doctor Fern brought them together."

"Did he mean to bring them together?" I said, slightly surprised that WS had chosen to impart all this information, not just about the feuding families and the physician called Hugh Fern but also, in a glancing way, about himself. I don't think I'd ever heard him say anything about his personal circumstances before.

"Mean to bring them together? Well, I suppose Hugh is a little like Cupid," said Shakespeare.

"He had Venus for a mother?"

"His mother was rather plain, God rest her," said Shakespeare. "No, Hugh is like Cupid in looks. I don't think he'd be offended if I said that, no. He has plump enough cheeks, and a mischievous glance sometimes, and he used to hunt with bow and arrow when he was young. We used to hunt together. Shooting harts with horns rather than *hearts* with an 'e' . . . "

He paused to see whether I'd got the joke but, being familiar with his style of humour, I just made a grimace, so he carried on, "Of course we were not permitted to shoot harts or anything else."

He paused to see how I was taking this admission that he'd once poached deer. I was a little surprised but struggled not to show it (and so most likely did show it).

"Anyway," continued the poacher turned playwright, "when it comes to people in love or those who might be, only a fool would attempt to bring them together, and Hugh Fern's no fool. He has Sarah Constant's best interests at heart too for he is Sarah's sponsor, her godfather."

I waited for WS to enlighten me as to why it was foolish to make matches for would-be lovers – since I was always ready to gather up the crumbs of wisdom dropped from his table, even if I could have left his puns to grow cold up there – but we were interrupted by the appearance of a doleful man, who stood looking down at us.

"Master Shakespeare," said this person. His voice matched his appearance, subdued and gloomy. "What are you doing here?"

"I am a guest of yours, staying in one of your rooms," said WS. "And if you mean what are we doing now, then we are innocently drinking, John Davenant. How are you?"

"Could be worse."

But his look seemed to say, not much worse.

"Business is good," said WS.

The tavern called the Tavern was full, and there were plenty of clamouring customers and much coming-and-going by the drawers and pot-boys, but this gentleman shrugged his shoulders.

"Could be better," he said.

"Landlords are like farmers," said WS to me. "They would find fault with a summer in paradise."

"I heard your company of players was in town, my wife told me," said Davenant, who I assumed was the owner of this place. "My beds are no worse than my beer. If *you're* staying here why doesn't the rest of your Company stay here?"

"Oh, your beds are more than good enough for me, Jack. But when it comes to the whole Company, it's because we are playing *next* to here," said Shakespeare, jerking his thumb in the direction of the Golden Cross further up Cornmarket. "We stay where we play, if it's possible."

"You'll draw all my trade," said this dolorous host.

"Nonsense, Jack. You know perfectly well that for every citizen who loves plays there's another one who can't stand them."

"So?" said Davenant.

"So," said Shakespeare, "all the regulars who normally go to the Cross and can't abide plays will come a few yards down the road to you. And they'll drink your beer and wine, and drink it all the faster because they won't be distracted by somebody spouting verse."

"Miserable sods," said Davenant. I wasn't sure whether he was describing those citizens who didn't like plays and would therefore come flocking to his inn or the Chamberlain's players who had chosen not to lodge with him. In fact the description best fitted himself.

"I promise you, Jack, that when we come back to Oxford, we'll put up with you."

43

"Put up with me, that is good of you," said Davenant, but he seemed slightly mollified by the promise.

"This is Nicholas Revill," said WS, perhaps to divert the conversation into a different channel. "Nicholas, this is John Davenant, whose fame is spread far and wide throughout Oxfordshire."

I muttered something about his being famous for being a tavern host, no doubt, but WS was quick to correct me.

"No, he is famous for his wife. She is the nonpareil of beauty."

I couldn't tell from WS's tone whether he was being mocking or not (though I rather think he was serious), nor could I tell from the expression on the landlord's face whether he was pleased to have his wife referred to like this. Probably not as, if anything, Davenant's expression grew longer.

"Take care you make your pieces boring and long-winded," he said to Shakespeare.

"Come and see for yourself."

"Perhaps I will. But I would still have your audiences desert you half-way through and come down to me for liquid refreshment."

"We'll do our worst," said WS.

And seemingly content with this, the landlord turned round and made his way to another corner of the tavern, probably to abuse more of his customers.

WS, however, didn't seem offended by Davenant's comments. Instead, he said, "He is a good fellow although a dry one. You get used to him in time."

"And his wife?" I said, greatly daring.

"No, you wouldn't get used to her, not in a lifetime," said WS. "Not Jane Davenant."

This was more than interesting and I waited for details. But nothing was forthcoming. Since WS seemed about to get up and move away, and being reluctant to lose his company, I ordered another drink for each of us and turned the talk back to the subject of the Constants, the Sadlers, and the ancient feud between the two families. From what the play-wright had said, it seemed as though there was no violent objection to the marriage of Sarah and William from either side.

"So what's the difficulty then?" I said.

"Oh, there should be no difficulty," said WS, "but our play will serve as a kind of warning, a gentle warning."

"Shouldn't they have a comedy at a wedding? I realize that *Romeo and Juliet* is about two families at war and two young people who want to marry. But it's a tragedy."

Even as I said these words I thought that it was foolish to be defining Shakespeare's own work to himself, but if the playwright was annoyed – or amused – at my presumption he didn't show it.

"I don't usually believe that we can learn anything at all from plays," said WS, "but, in the case of the Constants and the Sadlers, Hugh Fern considers that it might be instructive . . . for the two sides to watch a piece in which things go wrong . . . "

"So that they can avoid any actions which might lead to a similar conclusion?" I suggested.

"Yes," said WS. "Tragedy can be averted sometimes."

"Otherwise it would not be tragedy, but fate," I put in.

"Perhaps . . . " he said, apparently unwilling to discuss my interesting insight. "Besides we are being well paid for this. My old friend Hugh Fern has prospered since he came to this town. He is doing better than if he had become a player, much better. Being a good friend also to the Constants and Sadlers he is ready to subscribe to a private performance of my piece in the hopes of providing the two families with some diversion – and a very gentle warning. And the Chamberlain's with some cash."

I was always a little taken aback by the nakedness with which Shakespeare and the other shareholders referred to money. They made no bones about it. As if he could read my thoughts WS now said, "You know what our motto is in the Chamberlain's?"

"Our motto?"

"It is 'You pay, we'll play'."

"No, I didn't know that."

"That's because I just invented it, Nick. You ought to be a bit more wary of what you're told."

I must have looked a little crestfallen because WS put his hand on my arm and hastened to reassure me, "But it ought to be our motto. I'll have a word with Dick Burbage. Perhaps we could get up a coat of arms. Money-bags on an argent field."

"And are you playing in this story of the Montagues and the Capulets?" I said quickly.

"I've played Friar Laurence more than once. I may do so again on this occasion. We'll see."

It may seem odd that Shakespeare didn't know whether he'd be playing or not, but life on tour was more improvised than the scheduled playing at the Globe. The seniors had a rough idea of what we would be doing – and evidently the private production of *Romeo and Juliet* had been settled on before we left London – but we lesser mortals were kept in the dark.

"Have the other parts been allotted yet?"

"What are *you* going to do, you mean?"

"Yes, that's what I mean."

Ever since finding out a few minutes earlier that we were to perform *Romeo and Juliet*, a hope had been jumping around in my breast. Not so long ago I'd played the betrayed lover Troilus in Shakespeare's bitter tragedy of the Trojan war, and before that one of the youthful lovers in *Midsummer Night's Dream*. Could I now expect to take the part of Romeo the lover?

Apparently not, from what WS said next.

"Dick Burbage will play Romeo Montague – although I can see by your look that you think he's too old."

"I wouldn't be so presumptuous. Never entered my head."

"That's only because it's already on its way out the other

side," said WS. "What we have in mind for you, Revill, is Mercutio, kinsman to the Prince and friend to Romeo."

"Who dies in a sword-fight? Half-way through the action."

"But not before uttering a deal of words. He is a witty, brave man. Somewhat fanciful. The pivot of the action in the first half in some ways."

"Well, that's good," I said, not knowing what else to say since I figured that Shakespeare was delivering a compliment here.

By this time the evening had worn on a bit and WS announced that he should return to the Golden Cross Inn for a conference with Burbage and Pope and some of the other shareholders, no doubt to make the final preparations for our presentations in the inn yard and wherever it was that we were scheduled to play *Romeo and Juliet*.

I wandered out into Cornmarket, not having any conference to go to myself, not wanting to retire to bed just yet and not wanting to search through numerous Oxford taverns before I stumbled across Abel Glaze or Jack Wilson or some other of my fellows to drink with. Instead, I'd walk the streets in this busy, relatively well-lit area.

Mercutio . . . hmm. Kinsman to the Prince and friend to Romeo Montague. I struggled to remember the production of *Romeo and Juliet* which I'd seen not long after arriving in London several years before. At the time I'd thought that my ambition to join the players might be furthered by hanging around playhouses and seeing as many dramas as possible. I smiled to remember my greenness then. And wondered whether I appeared much more experienced now. But I must do surely . . . to be offered a part like Mercutio. He is a whimsical fellow, given to flights of fancy. He is a pivot, in some ways. He is teasing and changeable. Half-way through he dies in a sword-fight. I couldn't recall the details exactly but the fight begins somewhere between joke and earnest. All the same, Mercutio dies. Well, I would give them a good death.

And hot on the heels of this thought came another one, quite a different one. I'd been intrigued back at the Tavern when Shakespeare mentioned his boyhood friendship with Hugh Fern, and of how they'd both started out from the Warwickshire country to make their fortunes at the same time. And then there'd been that reference to poaching deer, to shooting the hart . . .

Now, I had little doubt that William Shakespeare was a great man, whose work and reputation would outlive his mere earthly existence by many years. I wondered whether anyone had yet thought to amass biographical scraps, the materials for a life of WS, for the edification and entertainment of future ages. I wondered whether N. Revill was the man to undertake this task (and in the process of memorializing a great man win a little reflected glory for himself).

In the middle of these thoughts, these dreams of mortal glory, I realized that I hadn't been paying attention to where I was going. Dazzled by Mercutio and then by the notion of writing about WS, I'd taken three or four turns and was now lost.

Wherever I found myself it was well away from the busy thoroughfare called the Cornmarket, away from noise and light and people. Instead I was in a dark and silent place, between high walls. Under my feet was close-packed earth, not the cobbles of a street. Overhead was a swath of night sky, glimmering with fitful stars. A breeze crept down this walkway and made me shiver. As my eyes grew more used to the dark, I saw that the walls were pierced by a few remote, high windows. I reached out for the nearest wall. The lower part was covered with a creeper that felt dead to the touch, last year's growth. I supposed that I was standing outside one of the colleges, or rather between two of them. The walls were more like those of a castle or a palace than a place of learning. I wondered what it would be like to be on the other side. I imagined scholars in lofty towers, surrounded by books and manuscripts, piercing the secrets of the heavens or turning their gaze inward on themselves.

These high-minded imaginings were interrupted by a strange shuffling sound from behind my back. I strained my ears. The sound resolved itself into that of feet, several pairs of feet moving uncertainly over the ground, together with an intermittent whispering. I shivered again although there was no draught of air this time. The shuffling feet were moving towards me, in the direction I'd just come from.

Honest citizens of Oxford? Possibly . . . although if they were honest citizens why were they whispering and slinking down a dim alley instead of sitting snug inside their dwellings or drinking the evening away in a tavern? Honest? I did not think so.

What I thought was that I had better make myself scarce. Not wanting to go forward, since I'd no idea what lay ahead, I looked about for a place to conceal myself. Luckily, the wall on one side was buttressed by thick ribs of stone, giving this spot an even more fortified appearance. The darkness was naturally thickest at the base of these buttresses and I made myself small where the nearest of these met the wall.

Looking back towards the mouth of the walkway, where there was a break in the surrounding darkness and from where the shuffling was emanating, I made out a confused mass of shadows, two or three, breaking apart and merging again into a single mass. The only certain fact was that they were advancing. I could tell this more by sound than sight. There was no moon, only the faintest star-fall. Even though I was able to see so little, there was some aspect to their appearance which was already provoking fear in me. I don't mean the fear of being found out in the street after dark by some ruffians who'll lift your purse or, if you're truly unlucky, deprive you of your life. That fear is, so to speak, a reasonable fear. What I experienced now was something deeper which took me back to the nightmares of childhood. And the nightmare grew worse as the shapes grew larger and more questionable instead of clearer.

What were they?

Then from overhead there was a sudden scraping sound. Instinctively I looked up at the noise. A frail light hung swaying in the air. It took me a moment to realize that the sound was a window being opened and that the light was a lantern being thrust out at arm's length, no doubt by the occupant of the room, curious about the movement and noise in the alley.

After a few seconds the light was withdrawn and the window closed with another scrape. Perhaps the lantern-holder hadn't been able to see anything from his position high up above the ground. Perhaps he had seen something, and did not want to see more.

But I had seen. I wished that I hadn't. I wished that I too was high up behind a wall, in a secure room.

For what the flickering, uncertain rays of the lantern revealed was that these shadows creeping towards my hiding place had no heads – or no human heads. Instead they possessed great beast-like snouts which wagged in the night air while, waving in front of each shape, was a thin extension like the horn or feeler of an insect.

This vision lasted only a moment but it set my heart thudding and made my hair stir. I might have tried to groan or to cry aloud but something swelled in my throat and choked off any sound. I'm not sure what happened next. I think that I closed my eyes, in order to shut out the slightest glimpse of the scene, benighted as it all was. I was more terrified of seeing than of being seen. I could not help hearing though. The padding of feet, of several feet, tentative but continuous, turned into a kind of slithering in my ears and made me to wonder whether I had dropped through the surface of the earth into a pit of monsters.

What saved me was a curse. Not loud and not mine, but issuing from the snout of one of the creatures now processing past my hiding-place at the foot of the buttress.

"God's bones," came a muffled voice, "but it's dark enough. And cold enough."

No more. But the oath and the workaday comments were enough to tell me that the creatures which were creeping past were human after all. Neither more nor less than human. Three humans to be precise. I stayed where I was, huddled up in the corner between buttress and wall, scarcely breathing, scarcely thinking, only listening until the last shuffle and slither had faded into the night.

After a time I unwound myself from my corner and stood up, stiff but shivering, in the alley. Now that I'd collected myself slightly, the scene reminded me of something but, in my still frightened state, I couldn't think of what.

Then I turned about and – walking more and more quickly before breaking into a run – I chased down winding walks and around corners until I emerged once more into Cornmarket, more by accident than intention. I slunk back to the Golden Cross Inn and up the stairs to the room where some eight or nine of us run-of-the-mill players were bedding down together. Since my fellows were either snoring after the day's journey or not yet returned from carousing in town there was no one to talk to or be questioned by. This was just as well because I couldn't have guaranteed the steadiness of my voice. I claimed an unoccupied corner in one of the three beds, recognizing the bulk of Laurence Savage next to me. He was well away, breathing easily. On the far side of him lay Abel Glaze, also well settled. But I stayed awake for a long time, staring at the low ceiling across which floated dark, devil shapes with snouts and insect horns.

I decided to say nothing of what I'd seen. Anyway, I probably wouldn't be believed. It would sound like a dream. Perhaps it had after all been some ritual, this dressing up and parading through the back streets of the town, quite normal here. Maybe the scholars got together to celebrate the arrival of spring or the birthday of the patron saint of scholarship (whoever he or she may be), maybe they dressed up as insects and shuffled through the streets at night in small, whispering groups. Who knew how they did things in Oxford?

In the next couple of days we gained a bit of experience in how they did things in Oxford, or at least in the yard of the Golden Cross Inn. They did them not so differently than they did in the standing-room and the galleries of the Globe playhouse. The Oxford citizens gasped, cheered, whistled and wept just like Londoners and generally at the same points in the action. After a single morning's rehearsal, the first play we put on was the late Richard Milford's *The World's Diseas'd*, a piece which had drawn good audiences in London during the winter and which went down well in this place too. It was a pleasing choice for me, since I played the revenger Vindice. I'd thought it a pretty absurd tragedy when I first read it at Richard's insistence, but Shakespeare had humanized some of the action and the characters while retaining the crowd-pleasing bits (usually involving amputation and incest). And when you realize that, whatever it might look like on paper, a piece is actually working on stage – to say nothing of having a good many lines in it yourself – it's strange how your critical faculties get blunted.

The next afternoon we staged a newish play by William Hordle, a shy writer with a large and still expanding family. For the Chamberlain's Company he was working his way through the lexicon of love. His *Love's Disdain* we performed in the summer of 1601 while *Love's Diversion* had appeared the following year. Now we were presenting *Love's Loss* which was the most cheerful of the three, despite its title. Doubtless he was already working on *Love Regained*. His play production had to outstrip the rate at which his wife produced children and so, while supplying the Chamberlain's with the light fare of love, he offered meatier matter to the Admiral's Men, pieces that climaxed in battle-scenes and the suicides of generals. In *Love's Loss* I played a simple soul, a contrast to the rampant avenger of *The World's Diseas'd*.

Love's Loss was also well received by the Oxonians. In fact our reception was so good that we considered that if things went badly in London – if, that is to say, the entire city fell victim to the plague or if the Globe playhouse burnt down – then we would be able to set up in Oxford instead. It was a paper dream, for the place was much smaller than London and could not have sustained a company of the size of the Chamberlain's, even at our present reduced numbers. And, once established in the capital, which person has ever *seriously* considered leaving London? Nevertheless, two or three of our number began to make connections and arrangements with some of the townsfolk, or (to be more precise) with some of the townswomen. It crossed my mind to do the same, if the occasion arose, but I remembered Lucy Milford back in London and thought she deserved at least a week or two of fidelity. Oh honourable Revill!

Playing at the Golden Cross Inn was much more basic than playing at the Globe, but we didn't mind. Give us costumes and a few simple properties (dagger or crown, for instance), give us the lines, above all give us a crowd, and we'll do it anywhere. All of this activity meant that I forgot my frightening encounter with the hooded group of men. However, I did not wander off in the evenings again but kept to the main thoroughfares.

As a treat the audiences were promised Shakespeare's *Romeo and Juliet* but not now, not yet . . . since we wanted word to spread that the Chamberlain's were in town. Of course we were also due to offer this tragic romance in more intimate circumstances, and those I'll come to in a moment.

No more alarming news of King Pest arrived from London. In fact some of the married men were receiving letters already – we had been easily outstripped by the posthorses in our gradual progress towards Oxford – and their contents were reassuring enough (although this turned out to be misleading). I would have welcomed a letter from Lucy Milford but she did not choose to write, and so whatever I heard was at third-hand. All the news, apart from domestic matters, was to do with the Queen, who was reported to be sinking at a faster rate.

Whether John Davenant, the gloomy landlord of the Tavern further down Cornmarket, was right in his fear that we would cause him to lose trade, or whether WS was right when he claimed that for every play-lover there's somebody who can't stand the things and will take shelter in the nearest tavern to escape them, I never discovered.

What I did discover was Davenant's wife, Mistress Jane.

Two or three days after our arrival in Oxford, I was standing in the Cornmarket in the early morning when I noticed a striking woman on the far side of the street. The sun was fast burning away the early mist, and it seemed as though this woman came striding out of the clouds. She was tall, with a fine head of dark tangled hair. She walked in a way which simultaneously suggested that she knew everyone's eyes were on her – and although there were only a few people about, I am sure they were – and that she couldn't care less. Handsome rather than beautiful, and not so young either, she was accustomed to being looked at without betraying the fact (as an actor is). Someone nudged me, and I turned to recognize one of the ostlers from the Golden Cross stables, a perky sandy-haired fellow. He had taken charge of Flem, the Company horse, after we arrived.

"I can see where you're looking," he said.

"Looking is free."

"That one's a gypsy. Plays at fast and loose."

"At fairs?" I said, thinking he meant it literally and was referring to that con-game involving knots and string.

"With her husband – and others maybe," said the ostler.

"Who is she then, since you obviously know her?"

"Everybody in Oxford knows Mistress Jane Davenant."

The name struck a chord, and just as I made the connection between Jack Davenant, landlord of the Tavern, and the wife whom Shakespeare had enigmatically mentioned, this tall and striking woman crossed the street and turned into the yard of the Tavern next door to us.

So that was Jane Davenant. What had WS said of her – that she was a woman you wouldn't get used to, not in a lifetime?

"So what else do you know about her?" I said.

"She is witty and of good conversation, they say," said the ostler.

"And what else?"

The little ostler giggled and tapped himself on his head in an odd gesture that conveyed, I suppose, that whatever knowledge he possessed was going to stay locked up inside his sandy skull. A penny or two would probably have unlocked it but I wasn't going to pay for gossip. The ostler seemed disappointed.

"Well, if you want to know more, you know where to come," he said. "Christopher Kite at your service."

"Thank you," I said.

"But you may call me Kit. Kit Kite."

I thanked him again, reflecting that it was a funny old world where ostlers gave you permission to call them by their diminutives.

It wasn't Kit Kite I was really thinking of anyway but the handsome woman. If Mrs Davenant was as famous or notorious as all that then I'd probably find somebody willing to tell me all about her for free. Perhaps I'd ask WS next time we had a drink together.

In any case I had other business apart from listening to an ostler's chat that morning. We all had other business since we were due to go to the outskirts of the city and inspect the house where *Romeo and Juliet* was to be privately staged. (There was no early rehearsal as we were merely reprising *The World's Diseas'd* that afternoon.)

When we Chamberlain's played away from home it was a requirement for all the players, as well as any hangers-on, to inspect in advance what you might call the field of battle, the arena of action. Each arena, whether it's a playhouse or an inn yard or a private dwelling or simply an open stretch of ground under the stars, has its own quality and smell. We need to grow familiar with the dimensions of the place, its entrances and exits, and most important of all, its peculiarities, such as the creaking floorboards on the left or the fact that there's a dead spot downstage where your voice never projects properly. And the only way to know your patch of ground is by walking it over, talking and declaiming to yourself while you're doing so.

William Shakespeare had already mentioned to me his friend Hugh Fern, the doctor who was on good terms with the Constant and Sadler families. Not only had he proposed a presentation of *Romeo and Juliet* and offered to pay for it, he had also offered a venue: the spacious hall of his own house. This was a sort of neutral ground where each family might come and go freely. It was a generous act of patronage and friendship by the Doctor. Private performances aren't so rare but they are usually requested by members of the nobility, and intended as a demonstration of the wealth or taste of the patron. But our *Romeo and Juliet* seemed meant rather as an upside-down warning, a way of averting a new outbreak of feuding between the neighbouring Oxford families.

When we'd all assembled outside the Golden Cross Inn, Dick Burbage led us off in the direction of the hill leading towards Headington, a suburb which lies to the east of the city. The mist which had swathed the streets was all burned off by now. Church bells clanged. There was a particularly fine spire on a church to our left. The morning sun dazzled our faces as we walked down the wide, gently curving road which runs through the centre of Oxford and is called the High. A holiday mood still clung to us. We swung along with a bit of swagger, aware that some locals were pointing us out as the players from London and commenting, "They're good, they're worth seeing," or "Don't miss 'em." At least I hoped that's what they were saying. On either side was a queer assemblage of shops and plenty of taverns with great hanging signs, mixed up with grander edifices, the halls and colleges.

After a short time the road passed through the city wall. Beyond it were more high walls guarding groves of trees, together with a fine tower – the tallest I'd yet seen outside London. As we were walking and talking under the shadow of this great tower, someone told me that it belonged to Magdalen College. I wondered what it would be like to spend one's life in study and contemplation, debating under the shelter of those old trees or gazing out at the world from the top of the tower. Wondered for a few moments only. I would sooner be in the public eye than buried among mouldy books, sooner be with my fellows on the road or on the stage than consorting with dry-as-dust scholars. Then we crossed a bridge over some willow-strewn watercourses before the road began to make a gentle ascent.

There were several large dwellings on either side of the road – close enough to the city for the necessaries of life (and, I suppose, the protection of those walls) but far enough away from any unpleasant town fumes – and it was towards one of these that we now turned. It was a handsome house, Doctor Fern's, no doubt fitting his standing in the town. It was surrounded by a garden, gently terraced on account of the slope of the hill. Perhaps this was what happened to you when you became middle-aged and respectable, and did well. You purchased a big house with a comfortable garden, you lived in it, you looked out at your views, and you sighed with satisfaction. I remembered hearing somewhere that William Shakespeare had bought one of the largest houses in Stratford-on-Avon a few years previously. And yet these two, playwright and physician, had apparently been on poaching expeditions together when they were growing up in Warwickshire!

By the time all of us – and there were more than twenty players and extras – had been admitted, a little welcoming party had assembled in the hall of the house. I easily picked out Doctor Fern. A smiling fellow with rounded cheeks and a cheerful glance, he was quite close to the Cupid that WS had described, apart from a fringe of prematurely white hair which gave him a tonsured monkish look. A stolid lady next to him was presumably Mrs Fern, while a younger, not unattractive woman remained in the background together with a pocky-faced young man. Shakespeare himself was already part of the group and I guessed he had arrived at the house some time before us. It was obvious from the way that Dick Burbage and one or two of the other seniors greeted the Ferns that they were well known to each another.

It seemed a happy household. You know how you can detect that straightaway sometimes. The Ferns had no children, I discovered later, but a clutch of dogs had the run of the place and were made much of by their mistress.

We were made very welcome, the Doctor shaking each of us by the hand and complimenting us on our reputation, with his wife adding further kind words. I couldn't help contrasting this with the frosty reception we've had at one or two great houses. Then, since it was shortly after breakfast time, ale was brought in for our refreshment. We started to examine the hall where we stood, for it was here that our private *Romeo and Juliet* would be presented. Although the house was quite new, the hall was rather in the old style, with linen-fold panelling and a fireplace large enough to accommodate half the household. There was a gallery at one end, and this was highly convenient since we could use it for those parts of the action where a balcony or a different level was required.

Thomas Pope instructed us to test out our voices with a few lines so as to get accustomed to the echoes and resonances. It would be a little different when the hall was full of people but still it gave a good idea what we, or rather what the room, was capable of. I observed that Doctor Fern and his wife, together with the younger man and woman, watched all this activity with interest.

Thomas Pope himself busied around in the part of Juliet's nurse and, inside a second or two, had brought that garrulous figure to life. Dick Burbage spoke to an imagined Juliet in the gallery – he was too old for the young lover but you forgot that fact within a few lines. Shakespeare delivered a handful of lines as Friar Laurence although I didn't know whether he intended to take the part for himself on this occasion. When it came to my turn, I did a bit of Mercutio. Abel Glaze, who was due to play the apothecary among other roles, had already mastered his brief scene and gave a good impression of that unfortunate tradesman, driven by poverty to sell a deadly poison to Romeo.

Everything seemed set fair for the actual production of *Romeo and Juliet*, which would take place in about a week's time in the presence of the Constants and Sadlers. Two mornings would be put aside for rehearsals in the house on Headington Hill. But before we performed privately for the benefit of the two families – whose enmity, by the way, seemed essentially a matter of history – we were to present the same play in the yard of the Golden Cross Inn. Any rough edges could be planed away. The number of public performances in town would depend on the popularity of the piece.

Well, as I've said, we weren't due to practise on this fine spring morning (our schedule was less pressing than at the Globe) and so were free to dispose of ourselves in the few hours before the two o'clock performance of *The World's Diseas'd* at the Golden Cross. The Company split up into separate groups, with William Shakespeare and one or two others remaining at the Doctor's house. I had the scroll of my part as Mercutio with me and was planning to return to the town and, if the sun lasted, find a secluded spot down by the river to continue memorizing my lines.

Abel Glaze and I spent a bit of time admiring the view from the Ferns' garden. Before us was a panorama of pinnacles and towers, gleaming in the bright air. From this distance the stone took on the appearance of lacework. Then we walked down the Doctor's drive and turned out of his gate on to the slope which led towards the town.

All at once there was a clattering and loud shouting behind us. Looking round I saw, some fifty yards further up the hill, a woman lying face-down in the road, together with a horse and cart slewed towards the opposite side. The driver had almost toppled off his perch. The woman wasn't moving and for an instant I thought she was dead until she shouted something, but still without moving. I couldn't make out the words or even whether she was hurt or simply distressed and angry. Righting himself, the carter jumped from his seat and made as if to help the woman but he thought better of it and went instead to retrieve a sack which had tumbled into the roadway. Rather than pick it up he dragged it awkwardly to the cart before heaving it into the back.

Abel Glaze, quicker or more charitable than I, ran up the slope. I followed. By this time the woman had rolled over on to her back. Her bonnet sat like an upturned helmet in the centre of the rutty road. She groaned when she saw us. It was plain what had happened. There were mud marks and grease across her skirts where the cart or its wheel had struck her and knocked her over.

"Are you all right, mistress?" said Abel, crouching down.

"Where is he?" said this woman. "I'll see him."

She was a red-faced individual, and not just on account of her supine position. Even though she was lying injured on the ground she radiated determination. There was a smirch of mud on her cheek. I didn't think she was badly hurt.

"Should we help?" I said, kneeling down on the other side of her.

Her eyes, small currant-like objects, swivelled between Abel and me.

"Yes," she said, raising her head, then, "No."

At which she lay back and groaned more loudly than ever. I'd forgotten about the carter but now a reluctant shadow fell across the scene as he drew nearer.

"I know you," she said, looking over my shoulder. "John Hoby."

"Oh, Mistress Root," said the carter. "Oh dear."

He stood there, holding his cap in his hands and twisting it in his fingers.

"I – I – didn't recognize – Mistress R-R-Root . . . "

"And what if you had," she said. "It would be all right, I suppose, to knock down poor old harmless women in the street as long as you do recognize them."

"I ca-ca-called out."

"And I did not hear you, you muddle-headed measle. I am deaf on one side."

"Mistress – you – you were wandering . . . "

"Yes! Wandering! Was I wandering!"

I moved back slightly, driven by the force of her shouts. She remained lying in the roadway. For sure she could not be badly hurt.

" . . . w-w-wandering about the r-r-r-r – "

The carter, twining his fingers more furiously in his cap, was unable to get the word "road" out through his teeth. He had a wen or growth of some kind on his exposed neck, about the size of a tennis ball, which bobbed in time with his efforts and made him look even more ridiculous. He made a series of whooping sounds and then gestured helplessly around him. By now a handful of passers-by, on foot or horseback, had slowed down or even stopped altogether so as to savour the scene. Abel Glaze had moved back as well, sensing that this Mistress Root was well able to take care of herself. Most likely she was enjoying the commotion.

"I suppose a poor old lady is entitled to wander down the road, you clay-brained coxcomb."

The carter didn't know what to say. His mouth opened but no sounds came out.

"I *know* you, John Hoby," said this woman again. She hadn't moved an inch from her position on the road. "You will pay."

The carter looked round helplessly at his horse and cart. The horse, a piebald nag that didn't look in much better condition than its driver, was browsing on the grass at the verge. The driver looked back at the fallen woman. It seemed as if he might burst into tears.

"A thousand plagues on you, you onion-eyed oyster," said Mistress Root, half getting up from the ground. Abel and I

moved to assist her. She groaned but it was for show only. There
was no satisfaction in her eyes at the effect she'd produced on
the carter but rather a kind of contempt directed at him. I had
begun by feeling concern for the woman but now I felt sorrier
for John Hoby. It was as if *he* had been run down by her.

Mistress Root was a short, quite elderly woman with a lot
of flesh attaching to her. Her arms, each of which was secured
by Abel and me as if we were taking her into custody, were
like bolsters.

"These two young gentlemen will see to me now," she said,
and I would not have dared to controvert this.

"My bonnet," she said, and Abel let go of her arm to
retrieve her headgear from where it lay.

"There is a doctor near here," I said, grasping at a way to
get rid of our burden.

"Oh, I know Hugh Fern," she said. She was the sort of
woman who would know everyone. "Take me to him."

We hobbled towards the Doctor's gate, leaving the hapless
carter to set himself in order and ponder how much he would
have to pay in blood-money. The onlookers moved off as
well, the show being over. Mistress Root enjoyed the
experience of being held up by two able-bodied men, judging
by the way she frequently paused to catch her breath and
slump against us.

I'd been wondering how to explain our reappearance at
Doctor Fern's but Mistress Root took matters in hand as we
entered the front door. Standing in the great hall was the not
unattractive young woman I'd glimpsed earlier, still in the
company of the pocky man. They had been talking together.

"Mistress Root," said the young woman, looking up,
surprised.

"Susan, I am sent by your mother."

"What happened to you?"

The young woman came towards us.

"An oaf of a carter ran me down and would have trampled
all over me if it hadn't been for these young gentlemen here."

The woman called Susan looked grateful. Abel and I smiled our oh-it-was-nothing smiles. Meantime I was trying to work out who Susan was and her relation to Mistress Root. Now the young woman turned to the individual with the pitted skin.

"Pearman, go and fetch the Doctor,"she said. "Mistress Root, you shall come into this chamber."

Abel Glaze and I would have released our hold on Mistress Root at this point – since she could certainly have walked unaided – but she seemed reluctant to be let go of, and we escorted her to a room on one side of the hall.

It was evidently the place where Doctor Fern carried on his business. Every surface was covered with little bottles and vials, with bowls and flasks, with mortars and pestles of all sizes, with steel and wooden implements, surgical probes and gauges, and with boxes containing little male and female figurines. On the walls were shelves of books together with planetary charts and drawings of human figures in outline pierced by arrows to indicate which areas were influenced by which signs of the zodiac.

I was reminded of an apothecary's shop I had once visited off Paul's Yard in London, not so much by the objects – everything here was much neater, newer and shinier than it had been in old Nick's emporium, and there were no crocodiles or unicorn horns hanging overhead – but by the smell of the place. A queer, sweetish smell, as of substances ground, mixed and distilled together, in which one could catch fugitive threads: of lavender, cinnamon and beer, for example, and underneath all, a kind of dungy scent. Not unpleasant.

We helped Mistress Root to a padded settle on one side of the room. She sat down heavily. We might have retreated at this point but she clutched at our sleeves.

"Who are you, chivalrous gentlemen of the road?"

There are some compliments you'd be just as glad not to receive, or people you'd rather not receive them from. This one was accompanied by a flirtatious wink of one of the currant-like eyes. Nevertheless we introduced ourselves.

"We're players," said Abel. "Of the Chamberlain's Company newly arrived in town. I am Abel Glaze."

"And I am Nicholas Revill, at your service, madam."

"Pardon?" she said, pulling me down. "I am deaf on this left side."

I repeated myself more loudly and nearer to the ear in question, although I think that rather than the information she wanted to have my breath on her muddy cheek. I would have wiped the mud away with my handkerchief but was afraid that such a gesture to such a ripe matron would be misconstrued. Horribly misconstrued.

"My second husband struck me on that side," she said, "so I went deaf afterwards."

"I am sorry to hear it," said Abel.

"Not as sorry as he was to have done it," said this dragon. "He did not rise for six hours from the floor when I was finished with him."

"You have a neat fist, mistress," I said. Her knuckles were dimples in the flesh, so ham-like were her hands. But I didn't doubt she could use them like mallets if necessary.

"He is dead now, Hopkins is dead," she said. "And so is the third one. Master Root is dead. I have seen them all into the ground. Root was the best – but none of them were any good in truth. 'Husband' and 'good' do not go together. Are you married?"

"Alas no," said Abel, who liked to play at being love-lorn.

"Not yet," I said.

"Good," said Mistress Root, "I would have no more marriage."

Before we could hear any more about marriage or about her husbands, bad and worse, Doctor Fern came into his chamber with the woman called Susan, the other man following at their heels. To my embarrassment, Master Shakespeare suddenly appeared in the doorway. Swiftly I explained the state of things to him while the trio fussed around Mrs Root. He pulled me into the hall.

"We were caught up in this willy-nilly. Who *are* all these

people? Do you know?" I said, reckoning that if anyone would be familiar with the *dramatis personae* of this business it would be William Shakespeare, the playwright. He didn't disappoint.

"The formidable woman called Root is the Constant nurse, the old nurse, I am told," he said. "Root is a fitting name for a nurse, considering how often she has to deal with herbs and plants."

"And the young one?" I said casually.

"The young one is Susan Constant."

"She's the one who wishes to marry?"

"No, that is *Sarah* Constant. This is a cousin, I believe."

"Oh . . ."

Then why had that woman, the formidable nurse, mentioned having been sent here by Susan's mother?

"While the other person is a servant or apprentice to Hugh Fern who goes by the name of Andrew Pearman," said WS. "Satisfied, Nick?"

"I like to know where I am or who it is I'm with."

"So it wasn't just a roundabout way of getting the identity of the young woman?"

I had wanted that, true enough, and what I wanted now was to shift ground.

"I saw the landlord's wife this morning, William. She was striding out of the mist."

"Who? Oh, Jane Davenant?"

"A nonpareil, like you said."

An odd, opaque look glazed WS's features.

"Nurse Root wants to talk to you, look, she's beckoning."

I turned round. The old woman was sitting on the settle with her back to one end and her legs stretched out in front of her. Her skirts were up, not much beyond the bounds of modesty, and the legs were being examined by Hugh Fern. She was gazing at me, however, and waving a mighty arm in the air. Pearman, the Doctor's apprentice, hovered to one side. My friend Abel Glaze was chatting to the woman WS had identified as Susan Constant. I went over.

Hugh Fern was saying genially, "There doesn't seem to be any great harm done, Mistress Root."

"No harm. No *harm*. Master Revill, you will testify to the harm that devil carter did to me."

It was a statement not a question. I looked at the legs. They looked back at me, plump and sound.

"Well . . . " I said.

"A poor old body like me," she said.

I'd scarcely seen anyone more robust in my life, of any age. I glanced over at where WS had been standing but he was already gone.

"I will give you a draught of something to swallow, Mistress Root," said Doctor Fern, "and a preparation of neat's-foot and other salves to rub on the afflicted area."

The old nurse seemed pleased enough and I realized that the wise doctor – to say nothing of the prosperous one – treads a line between his patients' claims and his own observations.

"You will cast again for me, Doctor Fern? As you did before?" said Mistress Root. "To see if I should proceed in a suit against that bad carter, John Hoby."

"That I will next week," said Fern, "when the moon is right."

A touch of reluctance in his tone suggested to me that he would advise her not to proceed, and my opinion of him rose.

"You would cast for me too, sir?" said Abel Glaze, who had been listening to the tail of this conversation. I was rather surprised that my friend wanted to have his future told, perhaps because it was something I wouldn't have chosen to have done myself (I was uneasy enough with Lucy Milford's prophesyings, and they came free after all). Possibly the surprise showed on my face, and was read as doubt or disbelief by the others.

"Doctor Fern cast for me when I lost a cup," said Susan Constant. She had a crisp, decided voice – almost mannish – which complemented her clear, sculpted features. "It was found where he said it would be."

The Doctor smiled at this testimony to his skill.

"For myself I haven't lost anything of value, perhaps because I have nothing of value to lose," said Abel disingenuously, "but I should like to know what I might gain in the future."

"The answer is nothing," I said. "We are poor players. Our future is simply enough told. It is pillar to post."

I don't know why I was so averse to what Abel was asking for. It was normal enough. People in every walk of life, from housewives to admirals, visit their doctors not merely for remedies but also for castings, and most doctors are happy to oblige.

Hugh Fern obviously regarded me as a sceptic about horoscopes – which I wasn't altogether, only wary – because he stroked his round cheeks and looked at his assistant.

"What would you say, Pearman? What is this gentleman's sign?"

I hadn't paid much attention to this individual up to now but, as he began casting his eyes up and down my form and moving his raw head from side to side as if to catch me at all angles, I began to examine him too. He was of middle height, with a small ball-like head, a raw and pocked one. He looked to have been rubbed around the noddle with a nutmeg grater. He got more out of me than I got out of him, however.

"Hmm . . . tall enough . . . lean . . . may I see your teeth, sir?"

"Like a horse," I said and treated him to a bare grin, without much good humour in it. Still, I suppose I should have been grateful. He might have asked to examine my urine like a piss-prophet.

"A player . . . and a traveller therefore," said Pearman, although he knew this already before checking my teeth. "I should say that the gentleman was born under the sign of the Archer."

This last part was delivered with a flourish. Despite myself I was impressed, or at least surprised, at what was little more than an ale-house trick. I wondered what comment William Shakespeare would have made about the whole business.

"Sagittarius? I should say so too," said Fern, clapping his assistant on the shoulder with pleasure and looking to me for confirmation.

"He is correct," I said.

"And from your grudging way of showing it, Master Revill, I would add that you were born near to the secretive sign of Scorpio."

"Near enough," I conceded. "But my father was a parson and did not believe in having nativities cast. He preached against the things."

"And I?" said Abel Glaze, ignoring my comment. "What am I?"

Why are we so eager to be told who and what we are, to know what lies around the corner for us?

At that moment there was a groan from the settle where Nurse Root was lying. It was a groan of neglect rather than of pain, but it was sufficient to cause the company to pay attention to her welfare once more and to enable Abel and me to escape from the Doctor's house, his future still untold.

As we made our way down the path that led from the door I was surprised to see the carter and his piebald nag driving slowly towards us, driving with furrowed brow and bobbing wen (the man, that is). It had taken him all this time to set himself in order and resume his business. I wondered why he was going to the Doctor's house. Perhaps he intended to apologize more fulsomely in front of Mistress Root, throwing himself on her mercy. A bad move, if so. He'd probably do no more than stir up her wrath again. I thought of calling out to him, telling him that it would most probably be all right and that Mistress Root was unlikely to go to law (since Doctor Fern would advise against it). But the poor fellow looked so worried as he trundled past us that I reckoned he was immune to comfort.

Beautiful Lady

The root is the most effective part. White and fleshy when disinterred from the ground, it shrivels as it dries out. You wear gloves at all times when you handle it, knowing that the venom can creep through any raw or open place on your flesh. Dried, it looks like a miniature, malignant tree. Then you slice it with a little knife and grind it down with pestle and mortar until it is almost as fine as grain. A faint, disagreeable odour rises up. The naked taste of this preparation would not be agreeable so you must mask it behind something stronger and more palatable, using mulled wine or sack for cover. If you had the time you would go about this as carefully as a royal cook, preparing a meal for the monarch. In the proper way, the powder should be left to steep in solution somewhere warm and open – on a window sill, say – for a month or more. But you have not got the luxury of time. Events are peering over your shoulder. So you decoct the powder in wine over a gentle heat, until it has all dissolved. Then you decant the result into half a dozen stoppered phials, made of opaque glass. Here is your arsenal.

Belladonna. Bella donna. Beautiful lady.

The Italians now, they are the past masters of poisoning. With them it is an art. For example, they have perfected the poisoned knife from which, when the slightest pressure is applied to the blade, three little envenomed spikes spring out to nip the unsuspecting knife-holder in the palm. What you are doing is simple enough stuff, however, only the beginning. For you have ambitions in the field of poisons. There are so many compounds, so many methods of delivery apart from the poison knife. You might take a quill and blow a powder into the ear of a sleeping man, or pierce another one's windpipe with a poisoned needle, or soak this gentleman's doublet in cantharides, or give that fine lady a pomander which is impregnated with arsenic. (Although there are different views on arsenic, you have learned, some saying it is a preservative.)

To administer poison is to deal death from on high. Although you must be ready to confront your victims directly, as with old mother Morrison, you have the comfort of knowing that, if all runs smoothly, you can put a distance between the two of you. You are able to keep your hands clean. As for your conscience, that can go whistle. What are two or three or five deaths when so many more are in prospect during this time of plague?

This easy interlude in Oxford was too pleasant to last long. We continued to play in front of appreciative audiences at the Golden Cross Inn and had the first practice for *Romeo and Juliet* at Hugh Fern's house on Headington Hill. The rehearsal went well enough – although there was an odd consequence to it – and I considered that I acquitted myself respectably as Mercutio.

But the mood of the Company was darkened by some news which had reached us that very morning. It was all the talk of the ostlers, the drawers, and the other servants before we were ever up, and it was to do with the plague. King Pest.

Well, there was a lesson here, for if we'd believed we could trick fate and outrun the infection we were deluded. An outbreak of the pestilence had been reported from the south side of the town. News of such an event spreads even more quickly than the disease itself and, like the disease, usually has no obvious source. It simply became "known" that an entire household had been struck down near Folly Bridge.

The response of the players was perhaps a little offhand. We had come, after all, from a populous city where the disease never quite died out. You got used to it, as I'd said to Abel. Certainly you didn't show fear. A more immediate concern for us might have been the suspicion directed at outsiders. Since the Chamberlain's Company had crossed Folly Bridge only a few days before – and since we might therefore have been blamed for importing the infection with us – it was just as well that the road across the bridge was the principal route into and out of town and constantly busy. In other words, if the disease had come from the outside, it might have been brought in by any of the hundreds of travellers who arrive at the Athens of England at all times of the day.

We didn't know whether the city authorities differed from those in London in the way they would handle the outbreak, apart from the inevitable step of isolating the household. The general opinion was that we, that is the players, would be permitted to ply our trade in the inn yard for as long as the death toll stayed low. But, if it started to rise (and bearing in mind that Oxford is a much smaller place than London, not partitioned into many suburbs and wards), then we could find ourselves on the move once more. I'd said to Abel Glaze, half in jest, that the player's future was never other or better than a matter of pillar to post. This staggering insight was likely to be proved true once again.

However, we dismissed the plague and its threat to our livelihoods, not to mention lives, as soon as we reached Doctor Fern's and began practising for *Romeo and Juliet*.

This is a queerly affecting play, a sugared tragedy. The story is surely known to you. If the theatre survives and the Puritans or the plague do not triumph over all of us then this tragedy will be played out down the centuries, and keep WS's name fresh to succeeding generations. But – wherever you live, whenever you live – you are doubtless already familiar with the two rival families in the city of Verona, those Montagues and Capulets, and the young couple who reach across the divide which separates them. You recognize the couple's fear that their parents would hardly allow them to meet, let alone marry. You remember the intervention of Friar Laurence, Romeo's friend and father-confessor, who encourages Romeo and Juliet to wed in secret, partly for the sake of propriety but also in the hope that the union of such young lovers might bring about a reconciliation of the feuding families (which it does, but in the last way that anyone would have desired).

The youngsters enjoy one night of wedded bliss. Their whole marriage is contracted into the hours between a single dusk and dawn, hardly more than an eye-blink. Then Romeo must fly from Verona for the killing of Tybalt, and Juliet must feign death with the help of Friar Laurence's potions, and Romeo must believe her really dead, and return to kill himself over her drugged body in the Capulet family vault, and then she must awaken – too late, just too late! – to see her husband truly dead and gone, before taking up his dagger and sheathing it in her own body. So perish the young lovers and so are their old families brought together in grief and self-reproach.

Love and death, it is a most infallible mixture.

It is not just the deaths of the young lovers, either. There's also the odd fight on the way, with the occasional casualty. On the road to that love-tryst in the Capulet tomb others will perish. Mercutio is mortally wounded by Tybalt's rapier before Tybalt himself dies at the hands of Romeo. The real hatred is between these two, since Tybalt has just killed Romeo's friend. By contrast, the bout between Tybalt and Mercutio starts in a relatively light-hearted vein before digging deeper and opening real veins, so to speak.

Now, I was playing Mercutio and so was required to fight and die in the public eye. When it comes to fighting, the public eye is sharp and wants value for money. Londoners are used to pageants and jousts, and any stage company worth its salt must make a good fist of fighting. Not every player is an accomplished swordsman, even though it's one of those skills – like dancing and singing – which you tend to pick up as the years go by, however useless you are to begin with. In my opinion Mercutio is not that good a swordsman, in fact he's more of a *wordsman*. Or perhaps it was rather that I knew myself to be clumsy with a sword and was projecting this on to my character. Unlike Richard Burbage, for example, who still gave Romeo a professional edge when he flashed his blade. And unlike Jack Wilson who was taking the part of Tybalt, and against whom I was scheduled to fight.

True, I had played a fighter during a performance the previous winter as Prince Troilus. But, though there's plenty of talk about Troilus's prowess as a fighter we don't actually *see* much sign of it on stage, and I'd been able to hide behind Shakespeare's lines. Now, however, I would have to give a good account of myself, not only with words but with the sword. I also knew that if I ever wanted to progress to the larger parts – Hamlet the Dane, say, that noble duellist – then I would have to prove my dexterity with the foil.

So, after the half-way point in *Romeo and Juliet* when we weren't needed at practice, I suggested to my friend Jack Wilson that we might run through a few passes and thrusts outside. The reason we weren't needed was that we, as Tybalt and Mercutio, were both dead. And the reason I suggested a practice was because I'd noticed Dick Burbage frowning a little at some of my strokes and slashes. You need to learn how to handle a foil, his frown said, confirming what I already knew.

The others remained indoors while Jack and I found a secluded spot on one of the Doctor's untilled lawns. Hugh Fern had given the Chamberlain's the run of the public rooms of his house and of its gardens. His generosity towards us was marked. I suppose that it was connected to his one-time wish to become a player, which Shakespeare had mentioned. The morning was fine and clear, with that pleasant view over Oxford's towers and spires. We soon worked up a sweat, or at any rate I did.

Jack was trying to instruct me in the niceties of the various strokes. This was necessary since Mercutio, good swordsman or not, is certain to be familiar with all the terms and poses which will enable him to cut a good figure in the piazza. He is an Italian after all.

"No, Nick, no," said Jack, standing next to me and grasping my right hand. "*This* is the *stocatta*. You go under your opponent's weapon, and up. So."

"I thought that was the *imbrocatta*."

"That is *over* your opponent's weapon. The *stocatta* is usually directed to the belly. So . . . "

And he lunged forward, taking my arm and the foil along with him.

"The *stocatta*," I said. " *Stocatta.*"

"Forget the terms," said Jack. "Unless you think you will one day be a gentleman and fight duels and get left for dead on the field or clapped up in gaol for your pains."

"How did you learn them then?"

"My father. He had ambitions for me as a gentleman, not a player. He would have preferred me to hunt and ride, not strut about on stage in front of the common people."

It's surprising what you learn about people you thought you knew. I would have heard more but Jack, perhaps suspecting me of time-wasting, returned to the practice.

"Concentrate instead on the moves, the thrusts. Not the names. So – like this! And this! Now let me see you do it unaided, Master Revill."

Jack stood watching me like a fencing-master until I had grasped the strokes to his satisfaction – or at least to my satisfaction, which was considerably easier to obtain.

"Now we ought to move on to the *volte* and the *punta riversa*," he said.

"Unless we are required inside," I said hopefully.

But Jack was enjoying his role as instructor too much and brushed aside my comment as easily as he brushed aside my blade. We thrust and parried, twisted and turned on the Doctor's lawn like a pair of dancers. It was one of those early spring mornings that seem to prefigure summer itself. The sweat was running down my face. Eventually, to my relief, Laurence Savage summoned Jack for a reprise of one of his scenes indoors and I was left to myself. I sank down, placing my gleaming blade in the long grass beside me.

"*Stocatta, imbrocatta*," I hissed through my teeth in true Italian style, and then, "*Volte, punta riversa . . . puuunta riverrrrsa.*"

Then I stood up once more, retrieved my foil from the ground and lunged and parried, all the time repeating the terms which Jack had used. I felt like a real Mercutio. All at once I stopped. I was being watched.

There was a little burst of clapping from above.

"*Bene*," said a voice.

I looked up and saw Susan Constant watching me from a bank above the lawn, a twitch of what might have been amusement on her clear features. Like anyone caught un-awares, and doing something slightly foolish, I laughed it off.

I knew who she was but did not want to acknowledge it (since she might think I'd been asking questions about her, which I had) so I simply bowed slightly and introduced myself.

"Oh, I think I know you, Master Revill. I saw you bring in Mistress Root the other day. And I was watching you inside just now when you were killed in the duel."

"That's why I need to practise, mistress," I said. "So that I don't get killed again."

"But it is written, is it not?" she said. "That you must die."

"Only in this piece. As a player, I will rise to live and fight another day. I've died and risen again many times."

"Then perhaps you are the person to help?"

"Help who?"

"Help us. Help me."

"Help you, lady? But I am not even certain whom I have the honour of addressing."

"Aren't you?" she said. "Well, I am Susan Constant."

All this time she had been standing above me on the bank and now she ran down the slope until our heads were on the same level. I waited for her to speak first, because I really hadn't any idea what she wanted.

"Your Company is here to perform *Romeo and Juliet*, to smooth any obstacles on the road to my cousin's marriage?"

"Your cousin is Sarah Constant? While it is her marriage to William Sadler you mean," I said. "Yes, that's why we're here although we're also playing at the Golden Cross Inn for the public. But you should talk to one of the seniors or to Doctor Fern. They know more than me. I'm just a simple player."

"Your friend Abel Glaze told me about you," she said.

"I could tell you a thing or two about him."

"Are you playing at the Golden Cross today?"

"This afternoon at two o'clock. *Love's Loss.*" Seeing her

puzzled look I added, "It's the title of a piece by William Hordle."

"Who is William Hordle?"

"A playwright. His name is growing in London."

"It's a tragedy?"

"Veering nearer to comedy despite the title. You will leave happy."

"You are in it?"

"Madam, we are not such a large company, and so almost all of us are in almost everything the whole time," I said, wondering where this catechism was leading.

"Then I shall be at the Golden Cross this afternoon. Master Revill, I would welcome the opportunity to speak with you afterwards."

"I would be honoured to speak with you afterwards or at any time, Mistress Constant," I said, "but can you not give me some – indication – some hint of the help which you say you require?"

For the first time Susan Constant looked uneasy. She glanced over her shoulder in the direction of the Ferns' house.

"No," she said, "not now, not here. This afternoon after your *Love's Loss*."

She turned and ran back up the sloping ground.

I stood there, wondering if I should simply have refused to meet her after the play. How many men can turn down a woman's appeal for help, though? The answer is, plenty of us can. But what if the woman is young and – if not exactly pretty and definitely not beautiful – yet handsome in her own style, like Susan Constant? To say nothing of well-born, also like Susan Constant? Ah, then it isn't so easy to turn her down, is it? Mistress Constant displayed a briskness in firing off questions and indicating her requirements which suited her clear-cut features and her trim shape, and which I found ... not unengaging.

Curiosity played its part too. What was it she wanted to tell me? What "help" did she require? And just what had Abel Glaze been saying about me?

I looked down to discover that I was still holding the foil in whose use Jack Wilson had been instructing me. I tickled the long grass with the tip of the foil. The grass did not fight back. Perhaps Susan Constant had glimpsed in Nicholas Revill a chivalrous figure, a rescuer of damsels, a knight-at-arms who would leap on to his horse and come galloping to her rescue. In a way I hoped not, since my horsemanship was about on a par with my swordsmanship.

I tried one or two experimental slashes with the foil. Again I became aware that someone was watching me. I looked up to see Doctor Hugh Fern, standing atop the bank where Susan had been standing. I smiled up at the good Doctor and he gave me his cherubic grin in return.

Well, we played out William Hordle's *Love's Loss* that afternoon in the yard of the Golden Cross Inn and our audience was generous in its laughter and applause. Afterwards I half expected to find Mistress Susan Constant waiting for me outside one of our makeshift tiring-rooms. These were a row of tiny chambers in a corner of the yard where our clothes were hung up amid the unwanted items and detritus of the inn. But the female who hangs about outside the place where the players get dressed and undressed is usually confined to a certain sort of woman (and sometimes a certain sort of man). Mistress Constant was probably not that sort of hanging-about woman.

After quickly changing into my street clothes, I left the Golden Cross and turned out into Cornmarket without encountering her. I hadn't spotted her at the performance either. At first I'd been gratified by Susan's request for an interview, then I was irritated by it and slightly troubled. But now that it appeared as though she'd changed her mind about talking to me, I grew disappointed. I'd already spoken to Abel Glaze to discover what secrets of mine he'd let slip but he insisted he'd said no more about me to the woman than terms of general praise.

"Master Revill."

A hand touched me on the shoulder. I'd looked round a moment before and hadn't seen her in the street.

"Nicholas," she said.

"Mistress Constant. I thought you weren't coming after all."

"Let's walk down this way," she said. "It's emptier."

"Don't you want to be seen with a player?"

She did not answer but briskly led the way through Cornmarket and across the place called Carfax where it intersected with the High Street. I followed, curious now.

"Did you see the play?" I asked.

"Yes. It was witty enough."

This was very mild praise. I suspected that Mistress Constant probably had little time for plays. Some people don't. I did not bother fishing for compliments on my performance, not being so desperate to hear them as I had been in my earlier acting days. Besides, I only played a simple soul in *Love's Loss*, a small part.

After a short time we found ourselves in a street lined with town houses and then turned down an alley on the right-hand side of it and so on to a selection of meadows framed with walks and fringed with trees which were beginning to turn green. My companion told me that we were in the meadows of the Cardinal's College or Christ Church. A few people were strolling about the walks, some of them threadbare scholars but others more plushly dressed.

It was late afternoon. The sky was overcast but there was still warmth in the air. I was not averse to walking out with a handsome woman.

But what did she want from me?

"What do you want from me?" I said.

"To find a murderer," she said.

This was said so matter-of-factly that I thought I'd misheard. I looked sideways at her, but she did not look at me. For the first time I noticed her jaw-line, clear-cut and composed.

"Who has . . . died?"

"No one has died."

For certain, she was mad – even though she might not have looked or sounded it.

"It is more a question of who will die."

Either mad or, like my friend Lucy Milford back in London, she had the "gift", was able to peer into the future. God forbid, not another seer, I said to myself.

"I am sorry to say this, Mistress Constant, but are you sure you're speaking to the right person?"

"Perhaps you think I need a divine or a physician instead," said Mistress Constant.

This was what I did think, but it's not altogether polite to recommend someone to a priest or a doctor unless they are in extremity.

"I am serious and I am in my right mind," she said. "Listen while I explain."

So I listened as we paced the walks of Christ Church meadows. Having agreed to meet her, I owed her that much.

She explained that her own family were cousins to the main branch of the Constant family which had lived in this city for generations. She was born in Ipswich but her parents died within a few months of each other when she was young, very young, and she had been taken in by the Oxford Constants – that is by James and Sarah Constant, the parents – and brought up as one of the family.

"Oh, but I thought your mother was still alive," I said.

"No, she is not. Why should you think so?"

"Because I remember the day when we brought the injured Mistress Root to Doctor Fern's house. She said that she'd been sent there by your mother."

"That is easily explained," said Susan. "I have no memory of my real parents, none at all, so it is natural for me to think of the older Sarah and of James as my mother and father, and they have been gracious enough to allow me to call them that. And I have been like a sister to their daughters, Sarah and Emilia and the others, like an older sister. Emilia wasn't even born when I arrived in this place. We had the same nurse in

Mistress Root. We shared the same memories, played the same games as children, we wept and laughed over the same childish happenings."

By now we'd reached the river which was flowing fast and high at this time of year. So special is this university town that the river is dignified here with the name of the Isis, although we ordinary Londoners know it as the ordinary Thames. Obviously the water has come down in the world by the time it's floated as far as the capital. I was still in the dark as to why Mistress Constant wanted to talk to me. So far, the story she'd told was usual enough. You might say that she was lucky to have been taken in by loving cousins. I said as much to her, in fact, while we paced along the bank.

Yes, she knew that she was lucky. She had obligations towards those who'd taken her in all those years ago, she said, speaking in her low tones and in an oddly formal way. And those obligations were the reason she had to do something now since she believed that her cousin Sarah, young Sarah, was being poisoned.

"Poisoned?"

"I believe so."

"Sarah is the woman who wishes to marry William Sadler," I said, thinking it was odd to be talking in an almost familiar fashion about two people I hadn't even seen, let alone met. "There is some opposition to the match?"

"Yes, but not so much," said Susan. "I think that the two families are almost ready to lay down their, ah, arms. The union of the young would bring about the final reconciliation of the old."

"What do the two young people think?"

"William is . . . careless," she said. "He will accept what is put on his plate. While Sarah, she is glad enough."

This was an odd way of talking about a prospective match. Still I pressed on.

"So – so – why do you think Mistress Sarah Constant, your cousin, is being poisoned?"

"Because she has an enemy who is determined she shall not marry William Sadler. I believe in this – this enemy also."

"And she has actually talked of enemies, of being poisoned?"

"Not in so many words, although she did once mention discoloured or strange-smelling food," said Susan Constant. "She is a delicate woman. She would weep plentifully over the death of a favourite dog. She has done so before now."

This distress over a dog's death didn't seem to me so unreasonable, though Susan Constant's tone suggested that *she* would not have been so easily affected. She continued, "But I have only to look at Sarah to see that something is working away at her from the inside. She has grown thinner and careworn, she has complained of pustules and blisters on her back. She says she is sometimes hot and feverish."

"And this is making her suspicious?"

"It is making me suspicious. *She* has a trusting nature. Since she will not look out for herself, someone must be suspicious on her behalf."

"Maybe she's anxious about the prospect of marriage," I said. "Even if the opposition to it is really quite small, she may still be troubled by the idea of going against her parents' wishes."

"Oh she is sick, believe me," said Susan.

I was affected by the helplessness in her voice. I was inclined to believe her, or at least half-inclined. I watched a heron take off on the other side of the river, its boxy wings casing up the air.

"Has anyone else detected these symptoms you talk of?"

"No one knows her as I do, not even Nurse Root. If they noticed anything wrong they would probably put it down to an anxious mind and heart, as you have just done."

"And has *Sarah* mentioned the signs to anyone else? Her intended husband, for instance."

"She – she would not say anything to him. Anyway, I do not think she is aware of her true state. Or does not want to be aware of it. She tries to laugh it off."

"What about consulting a doctor? Doctor Fern?"

"Not him," she said.

"Why not? After all, you must trust him."

"Why so?" she said, sounding genuinely curious.

"You described how he was clever enough to find your missing cup by casting for it."

"Cleverness is not trust. There is a world of difference between a missing trinket and an attempt at poisoning."

"Someone else then? Oxford must be full of wise men for you or your cousin to speak to."

"I tell you she will not take her condition seriously. She would rather think of her wedding day. Dream of it."

"When will it be, this wedding day?"

"There are negotiations taking place between my family and the Sadlers. If they are satisfactory the wedding will be celebrated soon."

"I still don't see why you are telling me all this. What can I do?"

"I do not know where else to turn," she said, and so naturally won a small quarter of my heart if not my head.

"I'm just a player."

I avoided the "simple" addition this time.

"Another member of your Company told me how you once helped a family in Somerset when they were in distress and how you brought light into a dark place. It is reputed that you can do these things."

"Who told you?"

"Abel Glaze is his name."

So that was it! That was what she and Abel had been talking about at the Ferns'. Well, it was my fault for having hinted to my friend that I had been instrumental in resolving a problem to do with the Agate family and the deaths which had occurred in it.* Of course, I might just have let slip details of one or two other riddling affairs which I'd been involved in. Now I was repaid for my casual vanity. If you have a mystery then bring it to N. Revill and watch him fumble his way to a solution.

*see *Alms for Oblivion*

We were still walking side by side along the river bank. Now I stopped, forcing Susan Constant to a halt as well, and turned to face her.

"Mistress Constant, I do not think you are being altogether straightforward with me."

A baffled look crossed her face.

"Why not . . . Nicholas? And you should call me Susan."

I grew a bit warier at this.

"Whatever I should call you, you are not telling me everything. You are fearful for your cousin Sarah because she is sick, and because you think that someone is determined she shouldn't marry. But there is no evidence for any of these beliefs – apart from the fact that she's grown thin and careworn – and the – what was it? – the blisters on her back. Where does this talk of poison and enemies come from?"

"You will compel me to say more, Nicholas?"

"If there is more to say."

"Listen and you may judge. But if you didn't believe me earlier then you are even less likely to believe me now."

She'd nimbly put me in the wrong by accusing me of outright disbelief – when what I really thought was that she had probably dreamed up a plot and enemies where none existed – but I didn't protest. Instead I waited. Avoiding my eyes, she looked out over the fast-flowing waters of the Isis.

"There was a woman died recently outside the city walls, on a farm near the Constant grounds."

"Poisoned?" I said.

"Perhaps," said Susan, ignoring the touch of mockery in my remark. "But she was old and ready enough to die."

"You knew her?"

"Everyone knew old mother Morrison. She and her family have been tenants of the Constants for ever. But, listen, that is not the point of my story. On the day of her death I was out walking close to this farm. It was a fine morning and I was out early because I had not been able to sleep. The birds were singing with the spring. The sky was clear."

She turned away from the river and suddenly grasped my upper arm.

"Then at once there was – was – a figure crossing the path directly ahead of me. I saw a figure."

"What figure?"

"It was dressed in black. Some kind of black coat or cloak that was shapeless. It seemed to drain the light from all around so that wherever it moved there was a dead, dark space."

Her grip on my arm tightened.

"It was carrying a long thin stick, held out in front of it. Like a probe."

She did not need to grasp my arm so tightly. She had all my attention now.

"On this fine morning to see such a figure cross my path! Like a fragment of the night! But that wasn't the worst aspect of it. The worst of it was the head. It had the head of a bird, a head all cased up in black. There was a snout which stuck out like a fat beak as if it had just crammed its maw. There were its eyes, glassy eyes, wicked round eyes which caught the glitter of the morning sun."

As she said this, Susan Constant was staring not at me but staring inwardly, remembering her vision of the bird-figure.

"It gazed neither to the right nor left but moved across my path, within two arm's length, three at most."

"It did not see you?" I said, struggling to keep my voice level.

"Thank God, it could not have done. It was intent on other business. It glided on and disappeared among the trees and bushes by the side of the path. I – I did not want to turn my head and see it vanish into the woods."

"Are you certain of this?" I said.

"I felt the passage of the – the thing," she said. "As it moved across in front of me I felt a draught of air. And smelt a smell, a musty dead smell. Then I heard the noise of a body moving among branches, a slight noise, a rustling. It was not a spirit. I did not dream this thing, I'm certain."

She shuddered. Then it seemed as though she came back to herself. She looked down at her hand where it still grasped my arm. She even managed a quarter-smile.

"There . . . Nicholas. I said that you were even less likely to believe me now."

"But I do believe you."

I did not say that the figure she'd described was the same, essentially the same, as the ones I had half seen in a back street on my first night in Oxford. A figure garbed in black with a bird-shaped head, holding out in front of it a stick like a probe or an insect's horn. I had glimpsed several of them by night while Mistress Constant had seen a single one by day. But could there be any doubt that, separately, we had witnessed the same . . . prodigy?

Perhaps encouraged that I hadn't dismissed her story out of hand, Susan went on.

"I stood there for I don't know how long. I think I was afraid to move, and also afraid that the figure would come back, and between one fear and the other I did nothing. The sun shone and insects were buzzing about my head. Then I heard a terrible cry from the direction of the farmhouse where mother Morrison lives, where she lived rather, and that must have brought me to my senses because the next thing I knew I was running – not towards the house, but away from it. I ran and ran until I got home . . . "

"Did you tell anyone about this?"

"I said no words but crept up into my chamber, my legs were trembling so much that I could hardly stand. So I knelt down and spent some time in prayer and eventually grew calmer in my mind and body. For a time I hoped that it had all been my imagination, that I'd never seen the figure cross my path or heard the cry from the farmhouse. But I know that I saw that shape as surely as I can see you now, Nicholas."

I put out a reassuring hand.

"I said I believe you."

And now I briefly described the vision which I had experienced, the shapes shuffling along the dark alley, the flash of lantern-light from above, the nightmarish sight of the hooded and snouted heads. Susan Constant looked shocked, as if taken aback to have her own vision confirmed by someone else.

"What did you do?" she said.

"Like you, I went back to my room, to the inn where we're staying in town. I ran back, if I'm honest. No one asked me any questions, my fellows were mostly asleep. It took *me* some time to get to sleep though."

"You told no one afterwards?"

"Not until now."

"I'm glad."

"Glad I haven't told anyone?"

"Glad that I am not alone. That you have seen this thing too."

"This old woman you mentioned," I said, "the one in the farmhouse, she died?"

"Her death was reported the same day. She was found in her bed at the dinner hour. So the cry I heard must have been . . ."

She let the sentence fall away.

"You've no idea what the shape was?"

"No. But listen, I have seen it since and near to our own house too."

For the first time in her account I felt myself go cold.

"Early one morning I was looking out from my chamber window – I could not sleep again – I do not know why but I have been restless and wakeful recently – when I caught sight of it, black-clad, bird-headed, outside among the yew hedges. It was there one moment and I turned away in terror and when I turned back it had gone."

I didn't ask her what "it" was doing out among the yew hedges but my look may have been enough because she went on, "Later that day Sarah received a parcel. It contained a clay figure, like a plaything."

"A present? Who sent it?"

"There was no mark of any sender. The parcel was left outside a back entrance to the house, with my cousin's name on it."

"What is so terrible about a play figure?"

"This one had a pin stuck in its belly."

I had heard of such attempts at magic cursing before. It is not too difficult to shrug them off as the work of ignorant country dwellers, but not perhaps if you are the recipient.

"What was its effect on Sarah?"

"She said at first that the image wasn't meant for her but for someone else. Then she said that the person who made it must have simply left the pin in its belly by accident. And then she took to her bed with stomach cramps and a fever. Nurse Root was able to mix a preparation of saffron for her."

"You are linking the figure in black with this item? Just as you link it with the death of the old woman in the farmhouse?"

"I don't know," said Susan Constant. "But it seems likely. What else can I do?"

The effect of these visions and happenings was plain enough. They had made Susan Constant a frightened woman, not so much for herself but for Sarah. I couldn't understand any way in which these events and surmises might be connected but it was obvious that something was not right in the Constant household. But neither could I understand the role which I was destined to play, or what Susan had in mind for me.

"I don't know exactly what I want from you, Nicholas," she said, when I reiterated this point. "Simply to talk to someone else is a relief and then to find that you also have witnessed these things! And you are a player and so a resourceful man . . . and your friend Abel told me how you had helped to solve a mystery once . . . and I know that you are an observant individual."

This praise wasn't altogether welcome (because I did not yet see how I could assist her) but I must have raised my eyebrows at this last comment.

"You noticed that Mistress Root referred to my mother, and you picked up on it when I said that my parents were dead. That is all I meant, Nicholas. You're a sharp-eyed person, a sharp-eared one too."

We moved back along a path leading towards the city. There were few people about now and it was growing dusky.

"Are you superstitious?" she said. "Do you believe in spirits and such?"

"It depends on what time of day you ask the question – or what time of night perhaps."

"Just so. You bring reason to a situation, if you are able to. So do I. Yet you can be overtaken by fears. So can I. I tell myself that what I have seen is not an apparition or a monster but a human being who, for motives of its own, chooses to – disguise itself in such a manner. And if it has reasons they are likely to be connected somehow to my cousin's forthcoming marriage. And if there are reasons then, whatever they are, they can be uncovered by the application of reason."

I looked sideways at my companion's profile. There was a clear, determined set to her expression. She was moving briskly. There was something almost masculine about her process of argument. I was willing to be impressed. I was ready to give a hand.

"So what do you want me to do?" I said.

So she told me.

As we were walking back along the meadow paths towards the town, the calm of the early evening was broken by the ringing of a church bell. Nothing unusual in that. Oxford, like London, is a city of towers, steeples and bells. But on this occasion there was an eager, even frantic quality in the sound.

"That is St Martin's," said Susan Constant. A true town-dweller, she knew the character and whereabouts of each bell.

"The church at the crossroads?"

"Yes, at Carfax."

She paused on the shadowy path.

"Is there something wrong?"

"Wait."

In a moment another bell rang out from a slightly different quarter. As with the first ringing there was an excited, jerky note to the sound.

"But that's St Mary's," she said. "The great church in the High Street. I knew it."

"What's happening?"

"A dispute, most likely."

She set off down the path at a brisker rate. We threaded through the alleys by which we'd emerged on to the walks until we were once more on the public ways near the town centre.

The church bells continued to toll irregularly but from underneath that sound came a buzzing, like a thick cloud of insects, which grew louder as we approached Carfax. I knew what it was long before we arrived on the scene. I've lived in London too many years not to recognize the sound of honest citizens smashing up property, battering each other about the head, and generally behaving in an excitable fashion.

In London it's usually the apprentices versus the rest of the world. But this is Oxford, and they do things slightly differently here.

It was dusk by this point and there was a haze of chimney smoke about. Enough light remained to show a confused mass of individuals heaving itself backwards and forwards over the place where Cornmarket runs into Carfax. Susan Constant and I stopped at the nearest corner. The pushing and pulling of the crowd might have been a game – with each group set on preventing the other from reaching the opposite side of the street – but, if so, it was a particularly vicious, lawless game. I saw sticks and staves being brandished in the half-light. Undetermined objects flew through the air. On the fringes of the shifting group some people were tussling on the ground.

The bell from the tower of St Martin's, which stands to one side of the Carfax crossroads, clanged above this scrimmage of bodies, almost drowning out the yells and groans and oaths. At a little distance two women were tugging on a man, one at each arm as though they meant to divide him down the middle. Right in front of us a young, soberly dressed fellow ceremoniously removed his tufted cap before lowering his head like a bull and charging at an older gent. The young head hit the middle-aged belly, and both men over-balanced and fell down, winded.

"A dispute, you said," I said to Susan. "Is this an Oxford dispute?"

"Town and gown will never agree," she said. "Any occasion serves for a quarrel."

"Town and gown". I'd heard that expression several times since we'd been in Oxford. It didn't take much to detect the uneasy relations between the students of the university and the town-dwellers. They were obvious in the insults or taunts – or in the simple, glaring looks – exchanged across a street. But this was the first time I'd seen hostility break out into open violence. From the resigned, almost amused way in which Susan referred to the scene, it appeared to be a not unusual occurrence.

"And the bells are calling them to arms?"

"St Martin's alerts the citizens of the town while the bells of St Mary's summon the scholars. You wouldn't have to stay very long in this place, Nicholas, before you become familiar with the clangour of those two."

It wasn't difficult to distinguish between the two sets of bells, the graver tolling of St Mary's being just audible beneath the more jangling note of the Carfax church. Equally you could tell the difference between the two sides, since the students were mostly younger than their opponents and some of them were wearing their academical gowns. There was something a little comic in seeing the scholars whirl about in the dusk like tattered bats – but also (to a person like me with an innocent belief that learning should bring polite behaviour in its train) something a little shocking.

"I thought they used their heads for thinking with, not as battering rams," I said.

"They're a turbulent crew."

"The townsfolk?"

"The students."

I observed that she was watching the scene with close interest. Most women of her class will steer clear of trouble in the streets. But Susan Constant, hearing the warning bells, had headed directly for the source of noise and tumult.

We were standing at a safe distance from the conflict, or so I thought. But at that moment a missile came arcing through the gloom and bounced near our feet. Instinctively I jumped back and an instant later hauled Susan out of harm's way. The object, round and solid but with dints in it like a cannon ball, rolled after us as if in pursuit. Susan bent down to examine it. She picked it up and laughed.

"It's a loaf. Look, a very stale one. This is an economical fight. You throw only what you can't eat."

"It might have been a stone though," I said.

"Worse, it might have been a piece of offal."

"Stand further back in any case."

She shrugged off my restraining hand, and let the hard loaf drop to the ground, although for a moment she looked as though she was going to lob it back into the fray. Here was a woman who knew her own mind. Well, if she wanted to stand within the range of loaves or stones, so be it. I might even have left her to it. But the way back to my inn and shelter lay through the middle of this rampaging mob, and until things calmed down I had nowhere else to go.

I looked out for the bull-headed student and the older gent but they had merged into the swaying crowd once more. In their place was an even more ill-assorted couple. A few yards away, a tall young man in student garb was being struck about the head by a squat woman. She wasn't using her hands but some elongated object which I couldn't identify. The student was holding up his hands to ward off the blows. With each blow from the improvised weapon, the woman delivered an unfavourable opinion on her opponent, an opinion which carried clearly above the clanging of the bells and the noise of the mob.

"You craven codpiece!"

Thwack!

"You stupid student!"

Thunk!

Now where had I heard that kind of language before? Ah yes . . .

Just as I was about to say something to my companion along the lines of "Isn't that the woman . . .?", Susan Constant stepped forward and yelled out on her own behalf.

"William! Will Sadler! Nurse Root!"

The man and the woman stopped what they were doing – which was cowering and striking, respectively – and looked at Susan. Recognition came simultaneously to everyone. I didn't know the young man but the squat woman was Mistress Root, the Constants' old nurse. She lowered her striking implement and peered at her victim. In the background the crowd continued to swirl about like demented dancers but this couple was standing downstage, as it were.

"William Sadler, is it you?" she said.

"Mistress Root, it *is* you," he said. "I thought so."

This was an odd way to go about things: to exchange names after exchanging blows, even if the blows had been going in one direction only.

"Why didn't you say, you silly student? You know I cannot see well."

"I was too busy defending myself from your weapon."

"Weapon, William Sadler! This is a simple stockfish. It's not even fresh. You cannot claim to be hurt."

In the gathering gloom the matron held up an item which might well have been the dried cod to which she was referring. Speaking for myself, I didn't know whether it would be worse being slapped around the head with a fresh wet fish or an old dried one – although no great harm was likely to occur in either case – but Mistress Root spoke with a certain authority in the matter. Who would dare to contradict her?

"This is a fine battle," said Susan Constant, speaking for the first time since she'd called out the names of the student and the old nurse, and at the same time kicking at the round loaf with her foot. "A fine battle if it's being fought with loaves and fishes. Perhaps they will miraculously multiply."

The student laughed at this, a barking laugh, a single "Ha!" Plainly he had not been much injured by the stockfish.

"What's the cause of all this?" I asked, acknowledging Mistress Root with a tilt of my head.

The question seemed to cause the three of them further amusement.

"You might as well ask why a cat and a dog spit or snarl at each other," said Susan. "Are you all right, Will?"

"Who is this individual?" said the student, not bothering to answer the question.

While the battle raged on, Susan Constant introduced us as calmly as if we were supper guests.

"It is Nicholas Revill, a member of the players who are here to entertain our families. Nicholas, this is William Sadler, the man that my cousin Sarah hopes to marry."

"Ah, Master Revill," said Mistress Root. "You helped me when I was wounded. I remember you."

"And I you, madam."

"You are to play in *Romeo and Juliet*?" said William Sadler.

"And other things besides," I said.

"Where is your nice young friend, the other one who bore me up when I was wounded?" said Mistress Root. I noticed that she was still holding the dried fish in what you might have called the half-cock position, ready for the next enemy.

But before we could get involved in a chat about the niceness of Abel Glaze and the plays which the Chamberlain's were scheduled to perform and other conversational diversions, we were interrupted by a new stage in the Carfax brawl. The shouting had been growing louder, the bells clanging more furiously, and the miscellany of objects flying through the air thicker. Among all this tumult the blare of a trumpet suddenly erupted from one side, like a fanfare played off stage. Oh, just like a real battle, I thought (not that I've ever been present at one of those).

Automatically we turned in the direction of the trumpet sound. Coming up the High Street behind us was as finely dressed a group of men as I've seen outside the court of Queen Elizabeth. They were illuminated by torches held by attendants on the fringes of the group. The smoky light flickered across faces that were grave and wrinkled, and bodies that were mostly stooped and shrunken. But their robes! Bright green robes, sky blue ones, deep blood-reds. It was as if so many flower-beds had decided to get up and go walking about in the middle of the night. The Chamberlain's tire-man – fussy Bartholomew Ridd who had charge of our players' costumes – would have gone into ecstasies over such a display of finery.

I didn't have to be told the identity of these gents. This was the walking majesty of the University, the heads of the halls and houses and colleges, accompanied by their torch-brandishing escort. One of that escort, standing to the fore, was clutching a brass trumpet, while another grim-faced one toted a great pole-ax. Others carried staves as well as the sooty torches.

"The bulldogs, by God," said William Sadler.

I couldn't see any dogs but was willing to take his word for it.

Then from the opposite corner, from the road which emerged into Carfax by St Martin's church, entered a second body of men. They weren't as gorgeously dressed as the first bunch but they too carried the stamp of authority. That is, they were middle-aged or worse, had serious expressions and were kept company by their own armed, torch-carrying attendants. The man in the lead was wearing regalia which glinted in the light, and I guessed that he was the mayor of Oxford. These were the leading citizens of the city, therefore, the aldermen and burgesses, part of whose commission would be to ensure that the civil peace was maintained and that any offenders against it were duly punished.

Both groups halted warily within a few yards of each other. For an instant I wondered whether they, or more likely their escorts, would come to blows as well. But they were respectable beings, conscious of their dignity, to say nothing of the unblemished glory of their robes. They were here to stamp out the flames not to blow on them. The four of us – Mistress Root, Susan Constant, William Sadler and I – were uncomfortably exposed almost in the middle ground. I noticed that William Sadler half hid his face in his gown. I too felt obscurely ashamed, although I'd come late to this fight and had taken absolutely no part in it.

Awareness of the presence of these two groups of oldsters seemed to spread quite fast among the tussling crowd. People who'd been tumbled on the ground picked themselves up, with an attitude suggesting that they'd fallen over by accident. Some individuals on the edges started to melt away into the darkness. All at once the air, which had been thick with oaths and groans, with sticks and flying bread (and probably with flying fish too), turned still and empty. Even the wild tolling of the church bells subsided until, with a final clang, it halted altogether. Then the two sets of attendants moved, as if by a single command, into the heart of the rapidly dissolving mass. The grim fellow with the pole-ax passed close by me.

"Come on!" someone hissed at my ear.

It was William Sadler. He pulled at my doublet.

"What about – ?"

But Susan Constant and the old nurse had already vanished.

I started to follow Sadler as he sped off in the opposite direction, away from Cornmarket and down the street known as Southgate. We weren't alone. Other figures were doing their best to make themselves unobtrusive in the gloom. From my little experience of London misbehaviour, I know what you ought to do when faced with authorities carrying big sticks. It is simple. You take to your heels. The authorities probably won't be too particular about who they lash out at, and they have all the licence of the law on their side. In this case there were two sets of authority, town and gown, and so a double chance of getting beaten about the head.

We hadn't been going for more than a few moments when a bell began to clang out once again. This time, instead of the excited jangling which had summoned students and citizens to the Cornmarket fray, it was a steady, insistent beat.

"The curfew bell," said William Sadler.

I allowed myself to be directed by him. What did I know of Oxford and its peculiar customs? Perhaps anyone caught out on the streets after the curfew had tolled would be hung, drawn and quartered by bulldogs, or pressed to death under thousands of books.

We turned left through a postern gate and found ourselves in a great open square surrounded by an unbroken line of buildings on all sides. The noise of running water, audible despite the bell, surprised me until I saw the glimmer of a fountain in the centre. I assumed that this was William Sadler's own hall or college. He seemed to confirm this by knowing his way about the dark quadrangle in which only a couple of windows on the far side showed pin-pricks of light, all calm and remote after the turmoil in Carfax. The front of the building down which we were passing was pierced with darker entrances which appeared to my over-stirred imagination like the openings to caves. Sadler stoppped at the third or fourth of these.

"Here," he said.

"Where's here?"

"Christ Church, formerly Cardinal College and in between times King Henry the Eighth College. My room is on the second floor."

We groped our way up a dark staircase and I waited while he fumbled with a key. Then waited some more as he entered the room, found his tinder-box with practised hands and lit some candles. They were good candles, not tallow-y things. The room was warm from a coal fire which slumbered in the chimney.

"Come in, Master Revill."

"Nicholas. Nick to my familiars."

He indicated a stool on the far side of a table which was scattered with books. I sat down and looked around. The walls were panelled. There was a feather bed in one corner. It was not even shared accommodation. Properly furnished, well lighted and heated, there was no hard lodging here.

"Behold the scholar's chamber," said Sadler. "Is it what you expected?"

"Something more . . . monastic perhaps."

"We're not all cut out to be monks – even if they still existed."

"*Cucullus non facit monachum*," I said, and immediately regretted it since I was only showing off, demonstrating that I too had a touch of the scholar, together with his Latin, in my veins.

"'The cowl does not make the monk.' Appearances deceive. Too true," said Sadler.

I shivered for, across my mind's eye, there flashed that scene in the alley from my first evening in Oxford. The troupe of hooded figures feeling their way down the blind path. I remembered an illustration I'd once seen in a book, of a line of monks, cowled and creeping along – not religious at all but sinister, as the picture was probably intended to be. That was what the figures had reminded me of.

"Are you well, Nicholas?"

"Yes. Something unpleasant just crossed my mind."

"Then this might help to get it out again."

William Sadler poured two glasses of wine and passed one across to me before sitting down at a stool on the opposite side of the table. Rather unceremoniously he shoved the books to the far edge, careless that a couple of them thudded on to the rush-strewn floor. By the candlelight I saw a man perhaps a little younger than me, clean-shaven with a thin mouth. So this was the husband-to-be, the man who wanted to marry Sarah Constant. Did he look like a bridegroom? Did he look smug or distracted or besotted? No, although he did seem content with himself.

"It's good sense to get off the streets when the bulldogs are prowling," he said.

"I didn't see any dogs."

"The bulldogs are the gentlemen with staves. They keep order here by knocking student heads."

"How did the fight start?"

I hadn't expected him to be able to tell me but he claimed he'd been in on it from the beginning and gave me the story piecemeal.

"It was all an inn-keeper's fault. He's an arrogant, sour fellow. Some friends and I disagreed with him over the quality of the wine he was providing us with. That was sour too. It didn't compare with what we'd already drunk at the Bear and the Mitre."

I visualized a bunch of pissed, pot-valiant students strutting and staggering their way from inn to inn.

"So the whole town went to war because you didn't care for your drink?"

"Not by our choice," said William Sadler. "We didn't start it. Any excuse will serve for those townsfolk though. In truth Master Davenant gave us some very hard words. We were in a cheerful mood and he was not."

"John Davenant at the Tavern?"

"You're already qualified to be a student here, Nicholas, since you are familiar with the inn-keepers of the town. Do you happen to know Davenant's wife too?"

"I saw her in the street recently."

"A fine piece."

"Was she part of the disagreement as well?"

"Not directly. Though one of our group may have made a couple of comments about Jane Davenant which, ah, didn't help matters," conceded Sadler, putting his fingers to either side of his forehead in the sign of the cuckold's horns. "But the real cause of the dispute was the quality of the man's wine, not the calibre of his wife. Ha!"

I must have looked sceptical because, with a grin, Sadler continued, "All right, I admit he might have been provoked by the way in which we returned his sour drink to him."

"How was that?"

"By throwing it and the vessel in the direction of his head. But it fell far short and landed on the floor and did no harm to anyone."

I tried to laugh but not very hard. Something about the student's manner – a kind of amused arrogance – was putting my hackles up. I wondered what Sarah Constant saw in him.

"Master Davenant grew very passionate at that," said Sadler, "and called several of his friends and neighbours together, and instructed one of them to go off and ring the bell of St Martin's. He's an influential man in Oxford with his eye set on becoming mayor, they say. As we were trying to make a peaceful exit we were set upon by the good citizens of this place. By that stage, of course, some more of *our* side had joined us and, well, you saw what followed."

Personally I was sorry that Mistress Root hadn't found something harder than a dried fish with which to beat him about the head. Still, you can't sit in a man's chamber drinking his wine and utter such thoughts aloud. And I have to admit that I was a bit curious about William Sadler. How typical was he of the students at this university? My ideas of the lofty, self-denying nature of academic life were rapidly disappearing.

"Aren't you afraid of the consequences?"

"This wasn't a real battle, Nicholas. Nobody was killed like they were in the old days. It was just a skirmish, fought with loaves and fishes. A falling-out between town and gown over some spilt wine. Anyway, even if there is the prospect of trouble, it can always be . . . you know."

He rubbed his thumb and fingers together. To the other charges I was mentally laying up against William Sadler – arrogance, lack of respect for one's elders, heavy drinking and riotousness – I added the accusation of wealth. I felt older than my years.

Not greatly enjoying his company, I made to get up. Sadler's arm shot across the table and grasped my wrist. In irritation, I shook it free.

"Where are you going?"

"Back to my inn."

"The streets will not be safe yet. The bulldogs will still be on the prowl. Besides, you haven't finished your drink."

"I'm not so thirsty."

"We'll teach you to drink deep before you depart."

This time I couldn't help a half-smile in acknowledgement of the line (it is said by Hamlet to Horatio in WS's play) Suiting the action to the word, Sadler fetched the flask from the sideboard and poured himself another drink.

"Yes," he said, "we may not be encouraged to see plays but that was a popular one here. Every student regards himself as Prince Hamlet on leave from Wittenberg, full of delicious melancholy."

"I thought you were forbidden to go to the theatre, you students," I said.

"A regulation more honoured in the breach than the observance."

"Yet you are permitted to stage your own pieces?"

"Playing is an occasional recreation for a gentleman, but as a regular means of livelihood it is regarded with scorn. What use is it? What purpose does it serve?"

I couldn't tell if this was William Sadler's own opinion or if he was merely passing on, in a slightly mocking fashion, the opinion of the university authorities. In any case it was a standard enough view.

"What purpose does it serve?" I repeated. "Well, I understand that we're here to bind up your wounds. I mean in the matter of – of a marriage."

"Oh that," he said. "To tell you the truth, Nicholas, there's no such great enmity now between the Sadler and Constant families. This whole business of putting on *Romeo and Juliet* is more Doctor Hugh Fern's doing. He can't resist seeing a problem where there is nothing much wrong, and then interfering. Am I meant to be identified with Romeo? Ha!"

"Forgive me if I'm presuming," I said, and not much concerned whether I was or not, "but I thought that this was a love match conducted in the teeth of opposition. I thought there was once a question of elopement."

"Elopement!" said William Sadler, awarding himself another glass of wine from the handy flask. "That was a day's outing, a ten-mile ride to Woodstock! It set one or two tongues wagging and someone foolish like Mistress Root made a joke about us running away together. As for a love match, well, Sarah Constant is devoted to me. It runs in the family. Her cousin Susan was once . . . "

I waited but, having said so much, discretion or gallantry or something got the better of him and he abruptly changed the subject.

"Anyway, what does it matter to you? You're just players, after all, and we're just your audience. What does it matter to you as long as the coin is good?"

"One or two of our shareholders would agree with that," I said.

"And aren't you players only here to escape the plague anyway?"

"If so, I'm told it's followed us to Oxford."

"True, a household has been affected below Folly Bridge, near this very place."

He said this without concern. Susan Constant had described him as careless. I wondered whether anything troubled him very much. I stood up before he could detain me any longer.

He gestured towards the flask. Although there was no sign of drunkenness in his manner, he was – like many men who've sunk a few – evidently reluctant to be left to his own company.

But this wasn't to be necessary for at that moment the door to his room was thrown open.

"Why, William – "

The speaker, a well-dressed man in middle-age, stopped when he realized that Sadler was not alone.

"It is all right, Ralph. Master Revill is about to go," said Sadler standing up so quickly that he knocked his stool over and slopped drink out of his glass.

The newcomer just about acknowledged my presence but it was plain that he was waiting for me to leave.

I thanked William Sadler for his hospitality.

"When do you perform next, Nicholas?"

"In two afternoons' time we are putting on *Romeo and Juliet* for the townspeople."

"This is our *Romeo and Juliet*?"

"There's only one of them."

"Who is playing me?" said William Sadler.

"Dick Burbage, though he has a few years on you."

"A handsome fellow?"

"A fine player."

"Ha. It's the same thing, I dare say."

Again, I couldn't tell whether Sadler was mocking the whole business or whether his vanity was pricked by the notion of his situation, or that of his family, being presented on stage. Except that, according to his own account, it wasn't really his situation in the first place.

The visitor had said nothing all this while but stood waiting impatiently. For a second time I bade Sadler farewell and groped my way down the dark staircase. Once outside in the great quadrangle of Christ Church I waited for my eyes to grow used to the dark before heading to the right towards the postern gate. The stars were out and there was a crispness to the air. The city bells were all silent now.

I thought about the encounter with William Sadler. He was quite an arrogant fellow, but more indifferent than arrogant. Not exactly unpleasant. He had, after all, preserved me from possible danger on the streets. And he had responded with good humour to being beaten over the head by Mistress Root. Perhaps there was no great harm in him.

Concerning the other individual, the one who'd burst into the room, I was not so sure. I'd only had a glimpse of him in the candlelight but he was an imposing presence. He had bulbous eyes like a bullock's, and a jowly face to go with them. Was he a tutor to Sadler? He looked too well heeled, though, with his ermine hat and Spanish cloak. But then, as I've said, my notions of academic simplicity were rapidly being dispelled.

I walked up towards Carfax and then on to the Golden Cross. There was little sign of the battle which had raged over this spot barely an hour earlier. A few loiterers in the streets, and some squashy matter underfoot. I reflected on the automatic hostility between students and townspeople. They were all dry tinder, actively seeking for a spark. Because the play was on my mind I could not help recalling the hatred of the Montagues and the Capulets, so deeply embedded in each family that neither side knew – or cared – how the whole bad business had started.

I regained my inn and found my fellows in high spirits. None of them had taken part in the Cornmarket skirmish but most of them had been, like me, onlookers. For once there could be no question of any players being blamed for stirring up trouble. There was some amusement at the fact that university students could be so similar to the London apprentices – that is, easily given to riot. We're generally gratified to find that those with brains are just as capable of behaving foolishly as those who lack them. More foolishly sometimes, as though they have a point to make. If I thought I came hot-foot with news of how this particular riot began (William Sadler's tale of sour wine and a sourer tavern-keeper) it was merely to discover that there were at least half a dozen versions in circulation of how it had all started.

It was only as I was dropping off to sleep after this eventful day that I remembered my conversation with Susan Constant. Perhaps I had deliberately driven her strange appeal out of my mind, realizing that there wasn't really much I could do to help her. Even if she was correct in her belief that her cousin Sarah was being slowly poisoned how could I be expected to point a finger at the poisoner? I regretted that I'd said yes, a kind of half-hearted yes, to what she'd asked.

I witnessed an odd scene the next morning which I include here only because of what followed from it.

It was a fine morning. Like a butterfly in the sun, I was stretching my wings outside the yard of the Golden Cross Inn – there is something about this city of Oxford which seems to encourage hanging about – when my ears were seized by shouts and screeches close to. The source of the screeching was a woman standing next to a cart which was at the entrance to the Tavern on my immediate left. A wooden crate had fallen from the back of the cart on to the dirty road and, although it looked undamaged, this minor accident had been sufficient to provoke the woman into railing at the carter.

I recognized the carter by his horse, a clapped-out piebald nag.

He was the unfortunate John Hoby, the driver who had run down Mistress Root on the road from Headington and been roundly abused for his clumsiness. This expert in offending women sat on his perch, hapless and hangdog. I recognized him also by the wen that hung from his neck. Although he was, strictly speaking, higher up above the ground than the woman who was giving him a tongue-lashing he seemed on a lower level than her, if you know what I mean.

I recognized the woman also. It was Jane Davenant, the gypsy-like wife of the owner of the Tavern. She who was known to everyone in Oxford and who played at fast-and-loose, according to the ostler Kit Kite. She who might cuckold her husband, according to William Sadler's finger-horn gesture. Such women are always interesting, even when they are unpleasing to the eye – this was my rather worldly reflection – and Mistress Davenant was not unpleasing.

She didn't seem to mind that her ranting was drawing the attention of everyone at the lower end of Cornmarket, of idlers like myself, of stall-holders and students. She was probably enjoying it, since she shook her splayed fingers at John Hoby and wagged her fine, dark head of hair with an almost theatrical emphasis. From time to time odd phrases – "shotten herring!", "sad man" – emerged from the welter of abuse being poured over the carter. I was surprised that a woman such as Jane Davenant could sound like a fish-wife but perhaps it was part of her diverse charms.

The appearance of John Davenant on the scene did not affect her one jot. The landlord and husband looked gloomy, as usual. He put a restraining hand on his wife's arm but she shook it off unawares, as you might a fly's touch, and continued her ranting. So he stood by with folded arms, as if he was used to her fits, and waited for her to exhaust herself. Meantime the carter sat still as a mouse faced by a cat.

In the end Davenant made to pick up the fallen box himself but it was evidently too awkward for him to shift alone. He went round to the other side of the cart and tugged at the carter's sleeve so that the little man almost fell into his arms. Then together they hefted the box and carried it into the inn yard. His wife stopped her shouting and looked around at her scattered audience. I caught her eye but could not hold her gaze. Then she too went inside, although not before kicking out a stray dog that was creeping along close to the wall. I supposed that if she couldn't kick Hoby, then the next best thing was a vagrant cur.

After a short time Hoby emerged warily, as if he expected a fresh attack. He remounted his cart and urged his ancient nag towards the High Street. Having nothing better to do, I watched his departure and wondered what had been contained in the box that was too heavy for one man to carry.

Friar's Cap

There is a willow grows aslant the stream.

Well, there are many willows in this place, and a multitude of streams. During the winter the water rises here, and in midwinter the whole plain freezes over sometimes. But now we are on the edge of spring and there is an unaccustomed gentleness to the late afternoon air as it tilts towards evening. The tips of the branches are spotted with green and the birds are swooping low among the trees. The sound of the church bells, ferried across from the town, blooms in your ear.

Across this watery landscape run several tracks which are passable provided it has not rained recently. Some of them are like causeways, with pools and streams of water on either side. If conditions are good, these tracks provide a quicker route to the outlying villages of the town than the main road. But there are never many people travelling on these by-roads.

So it is now as you wait in the shelter of a stand of willows. Water gurgles at your feet, water cold from the winter. Nobody has passed along this path leading from the village of Whittingham to Oxford during the hour you have been waiting. At this instant, though, you hear the creaking of wheels and the heavy breathing of a horse. The driver is eager to get home before dark. But the horse is old and feeble, and has already dragged the cart around the edges of the town today. At least it is empty now. The carter has made his profit. A profit which he must now pay for.

Naturally, you have dressed for the occasion. You have grown used to your gear by now and are practised at slipping it on and off. At the last moment you tie the hood about your face, securing the points and buttons at the back. There is a comfort in being garbed like this. It is your armour against the world. The costume bestows power on you, of itself. You remember old mother Morrison's last moments. The look of terror in her eyes, the desperate struggle to raise herself from her narrow bed, the final spasm. You did not even have to touch her (although she had already been weakened by the tainted sweetmeats you had sent). When it came to the point she expired through sheer fright.

The horse and cart draw nearer. You glimpse them through the branches. The horse whinnies. It is uneasy, scenting your presence. The carter is muttering to himself under his breath. You cannot hear what he is saying, the hood prevents that, but even through the eyepieces you see his lips mouthing words. The growth on his neck seems to quiver with a life of its own. Abruptly, almost before you are aware of what you are doing, you step out from the clump of willows by the water's edge and stand there, in the way of horse, cart and driver.

The piebald horse shies away and then shuffles its forefeet. The driver looks – bemused. Then fearful. He begins to speak but can scarcely get the words out.

"Y-y-y-you. Is it you?"

He rears back on his wooden perch atop the little cart, and his cap falls off. He half stands up, as if minded to flee. But he cannot run without first getting down from the cart and that would put him on the same level as you. You move forward, waving your white wand from side to side. A slow but inexorable movement. The horse, profoundly unhappy now, attempts to turn round but it is hitched to the cart and the path is narrow. The creature's hooves slide on the muddy bank and it grows more panic-stricken.

Meantime the carter has decided to leap from the cart and in his confusion he jumps in your direction. Now he is trapped.

The cart is turned aslant the narrow track, with the slithering horse to one side. The carter tries to duck under the overhang at the back of the cart but, as he bends under the tail, you bring the cane down sharp on his back. It must be the shock of the blow, rather than the force behind it, which causes him to fall flat on his face in the mud at your feet.

He scrabbles around and looks up to see – the black bird of death hovering above him. If he were not so purely terrified he would scream or cry but, as it is, he opens his mouth and no sound emerges. He does not move or he cannot move, and you are reminded of the way in which a mouse will sometimes turn to stone in the presence of a cat.

You are far removed from this man, far above him. Through your eyepieces you observe your arm as it lifts itself up together with the stick it wields. Then the cane comes down again and again across the carter's exposed face. You strike at the disgusting growth which depends from his scrawny neck. He raises his arms to try to protect himself and, too late, scrabbles backwards to escape the blows hailing down on him. But he cannot see, cannot think. He flails about and falls into the water. His head, all battered and bloody, dips underneath the cold spring pool. He tries to rise but there is nothing for him to grasp hold of, and anyway you lean out over the water and strike at his waving arms. After a short period he falls back, exhausted, into the water. A trail of bubbles spurts to the surface of the pool and there is a great sighing sound. Then there is nothing.

You are gripped by a knot of sensations which, until later, you cannot unpick. It is excitement, a great excitement, but with a dash of pity. The pity redeems you but it is the excitement that drives you forward.

The peculiar request that Susan Constant had made of me was that I should use my eyes and ears to find out whether there was any truth in her belief that her cousin Sarah was being poisoned, slowly and secretly poisoned. An outsider might be helpful, she'd said, might see something she was blind to. It was of little use to claim that I was no expert and that she would be better off talking to a physician or at least unfolding her concerns to another member of her family. For some reason she was adamant that she would not speak to Hugh Fern. And I could only conclude that she was unwilling to involve her adopted family because – terrible as the idea was – she suspected someone within that family circle of being responsible.

The sensible course of action would have been for me to refuse to have anything to do with the business. But she had flattered me with mystery-solving powers, and just because a particular task is beyond our ability doesn't mean that we're immune to being cajoled into it. Also she had given a good impression of having no one else to turn to, she had appealed to my chivalrous nature. (Yes, I know, foolish Revill.)

Susan had informed me that I would have a good opportunity to observe both families together, the Constants and the Sadlers, at the performance of *Romeo and Juliet* at Fern's house on Headington Hill, which was scheduled for a few days after the first public performance. In the meantime, however, she contrived an encounter with Sarah for me. At least I assumed it was a contrived meeting, for I bumped into Susan and another young woman wandering one morning in a wide street which I'd heard called both Horsemonger Lane and the Broad. I had the feeling that she'd been keeping her eye open for me.

"Master Revill, you escaped from the riots?"

"William Sadler gave me refuge in his college. But I was concerned for you, madam."

"I was with Mistress Root. She lives nearby in Cats Street

and so we were not far from shelter. In any case she is worth a dozen bulldogs."

I laughed, remembering the way Nurse Root had beaten Sadler over the head with the stockfish.

Susan Constant seemed to have fallen into the habit of introducing me to others, and she did so now. I'd been right in my assumption that this was her cousin Sarah.

Sarah Constant was a pretty, slight thing. Delicate, as Susan had described her. She was wrapped up against a cold March wind which swept down this exposed street just beyond the old city walls. There was a sharpness in her features. She was pale, perhaps unhealthily so, and she was half leaning on her cousin as if for support. But not knowing what she looked like normally, as it were, I couldn't have said whether there was anything really wrong with her.

"This is a terrible spot," said Susan.

"Why is that?" I said, looking about. We were opposite the dour-looking tower gateway of the college called Balliol. Beyond the college were open fields, criss-crossed with overflowing streams. Oxford is very flat.

Sarah Constant said, "I can never pass here without seeing the flames and hearing the screams."

I wasn't sure what she was talking about but tried to be facetious by assuming that she was referring to more of the bad behaviour between town and gown.

"Obviously they make a profession of riot in this town."

"This is the place where the blessed martyrs met their end in Mary's time," explained Susan, with a stern look at me. "Hugh Latimer and Nicholas Ridley were burnt to death in this very street."

Taken aback, I looked about as if there might still be signs of the sacrifice. There were indeed a couple of charred stumps not many yards away which I did not want to examine too closely. A chaplet of flowers, now withered, had been draped over one of them.

"My grandfather told me that gunpowder was hung about

their necks," said Sarah. "He witnessed it. It was Ridley's brother-in-law who obtained permission to speed their end with gunpowder."

This was cheerless talk on a cheerless March day.

"Oh Mistress Sarah," I said. "All that was long ago. We should each of us pray that those dark days of persecution never return. But we are young, aren't we. Shouldn't we be looking forward? You have a wedding to celebrate, I believe."

For the first time a smile visited her face, and she was transformed. Susan Constant, I noticed, did not look so pleased. But then she wasn't the one who was getting married. I hoped that William Sadler would prove a worthy husband to this fragile woman.

We exchanged a few pleasantries after this, keeping off the gloom and martyrdom, and ending with an assurance from Susan that both cousins would come to the Golden Cross performance of *Romeo and Juliet* that very afternoon.

I protested that that might spoil the story for them, when we came to perform it in the Doctor's house on Headington Hill.

"Oh, everybody knows the story. It ends unhappily," said Susan Constant.

"That's no secret," I said. "The Prologue tells us so within a few seconds of the opening."

"Then we are really coming so that we can see your mettle," she said.

I think that the comment was intended to be a little flirtatious. But she couldn't really manage flirtation – she was too clear-cut and serious. Sarah Constant managed another smile which, in her white face, was like the sun on a snowfield but welcome for all that.

I must be very precise about the afternoon of the play performance. About all of it. "Every detail may be significant," someone said to me later. Judge for yourself.

The first surprise – but a very minor one in view of what

happened later in the day – was the information that Doctor Fern was to take part in our Golden Cross *Romeo and Juliet*. Shakespeare had hinted to me that his old friend had once had acting ambitions, and now our author proposed that, for a single performance, Fern should don his mantle (or his Franciscan cassock) as Laurence, the Friar who gives comfort to Romeo and provides the sleeping draught for Juliet.

"But he's not even a proper member of our Company," said Abel Glaze, with the outrage of the newcomer. Abel was playing the apothecary of Mantua who sells Romeo the poison with which he kills himself. My friend had a couple of other little roles as well but he felt aggrieved that a big part was going to a "play-dabbler" like Fern.

"Why has Shakespeare surrendered his own lines? I don't understand," he persisted.

"Because they're his lines so he can dispose of them as he wants," I said.

"And how does this doctor person, this play-dabbler, know these lines, anyway? Has he been in rehearsals? No, he hasn't."

"He knows the lines the same way we do. By rote. I hear he's been studying night and day since we arrived, and also that Burbage and Shakespeare have run through his moves with him."

Abel snorted.

"It's no use objecting, Abel. Master Shakespeare is a shareholder and may do as he pleases, provided the other seniors agree. And Doctor Fern is our sponsor too, we're here in this town mostly because of him. If he wants to tread the boards then he will be indulged . . . "

"Go on, Nick. You're very good at digging up reasons – or should that be excuses?"

"Also, he's a physician and that will give authority to Laurence's talk of herbs and remedies. And look at his hair and the way he's going bald. There's even something friarly about *that*."

"It's not professional," was the best that Abel could come up with in answer.

Since there won't be another opportunity, I may as well record here and now that – as far as he went – Doctor Hugh Fern provided a good performance as Friar Laurence. No one in the paying audience ought to have felt short-changed that this meaty part was being enacted by a man whom Abel Glaze had disparagingly referred to as a "play-dabbler". It was only a pity that the good Doctor was not permitted to deliver his lines to the very end.

For one thing, as I'd indicated to Abel, Fern looked right. With his round face and cheerful smile, he had the reassuring appearance of someone you would instinctively trust and turn to. Although he and Mercutio don't share any scenes together on stage, I was able to hear a few of his lines from off-stage, and there was some comment among the Chamberlain's afterwards that the day he decided to take up medicine was a decided loss to the English stage. (Mind you, people do tend to talk in that rather grand style about someone who's just died.) But they were right, he was a loss. To medicine, if not to the theatre.

If you think that I sound worked up about a man whose hand I'd shaken once and who'd only uttered a few words in my direction, then I should explain that I was one of the last people to see Hugh Fern alive. More than that, we had enjoyed a conversation together.

There was cause to remember that meeting later and I went over what we had said, or rather what *he* had said, several times in my mind to try to extract some clue out of his words. I even made some notes about our dialogue a few hours after his shocking death.

Although the Golden Cross Inn was a good place for playing as far as the audience was concerned – there was plenty of room for those who wanted to stand and, for those prepared to pay a bit more and hire stools or chairs, there was a wide gallery running round the entire yard – it was a little deficient from the players' point of view. The stage itself was a simple raised platform with booths for exits and entrances on opposite sides at the back, and a larger curtained area in the middle to simulate "indoor" scenes such as the Friar's cell or the tomb of the Capulets. The rear of the stage was concealed by canvas sheeting, painted with bright swirls of red and blue and green that were without meaning, and so adaptable to whatever action might be played out in front of it.

It was a simple set-up. There's nothing wrong with simplicity. In fact, there's an invigorating aspect to playing in an inn yard since it harks back to our origins as players (though not mine personally). But you get used to little comforts and amenities, only noticing them when they're gone. At our home in the Globe playhouse we had plenty of room to put our costumes on and off, just as we had secure nooks for the manuscripts containing our lines, and storage places for everything from pikes and pistols to coins and candle-holders, as well as offices for the tire-man, the book-man and the shareholder-players.

Naturally the Golden Cross possessed none of these amenities. It wasn't a haven for players but an inn where people stayed the night or chatted and drank away their waking hours. However, Owen Meredith, the landlord, had let us have a row of adjoining "rooms" convenient for the stage, in which we might change our costumes, store our few effects, & cetera. These spaces were little more than cupboards for the lumber of the inn, full of old barrel staves, discarded bottles, splintered bits of benching and piles of rag. A beery and vinous smell hung about them, not unpleasant. We tidied up the interiors and took them over for our costumes and effects but, even so, if the garments had had to remain there for more than a few days they would have picked up the mildew while our blunted foils would have gathered the rust.

These "rooms" were in the far right-hand corner of the yard as you approached it coming from the street. They occupied one side of a covered passage which led out into an unroofed alley which, in turn, would conduct you between the Golden Cross Inn and the Tavern next door until you emerged into the wider area of Cornmarket Street. Since there seemed to be a certain coolness between the two hostelries you might have thought of this short, narrow alley as the neutral territory between two rival camps. Certainly it looked scruffy and neglected, with the half-eaten corpses of a couple of cats at one end and live rats which were nearly as big as the dead cats and which scarcely bothered to move if you poked your head round the corner.

You could have gained access to either inn by means of this alley if you were coming from the street. There was an entrance directly into the Tavern about half-way along the alley wall as well as the opening to the covered passage at the far end which connected to the Golden Cross yard. You could have gained access to either inn by this means, I say, but it was unclear why anyone would want to do so, since the alley was dirtier, muddier and much less salubrious than the normal approaches via the yard of each hostelry.

There was a makeshift bench in the yard of the Golden Cross near the inner entrance to the covered passage and in the double shadow of the overhead gallery and the backstage cloth. It was nothing more than a couple of planks supported on two barrels, and put there, I suppose, for the convenience of those who might want to sit down after the labour of shifting stuff into or out of the store-rooms.

On this fateful afternoon I'd dressed myself in my costume as Mercutio. Because we were on tour we had no tire-man to help us into and out of our costumes. Or, more accurately, we had no fastidious Bartholomew Ridd to fuss and fret over torn lace and missing gloves. He'd chosen to stay in London. We had to see to everything ourselves. This included the laundering of our clothes – a significant requirement if you're playing in a tragedy and you are wounded or killed, and have to get the blood cleaned off.

There was about a quarter of an hour to go. An expectant, buzzing sound came floating out from the depths of the inn yard, as welcome to the player as the sound of bees to the bee-keeper. One way or another, that sound is honey to us all. Behind the platform or stage a couple of the pot-boys were busy sweeping the ground, making all neat and tidy for the players' comings and goings. Feet scuffled on the boards of the overhanging gallery. Some of my fellows were already mixing with the arriving audience. This is not something I like doing *before* a play. Afterwards is all right, when the action is done and you are about to resume your real self, but doing it before somehow seems to diminish the mystery.

This was the first time I'd played the role of Mercutio in public and I felt a fluttering in my stomach which was more intense – as if the little hive of bees was inside me rather than out in the yard – than the apprehension I usually experienced before going on stage. I'd grown accustomed to these feelings and the gradations in them over the last few years with the Chamberlain's. A familiar part in a play still provoked nervousness, but somehow it was a homely kind of nerves. A new part, on the other hand, produced a heightened state which sometimes had in it a touch of pure terror. In the early days I'd expected this sensation to get better over time, but the more experienced players denied that this ever happened. Indeed, some of them claimed that a player was nothing without his nerves, that they were required to keep him on his mettle.

I wasn't the only one suffering from apprehension, however. I was surprised to see a friar sitting on the makeshift bench slung between the barrels, then realized it was Hugh Fern in costume. The scroll containing his lines was partially unfurled on his lap and he darted frequent glances at it, at the same time plucking at the sleeves of his grey habit. His assistant Andrew Pearman was bending forward to catch something his employer said. I wondered whether Fern was repeating his lines and saw him clasp the standing man by the shoulder as if for reassurance. The other nodded then walked off in my direction. We passed with the slightest of acknowledgements.

The Doctor's expression was clouded, rather like the sky hanging over Oxford at this moment. I wasn't sure whether he remembered who I was but at least he should recognize me, in my costume, for a member of the Company. We started to talk (and here I must admit that part of my motive was to glean some details about Shakespeare's early life). I addressed him familiarly. It is wonderful how much of a leveller it is to act in a play together.

Nick Revill: Welcome to our Company, Doctor.

Hugh Fern: Thank you . . . Master . . . Revill, isn't it? Nicholas? Tell me, how do I do as a friar?

NR: Very well. Although perhaps . . .

HF: Yes?

NR: The shoes.

HF: Too many buckles? Too much decoration for a religious man?

NR: Well, now you mention it. But your habit is good.

HF: The habit belongs to William Shakespeare, but the shoes are mine.

NR: It's surprising how the audience notices shoes, how the groundlings do anyway. They're on the same level, you see.

HF: It looks as though it might rain. What happens if it rains? Will the play be postponed?

NR: No, we play on.

HF: Whatever the weather?

NR: I remember once at the Globe playhouse in London the fog was so thick that – some person – some foolish player – walked off the stage unawares and fell down with a terrible clatter among the groundlings.

HF: I hope it was during a comedy.

NR: Unfortunately it was a tragedy. It took the audience some time to settle down afterwards.

HF: And the player?

NR: No harm done, nothing worse than sprained pride.

HF: It is yourself you mean?

NR: Yes. I was that foolish player.

HF: Do not be too hard on yourself.

NR: I hear that you and William Shakespeare have been friends since boyhood.

HF: Since boyhood.

NR: Doctor Fern, I will be open with you. Such is my admiration for Master Shakespeare that I am eager to learn every detail of his life.

HF: Then surely you should ask *him*, Master Revill.

NR: He said once that in your younger days you went – went hunting together in company?

HF: Oh that. He has been telling you, I suppose, that we poached deer together – ?

NR: Well . . .

HF: On the estate of Sir Thomas Lucy near Stratford. Did he tell you also how he was caught by Sir Thomas and whipped and imprisoned but broke out of gaol with the help of some friends and then ran away to London, though not before penning a short satire against the Lucy family?

NR: Oh no. No, he didn't say any of that. Is that how it happened then?

HF: It's one of the stories I've heard. Stories tend to attach themselves to Master Shakespeare. People believe that they can say what they want about him and that he will not take offence.

NR: Is that true? That he would never take offence?

HF: Of course it's not. What would you think of a man who never took offence at anything said about him?

NR: Well, he was the one who spoke about the deer first.

HF: And speaking for myself, I have never taken a deer in

my life, Master Revill, nor have I ever been out poaching with William Shakespeare.

NR: Oh.

HF: You should believe nothing without the testimony of your own eyes, and not even then. I am very fond of William but he's a play-maker who lives in a world of kings and castles and murderers, and if he has to choose between a fat story and a starved reality then he will pick the first one every time.

NR: He would sacrifice a lot for a pun. He made a pun about hunting harts. He loves a pun.

HF: Very true. Never mind, Master Revill, if you have discovered that Shakespeare has stretched the truth and that you've been ready to listen to him. You're not the first. And you're a Sagittarius, I remember. It's one of the marks of your sign.

NR: Gullibility?

HF: Being open-minded.

NR: That's kind of you, Doctor Fern, to put it like that. I'm sorry to have troubled you.

HF: No, no, you've taken my mind off all this. I also remember now that your father was a parson, you said, and did not approve of casting horoscopes.

NR: He didn't. But I cannot see much harm in it.

HF: Doctors may be worse employed, believe me. Much worse employed. What's that sound?

NR: The trumpet which announces the beginning of the performance.

HF: Now?

NR: Imminently.

HF: Oh dear, I was afraid it was. You wouldn't think that I was eager to play yesterday, even this morning. But now . . .

NR: I am always frightened before I go on stage.

HF: That is heartening to know. If an experienced player can feel that . . .

NR: The most experienced feel it most of all, I'm told. And I'm on soon. I will let you alone to have a final look at your lines, sir.

So I left Doctor Fern to scan his part in peace. Even as I was positioning myself backstage (or rather joining my fellows where they were clustered to the rear of the platform in the yard) I heard the Chorus declaiming the opening lines of our tragedy.

> *Two households, both alike in dignity,*
> *In fair Verona, where we lay our scene,*
> *From ancient grudge break to new mutiny,*
> *Where civil blood makes civil hands unclean . . .*

The buzzing from the audience subsided. By the time the Chorus had reached the end of the prologue there was absolute quiet in the yard.

"It's a good audience," whispered Abel Glaze.

"It's a good play," I said.

I looked around for the author of this good play but there was no sign of him.

Things rolled smoothly from that point on. We had the street-fight (where the Montagues meet the Capulets), we had the ball (where Romeo meets Juliet), we had the first appearance of Friar Laurence. Hugh Fern entered through one of the curtained booths, carrying the basket in which he was gathering herbs and simples from the fields around Verona. I noticed that he'd changed his bright, buckled shoes for footwear that was altogether plainer and more friar-like. He started speaking too soon and too quickly – as inexperienced players often do – but any tremor in his voice was covered by the little burst of applause which greeted his appearance. Either some of the spectators recognized him under his grey habit or perhaps they were already aware that a local doctor was substituting for one of the regular players. Anyway, the clapping demonstrated his popularity.

As Mercutio I had two big scenes in particular. There is my speech about Queen Mab, which shows me up as a man of dreams and imagination, and then there is my fight with Tybalt, which reveals me as a man of action. The fight is a key moment in the story since it comes after the marriage of Romeo and Juliet but before that marriage can be consummated. In between marriage and consummation, Romeo will kill the man who has killed his friend and so earn himself the sentence of exile.

I was a bit nervous about the fight. My sessions with Jack Wilson had helped to polish the moves but I still didn't quite trust myself with a foil. And I wanted to die well since this was (obviously!) my final appearance. I would not be coming on again during the afternoon as a ghost or as another character in a different guise.

Laurence Savage, who was playing Benvolio, and I strolled on to the stage of the Golden Cross Inn, making pretend that this was a public place in Verona with the sun beating down on our capped heads. Even as Laurence was talking about "these hot days" I felt the first spot of rain on my sword-hand. The sky sagged above us. Still, I sensed that the audience was rapt enough. They knew that trouble was brewing.

Sure enough, Tybalt and a clutch of other Capulets soon swagger on and then Romeo enters, all bright and fresh (although not yet satisfied) from his union with Juliet. Tybalt challenges him to a fight but Romeo, softened by love, has no wish to take up arms against a man who is now related to him by marriage. Once again, I marvelled at the subtlety of Dick Burbage, of how he was able to suggest the conflict between love and honour within young Romeo – even though Burbage would never see the near side of thirty again and must be struggling to remember what youthful love was like. Why, I could hardly remember what it was like myself.

Now Mercutio steps forward. Unaware of Romeo's secret

marriage, he can't bear to see his friend turn the other cheek under Tybalt's goading. So Mercutio will fight on his behalf.

And so we go to it. *Stocatta, imbrocatta, punta riversa* and all that Italian cut and thrust. Swords flashing, we caper about the platform stage, Jack Wilson and I. The boards quiver under our buskins. The audience ignores the gathering rain, and oohs and aahs in sympathy.

Then: catastrophe for Mercutio (and for me).

Romeo intervenes in the fight, trying to part the duellists. He does it for the best of reasons, he wants to save his old friend just as he wants no harm to come to a member of Juliet's family. He steps between us and, under his arm, Tybalt thrusts up hard with his foil – maybe using that *stocatta* stroke – and gives me the fatal scratch. Perhaps sensing the damage he's done Tybalt quickly exits with his followers.

What happened next was entirely my fault. I wanted to die well, like I said. So I twisted away sharp from the touch of Tybalt's blade, burst the little bladder of sheep's blood which was snugged under my armpit and stood staring at Jack Wilson in full retreat. Then I looked down at the red stain spreading across my shirt, as if suddenly conscious of my true condition. Grasped what had occurred, fully grasped it. The fatal scratch. Staggered half-way across the stage, which by this time was fairly sprinkled with rain. So next thing I knew I was slipping in the wet and landing with a heavier thud than intended. My left foot doubled up under my body. I lay gazing out across the gaping faces of the audience, no doubt with genuine pain written all over my own face. From a horizontal position I delivered myself of my next line – *I am hurt. A plague o' both your houses* – and ordered my servant to obtain a surgeon. Then I tried to get up, almost managed it and fell over once more.

The audience thought this was real (that is, they thought it was all a matter of play) but for me there was a touch of earnestness in the business as well. Nevertheless, I gave my dry and witty farewell, with its talk of grave men and worm's meat, before being helped off-stage by Laurence Savage. The other players stood by, expressing shock at the turn events had taken. Laurence ushered me into one of the booths, waited for his cue to reappear then dashed on to announce my sudden death. Meantime I hobbled down the rickety steps to the yard. A couple of my fellow players, seeing that I was in difficulties, helped me to the bench. I sank down, leaned against the rough whitewashed wall and felt my foot throbbing.

Well, at least I hadn't fallen off the stage like I had that time at the Globe. I hadn't disgraced myself by disrupting the flow of the action or producing unintended comedy. Gingerly, I twisted my foot around.

"Let me look, Nicholas."

It was Hugh Fern. I hadn't been aware of his presence. He was still dressed in his Franciscan costume since he had much to do in the rest of the action. He made to reach for my bloodstained shirt.

"That is only pretend, where I was stabbed by Tybalt," I said. "But the injury to my foot is real enough. Real enough as a mark of my carelessness."

"Fallen again?"

I grimaced, the foolish player owning up. He felt my foot and ankle. His touch was comforting. The throb subsided slightly. All would be well.

"How did it go?" I asked. "Was it better than you expected, performing in public? I see you have changed your shoes."

"Thank you for the advice about footwear, Nicholas. As for the playing, it's something I could get a taste for. Though I would need to get my own costume, not use William's. He's about my height or a bit more but this is a little tight around the girth."

"Then it's more fitting for a friar, perhaps," I said. "They shouldn't be thin. They're too jolly for that."

Fern finished palping my foot.

"Nothing broken."

"My pride can only take so much, though."

"I will make up a poultice later."

"Are you speaking as Friar Laurence or as a physician?"

"There's not much difference between the two in this case."

"Thank you, whichever one you are," I said, warming to this kind, reassuring individual.

From the stage I could hear the thunderous denunciation of Escalus, the Prince of Verona, when he condemns Romeo to exile and, pointing to Tybalt's body, concludes:

> *let Romeo hence in haste,*
> *Else, when he's found, that hour is his last.*
> *Bear hence this body and attend our will:*
> *Mercy but murders, pardoning those that kill.*

A break in the action was scheduled at this point.

The audience was left with these questions to ponder: would the marriage of Romeo and Juliet be consummated? How would Romeo evade exile or, if he was caught in Verona, the sentence of death? What would happen to the lovers in the end?

At the Globe we would most likely have played the action straight through without interruption but staging plays at an inn imposes different conditions (not unrelated to the selling of extra liquor to the audience in the rest period). So now there was applause and a resurgence of buzzing from the audience. The rain hadn't dampened their interest.

My friends trooped down the steps from the platform and several came over to see how I was – since they alone perhaps were capable of judging how hard and unintended my fall had been. Some came in a spirit of amusement, but two or three with real concern. Both were welcome in their different ways but I almost preferred those who mocked.

Members of the audience were also strolling about back-stage and under the gallery, to get out of the drizzly air. Drawers and pot-boys darted around taking and delivering orders of drink. Susan Constant and her cousin Sarah had been as good as their word. I saw them, in company with

Mistress Root, at a little distance. Hugh Fern approached the group. The white of Sarah's countenance contrasted with the ruddiness of Nurse Root's. They looked in my direction and I gave a cheerful wave – to show that I had got over my injury – but all four were preoccupied in conversation. No doubt they were talking about the play.

The feeling between the two neighbouring inns, the Golden Cross and the Tavern, evidently wasn't so strong that it precluded Jack Davenant from attending a play in his rival's yard, for I noticed him walking about on the far side of the Constant cousins. He looked characteristically gloomy, his head swinging from side to side as if he was searching the crowd. Perhaps he was reckoning up how much business he was losing.

Luckily I was out of the action now. Mercutio was dead. I didn't think I would be able to take part in the jig which would end *Romeo and Juliet* but otherwise nothing was lost. In the capable hands of Hugh Fern I would soon recover to fight and fall another day.

I looked around for the good Doctor and caught a glimpse of his grey cloak and balding head slipping into one of the store-rooms further along the covered passage. I heard the door shut fast. I didn't think this strange at the time.

Everyone else in the Chamberlain's had slipped away by now, to make little adjustments to their costumes or touch up their face-paint or sink another pint or piss away the last one in a neglected corner. I was left alone.

The trumpet tooted to announce the commencement of the second half of the play.

I leaned my head back against the dirty white wall. I heard voices from the stage, clear but seeming to come from a distance on account of the backcloth. My eyes closed involuntarily and remained closed until I became conscious of the pain in my foot. I opened my eyes to see William Shakespeare standing over me. There was someone else behind him. He spoke in a breathless voice, aware that we were only yards from the stage.

"Where is the Doctor?"

"Who?"

"Hugh Fern. Have you seen him?"

"What? No ... yes, I have, he went down there a few minutes ago."

I jerked my thumb in the direction of the store-rooms. Shakespeare moved away to reveal the identity of the other person. I was surprised to see that it was Mrs Davenant, but not that surprised. I smiled lamely, not knowing what else to do and being confused about what was happening. I noticed her looking at my bloody shirt and quickly concluding that it was fake.

Something was wrong. Shakespeare almost ran down the covered passage – and this was a man who did almost everything at an unhurried pace – and peered into each of the tiny chambers. He rattled at the door of the one at the far end and then sped back to me.

"That one's locked," he said. "Is he in there?"

I was about to comment on the foolish nature of the question because if Hugh Fern was in the room then he would have heard the fuss outside and answered it, wouldn't he? And anyway why should he have shut himself inside? – but something set and serious in WS's expression prevented me.

"He's due to appear in minutes," said WS. "This is my fault."

"He was eager to play," I said.

"I didn't mean that," said WS, almost snappishly.

I got up from the bench and went to look for myself, careful about putting my full weight on my left foot. There were, to be precise, half a dozen little chambers opening off the right-hand side of the passage. I thought that Hugh Fern had gone into the last of these and, sure enough, the door was locked, although I couldn't imagine why it should be. The doors to the others were ajar or completely open. Inside were unused costumes and effects, together with the detritus of the inn. There were small grilled openings, more for ventilation than anything else, to each room. These openings were slightly above head height. I stood up on tiptoe and tried to peer into the locked room but it was too dim on the interior for anything to be clearly visible and my position was too uncomfortable to hold for long.

Shakespeare was already inside one of the open rooms, rummaging through the store of clothing there. Handsome, bright-eyed Jane Davenant stood to one side. I didn't know what she was doing there (but was starting to have my suspicions) and I certainly wouldn't have asked her straight out. I hadn't forgotten her attack on the hapless carter or the way she had kicked the stray dog.

"Help me, Nick," said WS from inside the dim little room. "Your eyes are better than mine, younger anyway."

"What are you looking for?"

"A friar's habit. We must have more than one."

"Perhaps next door," I said, and went into the neighbouring store-room.

This was the sort of situation where we really missed our tire-man. Bartholomew Ridd, fussy though he was, would have known exactly what was in stock. We carried certain staples, from a king's robes to a peasant's smock, and in many cases (although not the king's) several similar outfits. I sorted through the hanging jerkins, doublets, dresses and chain-mail before arriving at an item whose shape and texture felt right.

"Here is something."

I brought it out into the half-light of the passage. It was a religious costume, it was even a friar's garb, but not quite in the right colour, more dirty white than grey.

I said as much to Shakespeare.

"Never mind," said WS, already shrugging on the habit over his shirt. He was sparsely dressed for a damp afternoon in spring. "Needs must. It's a good enough fit."

"You're taking Hugh's part?"

I realized he was of course. What I wanted was some explanation.

"Yes," said WS.

"Where is he?"

"I don't know."

No more explanation than that.

Jane Davenant performed some smoothing and patting actions on Shakespeare as he adjusted his costume. She even secured the girdle about his waist. She was as good as our tire-man, nearly.

If Hugh Fern passed easily enough as a friar then so did WS, in a different way. With his high brow and his generally benevolent gaze, he looked the part – or would have done if it hadn't been for a manner that was unusual with him, somehow both abstracted and purposeful.

There was no time to stand about admiring looks and clothes, however. We were in the middle of a play. Now an anxious Dick Burbage appeared and there was a whispered conversation between the shareholders. I noticed that Dick ignored the presence of Jane Davenant. Shakespeare pointed towards the room at the end of the passage, the locked one. Then Dick Burbage gestured in my direction.

Shakespeare turned to me and said, "You were injured in the fight, Nick?"

I shrugged my "it's nothing" shrug but WS did no more than tell me to sit out the rest of the play and not to appear for the jig at the end, before he and Burbage returned to the area immediately behind the stage.

In the background all during Shakespeare's search for Hugh Fern and then for a friar's habit there had been audible the subdued shrieks of women. It was the sound of the Nurse and Juliet, or more precisely of Thomas Pope and the boy player Peter Pearce, as the former tells the latter that her cousin Tybalt has been killed by her lover Romeo. The Nurse has tried to console Juliet. Now the Friar must try to console Romeo.

Standing uncomfortably behind and below the platform stage, I watched Shakespeare go on through the booth and heard the small modification he made to his lines – "Romeo, come forth and speak to Friar Laurence" – to tell the audience who he was. I suppose they were aware of the substitution but there were no gasps of surprise or sounds of protest. It's strange how quickly audiences will accept what they're given. Then Dick Burbage entered as Romeo and everything proceeded smoothly once more.

Mistress Davenant had gone by now, though whether to watch the play or elsewhere I didn't know. I returned to my position on the bench and prepared to sit out the tragic unravelling of *Romeo and Juliet*. I was baffled by the scene which had just passed. Not so much that William Shakespeare had taken over the role of Friar Laurence half-way through. It was the playwright's part after all, Doctor Fern was no more than an afternoon substitute, and Shakespeare was only fulfilling the player's oldest obligation: appearing on cue. No, the baffling question was what had happened to the good Doctor.

The rain had slackened but the air was moist. So much for sun-kissed Verona. When I shivered in my thin, bloody shirt it wasn't altogether from the chill. It would have been sensible to go and look for my doublet in the store-room but I was in that inert, passive state where one doesn't want to move, even to avoid discomfort.

Instead I watched and listened.

From my place on the bench I watched the bustling exits and entrances of my fellows and listened to snatches of the stage-action as they brought the lamentable tale of the young lovers to its close. The double deaths in the tomb of the Capulets. The arrival of Prince Escalus and the two rival families to survey the scene. The final sentence of the Prince as he condemns the surviving Montagues and Capulets to live with what they have brought about, indirectly, through their bitter enmity.

So far, so good . . . or so bad.

Then the applause from the crowd in the Golden Cross yard. Heartfelt applause to warm a player's cockles, an antidote to this dull, wet afternoon.

As the applause was dying down the music struck up from above my head in the gallery and the Chamberlain's Company – all of them, living or dead at tragedy's end – came together and joined in a merry jig to dispel the glooms. The boards thudded and the air resonated with whoops and shouts.

My legs almost twitched in time. I longed to be up there with them. I felt alone.

But not quite alone.

Because now there appeared in front of me Doctor Fern's man, Andrew Pearman.

"Have you seen my master?"

There was a look almost of panic on his face.

"I have been searching for him everywhere."

"So have my people. He was not here to play his part in the second half."

"Please . . . Master Revill . . . have you seen him though?"

For the second time in less than an hour I indicated the covered passage which lay to my left. For the second time I gave the same sort of answer.

"Some while back I saw him enter a room along there. I don't know why he was going there."

Pearman at once started off. I called after him, not worried about shouting. Nothing could be overheard amid the music and the thumping. "But there's no one there now. It's no use. The door is shut fast."

I watched the servant pushing and tugging at the far door, quite desperately, but it would not give.

The noise of the cornets and drums from overhead, the stamping feet and the hurrah-ing crowd below, all swelled to fill the inn yard. Meantime another drama was being played out backstage. This was different from the anxious enquiries of Shakespeare about Hugh Fern. WS had been apprehensive because the Doctor was due to appear on stage and was nowhere to be found. He feared for the play more than for his friend. But on Andrew Pearman's face I could read a genuine worry or something worse than worry.

He hoisted himself up to look through the little opening into the room. Did it several times but evidently couldn't see

much. He was slightly shorter than me. He looked towards
where I was still sitting on the bench.

"Help me," he said.

I got up reluctantly. It was as if I sensed what was going to
happen next. No, not that exactly. But I knew the news was
not good.

"There is someone in there, lying down," said Pearman.
"Look."

I raised myself up and squinted through the barred space.
Knowing what I was looking for, I saw on the floor a shape
that might possibly have been a body, but the lack of light
made it hard to be certain. It was probably no more than a
carelessly heaped mound of clothes. All the same I felt my
stomach tighten.

"You may be right," I said.

"I fear so," he said.

There was a sheen of sweat across the man's brow. He
rattled urgently at the door, at the same time calling out,
"Doctor Fern! Doctor Fern!"

Though the door was flimsy, and there were gaps where
the boards had warped, it held fast.

"Perhaps it's bolted inside?" I said.

"Not when there's a keyhole," said Pearman. For all his
troubled state he was thinking more clearly than I was. I
suppose you might install a key as well as a bolt for extra
security, but you wouldn't put a bolt on the inside of a store-
room where there was no other exit. What would be the point?

Pearman moved a couple of paces to the opposite side of
the passage. I thought he was going to throw himself full-tilt
at the door but he gestured towards me, as if he expected
that I should do it.

"We ought to get Owen Meredith, the landlord," I said.
"This is his property. He will surely have the key."

"I am afraid for Doctor Fern," said Pearman, looking sus-
piciously at me as though I somehow bore responsibility for
this state of affairs. Then in an odd echo of WS's words earlier

he said, "Needs must," and did a little run and put his shoulder to the door. The boards shivered but still stuck fast.

Even now I was for going off to find Meredith but Andrew Pearman was already fiddling with the boards in the area of the keyhole. He squeezed his fingers into a gap, then got his whole hand in, curled it round and seized a piece of the planking from the far side so that his fingertips protruded. He wrenched it backwards and forwards. His face flushed and the veins in his forearm stood out. With a cracking sound a square chunk of wood splintered away. He drew it out and handed it to me. I placed it carefully on the flagstones of the passage. As I did so, something nagged at the corner of my mind. Perhaps I was troubled about the petty damage to the landlord's property. Well, if the Doctor's assistant was doing it in a proper cause, then no doubt the Doctor or someone would make it good.

I watched Pearman as he scrabbled blindly on the interior of the door, his forearm awkwardly angled though the hole.

"I can't feel anything."

His face fell, then brightened slightly. "Sir, your arm may be longer. Will you try?"

He stood to one side. By now I was thoroughly infected with his belief that something was wrong. I reached my own arm through the ragged gap in the door and groped about. I too could feel nothing at first, then suddenly my fingertips grazed something metallic. As my fingers closed around the slippery metal, I involuntarily cried out, "Got it!"

I might have tried to twist the key round from the inside and open the door in that way but it was hard to get a sufficient purchase on the head and shaft of the key. Instead I took a firm hold of it and inched it out of the lock, holding my breath for fear that it might slip from my grasp. I slowly withdrew my arm and clenched hand from the hole in the door. For the few moments which this process took I was completely oblivious of my surroundings. The dim passageway, the intent gaze of the Doctor's assistant, the remote sounds of drum,

cornet and stamping feet from the region of the stage. I only
registered these things again as I held up the key, in triumph.
The real purpose in retrieving the key was, for a tiny instant,
forgotten. I stood there wondering what to do next.

"Open it, Master Revill."

I turned the key in the lock of the battered door. It grated
rustily in the wards, suggesting that it wasn't often used, but
the door itself swung inwards at a little shove from my hand.
My heart beating faster and louder, I saw that the huddle of
grey on the dirty floor of the store-room was human. The
body lay on its side with its front turned away from us but
from what I could glimpse of the back of the head, I feared
that this was indeed Hugh Fern. I sensed Pearman crowding
behind me, felt his hot breath on my neck.

"Oh sweet Jesus."

He darted into the room and knelt down by the body. He
stretched out his hand respectfully and touched the man's
shoulder. Then shook it. There was no answering movement,
no sudden awakening. This was no sleeper. Still crouched
down, Pearman leaned over the body then turned towards
me. His face was rigid with terror. He forced out the words.

"Oh, it is my master."

"Is he dead?"

Pearman peered at the figure again, then moaned, a long
despairing noise.

"Yes."

"I'll get help," I said.

I hastened out of the passageway. As I went I heard
Pearman groaning and calling out the Doctor's name.

I wanted to get away from this place. Or, at least, before I
went back there I wanted witnesses, more witnesses than a
single distracted servant could provide.

Above all I didn't want to be found in the proximity of a
body.

(Not only was there a natural human resistance to this, I
was also, abruptly, conscious of the fact that I'd been one of

the last people to see Doctor Hugh Fern alive, that I was wearing a shirt streaked with stage-blood, that anyone finding Nicholas Revill together with a corpse might leap to the wrong conclusion. It's happened to me before and if that sounds calculating, well, I can't help it.)

As I emerged into the more open area at the back of the stage, I encountered my fellows milling around there in a happy back-slapping mood. The action was over. Romeo and Juliet were dead. The warring families were united in sorrow. The dances were finally done. The music had stopped. The audience was free to go home or to get on with their afternoon drinking and other pleasures.

I blurted out the name of Hugh Fern but didn't have to say anything else. My face must have registered something of the real tragedy which had been unfolding in the passageway of the Golden Cross. I pointed towards the covered passage.

I was swept up in a gaggle of Chamberlain's. A number of us had bloodstained costumes, Paris, Juliet, Tybalt, we had all been in the wars. We crowded back into the passage and round the door of the far chamber. I was at the rear but glimpsed, through the heads of my fellows, the essentials of the scene.

Andrew Pearman was as I had left him. He was on his knees by his master's body, which was by now rolled over on its back. Pearman was holding his hands to his face as if he could bear to look no longer. Hugh Fern, still clad in his Franciscan robes, lay gazing up at the ceiling of his last room. His face was distorted in an expression of horror, his teeth bared, his eyes bulging. There could be no doubt of the fact of his death. Nor of the means by which that death had been procured. Near the centre of his chest, surrounded by the folds of the blood-soaked friar's habit, stood the handle of a dagger.

The body was brought out and laid in the entrance to the narrow passageway, though not before a couple of the drawers had been despatched for a sheet to place on the ground. There was a strange sense of time suspended. People

– players, inn-servants, citizens who'd been slow to disperse at the end of the performance – ebbed and flowed about the corpse. Some came to gawp, some seemed genuinely shocked. Shakespeare held urgent consultations with Burbage and Thomas Pope, the latter still incongruously in his robes as Juliet's nurse. I considered leaving but there was a kind of comfort in numbers. Also, as one who had discovered the body, I felt an obligation to remain now. Andrew Pearman wandered distractedly round the yard. Like a bereaved dog he would not move far from his master.

The coroner was sent for but the messenger soon returned to say that he was busy about another death and that the body of Hugh Fern was to be put in store for a few hours. But where? Owen Meredith seemed reluctant to give house-room to the dead physician in the Golden Cross. Fortunately, the problem was solved by the arrival of a new actor on the scene.

Not new to me though. Barging through the press came the jowly individual I'd encountered in William Sadler's lodgings in Christ Church. He was as well-dressed as on that evening. His boots alone would have cost me many months' wages. He took out an expensive-looking octagonal watch and ostentatiously consulted it, I'm not sure why unless it was simply to impress us with his status and property. Having established the time, he stood over Fern's body, rubbing his hands together before bending down to examine the man's wounds. As he was doing so I noticed something odd, perhaps prompted by the newcomer's excellent boots.

The oddness was to do with Hugh Fern's feet. At some point before his first appearance as Friar Laurence he'd changed out of his own silver-buckled shoes and put on simpler footwear, more appropriate to the poor mendicant he was playing. I'd no idea where he'd got the plain shoes from, but I'd been half gratified, half embarrassed that he had taken advice from a young player. Yet now that he lay stretched out dead in the Golden Cross yard he appeared to have resumed his original shoes, the ones ornamented with

silver and cut from fine leather. For the rest he was still
dressed as a Franciscan, the grey robes disfigured with
bloodstains. It was only his shoes that had changed. I couldn't
understand it.

Meanwhile the dagger remained where it had been found,
towards the left side of Hugh Fern's chest. Squatting down on
his hams and taking out a handkerchief, the newcomer
wrapped it around the bloody haft of the dagger. Using both
hands and the counterweight of his own body, he pulled the
weapon out of the dead man's chest. The upper half of the
corpse quivered under the strain and rose slightly from the
ground while Fern's head fell helplessly backward. The other
man had to twist and tug at the dagger to get it clear but
eventually he succeeded. He stood up, holding the dagger out
before him. The blade, all dark and gouty with blood and other
matter, hung down between his hands. I noted that he did not
seem concerned about the damage he might do to his fine
clothes. He had the appearance of a conspirator in a play, an
impression reinforced by the ring of breathless bystanders.

This displaying of the dagger was too much for some of
us. A few turned away in discomfort, others groaned involuntarily. Perhaps I did too. But what I noticed was that the well-
dressed, jowly man looked more . . . interested in the scene
than anything else. It was plain that he had some authority
here as well as expertise. For an instant I wondered whether
he was the coroner after all – but if he was the coroner he
would surely have been greeted as such by the inn-keeper.

He wrapped the dagger up in the handkerchief (a fine silk
one) and positioned it on the sheet beside the corpse of Hugh
Fern. Then he gazed at the assembled audience, and said,
"What happened here?"

This was what had apparently happened.

Doctor Hugh Fern, a respected and prosperous physician
of the city of Oxford and a friend from boyhood of William
Shakespeare, had been invited to take the part of Friar

Laurence in a production of *Romeo and Juliet*. He had been a little nervous at the prospect – as I could testify, having talked with him on this very subject just before the play began. He had overcome his stage-fright, though, and started to enjoy himself. What had he said during the interval? "It's something I could get a taste for."

Shortly after he'd attended to my foot, promising to make up a poultice for it later, he had gone into one of the little changing-rooms down the passageway. Once inside, he had locked the door and left the key in the lock.

(Pearman was right, by the way. None of the rooms had bolts on the inside. In fact only one had a lock, the one that the Doctor had shut himself up in. There was nothing valuable in that room or any of the others, at least until the Chamberlain's costumes were put in store. Before that who'd want to steal old rags or discarded bits of seating? Meredith the landlord rather thought that there'd always been a key on the inside but couldn't remember it ever having been used – hence the rusty manner in which it had turned in my hand.)

Anyway the Doctor had entered the room and locked himself in, presumably to avoid being disturbed in his inexplicable purpose. Almost immediately Fern must have drawn out from under his friar's habit a dagger, a plain dagger such as a yeoman might carry, a plain and serviceable one. Or, if he hadn't taken the dagger with him into the room then he had discovered it there by chance. Or, if he hadn't found it by chance then he must have previously left the dagger in that place with the intention of doing what he did next.

What he did next was to hold the tip of the dagger at a little distance from his heart, perhaps searching with his left hand for the appropriate spot between his ribs. After he had found the spot – he was a doctor, more familiar than most with the right place to strike – he had grasped the haft of the dagger with both hands and driven it with all his might into his heart. Then, with his life-blood welling out of him, he had fallen to the floor.

The Doctor must have died in a very brief space of time because the play had hardly got under way in its second half before Master Shakespeare, trailing Mrs Davenant in attendance, had come rushing into the backstage area, agitated and in search of his friend. Perhaps he suspected something was wrong. At any rate, he was concerned that Fern was literally not in position to make his entry as Friar Laurence. So there was that frantic hunt for a costume that would approximate to a friar's, there was the hasty dressing, the just-in-time entry of Will Shakespeare and Dick Burbage for the next scene.

Meanwhile the poor Doctor was no more than a few yards away. At least three of us – WS, then Nicholas Revill and finally Andrew Pearman – had examined the outside of the room where he was lying. All of us were uneasy, but none knew that Fern was already dead or dying from his self-inflicted wound.

Convinced by all this?

No, I wasn't either.

Especially not by the self-inflicted wound.

Not that Fern *couldn't* have killed himself.

Suicide is a grave sin, but men and women have done it before and are doing it now, some on the spur of the moment, some after long premeditation. All you need is a rope, a knife, poison . . . and a strong despair mixed with courage. Why, Shakespeare's own Romeo and Juliet show their fortitude in this matter. They say that poison is a woman's weapon but it is Romeo who buys poison and drinks it over Juliet's body in the vault, while it is Juliet who, waking from her sleep, snatches his dagger to plunge it into herself – a masculine act surely? Well, if a young girl has the strength of mind and body for such a desperate action, then surely an old doctor possesses it too?

But why should Fern have killed himself? If there was a deep and hidden reason (debt, disease, despair) then why should he choose such a peculiar time and place as the middle of a play performance in an inn yard? Why not put an end to

himself in the comfort of his fine house on Headington Hill?
And he was a doctor. If he knew just where to strike home
with the dagger's point, then surely – with his knowledge of
herbs and poisons – he knew many less painful means of
making his exit.

I thought too of the last things he'd said to me. Of how he
was getting a taste for playing. Of how he would make up a
poultice for my foot. This was hardly the talk of a man who
was five minutes away from suicide.

So it wasn't that he *couldn't* have killed himself but rather
(I believed) that he *hadn't*.

And yet what alternative was there?

Here was a man seen entering a little room. I knew. I'd
witnessed him going in. The friar's robes, the fringe of hair
with the balding spot. I was as certain as I could be that it
was Fern. And then there was his corpse lying inside that
same locked room. I'd actually found and withdrawn the key
myself through the hole that Pearman had bashed in the
woodwork, then I had unlocked the door from the outside.
There was no other way in or out of the room, apart from a
barred opening that might have admitted a cat, nothing larger.

Still I wasn't convinced.

The question "What happened here?" remained un-
answered. Rather, those parts that could be answered (such
as the means by which the Doctor had met his death) did no
more than scrape the surface.

As for the man who had asked that question, the well-
dressed individual who had so confidently extracted the
dagger from the corpse: he, it transpired, was another local
physician and worthy. Doctor Ralph Bodkin by name, he
lived and practised at the western end of town, near the
Castle. Judging by his dress and manner, he was obviously a
prosperous member of the fraternity like Hugh Fern.

Doctor Bodkin had actually been a member of our audience
on the fatal afternoon, together with William Sadler. They'd been
sitting up in the gallery. I remembered that I'd mentioned in the

hearing of both men that the Chamberlain's were staging *Romeo and Juliet* on this particular day. Maybe this had sparked the idea that they should come and see the play together.

Now, it may be that the suspicious mind scents a conspiracy here – or at any rate an unnatural coincidence. What was Sadler doing at the Golden Cross Inn? And why should a well-to-do physician mingle with the common townsfolk, albeit from his position in a more expensive gallery seat? But there was nothing out of the way about their presence. William Sadler had decided to attend the play out of curiosity and perhaps a touch of vanity, for this was the narrative in which he had been cast as Romeo, if not by himself then by Hugh Fern. Ralph Bodkin accompanied him because the Doctor had once been a tutor to William, as I'd surmized, and now stood in some less specified position of guide or mentor. And to suppose that a man like Doctor Bodkin was somehow too superior to attend a public play was to contradict all our experience at the Globe playhouse, where we enjoyed a fine mixture of the rich, the respectable, the feckless and the downright dishonest.

And, if the really suspicious mind scents something . . . something too convenient, too opportune about Bodkin's arrival after the discovery of the body then this is simply explained as well.

Along with most of the audience, William Sadler and Ralph Bodkin had quit the Golden Cross Inn at the end of the performance, walking away together, quite unaware of the drama which was taking place off-stage. They'd been well on their way towards the church of St Ebbe's when they were intercepted by the messenger who had been sent in search of the coroner and was returning empty-handed. This breathless individual, a pot-boy called Percy, recognized in Doctor Bodkin an alternative authority and, perhaps confused, panted out his message – that the coroner was already busy – with another dead man – could not attend the Golden Cross for a few hours yet – meantime the body should be kept safe.

What dead man? asked Bodkin. Which one, the first or the second dead man? said Percy. The one in the Golden Cross, said Bodkin. Oh that one, said Percy. Yes that one, said Bodkin, who is he? *I* don't know, said Percy, before dashing off towards St Martin's and Cornmarket.

(I heard later that the dead man – the first one – who was already occupying the attention of the coroner was some individual who'd been fished out of the River Isis earlier in the day. Apparently a waterman. I thought nothing of it at the time, so preoccupied were we all with the death of Hugh Fern.)

So Doctor Bodkin turned round and walked back to the inn yard, reaching it shortly after the pot-boy. William Sadler, assuming that whatever had occurred was nothing to do with him, wasn't sufficiently interested in the notion of a corpse at an inn, and decided to continue with his afternoon business. He only found out later that the body in question was that of Hugh Fern, the old family friend of both the Sadlers and the Constants.

I had this part of the story from Sadler himself. I'll explain in due course how I came to be asking him questions about the sequence of events surrounding Fern's death.

"So although you didn't know about Doctor Fern's death," I said, "didn't you notice that he was no longer playing the part of the friar?"

"I noticed that his voice had changed," said Sadler. "And then I looked harder at the figure inside the habit and realized that he'd changed. I suppose I wondered why Fern wasn't playing the part any longer. I recognized *him* in his habit all right. He spent a lot of time looking out at the audience."

I refrained from saying that inexperienced players often do that, they are so thrilled to find themselves the centre of all eyes.

"Then I noticed how his part had been taken by someone else. But I thought that this was maybe how you professional players did things. Change horses in mid-stream."

"Not usually," I said.

"I tell you one thing though, Nicholas," said Sadler. "The fellow playing Friar Laurence – in the second half, I mean – he wasn't much good. Ha!"

"You're talking about William Shakespeare."

"He still wasn't much good."

He didn't expect to have to play that part, or not play that part just then," I said, wondering why I was bothering to defend WS and conscious that my excuse on his behalf was feeble anyway.

"He should stick to writing. Your man Burbage wasn't bad, playing Romeo. Very *active*, though."

"Did you notice your – your betrothed at the play?"

"My – oh, you mean Sarah. Yes, she was there together with Susan. And the battle-axe of a nurse, Mistress Root. They were sitting on the opposite side of the gallery."

"Did you communicate with each other?"

"Communicate? We waved," said Sadler.

This didn't sound exactly like Romeo-and-Juliet-style behaviour, two lovers waving decorously at each other from the opposite sides of an inn yard. Not quite star-struck. Yet I could hardly come out and ask William directly whether he felt passionate about Sarah Constant. Concerning her feelings, though, I had little doubt. I remembered the smile that had lit up her face in Broad Street.

Nightshade

You knew you'd have to kill him when you saw him looking at you.

There was no doubt that he knew. It was only a matter of time, perhaps, before he made . . . certain discoveries. Even so, the occasion caught you unprepared.

It was a perilous moment to act. You would have preferred to be in your disguise, in your armour. But it would have been even more perilous to do nothing, to allow Doctor Fern to expose you . . . and you have to admit to yourself that the danger, the fine timing of the business excited you. It nearly went wrong but a cool head and resolution snatched safety out of the jaws of danger.

The departure of the Doctor is to be regretted but it would have happened sooner or later.

And coming so soon after the death of the carter. In hindsight you should have stayed behind on the banks of the stream, should have ensured that the little man sunk out of sight in the water. Should have weighted the body down with rocks. As it was, Hoby's corpse must have been carried away and down towards the big river for it had been discovered at daybreak, snagged on a fallen tree where the river runs shallow by Folly Bridge. With luck the marks on Hoby would be attributed to the effect of a fast-moving current and the inevitable buffetings by logs and stones.

Anyway the corpse would not be closely examined by coroner or magistrate. The law does not permit it. That's the whole point, isn't it?

I was sufficiently troubled about the death of Hugh Fern to want to speak to Shakespeare about it. Maybe it was presumptuous of me but I chose him because, out of all the seniors, he was the one who had in the past rescued me from a couple of tricky situations, the one whom I most respected, and the one who was most ready to give advice or a listening ear to the junior members of the Company.

Also I believed that WS was more intimately involved with what had happened than anybody else. Doctor Fern was his particular friend and the Chamberlain's were playing in Oxford largely on account of that connection. In addition, Fern had taken the part which Shakespeare should have been playing. The playwright, together with Mrs Davenant, had been present backstage only a few yards from where Fern lay dead or dying.

WS was lodging in a chamber in the Tavern, next door to the Golden Cross. It was one of the best rooms, fitting a distinguished guest, with a view out over Cornmarket. The walls were of a glowing red, with white roses and Canterbury bells and bunches of grapes painted, as far as I could see, with a craftsman's assurance, not the journeyman work you usually find in such places. It was late in the evening of the day of Fern's death, a cold evening in spring. A fire was burning in the grate. WS looked tired and drawn, and I apologized for interrupting him, then apologized again when I saw he wasn't alone. Dick Burbage, our afternoon Romeo, was sitting in the half-light on the other side of the fire.

I made to go out again.

"No, come in, Nick."

Shakespeare indicated a stool and told me to pour myself a glass from a flask which stood on a neighbouring table. I refused, saying that I still felt queasy from the events of the afternoon.

"Good God, man, we all feel queasy," said Burbage. "What's so special with you? A drink will soon cure that."

He held up his own glass so that the red liquid glowed from the flames of the fire before gulping it down.

"Drink, unless you want to be like a green girl."

I wasn't welcome. Why should I be? I got up to leave.

"Sit down," said WS. "You injured your foot today, didn't you?"

"I don't want to disturb your council."

"You aren't disturbing anything. In any case we might value your opinion. Eh, Dick?"

Burbage shrugged. Whatever WS might have valued – and I thought he was just being courteous – Burbage had little time for the views of the ordinary player.

"Opinion on what, William?"

"Whether we should leave."

"Leave Oxford?"

"Leave Oxford."

"Because we're going to lose our audience, you mean, after the – after what happened today?"

Burbage snorted at this. I judged he'd already downed quite a few glasses. No more was he the youthful Romeo but the middle-aged shareholder.

"Nicholas, you have still got a bit to learn about audiences. We're likely to *increase* our numbers after what happened today. They'll come to gawp at the site of a recent death and incidentally they might watch a play. Owen Meredith could probably put an extra halfpenny on his beer."

Shakespeare raised his hand in Burbage's direction. Perhaps he considered the remarks improper or tactless, especially given his connection to the dead man. When he spoke, though, it was with weariness rather than irritation.

"Dick is right enough, I'm afraid. Audiences are human, for better and worse. But it's not just the death of Doctor Fern. Today has been a day of the dead. A man was found drowned in the Isis this morning for one thing."

"Yes, I know, a waterman. I heard it was a waterman," I said.

"No, this dead man was a carter," said WS, "and one known to the Davenants in this place."

I remembered the scene the other morning. Jane Davenant shouting at the unfortunate carter who had let fall a crate from the back of his cart, her husband helping him to carry it indoors. Was it the same man? Probably.

I felt cold. I was sitting at a little distance from the fire. I wondered whether to pour myself a drink after all.

"And this is not the end of it," said WS.

"Another murder?" I said.

Both WS and Dick Burbage turned their faces towards where I sat on the stool in the recesses of the room. The remark had slipped out but it was the first thing I'd said which really caught their attention.

"Murder? Who has been murdered?" said Burbage.

"Doctor Fern."

"Why do you say that, Nicholas? You believe Doctor Fern was murdered? How can that be? You were there when he was found."

"I – no, I don't know why I said it. Forget that I spoke."

Shakespeare had said nothing all this while though he gazed at me intently. There was a silence which I broke reluctantly after some moments.

"Is this what you meant by a day of the dead? This carter and Doctor Fern?"

"There's more," said WS.

"The plague is taking hold in Oxford," said Burbage. "There were four or five households sealed up this very morning, and there are others under watch."

I reached across to the flask and poured out a measure of wine.

"It will only be a short time before the city authorities prohibit all gatherings," said WS. "And the first thing to close down will be a company of players from out of town. We may not have much longer."

"So where should we go? Tell us," said Dick Burbage to me as if I was in possession of the answer.

"Back to London? I have heard that things are no worse there."

"Then you are misinformed," said Burbage. "Matters are worse there than ever. I received a letter from my wife today."

I suddenly saw – in one of those belated flashes of understanding which serve more than anything to illuminate our own obtuseness – the reasons for Burbage's bear-like manner. His wife and children had been abandoned in a plaguey town. (WS, by contrast, had his family tucked safely away in Stratford-on-Avon.) Nor was this all, this consciousness of a family rawly left. Dick Burbage, together with the other shareholders, carried the Chamberlain's on his shoulders, just as Hercules holds up the image of the globe on the roof of our playhouse. For me the question of the Company's next destination was an interesting speculation which had a bearing on my livelihood, but it wasn't my direct responsibility. But for Thomas Pope and Dick and WS and the rest, it was their decision and it affected all of us.

"Dick's wife says that the Queen is near her end," said WS.

"A matter of days," said Burbage.

The gloom in the room deepened. The fire flickered, casting a dying glow on the red and white walls.

"Are we still to present *Romeo and Juliet* for the Constant and Sadler families?" I asked. "Surely not?"

"That is a private presentation, not subject to the city authorities," said Burbage. "We do not yet know whether we can still stage it at the Ferns' house. William and I will pay our respects to his widow tomorrow. Depending on what she says we may quit Oxford very soon – or we may stay a few days longer."

"Then we could go to – to Gloucester," I said. Even as I spoke I felt the blood flood into my face. Why was I saying this? Only to fill the silence.

"Yes, we might go to Gloucester – or Worcester – or Leicester. What does it matter?"

And with that Dick Burbage carefully placed his glass on the floor, got up and left WS's room. He was drunk and angry, but in a closed-up fashion. Shakespeare made no attempt to stop him. There was another silence. I wondered how, and how soon, I could make my own exit. But it wasn't to be so easy.

WS motioned me to take up the vacant chair by the fire, then said, "Why did you say *Gloucester*?"

"I've no idea. It was the first place that came into my head."

"And why did you claim that Hugh Fern was murdered? And don't say you've no idea about that either."

Well, since this was why I'd come to see WS in the first place, there was no reason to hold back. Limpingly, I came out with the deductions I've already given, although they sounded even less convincing when uttered aloud. I couldn't see any reason why Doctor Fern should suddenly put an end to himself, I'd been one of the last people he'd talked to and he had given no hint of what he was about to do, and so on.

"Very well," said WS "And what makes you qualified to peer into another man's heart and pronounce on his intentions, if he has decided to keep them hidden?"

"I don't claim that. It's more a question of common sense."

"Common sense tells us that, if a man meets a violent death inside a locked room and there is no sign – or possibility – of the involvement of another, then it must follow that that man did violence on himself, particularly when the implement is so plainly to hand."

"I suppose so."

"I like the idea even less than you do, Nick. To do away with oneself is a dreadful course, it is a mortal sin. Perhaps it was all an accident."

This seemed an even less likely notion than murder but I said nothing.

"Hugh Fern was an old friend. Tomorrow I must console his wife. Hugh and I shared our boyhoods."

"I know," I said. "You went poaching together."

"Who told you that? Did he tell you that?" said WS.

I was about to say, no, you told me, but instead I shrugged and said, "So I've heard."

"Don't believe all you hear. Or even what you see. Don't leap to conclusions about what you witnessed this afternoon. Don't leap to – murder – or wrong conclusions about other things."

William Shakespeare glanced up at me from his chair on the other side of the slumbering fire and then covered the moment by raising his glass.

Other things.

Was this an indirect way of referring to his own breathless appearance in the inn yard with Jane Davenant? I recalled the way she'd helped him into the friar's costume, tugged on over the shirt which he was already wearing, a frail garment for a dull, wet afternoon. I recalled that earlier during the interval I'd seen Jack Davenant wandering gloomily about the Golden Cross. Perhaps the landlord wasn't mourning the trade which was being lost to his rival. Perhaps he was mourning a different type of loss. Perhaps he was in search of his wife. Who, at that very instant, was elsewhere, *perhaps* . . .

One idea suggested another. My eyes flitted about in the gloom, searching for the bed in Shakespeare's chamber. It was a capacious enough bed, but then this was probably the best room in the Tavern, one fitting a distinguished guest. Then I grew embarrassed when I caught WS looking at me looking round the room. Having been cold on my entrance into the room, I now felt hot next to the dying fire.

It never crossed my mind to say anything direct to WS. Or rather it did but I immediately suppressed the idea. I remembered what Hugh Fern had said to me about WS's capacity to take offence. Tolerant and easy he might be but everyone has limits. I grew hotter still. Fortunately WS switched topics. Maybe he felt uncomfortable too.

"Do not say too much about Dick's little outburst, Nick. He is anxious for his family."

I nodded a little harder than necessary.

"I guessed as much."

"When you come to get a family you will find that you have made hostages for fortune."

"Perhaps that is why I have no plans to get a family."

"*Plans*," said WS. "You plan what shirt to put on for the week or which tavern you might eat your lunch in, you don't plan marriage or a family. Not unless you're a prince or an heir to a great estate – and if you are then someone else does the planning for you."

If I was waiting for some little revelation concerning unplanned marriages, then I was to be disappointed for WS now said, "This has not been the best of days. And tomorrow morning Burbage and I must visit the widow."

I took the hint and stood up. WS said goodnight in an abstracted way. I left him sipping at his glass and staring at the embers, and went downstairs, intending to return to my own dormitory in the Golden Cross next door.

In the gloom at the bottom of stairs I almost collided with a figure who was waiting there. I mumbled an apology and expected him to climb the stairs now they were clear. But the man didn't move. He peered into my face and I recognized Jack Davenant.

"You have been to see Master Shakespeare?" said the landlord.

"Yes."

"Is he alone?"

"He is now," I said, then realizing this might be misconstrued I added, "Dick Burbage was with him but he left some time ago. I don't think Shakespeare wants to be disturbed."

"Oh, I shan't disturb him. I love the fellow."

This was such an odd thing to say, out of the blue, in the near dark, that I couldn't judge Davenant's tone. Was he sneering or did he mean it?

"You were there this afternoon, weren't you?" he said. "You were next door in the Golden Cross?"

"I'm a member of the Chamberlain's," I said. "I was playing in *Romeo and Juliet*."

"So was Master Shakespeare."

"Yes, he played the friar."

"The dead friar?"

"That was another player. Or not a player exactly but Doctor Fern. When he could not be found during the interval Shakespeare took over his part."

"So Master Shakespeare was around at that time?"

"Why yes," I said, not knowing where all this was leading, and on my guard for a trap.

"You confirm that he was there?"

"Is this a court of law?" I said.

"Not yet," said Davenant.

"You know that Shakespeare is one of our shareholders. He keeps an eye on us, even when he is not playing."

"Playing, hmm," said the landlord.

"If you'll excuse me, Master Davenant, I'll be on my way to my lodging. I'm tired and this hasn't been the best of days."

"Of course, Master . . .?"

We'd already been introduced on my first night in the town when WS and I sat drinking at a table not more than a few yards from the foot of these stairs. I didn't think I'd remind Davenant of this but, since I had no choice, I gave him my name once more. He stood aside to let me pass, then suddenly came up so close that we were almost touching, chest to chest.

"I am an important man in this town, Master Revill. I am a vintner and a broker. My word carries weight."

"I do not doubt it, sir," I said and slipped past him, across the main room of the Tavern and so out into the street. It was a cold, gloomy night, shadowed by the events of the day. I went the few yards up Cornmarket, through the yard of the Golden Cross (where the stage stood, looking bereft without the benefit of action), past the passage where Fern's body had been discovered, and so up the stairs into my crowded quarters.

I took off my shoes and moved restlessly about the room in my stockinged feet, unable to lie down straightaway. There were too many troubling speculations and questions.

Most of my fellows were in bed and asleep, judging by their little noises – a long, difficult day for them too. There was a window at the far end, looking out on the maze of narrow lanes and alleys which clustered at the back of the Golden Cross. The houses on either side overhung the alleys, leaning towards each other so that their upper storeys were almost touching. There was a candle glimmering in one of the chambers set at an angle to ours, and by its light I thought I saw those monkish figures once more. Two cowled heads and snouts shifting in the shadows. The bird-like monks. The monk-like birds. I went cold, and blinked and rubbed my eyes and looked again, but by then everything had disappeared, even the candle's glimmer.

I crept into bed, convincing myself that I was tired and that my eyes were playing tricks, trying to reason my fear away.

The day had provided plenty of other material for reason and reflection. Once in my shared bed, with Laurence Savage slumbering beside me, I chewed over the last twelve hours like a cow chews her cud, although without the cow's contentment. It wasn't only the sudden death of Hugh Fern and any suspicions which attached to that. It was also my recent encounters with WS and then with Jack Davenant.

My intention to pick up bits and pieces about Shakespeare's life had misfired early on. It had all seemed so easy. I should have remembered that the truth is as slippery as an eel. Already I had heard contradictory stories about poaching, with WS apparently confessing to a boyhood escapade and then Hugh Fern denying that he at least had anything to do with it.

And the same doubt hung around what you might call a different species of poaching, WS's connection with Jane Davenant. Was it what it appeared? A hurried appearance by the shirt-clad playwright during the interval of the play, accompanied by the landlord's wife. Had they been engaged in another kind of play, with a cast of two only? Was William

Shakespeare playing the afternoon Romeo, rather than Dick Burbage, with Jane Davenant as a Juliet well beyond her first youthful flush? There was also to be considered the apparently loose reputation of Mistress Davenant in Oxford, that gossip about cuckoldry, that ostler-talk about gypsies and playing at fast-and-loose. There was the strange manner of the landlord, questioning whether WS was alone in his room. But hadn't he also said of Shakespeare, "I love the fellow."

Shakespeare himself had warned me against jumping to conclusions. Did he say this because there *were* conclusions – obvious ones – to be jumped to, and because he wanted to forestall my suspicions? Was this a ploy? Similarly with his talk of not believing everything one heard or saw. Don't even trust your senses.

And did that self-distrust apply to the death of Hugh Fern? If you believed the evidence of your eyes it looked like suicide. (But a kind of intuition told me that it was not.)

Why was Jack Davenant so concerned to establish Shakespeare's whereabouts in the interval of the play? Was he trying to link his wife and WS together? Or was he insinuating that WS was somehow involved in the death of Hugh Fern? Suppose that you had a rival in . . . love, for want of a better term . . . and that you were a prominent local citizen, say a vintner and a broker, whose word carried weight . . . would you have scruples about linking that rival to a suspicious death, if it meant that he might be investigated and, at the least, put to some inconvenience, possibly worse than inconvenience?

As I was falling asleep, I recalled how WS had helped me in the past when I was in difficulties. I wondered whether he was still sitting up next door in his chamber in the Tavern, alone and pondering on the death of a friend, gazing into the relics of the fire and sipping at the dregs in his glass.

At once I resolved to come to WS's aid. I would look into Doctor Fern's demise and arrive at the truth. Then, having got this settled in my mind, I must have dropped off to sleep.

Like most late-night resolutions, this one looked distinctly threadbare, even stupid, by the light of morning. How could I have had the presumption to believe I could "help" William Shakespeare? How, in any case, was I supposed to come by the truth about Fern's death? Where to start?

Happening to fall into company with Will Sadler – Oxford is a small place, stand in Carfax and the world will pass you by sooner or later – I heard the student's account of how he and Doctor Bodkin had been intercepted on their way out of the Golden Cross, and how the physician had returned to examine Fern's body. But there was nothing out of place in his story. I grew inclined to think that there was nothing to discover.

We continued to perform in the Golden Cross yard. Another day, another play. As Dick Burbage had predicted, our audiences actually went up after Hugh Fern's death. But, as WS had also predicted, the players' stay here was almost certainly drawing to a close. The number of plague deaths increased quite sharply, and the fatalities were dotted about the city in a way that suggested that King Pest was operating to his usual pattern – that is, at random.

WS and Dick Burbage paid their visit to Mrs Fern. I don't know what passed between the widow and the shareholders but the upshot as far as the Chamberlain's were concerned was that our private performance of *Romeo and Juliet* was scheduled to go ahead in the Headington house on its due date. The Sadler and Constant families were to attend, as much in tribute to the dead Doctor as anything else.

I hadn't completely forgotten the story which Susan Constant had told me, of her belief that her cousin was being poisoned and that there was some malevolent presence haunting her house, leaving clay figures by the door, and so on. But I was inclined to put it down to an over-active imagination. (Yes, I can see the irony here, considering my own excited speculations about Hugh Fern.) If Sarah Constant was genuinely ill, then couldn't that be attributed to her apprehensions about marriage and to her high-strung nature? I remembered her shivering account of hearing the martyrs' cries, of seeing the flames which consumed them in Broad Street, even though this had occurred many years before she was born.

Besides, all of this business of poisoning and mysterious figures was overshadowed by the shock of Fern's death. What Susan had told me was only a story, but Fern's death was real, tragically so.

It was Abel Glaze who made a connection between the two strands.

I told him everything, you see. Well, not quite everything. I did not mention my own night encounter with the hooded trio or that recent glimpse from the dormitory window. But I described Susan Constant's fears for her cousin's welfare. She had not bound me to secrecy, although perhaps she should have done. I also went through my reasoning over the death of Fern. It was an alternative to doing nothing at all. The burden of unravelling mysteries lay heavy on me. I wanted to lighten the load.

I knew that Abel looked on me in the light of a mentor – at least I flattered myself that he did – if only because my own service in the Chamberlain's was rather longer than his. In a manner of speaking I had brought him into the Company. Compared to him I was an expert on plays and playing, just as he was an adept in the tricks of the road. I might have turned to Jack Wilson or Laurence Savage but I feared that they'd laugh at my speculations.

Abel and I talked while we were waiting off-stage during a performance. We were doing *The World's Diseas'd*, Richard Milford's violent drama of sudden death and cold revenge. It was odd to be talking about a real-life death so close to where it had actually occurred and to be playing about with stage-death at the same time. Particularly so since I was taking the part of Vindice, and occasionally had to break away from our dialogue and make an entrance to do a spot of brooding or avenging. Luckily, I didn't have to throw myself about the platform since my ankle was still delicate. You forget these petty infirmities, however, when you're in front of the crowd. Abel's parts in the drama were smaller but he too had to keep an ear open for his cues. This gave our conversation a rather piecemeal, fractured quality.

Anyway, when I'd come out with all this about the Constants and Doctor Fern in a muddled narrative, Abel Glaze was quiet for a time then he said, "Doctor Fern was Sarah Constant's godfather, her sponsor?"

"I believe so. Yes, he was."

"Do you think that she might have said something to him about her health?"

"Maybe. But according to her cousin Susan she refuses to believe that anything is really wrong with her."

"But suppose that the Doctor came to the same conclusion as Susan, whether she — whether Sarah, I mean – said anything to him or not. He was a doctor after all. Maybe he too detected symptoms of poisoning in her."

"Yes . . . "

"And suppose you're right in your belief that there's something strange about Doctor Fern's death. Strange to the point of murder."

"Yes."

"Then *suppose* . . . "

"Wait a moment, Abel."

I stopped him at this point since I had to make an entrance as Vindice and deliver a speech about the pleasures of revenge and then stab a cardinal. When I'd done my duty I returned and we carried on our secret, whispered conversation at the back of the stage platform.

"You were in the middle of supposing, Abel. Tell me."

So he did. And what Abel Glaze supposed was twisted enough.

It was that Doctor Fern had uncovered a plot of some kind against Sarah Constant and that the discovery put him into danger, mortal danger. That whoever was plotting against Sarah was about to be confronted by Fern and had therefore been forced to take drastic action. Even to the point of killing him in the middle of a play.

Oddly enough, the more Abel said, the more sceptical I became.

"What about the locked room?" I said. I pointed towards the fatal chamber. We were leaning against the wall only a few yards from it.

"Oh, the locked room is a detail."

"An insuperable detail."

"Let's leave it in the wings."

"Wherever you leave it, it will still have to be accounted for sooner or later."

"I have it! It could be that Fern himself turned the key in the door."

"A notable feat for a dead man."

"*Before* he died, Nick. He is badly wounded, dying but does not know it, or rather he is not aware of what he is doing at all in his final moments. Only instinct is left. He manages to bar the door against his adversary."

"If he'd any last bit of sense left in him, wouldn't he have gone looking for help?"

"Not if the person who stabbed him was still there, waiting outside the door."

"You're forgetting, Abel, that all this was taking place during the *Romeo and Juliet* interval. There were plenty of people around."

"You know what it's like during intervals. Nobody really pays attention to anybody else. They're too busy about their own affairs."

"But this wasn't backstage at the Globe, all private and shut away. There were members of the public wandering about as well."

"That just adds to the confusion. Nobody staying in one spot for more than a few moments."

"*I* was there the whole time though, sitting on that bench by the passageway. I'd injured my foot. I had nothing to be busy about. "

"So you ought to be in the best position to see what happened."

"I didn't see anyone brandishing a bloody knife."

"Of course not. This isn't a play or a story where the murderer struts around, cackling and showing off his weapon."

"The Chamberlain's doesn't indulge in that kind of crude stuff, Abel. You've been with us long enough to know that."

"Never mind that, Nick. Tell me again what you saw and heard. Every detail may be significant. Remember that I once made my living out of paying attention to tiny details, even if they were fake ones."

I sighed. I half regretted having revealed my misgivings about the death of Hugh Fern to my friend. But I owed him the story for a second and last time. He was enjoying playing the mystery-solver. So I went over everything from my first conversation with Doctor Fern in the yard, his uneasiness about appearing in front of the crowd, his growing confidence as he found his stage-legs (which Abel had witnessed for himself), the way I'd injured myself, how Fern had promised to make up a poultice for my ankle, & cetera.

Then I described how I'd seen Fern going into the far room where he was later found dead. I described WS's hurried appearance with Mrs Davenant. (Abel didn't seem particularly interested in this, fortunately.) I recounted how Andrew Pearman had come in next, urgently seeking his master.

"Wait a moment," said Abel. "This Pearman person now. What about him? He was standing by the door with you."

I hadn't realized it until Abel said this but his words chimed with some half-hidden suspicion of my own.

"He was with me at the door, yes, but I was the one who got hold of the key from the inside and opened it. And it doesn't make sense. If Pearman was . . . involved . . . then he wouldn't go drawing attention to himself, would he? And why should he want to stab his master anyway? It would leave him without employment."

"Let's leave motive to one side for the moment."

"It strikes me that we're leaving a great deal to one side. Anyway, if Pearman'd somehow managed to stab his master then he'd want to get as far away from the scene as possible. I would."

"Could be a bluff," said Abel. "Diverting suspicion by encouraging it."

"Why do that, when it's much simpler to avoid suspicion altogether?"

"Perhaps he is naturally devious."

"No, I don't believe so," I said.

"Oh, I see," said Abel. "When it's your theory we have to listen very carefully but when it comes to anything I say . . . "

"No, it's not that. There's another thing besides. Both of us, Abel, can tell when a person is genuinely shocked and distressed. A good player can counterfeit these responses – but a good player can also tell if another person is counter-feiting them. I may be wrong but I would swear to it that Pearman's distress was real. He didn't know that he was going to find his master dead any more than I did."

"All right then . . . "

Abel seemed disappointed that his idea had come to nothing. But his brain was working in wider and wider circles.

"What if Fern's murderer came from the outside? I mean, that he – "

"Or she. Since we're merely speculating."

"What if he – or she – was not part of the audience that afternoon in the Golden Cross yard? They might not have come through the yard, not come past where you were sitting at all. There's that other approach through the alley down there, the one between the two inns. You could reach the locked room that way."

"No," I said, "nobody came in that way, at least not after the interval had started."

"How can you be sure, Nick?"

"I hadn't even thought about it until just now when you mentioned it. But there was no mud in the passageway outside those store-rooms."

"So?"

"The whole area had been swept. I remember seeing a couple of pot-boys at work, making it neat for the players, or as neat as an inn yard can ever be. A person who'd walked down the alleyway would have come in with grime all over their boots. Have a look for yourself, that alley's filthy with rats and dead cats as well as mud."

"I'll take your word for it."

"And that afternoon it had begun to rain well before the end of the first half of *Romeo and Juliet* – so that would have made the mud even worse."

"There were no footmarks outside Fern's room?"

"It wasn't clean but there were no gouts of mud."

"So it follows that if Fern was murdered, then his murderer was a member of the audience that afternoon, someone *already* inside the inn yard."

"Excellent logic, Abel."

"Thank you, master."

"That reduces us to two hundred possibilities, give or take a few."

"Unless it was one of us players."

"There's a difference between playing a murderer and being one."

"Just a joke, Nicholas."

"So was my comment about two hundred possibilities."

"Let's restrict it to those we *know* were in the audience. Those people we can identify and who must have known Doctor Fern."

We had to interrupt ourselves at this point because we were both required to attend the finale of *The World's Diseas'd*. After the play was over – I was dead, like all good avengers, but Abel had survived as a minor courtier – we resumed the discussion, so caught up in our speculations that we didn't bother to change out of our costumes straightaway.

Abel asked me to search my memory for those people I'd seen in the yard around the time Hugh Fern died.

"Susan Constant was there together with her cousin Sarah. They were talking with Doctor Fern. So was Mistress Root, come to that."

"The woman we picked up from the road after she'd been run down by that carter? The one who called us chivalrous gentlemen of the road?"

"Yes, her. But I can tell you that the carter is dead. Hoby was his name. His body was found in the Isis."

"In the river? Drowned?"

"It's a fair assumption if you find a body in a river."

"You don't suppose Mistress Root drowned the man? After all, she did swear a thousand plagues on him."

"Seriously, Abel?"

"Everything must be considered. All stones must be upturned and the ground examined underneath."

"Then it's much more likely the carter drove straight into the river, seeing how much control he had over his horse."

(But had the horse and cart been found near where the carter drowned? I didn't know. This was a diversion from our main topic, however.)

"Mistress Root is a strong woman," said Abel. "Good with her fists. She floored her husband, one of her husbands anyway."

"She can hold her own in a scrap, no doubt about it."

"She hates marriage. She said she'd have no more of it."

"For herself, I think she meant. No more marriages for herself."

"Who'd have her in marriage or any other way, the great brawny old thing? But seriously, Nick, if we have to be serious now . . . Nurse Root is against marriage, against the marriage of Sarah Constant perhaps."

"What are you hinting at?"

"That she is the opposite of our Shakespeare's Nurse in *Romeo and Juliet.*"

"Instead of secretly helping the young lovers, she's trying to trip them up, you mean?"

"Worse than trip them up . . . "

"It is a ridiculous notion. A nurse as a poisoner and murderer."

"Who better placed to be a poisoner? And who knows what goes on in the mind of a woman like that? Perhaps she wishes to preserve her Sarah in a state of perfection, the eternal virgin."

I looked hard at Abel.

"Just an idea," he said. "Well, go on. Who else did you see backstage?"

"Jack Davenant and Mrs Davenant."

"Together."

"Not together."

"Ah," said Abel, tapping his nose. "She was with William Shakespeare, you said."

"Yes, but I don't think he was involved."

"You never know."

"William Sadler was also in the audience," I said quickly. "The student who is to marry Sarah Constant. He was sitting in the gallery with a man called Ralph Bodkin."

"Ah!"

"What?"

"Ralph Bodkin. A suggestive name."

"Ralph?"

"No, Bodkin. A bodkin is a little dagger, you know."

"I didn't think we were going to convict people on their names," I said, "but I suppose it's appropriate in a different way since Bodkin is a doctor, like Fern. It was he who came to examine Fern's corpse."

"If he's a doctor then he'd have enough to do with bodkins and lancets in his trade," said Abel. "That's suggestive too."

"Bodkins are used for bleeding and for lancing boils, not killing people."

"A knife knows no purpose," said Abel.

"True, it's a Jack-of-all-trades," I said.

That's more or less where our talk ended. And not before time, you may think, since we were getting ourselves stranded on the far shores of absurdity. Maybe it was the effect of whispering in the lee of the platform stage, discussing theories of murder at the same time as participating in the playing of murder. In my character of Vindice I was very bloody, and perhaps inclined to discover plots everywhere. For his part, Abel seemed eager enough to take my cue and come out with his own notions, however outrageous.

But the more we talked, the less plausible my ideas and suspicions appeared – even to me, especially to me perhaps. In the end, I concluded that I would do nothing since I could think of nothing useful to do.

The only step I took was a half-hearted attempt to fix the position of the room where I thought I'd glimpsed the hooded figures – the "monks" – by the glimmer of a candle. It lay somewhere to the back of the Golden Cross Inn and, gazing out of our players' dormitory during daylight, I saw several crooked windows at our level or a little above or below it. This was one of the oldest parts of the city, with cramped, winding passages threaded between houses whose overhanging tops almost obscured the sky. I couldn't have placed the "monk" window with any certainty, and I wasn't even sure that I wanted to. Probably it had been no more than a trick of tired eyes.

And there things rested for a day or two. If Jack Davenant had wanted to point an accusing finger at WS over Hugh Fern's death, he did not succeed. The Doctor was found by the coroner to have died as the result of falling on his knife in some inexplicable "accident". The unblinkered opinion might have been that Hugh Fern had committed suicide, even if the traditional motives (debt, disease, despair) seemed to be missing. But Doctor Fern was a prosperous and popular citizen of Oxford, and a well-connected one. He must have been on good terms, probably friendly ones, with the coroner as well as the local magistrates and other worthies such as Ralph Bodkin,

Suicide is a dreadful thing, as WS had said to me. An offence against God and man. We show our horror of it by burying the suicide at night in the public highway. While this may be good enough for the wandering veteran or the ruined shopkeeper, it will not do for an honourable man like Hugh Fern. If the influence of his friends could get the verdict shifted from intention to "accident", and so remove the shadow from the family as well as ensure that Fern received a fitting funeral, then nobody could say that this was really an improper course.

The other possibility – that of murder – was even more remote than suicide. I don't believe that it was even considered by anyone except two players with time on their hands and over-active minds.

Hugh Fern did receive his fitting funeral three days after his body had been discovered. Shakespeare, Burbage and some of the other seniors attended a service for him in St Mary's. Shakespeare himself composed the address, I was told.

That seemed to be that. Besides, the coroner and the magistrates had other, more pressing business than the half-baffling death of a local doctor.

Now the plague itself was firmly established within the city. No longer was it possible to pretend that it would be confined to a handful of cases on the outskirts. As I've said, we Londoners accepted it in a resigned, even relaxed way – or pretended to. But the city was on edge. The riot which Susan Constant and I had witnessed showed that town and gown liked beating each other over the head, but it also showed how touchy and moody the people were. They were tinder, ready for the spark.

I watched one of these sparks as it fell among the tinder.

Carfax is the closest Oxford comes to the area round Paul's Walk in London, a place where everyone gathers to gossip and to carry on trade, licit or illicit. Crowds form naturally, drawn by anything or nothing.

It was evening. The days were drawing out now. The sun was going down behind the tower of St Martin's, setting the sky on fire. At the foot of the church tower a man was having a similar effect on a crowd. He was standing on the back of a horseless cart and waving his arms about. A stocky figure, his voice was disproportionately loud. I could hear his booming tones from a distance although I couldn't make out any of the words. I drew nearer and heard what he was declaiming. Ah yes. It wasn't altogether a surprise. I'd been expecting something like this.

The plague brings prophets as surely as a dog carries fleas. They are mostly self-styled preachers who tell us that we are all doomed. I know the breed, because my father was one of them – although he was a proper preacher, not self-appointed – and so I've perhaps been inoculated against the worst effects of their ranting.

This man did not appear to be very different. He ranted and roared. He pointed to the cluster of bills which had suddenly been stuck over the doors of St Martin's. He didn't have to explain what they were. Everyone feared the appearance of the plague orders and the mortality bills, breaking out in public places like white pustules on healthy skin.

Then the speaker got down to business. The plague was God's instrument for the punishment of sin, he declaimed. It was God's angel – or his arrow flying through the air – or his hand stretched out to smite the wickedness of men – or all of these together and more. What was being punished was vice and sin. The very air which we breathed in was infected by human corruption, and so gave back to us our own taint.

The crowd, mostly made up of townspeople but containing a few students, was growing by the instant. Some of them looked up at this last remark and snuffed the air, which was hazy from chimney-smoke. They seemed to be enjoying the prospect of peril and punishment. They weren't really, of course, but there is a kind of initial thrill which runs through us in such a situation, as I'd observed when Abel and I had come across the plague-house in Southwark's Kentish Street.

If the man on the cart had confined himself to general condemnations and threats, then all would have been well. But he needed to find something or someone to blame the plague on. Possibly this had been the only motive for his harangue because when he moved on to the next stage in his denunciation, his voice became even harsher and his gesturing more emphatic.

He pointed with his left arm down Cornmarket in the direction of the Golden Cross, where I'd just come from. Throughout what followed he kept his outstretched arm as stiff as the post of a gibbet, or curled it up and brandished his fist in the same direction. It quickly became obvious that players and playhouses were his target.

I won't weary you with everything he said. I've heard it before. So have you, probably. Playing on the public stage was immoral. Men demeaned themselves by dressing up as women so that other men should pay court to them. Play-houses were sinks of iniquity, & cetera. This man managed a new twist when he said that playing *out* of plague-time drew down God's wrath and so provoked the plague while playing *in* plague-time made a bad business even worse. This was an ingenious argument since it linked the plague inextricably with playing, and made both the object of horror and loathing.

I hovered unhappily on the edge of the crowd, almost afraid that I'd be singled out. Heads turned towards where the speaker's accusing arm was pointing. He named the Golden Cross Inn. Repeated it as if he was naming one of the suburbs of hell. He referred to the Chamberlain's Com-pany as a bunch of out-of-towners, a gaggle from *foul*

London come to pollute this *fair city*, through the laxity of its own citizens. Hadn't God shown his anger at the citizens of Oxford by destroying the life of one of the most prominent of them in the very yard of the Golden Cross? This was Doctor Fern's just punishment for participating in a play. (No one objected to this slander.) The players had brought the infection with them. They should return to *London* forthwith. They should *be* returned if that was the only way.

Returned by force.

There was a shifting among the hearers at this, an uncertain movement a few yards up Cornmarket and back again. The light was fading. Dusk brought with it the promise of action and these people were ready for it. They were like wine slopped about in a drunk's glass. It wouldn't take much, just a flick of the wrist, a tremor of the arm, for the contents to spill over.

I contemplated running back to the Golden Cross and warning my fellows. They'd just about have time to make themselves scarce or shut themselves in their rooms. We hadn't long finished our afternoon performance. I'm pretty certain that some of those who were lapping up the speaker's words had attended that day's play (it was the comedy called *Love's Loss*). Play or riot, what did it matter? It was all performance, show, distraction. The crowd would be quite capable of applauding us one minute and tearing down our stage the next. Or even of assaulting the same individuals who'd given them pleasure half an hour before. Audiences are human, as WS had said, for better and worse.

I was about to sprint back to the inn when another man suddenly clambered on to the cart. The speaker – I found out later that his name was Tom Long – had actually managed to keep his mouth shut for a few moments while he surveyed the effects of his rabble-rousing. Now he looked round in evident surprise as the cart shook under the weight of the other man. His outstretched arm faltered and he twisted to face the newcomer. His mouth opened but he did not have the chance to speak again. The second man, the one who'd climbed up with considerable agility, now acted with even greater speed. Using both hands he shoved the stocky speaker hard in the chest, so hard that the man stumbled backwards. His feet caught on the side of the cart and he fell over it, his arms flailing in the air. He disappeared into the press of people standing closest to the cart and did not emerge straightaway.

The success of this action was in its suddenness. The second man hadn't said anything or given the speaker time to argue or respond. He'd simply pushed him off his perch. And now this individual stood, arms akimbo, legs braced against any attempt to dispossess *him*. He stared out over the now silent crowd. It was hard to be certain in the half-light but I thought that I detected in his expression an almost taunting quality.

He stayed silent though. He stared the crowd down, with his jowly face and bullock's eye.

He was lucky in that he'd caught them just as they were beginning to smoulder. He'd put his foot down and doused the fire. Another few moments, or another few words from the ranter, and they'd have been streaming down Cornmarket and into the Golden Cross yard, there to smash up whatever caught their eye.

But it was not just luck. There was courage as well as a kind of contempt involved in his response. Courage to face down many dozens of excitable townspeople, and contempt for the ease with which they had been stirred up.

It was likely that some of them recognized him too. Like Hugh Fern, Ralph Bodkin was a prominent citizen. Not only a physician but an alderman, he had authority in this town. Once again I realized that authority is not entirely a matter of robes and titles.

The plays-and-plague speaker had now found his feet once more. By the manner in which he was clutching his head, he seemed to have been injured although not badly. He looked up at the man who had pushed him off the cart but said nothing.

Doctor Bodkin spoke for the first time.

"Get yourself to bed, Master Long, and let your hurt be looked to."

Again, there was an odd mixture in his response, this time of solicitude and dismissal.

Obediently, Long stumbled off into the dusk, supported by some of the bystanders. The rest of the crowd was dribbling away. Last time there'd been trouble in this spot it had taken two armed escorts and a battery of scholars and councilmen to bring peace. On this occasion one man had been enough.

Ralph Bodkin stayed on the cart, moving his head ponderously about (I was still reminded of the bullock) and keeping his hands perched on his hips. He would allow nothing so vulgar as triumph to creep into his posture.

Eventually only a handful of us were left at the crossroads. Bodkin relaxed his stance, bent down, grasped the side-board of the cart and vaulted over it, landing lightly on the cobblestones. For a man in middle age, perhaps of any age, he was fit and supple. He set off round the corner of St Martin's tower and down in the direction of St Ebbe's. I dithered for several instants then started in pursuit of him.

"Sir! Doctor Bodkin!"

He paused and turned round, with deliberate slowness. Behind him the sky was a dying mixture of red and yellow. I ran until I drew level with him. I was still hobbling slightly from my ankle injury.

"Yes? What is it?"

I don't know whether he thought I was one of the crowd, perhaps a friend or supporter of Long, come to remonstrate with him or worse. If so, he gave no sign of alarm. But then this man had stared down an entire crowd!

"Thank you," I said.

I was slightly breathless, and not only from running.

"What are you thanking me for?"

"I'm with the Chamberlain's Company."

He peered at me more closely.

"You were in Sadler's room the other night, weren't you?"

"Yes. I am Nicholas Revill, a player."

"I remember. Well, Master Revill ..?"

"If you hadn't intervened and stopped that man, then the people would have ... "

"Yes?"

"Tried to harm the Chamberlain's. Torn us apart probably."

"They would not have been so particular. If they hadn't found you, then anybody would have done."

"Yes," I said. "I am familiar with the London crowds, the apprentices and veterans, and the damage they can do."

"Even so, Master Revill, you should take this as a warning, I mean your Company should. Get out. Tom Long is the first of many who will find a ready audience in this town."

"I think our seniors are planning our departure from Oxford. We have only one more commission to carry out, and it's a private one."

"They are wise then. Public performances will not be permitted for much longer."

Ralph Bodkin made to turn away. The faint red and yellow tints had almost disappeared from the sky. Beyond us was the thick thumb of the Castle tower and the great earth-mound where executions were carried out. There was something I wanted to say, yet was reluctant to ask.

"It's all nonsense, isn't it?" I said.

"What is nonsense?"

"Plays do not cause the plague."

"Do you believe that they do?"

"I – I cannot believe that God would punish something so nearly innocent with something so terrible."

"Even though a small voice tells you that he *might*?"

"I suppose so."

"It is superstition," said Doctor Bodkin with finality. "Good night, Master Revill."

I returned to the Golden Cross. The ostler Kit Kite was

standing in the yard in the posture of a sentry, armed with a pitchfork. I felt like a messenger, hot-foot from the battlefield.

"We heard there was trouble, Nicholas," he said, identifying me in his aggravating manner. "Meredith asked me to keep watch here."

The ostler was a perky, familiar fellow, referring to his employer by his last name and calling his guests by their first ones. I took care not to call him Kit, not to call him anything in fact.

"There might have been trouble but it was averted. One man started it and another man stopped it."

"I heard that old Tom Long was out there, waving and roaring."

"He was," I said. "But Ralph Bodkin simply stood still and said nothing, and he had the greater effect on the crowd."

"Oh, that was Doctor Bodkin stepped in, was it?" said Kit Kite. "If there's anybody who could've seen them off . . . "

A different note entered his voice. He sounded almost respectful. He referred to the Doctor by his title for one thing. I was curious about Bodkin.

"You know him?"

"He's a devil," said Kite promptly.

"Whatever he is normally, he was on the side of the angels this evening. He saved us Chamberlain's from a thrashing or worse. And he protected this inn from damage."

"He's still a right devil," said Kite, but there was admiration in his voice.

"You can stand down now, the danger is past," I said. "You can go back to your horses."

I left the ostler to get on with his business. If anyone could claim the name of devil, at least outwardly, it would be this perky familiar fellow, clutching at his pitchfork.

Naughty Man's Cherries

Once again you are near the old woman's house. Old mother Morrison. She is dead of course. You were the cause of that. She came after the dog and before John Hoby and Hugh Fern. Each death is a step further along, a step further up. But though the old woman may be no more there are others in the cottage to be . . . harvested.

Once again you make your way towards the house, the comfortable dwelling. It is only a few weeks since your first visit but it seems more like months or years, so much ground have you traversed since then. Now the costume that you put on so tentatively in the chamber that first day fits like a glove and you do not give it a second thought. You have even grown used to the strange, distancing effect of the eyepieces. You wield your wand with authority, like the magician that you are. You stride with assurance now.

As you approach the door you see that it is marked. The cross is painted in red and prominently displayed. You are pleased that your instructions have been so carefully carried out. The cross is more effective than a lock and bars, much more effective, since it not only keeps people out but drives them away. Who would think of entering or even coming close to an afflicted household? Not as long as they wanted to live . . .

You open the door and listen to the silence within. Once more the blood rustles in your ears and, beyond that, you hear again those little tapping and sighing sounds which every place makes. The house is empty now, and yet not empty. There is an odour which reaches into your nostrils despite the mask, despite the mixture of clove and cinnamon which is contained in the end of the beak. Nevertheless you will quickly get accustomed to the smell of the household.

You reach for your notebook and pencil. You enter the first of the rooms on the ground floor. Nothing of much value in the furnishings, although you mark down a green tapestry carpet that is draped over a table and a pewter jug which sits squarely in the middle. In one corner of the room is a chest but it contains nothing apart from linen, somewhat threadbare. In the opposite corner of the room is the body of a young man sitting up in the corner. His face is contorted. You do not touch him but note his presence also, not in your book but mentally.

Before you leave the room you pick up the pewter jug and, opening the casement window, tip out the dregs on to the ground outside. Leave all fair.

The process of inspection with occasional note-making is the same for the other two rooms on the ground floor and the three rooms upstairs. You account for the entire household right down to the old servant. They are all dead, all seven of them. Two of the bodies might be of use, the young man downstairs and an older woman who lies in one of the upper rooms, not the one where you last encountered old mother Morrison. She is resting on a feather-bed, this one, looking more at ease than the others. She is almost smirking. The feather-bed surprises you. Time was when a country household would have contained nothing better than straw pallets with a log for a pillow. Like the tapestry carpet, the feather-bed shows that there is a little wealth here.

Eventually you find it. Inside another chest in the room where the smirking woman lies you unearth a perfuming-pan and a pair of candlesticks, all of silver. You wrap them up in a blanket and place them by the front door, to be collected later.

You pass out of the house, pulling the door to behind you. It is late in the day. You might compare yourself to the angel of death, passing over these remote dwellings. Wherever you go, whatever you touch, is marked for destruction or for use.

The final commission which I'd mentioned to Doctor Ralph Bodkin was, as you've probably guessed, our private performance of *Romeo and Juliet* at the house of Doctor and Mrs Fern. Soon after this we were due to quit Oxford, the local authorities having been as good as Doctor Bodkin's word and prohibited further playing in the Golden Cross yard or anywhere else in a public place. By doing this they had anticipated the seniors' decision to leave. Where we were going next I had no idea. Perhaps the shareholders didn't either. Our departure from Oxford – or our dismissal – was expected since the plague deaths showed no signs of abating. Most of us were relieved, given the likely hostility of the townspeople if the Carfax demonstration was anything to go by. And yet these were some of the very citizens who'd been so loud and appreciative in their welcome only a fortnight earlier!

Surprisingly, the performance at the Ferns' wasn't a subdued affair. Mrs Fern, the Doctor's widow, might not have been merry in her black weeds but nor was she obviously grieving. There was a proper air of decorum but no exaggerated solemnity about the house. The funeral and the feast which followed had taken place a few days previously. Some of the pictures were draped with black but there was no other mark of mourning apart from the bands worn by the servants, including Andrew Pearman. The last I'd seen of him he had been pacing distractedly round the inn yard. He still looked sombre, understandably given that his position as the Doctor's assistant no longer existed. I wondered what would happen to all the gear contained in Fern's consulting room, all the bowls and flasks, the surgical probes and gauges.

We were to play *Romeo and Juliet* on the flat, that is, at floor level, while the (smallish) audience would sit on three or four tiers of raised seating. It was an evening performance and the massed candles glowed in the wall-sconces, their light reflected in the linen-fold panelling. There was a fire in the great fireplace. I foresaw that we'd all get very heated in our costumes.

The two families for whose benefit this play was being staged were milling around together, drinking and talking with some additional guests. They maintained a kind of reserve with each other, but not much. The parents on each side could have been cast in one of our plays, so neatly did they seem to fit their moulds. The fathers were grave and grey-bearded, the mothers matronly. There were a handful of brothers and sisters, younger Sadlers, smaller Constants, and I recalled now that Sarah had a sister called Emilia among others.

I found it hard to credit that there really was a feud between the Constants and the Sadlers, however muted. What was it supposed to have been about originally? I struggled to remember. A patch of useless land somewhere out in Cowley Marsh? Surely these two households were much too civilized and comfortable now to fall out over a bog? I also recalled that William Sadler had said that Hugh Fern could not resist seeing drama where there was none.

Those love-birds Sarah Constant and William Sadler seemed quite restrained with each other but perhaps that was natural. The couple were on public display, as it were. I didn't consider there was any great passion between them, at least on his side, although Sarah cast frequent fond glances in his direction. She was still pale but less tense-looking.

I'd been thinking about the poisoning story and whether Susan Constant still expected me to use those skills of detection which she had misguidedly attributed to me. Was I meant to try to uncover some hidden poisoner even at this late stage?

Fortunately, I was not. It was Susan herself who relieved me of that task before the play began.

"Nicholas, can I speak with you?"

I noticed some of my fellows looking at us while we whispered in a corner of the hall where, in the next hour, we were to perform our *Romeo and Juliet*. If she'd wanted to draw attention she could hardly have picked a more public spot, particularly as she put her head close to mine. She had sweet breath. Perhaps people would assume there was some liaison between us. I didn't mind. She was a handsome woman. But it turned out she had other things on her mind.

"You remember our conversation in the meadow by Christ Church?"

"When you talked about your cousin – and poison and clay figures?"

"Yes."

She paused. Whatever she wanted to say next would not come easily.

"I have been at fault in this."

"You mean that you . . .?"

"I mean that I have decided I was mistaken and you were right. I want to unsay what I said then. Since I cannot do that I would like you to forget it. My cousin is not sick. There is no enemy who is trying to come between her and William."

"Although you were so certain there was someone."

I struggled to remember a few of her words to quote back at her but she leaned in closer, her voice sounded deep and low in my ears, and I grew confused.

"There was no one."

"What about – what about the figure you saw that morning by the farmhouse. The bird-headed figure?"

"I was tired. I had not been sleeping well. It was only a farm labourer on his way to work, I expect."

"And the figure, the image that was left by your door. That was real enough surely?"

"A child's plaything, discarded."

Now I was even more confused. But it was none of my business if Susan had decided that she'd been imagining things and didn't after all require my help. I was relieved, to be honest.

"You haven't told anyone, have you, Nicholas?"

"I told my friend Abel Glaze."

"But you have not said anything to William Sadler?"

"Not a word to him."

"Promise me you will not say anything to William. I would not have him disturbed."

"Very well. I promise."

I looked over to where William Sadler was chatting with his father (or so I assumed, there was enough likeness between them). They were laughing together. Young Sadler looked unlikely to be disturbed by very much. As I watched, he upturned a goblet and drained it. I glanced back at Susan. She too had been gazing at William. Her whole expression, which I can best describe as one of fond impatience, told me what I needed to know and solved the puzzle, or a small piece of it anyway.

What had Sadler said to me in his college room? He had complacently accepted Sarah Constant's devotion to him and made some comment about it running in the family. Then he had mentioned not Sarah but *Susan*, before thinking better of whatever he'd intended to say next.

I might have prised the secret out of her, I suppose. She owed me that much at least after the tales of poisoning and men in bird-masks. But no force or subtlety was necessary to get at the truth. The secret was written plainly enough on her face. She was the one who was in love with Sadler. Perhaps it had been stronger in the past but there were still traces of affection in her face for that careless student.

Now she looked back at me. Our heads were still close together. We were sharing a secret, or that's how it must have appeared. I suddenly thought that she wanted William to catch her – to catch us – like that, heads close together, whispering. With luck he might experience a twinge of jealousy. But Sadler was too busy pouring himself another drink from a convenient flask. He didn't so much as notice Susan noticing him.

"Yes," she said finally. "Think of me as Rosaline."

"Rosaline? I don't understand."

"But you do understand, Nicholas Revill. Your look tells

me that you do. Think of me as Rosaline in your play, I say, in *Romeo and Juliet*."

At that moment her cousin Sarah came up and claimed her attention by grasping her arm and wanting to talk. I must say that Susan put on a good show of cousinly affection. She smiled gently and listened patiently.

I moved away. I was already late for changing into my Mercutio costume.

As I was getting prepared in the side-room which was our dressing area, I puzzled over what she had said. Jack Wilson was next to me, getting into his clothes as Tybalt. Laurence Savage was also there. Since he appears in the very beginning, Laurence was already spruced up as Benvolio, cousin and friend to Romeo.

"You have your strokes ready, Nick?" said Jack. "This is likely to be the last time we fight in this particular play."

"At least there is no stage for me to fall off."

"*Alla stocatta.*"

He lunged at me but I was busy doing up my points and in no particular mood for levity.

"Jack, you know this piece of ours better than I do. There is no female called Rosaline in it, is there?"

It may seem odd that I had to ask about the identity of a character in *Romeo and Juliet*, although it's true we can't see a play from the outside as long as we are in it, and we almost never read or study the thing in its entirety but only our own parts and scenes. Still, it was even odder that I'd somehow overlooked a significant character. But Jack too seemed baffled.

"Rosaline? There is one Juliet, one Lady Montague, one Lady Capulet . . . the Nurse of course . . ."

"There *is* a Rosaline," said Laurence, "but she never appears on the stage."

Jack clapped his hand to his head.

"Of course there is," he said.

Seeing I wasn't going to get it, Laurence Savage looked a bit smug while he kept me waiting for an explanation.

Then he recited some lines.

> *"At this same ancient feast of Capulet's*
> *Sups the fair Rosaline, whom thou so lov'st,*
> *With all the admired beauties of Verona."*

When he saw that I still wasn't following him, he sighed. "Rosaline is Romeo's first love. I should know because Dick Burbage will pour out his heart to me in about, oh, half an hour. Remember Romeo doesn't take part in the fight at the beginning of the play because he is wandering love-sick among the sycamores on the edge of the city. He is pining for his *Rosaline* under the sycamores."

"But when he claps eyes on Juliet he forgets all about Rosaline," I said.

"Despite Rosaline's 'bright eyes and quivering thigh'," said Jack. "I should have remembered Rosaline. That is *my* line about the bright eye. Personally I would have been pleased enough with a quivering thigh."

"Why do you want to know, Nick?" said Laurence. "Are you thinking of ways you could improve on William Shakespeare? Have Romeo not kill himself after all, but go back to Rosaline at the end?"

I had a sudden vision of a different tragedy – one that wouldn't be a tragedy at all. Romeo survives and goes off to marry Rosaline.

"I don't think the audience would accept that," said Jack. "A *happy* ending to *Romeo and Juliet*? Come on."

"Only curious," I said.

But now I understood Susan Constant's reference and kicked myself for my slowness. She had seen the play in the yard of the Golden Cross Inn. The lines about Romeo and Rosaline must have struck home – and struck hard. Susan saw herself in the mirror of a character who is talked about but who never actually steps on to the stage.

Rosaline is displaced in Romeo's affections by Juliet.

Perhaps in the same way Susan had been displaced in William Sadler's affections – if he was capable of anything so selfless as affection – by her cousin Sarah. If that's what had happened. What evidence did I have? A glancing reference by Sadler and (much more significant) the look which Susan had given him just now across the hall, a look combining impatience and fondness.

When she is thrown over by Romeo what does Rosaline do in the play? Nothing. Or if she does do anything we never hear of it for *Romeo and Juliet* is not her story.

What does Susan Constant do in real life?

Does she invent a story about her cousin being poisoned, about the "present" of an image being left by the door with a pin sticking into it?

If it was all invention . . .

She seemed pretty certain that it was now. Had told me to forget all about it. The figure she'd glimpsed in the field was a labourer on his way to work. The clay image was an abandoned plaything.

In some part of her mind did Susan dislike – even hate? – her cousin sufficiently to wish harm on her? Did she claim that Sarah was being poisoned because it was what she herself wanted to do? And, unable to contemplate such a horrendous course directly, had she transferred the wish to some imagined enemy? I had no idea whether this speculation was right. It was too deep for me, this attempt to see into the recesses of another's heart and mind.

And, whatever Susan Constant was saying now, at the time she had believed in her story. I could not forget that I too had had more than one glimpse of those hooded figures.

Jack Wilson and Laurence Savage and the others had left by this stage. Not yet fully costumed as Mercutio, I must have been standing there in a brown study (perhaps remembering those hooded figures) because I wasn't aware that Shakespeare had entered the changing-room. He was dressed in the garb of Friar Laurence, and for an instant I didn't recognize him. The gloom that had shrouded him when we'd last talked in his chamber in the Tavern was dissipated. He was generally a sunny individual.

"You look as though you've seen a ghost, Nick."

"It's nothing," I said.

It was on the tip of my tongue to tell him what was really on my mind but instead I said, "This is a strange business."

"How so?"

"We are supposed to be bringing two families together by playing, but I do not see any great signs of hostility, even of dislike between them. Did Hugh Fern imagine this thing? William Sadler suggested that to me."

"Does it matter why we are playing?"

"Oh, it's only money, I suppose. What does anything matter as long as the coin is good?"

There was an unexpected sharpness to my tone and WS looked taken aback. I don't know why I felt like this. Perhaps it was the result of having been taken in by Susan Constant with her stories. No, not taken in . . . but . . .

"There was once a coldness between the Sadlers and the Constants, that's true," said WS, seeing that I needed an explanation. "But it was years ago. I think my friend Hugh Fern saw himself as a peace-maker, where a truce had already been declared. Or it may be that . . . "

I waited.

" . . . he wanted to encourage the young lovers."

"By having them watch a tragedy where the young lovers perish?"

"By displaying true passion to them, perhaps," said WS. "I do not know. If you've talked to Will Sadler at all you must have noticed that he's a somewhat – lukewarm young man. Maybe Hugh wanted to encourage him in love."

"Someone told me recently that only a fool would try to bring two people together," I said.

"I wonder who that was," said Shakespeare. "Well, all we know is that none of us is consistent. Nothing is certain. Had you not better finish your dressing? We are beginning soon."

I half smiled and resumed doing up the points of my costume. Seeing that I was pacified, WS moved away, saying that he had guests to welcome.

Our chamber production of *Romeo and Juliet*, played out in the hall of the Fern house, was a notable success, small though the audience was. Quality made up for quantity. They laughed, groaned and wept in the right places, but all in a refined fashion. *Romeo and Juliet* can hardly have been unfamiliar to them, since several of the audience had been in the Golden Cross on the afternoon of Hugh Fern's death and others had doubtless seen the play before. However, the story comes fresh even when we know the ending.

In fact our audience too was familiar, apart from those members of the two families whom I hadn't glimpsed before. There was Mistress Root, gaudily dressed and laughing at the bawdiness of Thomas Pope playing the Nurse to Juliet. There was William Sadler sitting close to Sarah Constant. I could not see the expression on his face but hoped that the play was working its magic and causing him to fall into a grand passion for her. There was Susan Constant, who had already told me that she was to be identified with Romeo's discarded lover, Rosaline.

Other familiar faces in the audience were Doctor Ralph Bodkin and, more surprisingly, John and Jane Davenant from the Tavern. What was going on inside their heads I haven't the slightest idea, but I presumed they were here as friends to the Company or to the Ferns. It was a private performance but also our farewell appearance in Oxford, and who knew when a troupe of players would pass this way again?

The tragedy finished with our jig. I was able to join in this time, my ankle being almost healed. Nothing untoward occurred. Nobody was found dead in a cupboard afterwards. There was more food and drink at the close. The Sadler and Constant families mingled cheerfully with the other guests. From fragments of conversation, I gathered that a wedding would soon be celebrated (unless the plague took a real hold of the town and brought everything to a stop). Sarah Constant's face was lit up by her smile, sun on a snowfield. Will Sadler had his face buried in a glass. There was no sign of Susan.

We packed up our gear and prepared to make the journey back into town for the night. Like any travelling after dark, this was best done together or at least in groups large enough to deter thieves and worse. We walked down the hill under the moon, but guided as well by several lanterns. We entered the city through the east gate and went down the High Street. The town was quiet.

A few of our number detached themselves from the party at various stages along our route, including Laurence Savage and Jack Wilson. They had private business to attend to, no doubt. I'd heard that Jack had picked up with the wife of a wool merchant who was conveniently absent in Peter-borough. Her name was Maria and she had much admired his skill with the foil when he was playing Tybalt. I knew no more than that. Even bland, mild-mannered Laurence had apparently secured himself a friend of that kind, or so he'd hinted to me. For the first time in several days I thought of Lucy Milford and wondered how she was managing in London. Managing without me, that is. (But of course, she'd be perfectly all right without me. Sad but true.)

For reasons I couldn't fathom I kept expecting something to happen, but it didn't. We got back to the Golden Cross Inn, those of us who hadn't anything more urgent or interesting to do than go to bed. I thought that it was all over. We were to leave the city within a day or two.

I found the note as I was unpacking the scroll which contained my lines as Mercutio. You probably know that these scrolls are among the most precious items carried by a player. Anyone who mislays his lines must not only pay for a new copy but also face the wrath of Master Allison, the book-keeper. So we treat our parts with care. I was about to stow it in the scrip or wallet which I kept under my bolster when a piece of paper fluttered to the floor. I picked it up and held it near the candle.

The writing was unfamiliar – not the clear hand of the play copyist – and I had to angle the page so that it caught the light. It was a simple messsage, simple in one sense. It said:

You are right to suspect foul play in the death of Hugh Fern. We must talk in private. Say nothing beforehand but come to my house on the corner of Cate Street tomorrow morning.
Angelica Root.

I carefully folded the note inside my scrip and thought.

This was a baffling communication for several reasons. For one thing I'd mentioned my suspicions about Doctor Fern's death only to Dick Burbage and WS, and Abel of course. How had Mistress Root got to hear of them? For another, I'd assumed that the problem of Hugh Fern was dead and buried, so to speak. Whatever the questions which surrounded his death, the coroner had pronounced it to be an accident, misadventure.

Then, if Mistress Root wanted to talk to me, why hadn't she taken the opportunity this evening when we were all together at the Ferns' house? (This at least was more easily answered. Presumably she did not want the two of us to be seen talking together in public.)

And how had she contrived to put the note inside the Mercutio scroll? A moment's reflection, however, suggested that this would have been relatively simple, since the scrolls had been left in the "dressing-room" while we were mingling with the audience at the end of the performance. Anyone might have slipped in and secreted a note inside my scroll.

"Getting love-letters again?"

It was Abel Glaze, who, sleeping in the same bed as me, noticed my scrutiny of the note from Mistress Root and the thoughtful way I'd folded it up.

"Something of the sort," I said.

Luckily the light in our large room was so feeble – candle economy – that he wasn't able to see much. *Say nothing beforehand.*

"Is it from Mistress Constant?"

"She is engaged to be married."

"I mean, from *Susan* Constant."

"No, it is not. Not from anyone like that."

"Oh well," said Abel with a sigh, "and I thought we were the only two in the Chamberlain's not to have found ourselves a mistress in this place and be busy tonight."

This was not completely accurate – at least half the bed spaces in our dormitory were occupied at this very moment, and solely by their rightful owners – but I detected a rueful note in my friend's voice. Perhaps his love-lorn pose was not altogether a pose.

I blew out the candle and lay down. One advantage of Laurence Savage's absence was that I had more space in the bed, as did Abel.

"Where is Laurence, do you know?" he said.

"No."

"I hope he has found himself a more comfortable nook than this place."

I refused to rise to Abel's speculation. The question was not interesting (or not *that* interesting). The real question that was preoccupying me, of course, was whether I should respond to Mistress Root's summons to her house in Cats Street. I had more or less put the business of Hugh Fern's death out of my mind. The coroner had sat, everyone seemed satisfied. Yet here was the promise of further secrets.

We must talk in private.

I could ignore the request. We'd be departing from Oxford in forty-eight hours or less.

Caution counselled, well, caution. What did this have to do with me?

But curiosity said something different. To leave the town without having got to the bottom of this mystery would be like quitting a play before the fifth act. You stick it out even though you know it's going to end unhappily.

So early next morning, after breakfasting on a little ale and brown bread, I slipped out of the Golden Cross and made my way to Cats Street. It wasn't far, just a few hundred yards down the High Street and to the east of St Mary's, the church with the great spire. The mist from the river was lifting but shreds of it still hung in the air. The highways were almost deserted.

I had the note in my pocket. The house on the corner. This must be it. A quite handsome dwelling on two floors, half facing on to the High and half on to Cats Street, which was more of a lane. It was a large place for one woman, though Angelica Root may have had dependants or lodgers for all I knew. Certainly large for a nurse, but then I recalled that she'd been married at least three times. Perhaps the late Mr Root had left her well provided for.

I knocked at the door, expecting to be capeniel. Waited. No one came. Knocked again. I pushed at the door but it was shut fast. I turned to go away, half relieved.

Then I saw that one of the casement windows on the side of the house which faced Cats Street was ajar, more than slightly ajar. I peered into the room, which was unoccupied apart from a dining-table, a few chairs and some decorative odds-and-ends. If you're a town-dweller it is not wise to leave a window unlatched during the night for obvious reasons, and if you live in the country then you probably believe that the night air is bad for your health. So I concluded that there was someone in the house, or that there had been someone here earlier this morning.

I returned to the front door and rapped on it once more.

When no answer came, I walked back down the lane and stood in front of the open window.

Before I was properly conscious of what I was doing, I had swung the window right open and hoisted myself over the sill and into the dining-room. Getting in was not difficult.

The sill of the window was only three feet or so from the ground.

Once inside the house I paused. I wondered whether anyone had seen me climbing in. So impulsive had the action been that I hadn't even bothered to check. I closed the window.

I called out Mistress Root's name. The boards creaked as I made my way across a dark lobby and towards a room on the far side. The curtains were drawn but some light squeezed through a gap. In one corner was an ample bed, the marital bed I assumed. Mistress Root was lying on the bed under the shadow of the tester overhead. She was fully clothed, in the same rather gaudy robes she'd been wearing at the Ferns' last night.

I called out her name, more softly this time. But I knew that she was dead. Even by the meagre light I could see her staring eyes, like currants popping out of a cake. She was still red in the face, but blotchily so. On the bed beside her lay two figures, simple clay things that a child might play with, miniature humans. I picked them up, for want of anything else to do. They had featureless heads and gestures for limbs. They seemed familiar, and I remembered Susan Constant's description (now retracted) of a figure left outside a back door. One of these images had a pin stuck into its belly while the other had a pin jammed into its head.

I felt hot, then cold. I don't know how long I stood there in the house of a dead woman, before I was brought back to myself by the squeaking of cart wheels from the lane outside. The mind is odd, because I remember thinking to myself that the carter needed to grease his axle. The squeaking stopped. There was the sound of a key scraping in the front door, then the creak of the door opening and a gust of cold air. There was a little hanging moment, when time seemed to stop altogether. Then a whispering and the soft click of the door being closed again. Too soft a sound, too surreptitious.

In such moments instinct takes over. Thank God it takes over. And thank God too that Mistress Root was a woman who'd come up in the world or married well or been left comfortably off. Whatever the reason, she was the (dead) occupant of a fine bed, elaborately carved with recesses for candles in the headboard and with solid plinths supporting the pillars which held up the tester. But what mattered to me at that moment wasn't the carving or the embroidery but the space underneath the bed.

Before I was really aware of what I'd done I found myself beneath the bed, burrowing like a frightened rabbit pursued by dogs. It was dark and dusty down here. I waited. The top of my head grazed against the leather webbing which supported the feather mattress and the wool blankets (no fustian for Mrs Root) and their late owner. However terrible the circumstances, there was something almost comforting in all this weight above me, particularly when I heard the floorboards creaking right outside the room.

"There's nothing to see," said a muffled voice.

The light was poor but, for myself, I could see quite enough. There were two of them. I'd been saved by the fact that before they reached the bedroom they had gone into at least one of the other rooms on this floor. I'd also heard feet mounting the stairs and, after a few moments, coming down again. If they'd headed straight for this room I would not have had time to get lodged out of sight beneath the bed.

But now the four feet advanced towards my hiding-place and I breathed slow. Not just feet. Also in my line of sight were the bottom of their dark cloaks and a pair of pale sticks, too thin and whip-like to be aids to walking. The feet stopped. Then came the same muffled voice.

"Naughty man's cherries," it said.

Naughty man's cherries?

At least that's what it sounded like. And there was something familiar about the voice which had uttered these words, although I couldn't place it. This peculiar remark was followed by a giggle.

The other person made an impatient, shushing sound.

The feet positioned themselves wide apart and there was a grunting and heaving from above. The two intruders pulled the body of Mistress Root off the bed, none too gently or respectfully. It landed with a thump on the floor. Shadowy figures bent down and half carried, half dragged the body from the bedroom.

I caught a glimpse of the pair as they reached for the corpse. Only a glimpse but it was enough to confirm that they were the hooded, beaked figures I'd seen on two other occasions in this town. The white sticks or wands were the insect-like horns they carried. Seeing them, I was frightened, even more frightened than before, but somehow not surprised by the sight.

As they moved the woman's body one of her shoes fell off. If either of the men noticed, neither came back to retrieve it. There was a slithering and thumping from the lobby before the house door opened and closed with a bolder sound than previously. I waited, expecting to hear the creaking of the cart. But no sound came. I concentrated on a feather which was hanging down from the mattress in front of my face. It quivered with my breath. The door to the bedroom was still open. The stretch of floor between where I was lying and the way out seemed as big as a ploughed field. In the middle of the floor Mistress Root's shoe lay abandoned.

Eventually I heard the cart departing. I counted to a hundred, and then to another hundred for safety's sake. I eased myself out from under the bed. I was covered in dust and feathery stuff. I brushed myself down, taking longer over it than was perhaps necessary. I picked up Mistress Root's shoe and placed it carefully on the bed. It was a smart chopin, with a raised sole to keep the wearer out of the mud or, in Mistress Root's case, to give her an extra inch or so in conversation. I felt a sudden jolt of anger. She might have been a formidable creature, but what had she done to deserve to die? There was a hollow where her body had lain. The two images, run through with pins, had been left behind by the hooded figures.

There was nothing more to be done here. I went into the dark lobby and tried to open the front door but it was locked. The "visitors" had arrived with a key and they had evidently departed with it too. So I passed into the dining-room, paused and looked around for a moment before moving on to the casement by which I'd made my illicit entrance in the first place. Once again I opened the window. This time I checked in each direction. My luck was holding. Cats Street was empty. I swung myself over the sill and hopped out into the lane, then strode off towards the High.

Or rather I made to stride off but my attention was immediately caught by the front door. A cross had been daubed in red on it. The paint was fresh and glistened slightly. Even as I watched, a streak ran down like blood from a wound. It was a careless job. I don't suppose that Alderman Farnaby back in Southwark would have approved, it would not have fitted his feet-and-inches specifications. But the cross did its job of warning off any curious neighbours or passers-by from this solid house in Cats Street, since it announced that the place was sealed up on account of the plague indoors. This explained the pause between the departure of the hooded men from the house and the noise of the cart retreating. One of them had been employed in daubing this crude sign on Mistress Root's door while the other had no doubt been loading the body on to the cart. I wondered what had happened to the third man, since I'd definitely seen three of them on my first night in Oxford.

My heart beating very fast now, I walked down the High. It was still relatively early on this cold spring morning, but a few more people were about. There were half a dozen carts trundling by in both directions, ordinary conveyances loaded with ordinary goods and driven by ordinary folk. No hooded individuals with a corpse for luggage. They would have been rather noticeable, after all. They would surely have wished to avoid being noticeable. I assumed therefore that these anonymous beings had not driven off in this direction.

I needed to get away somewhere, and think about what I'd just witnessed.

It took me only a few minutes of threading through back streets and alleys to gain the isolation of the meadows by Christ Church where I'd walked with Susan Constant several days before. Then we'd talked of her suspicions that her cousin was being poisoned and of hooded figures and of images stuck through with pins. She'd retracted everything that she'd said, but that didn't mean that it wasn't true. I could testify to the truth of at least two of these items.

Scarcely aware of the rushing water at my side, I walked furiously by the river bank, trying to order my own headlong thoughts.

First of all, there was the distress of discovering Angelica Root. A little debt of grief and silence was owing to her, even from one who had scarcely known her.

Close on the heels of this distress, very close, was the fear that I had been left vulnerable to the plague by being inside the same house, the same room, as the late Mistress Root. This fear – more properly, this terror – would have been enough to make some men run wild through the streets, tearing off their garments and throwing themselves on their knees with supplications to the Almighty for deliverance. With others, it might have driven them not to frenzy but to a final debauch. And others still would simply have curled up and waited to die.

I dare say I would have reacted in one of these ways, if I'd genuinely thought that I had been exposed to a plague victim. But, however Angelica Root had met her end, I did not believe that she had fallen under the scythe of King Pest.

For one thing, judging by my brief view of her while she lay on the great bed, she did not show the tokens, the swellings and buboes. For another, if she had been surprised by the infection, then it had been a sudden attack, remarkably sudden. Why, I had seen Mistress Root laughing her head off at the bawdiness of Thomas Pope as he played the Nurse in *Romeo and Juliet* scarcely more than twelve hours earlier. No sign of anything amiss there. I am no physician but, like everyone, I know that one of the worst aspects of the pestilence is its tendency to *toy* with its victims, to stretch them out on the rack of suffering rather than ending their lives with one certain stroke. So if Mistress Root had succumbed to the plague and died in less than a single circuit of the clock then she had been – in one sense – a lucky woman.

No, although I didn't know what had happened to her, I did not think that this was the cause of her death.

Leaving aside the question of how she died, I grubbed around on the edges of the business, trying to pick up a few conclusions.

To start with something small.

Like the two clay images, transfixed by pins. These were similar to the one described by Susan Constant as having been left outside her family's house, apparently directed at her cousin. Too similar for coincidence. Did the presence of these figures on Mistress Root's bed point to a connection between the nurse and her one-time charge? It was Abel Glaze who'd suggested that the old woman might have been so hostile to the notion of marriage that she'd resorted to extreme means to keep Sarah away from it. A ridiculous idea, but even ridiculous ideas turn out to be true sometimes . . .

Then there was the question of those shoes.

(This was the second time within a few days that I'd stopped to consider a dead person's shoes. I recalled the strange business of Hugh Fern's changing his footwear twice, before his appearance on the stage of the Golden Cross Inn and then once more before his death.)

The chopin discarded in the bedroom in Cats Street was for wearing outdoors, unlike the pumps or slippers which you might have expected a woman to put on when she enters her own house, for comfort's sake or to keep the mud and muck from her floors. The fact that Mistress Root was still wearing her street shoes when I found her could suggest that she'd died not long after returning home the previous night. Perhaps the hooded figures were lying in wait for her outside. That would explain how they'd obtained a key to the house.

This chain of reasoning wasn't very strong but it tended to reinforce the notion that, whatever the cause of death, it wasn't the plague. A doctor might have been able to tell – had any doctor been permitted to examine her, to anatomize her – but the unfortunate woman would already be on her way to a burial-pit, a place somewhere on the edge of the city well away from the most populous areas and set aside for plague victims.

For Angelica Root had been presented as a victim of the plague. That was the clear message of the red cross on her door. It was the only explanation for the presence of the hooded figures, whose garb – I now realized – might have been protective. I had never seen such garments before but they could have been put on for a practical purpose, as well as for the purpose of instilling fear. This pretence of the plague would account too for the way in which they'd been able to remove her body with relative boldness in broad daylight and from a house adjoining the busiest thoroughfare in the town.

The assumption I'd made earlier about hooded figures carting off corpses and their need to avoid being noticed was wrong. It didn't matter if they were noticed.

They were not worried about being stopped and inter-rogated on the contents of their cart, because anyone seeing them would do nothing but avert his eyes and say a prayer under his breath, perhaps crossing himself. Not a person would think of intercepting a plague-cart in a town where the disease was beginning to take hold. Nobody would question these drivers, however outlandish their costumes.

They could get away with murder.

The murder of Mistress Root, for example.

That Mistress Root had been murdered was not a com-pletely implausible speculation. She wasn't exactly a harmless

old woman. I wouldn't have liked to be on the receiving end
of her meaty fists. However, it was not her prowess in a fight
but the secrets she kept which made her dangerous. More
particularly, she had summoned me to a meeting to pass those
secrets on, maybe. The note was still in my pocket. By the
fast-flowing Isis I took it out and, although I knew the words
by heart, re-examined the wrinkled paper as if it might yield
more information.

*You are right to suspect foul play in the death of Hugh Fern.
We must talk in private.*

Here was sufficient reason for her death, surely. But what
had she been going to tell me? And why *me*? Because I was
the only one to be suspicious over Fern's death? How had
she discovered my suspicions?

A sudden idea flew into my head. Not a welcome one.

How could I be sure that the note had actually come from
Angelica Root? I'd not seen anything in her hand before. I
held up the paper against the thin sun which was beginning
to break through the clouds. I sniffed at the writing. I tried
to decide whether it was in a woman's hand – or a man's.
There was a firmness to the writing. But then, if the old nurse
had penned it herself, the hand would have been firm. Nor
was there anything special about the wording of the message
except for a certain directness – again, typical of Mistress
Root. I felt the texture of the paper, rubbing it loosely
between my fingers. Unfortunately, as I was doing so, a gust
of air lifted it from my hand. I made to grab it but it skittered
out of reach and over the water, and the little piece of evidence
connecting me to Mistress Root and the house in Cats Street
disappeared downriver. It wasn't much use that I could recall
its exact wording.

Well, if the vanished note had been written by someone else
then that person could have had only one motive. To trick me
into coming to Mistress Root's house and once there to . . .

I thought of the way the casement window had been left
conveniently ajar, almost inviting me to climb in. I recalled

the way in which the two "visitors" had let themselves in with the key and proceeded to go into the other rooms as well as upstairs before reaching the bedchamber. Were they looking for Mistress Root, since she might have expired anywhere in the house?

Or were they looking for Nicholas Revill?

There's nothing to see, one of the hooded individuals had said.

But there was something to see, there was a body lying on the bed in front of them. Did he say that before glimpsing the dead nurse, or were the two of them looking for another somebody?

Had they thought to trap me in the house, to take me by surprise and then to deal with me?

Only one of the hooded figures had spoken. As well as the comment about seeing nothing, he had made that riddling reference to "naughty man's cherries".

There was something half familiar about the voice, muffled though it had been by the hood.

My thinking being more or less done for the time being, I left the meadows by the river and made my way back towards Carfax and the Golden Cross. It crossed my mind that I should report my discovery of Angelica Root to the authorities, but now there was no body to be produced, and the only evidence of any wrongdoing, a crumpled note which might or might not be in the dead woman's hand-writing, was lost. Anyway, if poor old Root really had perished of the plague then the last thing the coroner or magistrate would wish for was an investigation into her death. What would be the point? What was one death among so many?

I encountered that familiar ostler Kit Kite in the deserted yard of the Golden Cross. He was idling his time. I stopped to idle it with him.

"Good day, Nicholas," he said.

"Master Kite."

"Out and about early?"

"I have been exploring the town."

"I hear you are leaving soon."

"Only me?"

"Ha, I mean your Company is leaving, Nicholas."

"Then I'm sure you are better informed than any of my Company – apart from the seniors. There are no secrets in an inn."

"I keep my ear to the ground."

The little ostler tapped himself on his sandy head, and giggled.

"An odd expression, that," I said. "I mean, no one really keeps his ear to the ground."

"I dare say they don't, but it is a figure, you know," said this learned handler of horses.

"A figure of speech, just so," I said.

"Such things don't deserve to be looked into so closely."

But I observed that Kit Kite was looking at me closely. His eyelashes were sandy too.

"I heard another expression recently in this town," I said. "I had not heard it before, and I wondered whether it was particular to this place."

"What might that be?"

"Something about . . . let me see . . . about dead man's cherries, I think."

"Where did you hear it?"

I bypassed the question, saying instead, "It would be more accurate to say that I *over*heard it."

Kit Kite screwed up his eyes and scratched his head in a quite convincing display of ignorance.

"It means nothing to me either. Perhaps you misheard, Nicholas."

"Perhaps so."

I made to walk on, leaving the ostler to his feigned uncertainty. After a couple of paces, I snapped my fingers and turned about.

"I have it! It was not a dead man but a naughty man. *Naughty man's cherries*, that was it."

"For sure you misheard, Master Revill," said Kit Kite.

"I don't believe so. Like you, I keep my ear to the ground."

Then I entered the inn before he could say anything else by way of denial or incomprehension. But I did not go upstairs to my quarters. I stayed just inside the entrance and watched the reaction of Master Kite in the gap between the door and the jamb.

The ostler remained standing in the middle of the yard. There was no look of bafflement on Kite's face now. I could see his expression clearly since he was gazing in the direction I'd gone in. His face registered something more decided, something tougher.

I jumped as a hand grasped my shoulder.

"Spying?"

"Ah, er, Master Davenant."

The landlord came up close to me. His face was as long as a beagle's. I wondered what he was doing in the Golden Cross, in Owen Meredith's establishment.

"Revill the player, isn't it?"

He smelled as though he'd been sampling some of his own produce or some of the rival landlord's. Wafts of warm, liquorish air occupied the space between us.

"Do you know anything about that man out there?" I said. "The ostler."

"Ostler? What ostler?"

"Kit Kite."

"Hardly know the man."

Nevertheless Jack Davenant poked his head round the door-frame.

"What are you talking about, Revill? There's no one there."

"It doesn't matter."

"You are leaving," said Davenant, echoing the words of the ostler he hadn't seen. His tone hung somewhere between command and question. I assumed he was referring to the whole Company rather than to one middling member of it.

"Leaving, yes. There is no more for us to do here," I said.

"No more playing," said Davenant. "No more mischief."

He wandered off into the yard. I saw him give a kick to one of the supports of the platform where we'd so recently performed *Romeo and Juliet* and the other pieces. I wondered what he'd been up to in the Golden Cross.

But it wasn't the landlord of the Tavern whose behaviour was puzzling me at the moment. It was the reaction of Master Kite, the knowing ostler. For sure, the expression "dead man's cherries", deliberately misquoted at first, had put him on his guard. Most people, if asked to explain a word or phrase, will repeat it with a frown. Kite, though, had simply enquired where I'd heard it.

I knew exactly where I'd heard it. Lying under the bed in Angelica Root's chamber.

And I was pretty certain whose mouth I'd heard it from: Kite's mouth.

Despite the muffling effect of the hood, it was his voice, and his giggle following after it.

The chamber which I shared with Laurence Savage and Abel Glaze and others was bustling. Jack Wilson looked particularly perky. I recalled the wool merchant's wife who had admired his way with a foil. Jack looked as though he hadn't slept a wink and had enjoyed every second of it. Which was more than you could say for my last couple of hours.

I soon learned that we were to leave Oxford the next day.

"Where are we going?"

"Where you will," said Jack. "We are released. Personally I shall stay here in town for a little. I have been offered lodging for the time being."

"I don't understand," I said.

"It's very simple," said Jack. "There's this woman in Grove Street, you see. She is a wool merchant's wife, and I must strike while the iron is hot. I fear that her husband will soon summon her to Peterborough when he finds out what's happening here. When he finds out about the plague, I mean, rather than that she is consorting with a member of the Chamberlain's."

"Not that," I said, faintly impatient with Jack's complacent elaboration. "What I don't understand is why all of us are being released."

"That's because you missed a meeting which the shareholders convened this morning. You weren't there, Nick."

"I was – busy."

"Well, Dick Burbage announced that we are to assemble in London again at the end of Lent."

"And then we shall take stock," said Abel Glaze.

I must have looked a bit baffled still because Abel added, "Burbage tells us that the Queen has only days left . . . they say that she cannot be persuaded to go to bed but sits up without speaking. To think that she should die!"

"And the plague rages on in London too," said Jack. Try as he might, he was unable to keep a touch of cheerfulness out of his voice.

Of course, I realized that Burbage and many more of the married men would want to get back to London, now it was clear that things weren't going to improve up there. Some would probably want to arrange for their wives and children to quit the city altogether.

But there was more to our return than a natural concern for families. If Queen Elizabeth was really on the point of death, then it might well seem to the Chamberlain's shareholders that the appropriate place for them was in her capital city. There was common sense here as well, for who knew what turn affairs would take after her death? Safer to be prepared for the future at our base in Southwark rather than elsewhere, several days' journey away.

"What are you going to do, Nick?"

"Unfortunately I haven't found your kind of accommodation yet, Jack," I said.

"Oh, and what kind is that?"

"The close-clinging-female kind. In Grove Street."

"You may say so," said Jack, liking to talk on this topic. "She does cling close, this merchant's wife. Maria. Ma-ri-a. A lovely name. She is younger than her husband."

I moved away but Jack kept babbling.

"What?"

Jack had said something but I wasn't listening.

"I tell you gentlemen, this plaguey period is a great increaser of fear and desire – for both sexes."

"Well, even without your diversions I may stay a day or two longer as well," I said. "I don't suppose Owen Meredith's rooms are going to be in great demand."

I was looking out of the window at the end of our dormitory room. As I've already described, there was a jumble of old houses and alleyways to the rear of the Golden Cross. What had distracted me was the sight of Kit Kite entering one of the houses down there. There was no mistaking that little sandy-haired figure. Naturally I linked his appearance with the night-time glimpse of the cowled figures at a nearby window.

This chimed with my suspicion that he was one of the pair who had removed Mistress Root's body. What I must decide now was what to do next. Or rather, whether to do something – or nothing. While the rest of my fellows continued their preparations for departure I pursued my thoughts.

I'd no doubt that I had stumbled on some ingenious and murderous business, even if it was one whose purposes and methods were still obscure to me. Just about everything which I'd seen and heard since arriving in this town – Susan Constant's story (later withdrawn) of the poisoning of her cousin, the mysterious deaths of Hugh Fern and of Angelica Root, the band of hooded figures, the convenient appearance of the plague cross on the house in Cats Street – seemed to be connected. But what were the threads that tied it all together?

There was no real story to take to the authorities. I had no proof – the vanished note would have been useful here – nothing except the testimony of my own eyes. I couldn't even call on Susan Constant, for she had denied her earlier suspicions and sworn me to silence. (And that was a minor mystery too.) It crossed my mind to approach Ralph Bodkin. He was a physician and a local alderman, a man of influence. I had seen for myself his bullish courage while he disposed of the ranting individual who was stirring up the crowd in Carfax. But there was a no-nonsense, almost intimidating aspect to the man. I recalled the way in which he'd dismissed as superstition the connection between plays and the plague. If Bodkin asked me for evidence, or even for a clear account of what was going on, I couldn't have obliged him.

No, if anything was to be done then it rested on the shoulders of one N. Revill.

Straightaway, before caution or second thoughts could intervene, I set out from the Golden Cross. After several false turns and blind alleys I found the area of the town which lay behind the inn. The houses here were old, mean and narrow. Only a little light penetrated between the overhang of the upper storeys. The roadways, more like ditches, were littered with household waste and the stench was stronger than it would have been in open places. I looked back and upwards to see the rear windows of our inn.

I identified the door which Kit Kite had gone through and knocked on it, aware that this was the second time in a single morning that I'd arrived at an unknown dwelling. Please God, there would be no bodies in here –

"What you want?"

A small, hard-faced woman clung about with children. Two – no, three – were holding on to her legs like miniature gaolers taking her into custody while a baby's wailing filled the background.

"I'm looking for lodging."

"There's none here. This is a house of mourning."

The comment was more like a threat than an appeal for commiseration.

"I'm a player."

"I don't care if you're the angel Gabriel."

She made to close the door.

"Wait!"

The door was half closed.

"I was recommended this place by Christopher Kite. Maybe you – "

Then she shut the door full in my face, although not before giving me a curious look or so I thought.

Not much revealed by her. But useful in one way. In the gloomy little lobby, behind the woman and her brood, I'd noticed a thin white cane propped against the wall.

"There's no proof of any of these things, Nick."

"You believe me though?"

I had got as far as telling Abel Glaze of my discovery of the old nurse and of the departure of the hooded figures with her corpse. I reported some of the conclusions I'd arrived at down by the river.

"Of course *I* believe what you say, though many might not," said Abel. "Even so, to withhold it from your friend until now."

"I'm sorry, Abel."

I was sorry but what I needed more was to pacify him since I required his assistance. I had changed my mind about shouldering the burden of this mystery by myself. As when we'd discussed the death of Hugh Fern, I wanted to lighten the load. But Abel, while not exactly sceptical, seemed to be making a show of his willingness to believe me, and wanting credit for it. Perhaps he was right to do so.

"It is a pity that you lost the letter from Mistress Root," he said now.

"I've told you what she said. If it was from her."

"But last night you claimed it was a love-letter."

"I think you were the one who said that first, imagining it was from one of the Constant cousins or something. You're always ready to believe in a love-letter."

"But you didn't deny it altogether."

"Because that's what the note instructed me to do: *say nothing beforehand.*"

"Even so . . . and what do you mean, I'm always ready to believe in a love-letter?"

"Oh, other men's cherries," I said. "Which reminds me . . . "

So I told Abel of the queer remark which I'd heard from my hiding-place under Mistress Root's bed, and of the little test to which I'd subjected Kit Kite. For sure, the ostler was familiar with the phrase. So was Abel Glaze, as it happened. All at once he grew excited.

"*Naughty man's cherries*, Nick. I know what they are."

His irritation that I had not revealed the full story earlier was swept away by his eagerness to tell me something.

"It is a name for a poison. For the deadly nightshade. And there are other names for it as well."

"Nightshade will do to be going on with," I said.

Nightshade. It was as if someone had opened a window in my head.

Nightshade. Of course. It was a common plant, you hardly had to go far looking for it. So they called it "naughty man's cherries". I thought of the purple berries, carrying destruction in their dark hearts but like enough to cherries for the term to be used mockingly by those possessed of no good intentions. The dark heart of nature.

A clump or two of it grew not far from the Somerset parsonage where I was brought up. I knew about it before I could speak, almost. How is it that we learn to avoid these fatal fruits when we are small? Instinct? Had my mother warned me about it? When we are children we are guarded by agents, they say, seen and unseen. But who is there to preserve us when we are grown men and women, and someone chooses to slip a mortal dose into our meat or drink?

I thought of Mistress Root stretched out on the marital bed, her eyes like popping currants, her shoes still on her dead feet. Truly it is man, not nature, that has a dark heart.

"What?" I said.

"I said," said Abel, "so you think that the old woman was poisoned?"

"Yes, and then that it was made to look like the plague."

"But why?"

"That is what we have to find out."

"We?"

Yes, *we*.

Us.

Nicholas Revill and Abel Glaze, middle-ranking players of the Chamberlain's Company, set down by chance in the middle of Oxford and thrown into the heart of a mystery which involved plague and poison. After a little resistance Abel had agreed to help, or at least to keep me company.

It was the middle of the evening. Abel and I were standing in an alley almost opposite the "house of mourning" where the hard-faced woman had answered the door to me earlier that day. We'd been loitering here for about half an hour, our eyes by now accustomed to the dark. Fortunately there was a good deal of coming and going at another house further up the street and this activity did something to mask our presence. It hadn't taken long to realize that this busy dwelling was a brothel or stew, but one of a particularly dilapidated sort.

The street was called Shoe Lane, I'd discovered, but any kind of respectable activity such as cobbling had long since quit the place, and now another kind of hammering and fitting was going on. The brothel had a little, low door so that those entering had to stoop as if they were making obeisance. By contrast with the stews of London – establishments such as the Cardinal's Hat or the Windmill, and above all Holland's Leaguer (where my friend Nell once plied her trade) – this place looked to be a sad, provincial affair. Its occupants were probably squinty-eyed country girls and dispossessed serving-women, or so I imagined. I'd no intention of finding out.

The customers, however, appeared more respectable from the occasional glimpse we had as they hurried, singly or in little groups, by the mouth of the alley. Some of them glanced in our direction then hurried on again without paying much attention. If they noticed us at all, two figures in the shadows, they presumably thought we were plucking up courage to visit the house ourselves. The more fearful might have imagined we were vagrants lying in wait to rob them (though if we were going to do that, we'd only do it while they were on the way *in*, not when they were leaving with lighter purses).

Again, it was fortunate for Abel and me that there'd been no sign of any beadle or watchman while we were hanging about. They'd doubtless been bribed to keep away from this quarter of the town, maybe with the offer of free samples. That's how it works in the borough of Southwark anyway. Abel was slightly surprised that the tightening grip of the plague in the town hadn't interrupted the flow of business at the brothel – he could be a bit green sometimes – but I whispered to him that the threat of King Pest was most likely to bring about an *increase* of trade not a diminution. Seize the day, make hay while the sun shines, & cetera, even if it's a pretty mouldy kind of hay.

We were here because we'd been spying intermittently on the ostler Kit Kite. That sandy-haired gentleman was, in my opinion, if not exactly the key to the mystery, a means by which one might get at the key. Kite had returned to his post in the stables during the day but Abel had seen him, from our vantage point in the inn chamber, once more entering the back-street house as the light faded from the sky. From the fact that the ostler had rushed off there earlier after I'd tantalized him in the Golden Cross yard with the reference to "naughty man's cherries", as well as from my observation of the white stick or cane propped against the wall in the lobby, it was evident that this pinched dwelling was serving as some kind of base for . . . for what exactly?

I didn't know. That's what Abel and I were doing here, loitering in the alley, trying to find out. But this wasn't entirely a shot in the dark.

While most of my fellows were packing up to leave Oxford, I'd spent the afternoon in pursuit of one or two notions. My first call was on a bookshop in Turl Street. I'd already dropped into this place a couple of times. The shopkeeper, one Nathaniel Thornton, was a dusty old man with a straggling white beard. He was very ready to chat with me – booksellers seem to fall into two classes, the very talkative and the very silent. He was not impressed to find that I was a member of a company of players since he shared the prevailing Oxonian view of acting as no profession for a gentleman. When I pointed out to him that he had William Shakespeare's poem *Lucrece* on his shelves as well as a battered copy of *Venus and Adonis*, and that this Shakespeare was our very own author, Master Thornton said, "Ah yes but the poems will last, mind you, unlike the man's plays." (I might have disputed this but wasn't sure enough of my ground.)

On this occasion I explained to Thornton that I was looking for a book that might give advice on devices and preservatives to keep off the plague, since I was returning to London, an even more plaguey spot than Oxford if that was possible. There was some truth in what I said – anyone would be glad of any instrument that might keep the thing at bay – but I was really in search of information on poisons and thought it best not to come straight out with this, rather to work round to the subject.

"Some say that a unicorn's horn is the best specific against the plague," said the bookseller.

"What's your view, Master Thornton?"

I was humouring the old fellow but I was also curious. It seemed to me that a lifetime spent selling books, especially in a learned city, must impart a certain wisdom.

"They say that Alexander the Great went to immense labour and expense to procure a unicorn, and even so could not find one alive. That being the case, Master Revill, it is strange how frequently one finds the horn of the beast ground up into a powder and on sale at street corners. You'll have to pay for it, mind you – but it is common."

"What do they use?"

"A shoe-horn usually, broken and ground up and mashed with something else. The ignorant are easily deceived."

I smiled smugly, as one of the non-ignorant, the undeceived. Master Thornton continued in his ruminative way, "When it comes to warding off the plague now, some people make great claims for the onion. Peeled and left to lie in the rotten place."

"At least it's cheaper than unicorn," I said.

"And more effective, since your onion is a great sucker-up of infections, which is more than I have ever heard said for a shoe-horn. But I have a different preservative."

"So what would you use, Master Thornton?"

He reached into a drawer of the desk behind which he was sitting and extracted three soft leather pouches attached to cords.

"When I go out I wear one of these about my neck. It is recommended by several authorities such as Doctor Bodkin in this very town."

Naturally my ears pricked up at the mention of Bodkin. The bookseller opened one of the little pouches to display its contents but I could see only a grey powder.

"This is arsenic. Ratsbane. So far I have been preserved, but I do not go out much, mind you."

The reference to arsenic was my cue and I asked Master Thornton whether he could recommend any herbals which dealt with poisons and other noxious substances, since it is frequently observed that a little danger will often work to keep off the greater. The bookseller knew his stock and indicated three or four volumes at the end of a shelf in the corner. He did this without moving from his station behind the desk, and I didn't wonder at his claim that he rarely stirred from his shop.

The most promising volume looked to be a *Herbal* by one Gerard Flower, a graduate of this very university as I saw on the title-page, and a highly appropriate name for an author writing about plants and their properties. But I realized that I would need more than a few minutes flicking through its pages in the corner of Nathaniel Thornton's shop. It cost five shillings, however, and I was not willing to part with so much money for a book that I needed only for one particular purpose and would probably not consult again.

We entered into negotiations. In the end I came to an agreement with Nathaniel Thornton that I could *borrow* Flower's *Herbal* on condition that I *bought* a copy of WS's *Lucrece* for two shillings, which I did on the spot and willingly enough. For an additional sixpence Thornton offered to throw in another item which, after a moment's hesitation, I accepted. I promised to return the herbal book within a day or so, and was pleased that he was willing to trust me with it.

As I was leaving the bookshop I encountered William Sadler. In his high-handed way he reached for the two books I was carrying and examined them cursorily.

"Poetry I can understand since you are a player, Nicholas, but a herbal . . .?"

"Perhaps I am trying to educate myself, William. About mixtures and preparations."

"Potions and stuff such as Romeo used?"

"Perhaps. You enjoyed our play?" I said, since he'd given me the cue.

"Oh, it was well enough, although personally I could not swallow dying for love."

"Only a play," I said.

Sadler disappeared into Thornton's shop, leaving me to reflect that if it had been part of the intention of the late Hugh Fern to encourage this man to feel the force of passion then the Doctor's shade must be feeling disappointed.

I returned to Carfax and consulted the plague orders which were posted on the church doors of St Martin's. Even though the information also appeared in other public places, there was quite a gaggle of townspeople in this central crossroads, bad news being infectiously attractive. The mortality bill showed how the numbers of the dead in the various parishes had increased in the two weeks or so since the Chamberlain's Company had been in Oxford, after that first reported outbreak in the Folly Bridge house. Angelica Root did not figure on the list yet, her death presumably being too recent. Although the numbers of dead were small by London standards, the increase was rapid, probably on account of the compact nature of the town.

The plague orders, as opposed to the mortality bills, concerned the appointment of scavengers and examiners and watchers and the like. These are people enlisted from the ranks of ordinary citizens, who find themselves with (generally) unwelcome duties to perform in time of plague, such as ensuring that the streets are kept clean or seeing that no one enters an infected dwelling. The orders were not so interesting to the bystanders as the list of the dead, which caused much finger-pointing and tutting and whispering but little open grief as far as I could see.

I couldn't find Kit Kite's name on the published orders, although that didn't necessarily mean that he and his accomplice were self-appointed to their role.

I wasn't absolutely sure what that role was ... though I was beginning to have an inkling of what it might be.

I remembered how, when Abel Glaze and I were walking along Kentish Street on the edge of Southwark, we'd encountered the group of neighbours outside the infested house, together with Alderman Farnaby, the beadle and the constable. There'd been a near fight between one of the locals and the old women, the sisters who'd been appointed as nurse-keepers. And I recalled the words which the neighbour had uttered: something about preferring to have rats at her linen or moths in her cupboard rather than letting any keeper inside her house.

And what was more to the point regarding this business unfolding in Oxford now – the neighbour had as good as accused the nurse-keeper of being prepared to commit murder on her charges, or at least to speed them on their way with a smothering pillow or a pinching shut of the nostrils with fingers.

I'd no idea how justified such an accusation was. But the fact that it could be made suggested that there was probably some truth behind it. It didn't take much cynicism about human nature to suppose that not all the persons appointed to watch over a dying household would be shining models of honesty, that some might be tempted to snaffle up the odd, portable item. They might even consider themselves entitled to do so, on the grounds that they were putting their own lives at risk by their charitable work, that the dying had no further use for said portable items, & cetera. It didn't take a much further descent into cynicism to imagine other persons – more ruthless ones – crossing the boundary and deciding to hurry on nature's work by the application of pillows or fingers.

Or poison.

A poison known as "naughty man's cherries".

Deadly nightshade.

I was fairly certain that Mistress Root had not perished of the plague. Of course, she might have dropped down dead from an ague or some other cause – I couldn't tell, I was no doctor, and even a doctor might not have been able to say. All I could say was that she'd appeared in rude health the previous evening during our *Romeo and Juliet*.

A natural death might still have been the natural assumption, however well she'd seemed. We all know that death can strike like a thief in the night when it's least expected. But thieves in the night can be human ones too. So I was looking not to an act of God but to the hand of man. And in this case there was the "cherries" comment made by the hooded individual whom I believed to be Kit Kite. There was also the note to consider. The note unfortunately lost to the fast-flowing Isis but whose teasing hints I could easily repeat. *You are right to suspect foul play in the death of Hugh Fern.*

If the note really had been written by her and if she had been intending to pass on her suspicions to me, possibly going so far as to name someone she considered responsible for Fern's death, then that *someone* had ample motive to want her out of the way. The assumption of foul play in her case as well as Fern's became even stronger if the note had been penned by another, by the unknown *someone* in fact, with the purpose of luring me into a trap.

This reasoning may seem a bit thin on paper, written down in black and white. But I had another supporting piece of evidence which pointed to wrong-doing, albeit without proper proof. When I'd climbed through the window of the house in Cats Street I had noticed in an abstracted way that the dining-room contained some decorative bits and pieces, including an item in the centre of the table, probably a salter, probably a silver one. I couldn't be certain since I had other things on my mind at the time. But before I'd made my exit through the same dining-room window, I had taken a longer look round the room and registered that the table was bare. Other items – portable ones – might have gone too from elsewhere in the chamber.

So it seemed as though the "thief in the night" description was appropriate in a different way. Angelica Root had not merely been struck down by death but had been robbed by him as well. A dangerous witness had been silenced, and a profit taken in the shape of a silver salter and other objects.

My next step was to consult the book which I'd borrowed from Nathaniel Thornton.

I was taken aback by the poison contained within its pages. Even though I'd acquired a smattering of knowledge about dangerous plants from my mother or my playfellows or simply from instinct, I had no idea that I'd spent every waking moment since birth on the edge of an abyss. Flower's *Herbal* opened up a perilous gallery in which almost every root, every bud, every leaf and seed could be employed for nefarious purposes. Nature was a veritable arsenal, and the cautious man would never eat or drink again for fear that, by accident or another's malicious design, he might swallow one of her fatal gifts.

However, it was only one little area of this great, wild world that I was concerned with. I discovered that "naughty man's cherries" was another name for the nightshade, as Abel had said, and also that it was known under several other guises such as belladonna, and beautiful lady, and devil's herb, and dwale. Gerard Flower – whose word had to be believed since he was a Master of Arts at the University of Oxford – said of the nightshade that it had been the "ruin of many a simple unwary soul, tempted by its dark and clustered fruit". It was only outdone in efficacy, he claimed, by monkshood. This plant, familiar to the learned as aconite, was an even more potent and quick-acting poison. Monkshood could also assume various names – like some human malefactors – being known as wolf's bane and friar's cap as well as having softer, more deceptive appelations such as Cupid's car. *Cupid's car*? Well, there's no accounting for names sometimes. In short, Master Flower instructed me, monkshood might be termed the Queen-mother of poisons.

And in short, it seemed to me from my reading and from the phrase I'd overheard that Angelica Root had been poisoned with a preparation of nightshade, perhaps mixed with wolf's bane (since the two combined well and were more than twice as noxious together). She had surely been murdered to silence her, and her abrupt death was connected – though I couldn't yet understand how – to the mysterious end of Hugh Fern. I was convinced now that, contrary to appearances, the Doctor's death had been no suicide. Equally, I was determined to sink my teeth into this mystery before it sank its teeth into me.

So this is how Abel and I came to be loitering in an alleyway in a dingy maze of streets at the back of the Golden Cross Inn. We'd been waiting here for the best part of an hour now and so far had seen nothing more than the trickle of customers to and from the bawdy-house.

Then Abel tugged me by the sleeve.

"Look, Nick," he hissed.

A shape, a familiar shape, was passing by the mouth of the alley, coming from the direction of the brothel.

"Isn't that . . . ?"

"Yes," I said. "That is Laurence Savage."

We paused to take in the information that a fellow player had been availing himself of what the town had to offer in the way of flesh.

"So the old Savage has been making a pig of himself in the pleasure house," said Abel.

I was mildly surprised, Laurence never having expressed much interest in these matters, but it would be convenient to have something to twit him with in future.

"He told me that he had a friend," I said, perhaps a bit priggishly, "but I did not know she was a whore."

"I have heard that *you* were close to a whore once, Nick."

"That was completely different. Nell was a city girl, refined and capable, working in a place that was like a mansion. She could even read and write – after her fashion. Not like the country girls and clapped-out serving-women they've got in there. Probably got in there, that is, how should I know?"

"What's that line about protesting too much?"

We were so carried away by this friendly dispute that our voices had risen above a whisper and we were neglecting our watching duties. It was dark, of course, but suddenly it seemed to grow even darker as two more shapes swept across the alley-mouth. By the time we'd gathered ourselves to peer out they were rounding the corner at the top of the narrow little street. But the brief glimpse of their backs was enough to show that they were cloaked and hooded, like the figures I'd seen on my first night in this town, like the figures I'd half seen from under Mistress Root's bed. Since we hadn't been watching the door of Kit Kite's house (as I thought of it) it was impossible to say whether the figures had come from there or whether one of them was Kite himself. But I would have bet heavily on a "yes" in both cases.

Abel clutched at my arm.

"My God, you were right. What are they?"

"Later," I said. "Let's see where they're going."

For it was evident that the two men, garbed in outfits that were a cross between a monk's and a bird's, were going *somewhere* and were surely up to *something*.

But we were not destined to go much further in our pursuit.

As we emerged from the alley which had been our skulking-place, there was a cry from the front of the stew.

"There they are!"

"Peepers!"

"Spies!"

I'd been wrong to suppose that our presence in the alley had not provoked much attention. A gaggle of customers from the bawdy-house were massing at its tight little entrance. By ill fortune Abel and I had emerged at exactly this moment. They couldn't have seen much perhaps, but I could imagine the comments that had been thrown about inside concerning a couple of dubious characters outside. Obviously they'd think of us as . . .

"Stew kites!"

"Queer-birds!"

"Punk watchers!"

... that odd brand of man which – so Nell had once told me – loiters about outside houses of ill-fame sniffing the air and hoping for a glimpse of naughtiness, but without ever going inside; a brand which is (rightly) regarded with resentment and suspicion by the madam and her brood as being bad for business.

Whether it would be enough for this crew to stand and hurl insults in our direction or whether – their baser appetites not yet being sated by their activities indoors – they wanted to do us actual damage, I don't know. We didn't wait to find out. Or rather Abel didn't. Some panic overtook him and he started off down the filthy street. After a moment's hesitation I followed him close at heels.

In the noise and confusion the hooded individuals may have run off or it may be that we took a different turning from them. Anyway, we lost sight of the pair, being more concerned with preserving our skins from a gaggle of brothel-creepers.

We got away from the outraged customers of the stew easily enough but returned to the Golden Cross with only one solid piece of information to show for our skulk in the alley: that our fellow player Laurence Savage, who was now tucked up in one of the communal beds and snoring blissfully, frequented stews. Well, he had gained more satisfaction than we had this evening. At least I hoped that he had.

Dwale

A good harvest – yet in this upside-down world it is only the springtime not autumn. And another strange thing, this is a crop which grows the more you reap. The dead pile up, and your hand is not always needed now to put them in their place on the pile. Now nature will handle them by herself. In some ways this is to be regretted since the pestilence is a crude instrument while you are continually refining your methods, ever since the early demise of the dog and the death of old mother Morrison. Now you can judge doses to a nicety. The only "crudeness" came in the way you dealt with the carter Hoby but that was inevitable. He was stealing your profit. Besides he was a frightened little man and sooner rather than later would have revealed himself or been revealed.

You are immune, though, in your armour. You will not suffer yourself to be discovered, to be revealed.

This is as well since there are stirrings of suspicion. In particular Revill the player is pushing his nose in and you have decided to cut it off – to cut him off – if it can be managed discreetly, as it should have been in the case of Doctor Fern. You had hoped to decoy Revill to that old woman's house and deal with him there, but something went wrong, he smelled a rat and did not appear. Or could not be found. Then Kite took fright at some provoking words of the player – most likely uttered only to test his response – and scuttled off to the house in Shoe Lane.

All that is required is calmness and self-control. You are very much afraid that Kite is no longer capable of showing such qualities. Underneath his cocksure surface there is a well of fears. It is only a matter of time before he too is invited to join the pile of the dead. Then it will be a fitting moment for you to decamp with your goods, your pot of money.

More important than goods and money, you will depart with your precious preparations and potions, which give you the power of life and death. With belladonna and beautiful lady, with devil's herb and dwale. With monkshood, wolf's bane and friar's cap. The words are a spell. Merely to recite them is comforting. They can open the doors to the other place.

They say that poison is a woman's weapon. Why is that? Is it the domestic preparation, the kitchen utensils, the grinding and mixing, the "cooking" that is sometimes needed? Is it that poison is most efficiently and painlessly served under the cover of necessary food and drink, the woman's province? Or is it, as a fool would claim, that poison suits the fainter heart of a woman? Yet it is not a faint-heart's instrument. Which requires the greater courage, the stronger nerve? To administer the fatal dose, either all at once or piecemeal, and then to wait in an agony of suspense which is almost as great as your victim's? Or to act when the blood is up and to run your victim through with a knife or sword, scarcely aware of what you're doing? You have done both so you know what you're talking about. The first deed demands coolness and premeditation, while the other one needs nothing more than a hot head and a nimble wrist.

These are . . . interesting reflections. Some time, when this present trouble is over, you must write them down.

"This is a dangerous course, Nick."
I'd lost count of the number of times Abel Glaze had said this. He meant well all right, but his words were only making me more frightened, something which was very easy to do at this moment. I was lying on a couch in a stranger's house. Abel was kneeling on the floor, his wallet unfurled in front of him. We had a small amount of light from a few candles, gross quality ones. It was still daylight outside but, being trespassers, we did not dare to open the curtains.

"Tell me again about the . . . what did you call them? . . . the pallets?" I said, more to stop Abel talking about the dangers which I was running than because I really wanted to be informed about the strange individuals he'd mentioned a few minutes earlier. He was outlining some of the methods which can be used to create a false impression of sickness or disease.

"Palli*ards* they are called. Or sometimes clapperdudgeons. I'm surprised you've never heard of them."

"I haven't got your underworld experience, Abel."

My friend bristled slightly at this. He didn't always like to be reminded of his coney-catching days or rather, if he did talk about them, it had to be on his own terms. He refused to look at me but knelt over the outspread contents of his capacious wallet, drew a candle closer and, with the aid of a couple of tiny wooden scoops, mingled the sticky ingredients of two or three tiny pots. Pots of grease and pouches of herbs were the tools of Abel's one-time trade. They'd been as essential to his old business as a hammer and chisel were to a mason but my friend still carried them everywhere with him. I'd twitted him once about the way he clung to these relics of his life on the road, conning the public, tricking charitable passers-by. He responded with some mangled proverb about any rabbit worth its salt having two holes to go to. I took this to mean that, if he ever grew tired of play-acting (or if play-acting grew tired of him), then he could resume his life as a wandering coney-catcher.

219

"*Palliards,*" I said. "What about them now?"

"Palliards fall into two classes," said Abel, talking in that abstracted way which people use when their hands are engaged in tricky operations. "The real ones and the artists."

"Artists?"

"Fakes, you would probably say. But they show great skill in adorning their bodies with sores and raw places."

"How?"

"With crowfoot and salt usually, sometimes mixed with spearwort. They rub these items together and then lay them on the part which they wish to afflict. Afterwards they cover the skin with cloth which sticks to the flesh, so when the linen is torn off the place is all fretted and raw."

"Ugh."

"That is nothing. The real artists will sprinkle ratsbane on top of the wound."

"Like sugar on comfits – very tasty," I said, divided between interest and disgust, and remembering Thornton the bookseller and his pouches of arsenic or ratsbane.

"Except that the palliard aims to make himself *un*tasty," said Abel, glancing up at me. "The ratsbane causes the sore to look even uglier and so excites the greater pity."

"And the more alms."

"Of course. These people aren't in it for love of their art."

As he'd started to expound these methods of trickery Abel's tone had grown less abstracted and almost eager.

"After all, Nick, we players make ourselves up for money. We cover ourselves with bloody clothes, we blotch our faces and pretend to be sick or dying or dead, for cash."

"And love of our art."

"Tell me, Nick, what is our purpose in this house? For sure, we're not here for our art – or for cash."

"We're here to catch a murderer or two," I said.

Abel and I were in a stranger's empty house, courtesy of Jack Wilson. The house was in Grove Street, off the High. It was a fine house and belonged to the wool merchant husband of the woman called Maria, the one whom Jack had been seeing – or seeing to, perhaps. Our playing comrade had been looking forward to a few extra days in Oxford enjoying the delights of bed and bawd, and so he'd been disappointed and almost angry when the woman, taking fright at the tightening grip of King Pest in the city, left suddenly to join her husband in Peterborough. Or it may have been that the merchant, concerned for his wife's health, had summoned her to his side. Whatever the reason, her departure had left the house empty; shuttered and curtained and without servants.

The fault was mine. I couldn't deny that it was mine. Illicitly entering a man's house was a serious enough crime. The only excuse was that we – Abel, Jack and I – intended no harm, but were bent simply on righting a series of wrongs and uncovering a much greater crime.

In the normal way my conscience would have quailed at the notion of trespassing like this on another's property. But these weren't normal ways or normal days. The pestilence was already making a difference to the ordinary, ordered life of the town. It was a strange season. There were many little indications of this, such as the more frequent tolling of the church bells and the abandonment of street markets as well as the stop which had been put on our playing at the Golden Cross. The highways were less crowded, except in the area around the Carfax crossroads where the mortality bills were published and where the prophets of doom were continuing with their God-given work. I'd witnessed another one that very morning and on this occasion there'd been no Ralph Bodkin to break up the crowd. The speaker, not Tom Long but another man, was comparatively subdued. He did not attack anyone but urged repentance on his listeners and they responded in a similarly muted fashion.

But the taverns were still full and, if the brothel in Shoe Lane was anything to go by, the stews were attracting plenty of customers. In a way this only served to confirm how serious the situation had become, for there was a hectic quality to the manner in which people took their pleasures as though they were determined to snatch at what might be a last opportunity for enjoyment. I dare say some of those who were laying out their final shillings on a final whore or their tenth mug of beer were the same gents who'd been listening, with nodding heads and contrite hearts, to the penitent urgings of the Carfax preachers. One more beer before the bier, eh? I'd have felt the same contrary tug myself: to prepare myself for heaven, but also to waste my last few hours on earth. I would have felt this, I say, if I hadn't been engaged on a more personal quest to get to the bottom of the Oxford mystery.

Anyway, all of this perhaps doesn't excuse our illegal entry into the fine house in Grove Street. But it may explain it. Fortunately I wasn't alone in this enterprise. I hadn't had to work too hard at persuading Abel Glaze to help me. For one thing I no longer needed to convince him of the truth of my story – he'd seen for himself those hooded figures sweeping by under the mask of night, and may have felt that his own panicky flight had enabled them to give us the slip. Whatever the reason he seemed willing enough to remain in Oxford for another day or two, arguing that he was as likely to be exposed to the plague in London as here.

We'd confided in Jack Wilson, newly disappointed in his amour with the wool merchant's wife. I'd explained my suspicion that, among the legitimate body-bearers, there was a band of two or three individuals taking advantage of the sickness in this city, and contriving to enter plaguey houses in their hooded guises (which had the added benefits of hiding their identities and giving them an official, not to say frightening aspect). It wouldn't be difficult to play the part of a bearer unlawfully, or even to obtain the post with proper authority. It is dangerous work, and there is no great press of applicants.

Once they'd got inside a house on the pretext of fetching out the dead our false friends would help themselves to the choicest portable items, such as silver salters or candlesticks. These valuables were easily removed at the same time as they carted off the bodies for burial in one of the common pits on the outskirts of town. As if for their greater convenience the authorities, in a measure intended to lessen public alarm, had laid down in the plague orders that bodies were to be cleared away in the evening or early morning, as at Mistress Root's house. Such periods on the margins of the night made their discovery even less likely. Anyway who would think – or wish – to challenge a couple of corpse-carriers in a cart?

What these two or three felons were doing was exactly what the Kentish Street nurse-keepers had been accused of planning to do by their Southwark neighbours, albeit on a smaller scale. They were robbing the dead.

Talking to Jack, I didn't enlarge much on my further suspicions that something more than mere robbery was involved in this business. I was fairly certain that several of the "plague" victims had been helped on their way by doses of poison and also had a feeling that robbery wasn't the sole motive. It wasn't so much that the theft of a few valuables was insufficient reason for a series of killings. Men have killed each other over a single shilling or less, while the haul of goods from the dead houses would be worth many hundreds, even thousands of shillings. Furthermore the penalty of the law is the same whether you steal a shilling or another's life. So if you're going to be hanged for the one offence you might as well be hanged for a string of worse ones . . .

Even so, this reasoning didn't quite fit the case. All this wickedness and elaboration – the bird-monk costumes, the ingenious application of poisons, the use of pestilence as cover for murder – appeared somehow excessive. It was out of proportion to the objective, which was nothing more than the amassing of a heap of items, however valuable. Yet a bad thief might think it a good bargain. Who knew how such an individual might choose to balance his scales? Despite all this I was certain that there was more to be discovered.

Anyway, Jack and Abel and I conferred about some of these things. I'd described the failure of the plan to track Kit Kite and his confederate from the house in Shoe Lane. Our quarry had eluded us then. Jack promptly launched into some rambling episode from his childhood about how, when out hunting, his father had advised him that the most effective way of catching your quarry was not to pursue it but to trick it into running or flying in your direction. And somehow the idea emerged of enticing Kit Kite and the other hooded figure into coming to us – or more precisely, to me – and seeing where that led us (or, more precisely, me). Which might happen if it was put about that I was dying of the plague, since these individuals were drawn to plague victims like flies to rotten meat.

"All right," I said, "but there is one small objection. I am not – as far as I know and God be thanked for it – dying of the plague."

"You're a player, Nick," said Jack, "while I've noticed that Abel here is a dab hand with the face-paint. He could make it appear as though you were sick or dying."

"I've done it often enough," said Abel, causing Jack to look puzzled.

"It won't work," I said. "For one thing, if I'm right and this pair are robbing the dead even while they're taking away their corpses, then they'd have nothing to gain by carting off a defunct player. I've got little more with me than a spare shirt and a couple of books – and precious little more than that back in London. No, we need a better bait than this. We need a prosperous citizen of Oxford."

"Like Edmund Cope."

"Who?"

For answer, Jack Wilson made the sign of the horns in the same way that Will Sadler had when referring to another Jack – Jack Davenant the landlord of the Tavern.

"Oh, your wool merchant. His name is Cope?"

"The one whose wife you've been *coping* with," Abel added.

Jack's grimace showed that this was a sore point. He no longer referred freely to Maria. Evidently he'd been hurt by her abrupt departure, as if she didn't have the right to save her own skin.

"Cope is a prosperous citizen of Oxford. He has a fine house in Grove Street," said Jack.

"And it's empty, you said," I said.

There was a pause.

"Well then . . . " I said.

So this is how I came to be reclining on a couch in a stranger's house while my friend Abel Glaze was kneeling on the floor, with his make-up wallet spread out in front of him. I was about to be made dead.

Getting into Edmund Cope's house hadn't been difficult. In fact it had been a simple matter of turning a key in the door. Somehow or other Jack Wilson had obtained the key, either given him by the pliant Maria or got hold of in some other fashion which I didn't choose to enquire into. In the rush to depart, the wool merchant's wife had decamped with her servants (no doubt even more eager to quit plague-ridden Oxford than she was) and left the place less secure than they might have done. So a single key sufficed.

Jack didn't seem over-bothered that we were entering into another man's house. I suppose that when you've already trespassed on that man's wife, then his estate seems rather secondary, mere goods. Or it may have been that Jack felt so aggrieved by Maria's fearful departure that he was searching for some way to get back at her, and that occupying her and her husband's house was as good as any other. As I said earlier, this was a strange season in Oxford. Ordered, everyday life had begun to break down.

Anyway, here we were in the house of the prosperous citizens of Grove Street. It was well furnished, with many valuable items, portable items.

Abel advanced towards me, carrying a candle in one hand and a little earthenware pot in the other.

"I am ready," he said.

"Make me dead, Abel."

"I could whiten your face first with egg-shell and alum like a fashionable lady's, but to my eye you look white enough already."

"I expect I am. Fear."

"Then I shall simply apply a few tokens on the visible places, Nicholas, but they will not stand much inspection."

"Just as long as they don't recognize me."

If our scheme worked, then my hope (hope – ha!) was to be carted off by the bearers without their paying too much attention to the nature and quality of the corpse they were carrying. Because if I was right in my suspicion that their primary purpose was to rob the victims' houses of valuable stuff then they wouldn't be too interested in the dead themselves, only in their belongings. Also I'd seen the casual way they manhandled Mistress Root's corpse.

In fact, I didn't believe that it would get to the stage of my being carried off in the dead cart. I intended otherwise. The cart would not be good for my health. No, my intention was to surprise these malefactors in the act of stripping the house of its more precious portables. Then I would unmask them in the midst of their malefactoring. My good friends Abel Glaze and Jack Wilson would be deeper inside the house but close at hand, ready to pounce on Kite and his confederate, ready to tear the disguises from their faces and haul them before the magistrates. I trusted Wilson and Glaze. They were my friends. Jack was a good swordsman – hadn't he taught me (a little of) that noble art, hadn't he played Tybalt and thereby attracted the attention of a wool merchant's wife? While, as for Abel, he was a resourceful fellow, able to *cope*.

Maybe this course appears foolhardy. It was foolhardy. I can only suppose that there was some infection in the air apart from the pestilence, tainting all of us, making us reckless and irrational.

Abel told me to stretch out my arm and, using the tiny

wooden scoop, started to apply the ointment in dabs across the back of my hand and wrist. He paused to admire his handiwork.

"These are the tokens of the plague. When they appear the poor person knows that he has only hours left to live."

I laughed, but felt sick to my stomach. I touched the dabs which were about the size and colour of a little, tarnished silver penny. Already they were starting to harden.

"What are you using?"

"It's a trade secret," said Abel. "Lie back now, and I shall put some across your forehead and cheeks."

He leant over me and, with a craftsman's care, dabbed at my face. Several times he stopped, stepping back a few paces to check on the result, squinting in the candlelight.

I was used enough to this procedure in the tiring-room at the Globe. With a shortage of mirrors, we usually helped each other to paint our faces – for example, white for a ghost, or with streaks of sheep's blood for head wounds. But there was a jollity about making up in the playhouse, even to act the ghost's part, which was completely absent in this situation. With each darting touch which Abel made, I felt as though I was truly being infected with the pestilence and I struggled not to flinch. He bent over me, as close as a lover.

"Abel, you remember when we went to meet Will Kemp, the old clown in Dow-gate?"

"Yes."

I talked to get my mind off what he was doing but I was also curious.

"You were moved by the sight of him. You kissed him farewell."

"He reminded me of my father," said Abel. "There! One or two more spots in the centre of your forehead should do it."

"Your father?"

"I left my father as he slept," said Abel. "I crept out of the

227

1311234567

house without saying farewell when I went off to fight in the wars."

(He meant the Dutch wars back in the middle '80s.)

"How old were you?"

"Twelve or thirteen, I suppose."

"Then we are of an age."

"I know it, Nick."

"You did not see him again?"

"No."

Abel stepped back for a final time.

"That'll do, but only in a bad light."

"Remember that the thieves are dressed in hoods with eyepieces for protection. I shouldn't think they could see too clearly through those in any circumstances. And they won't want to touch my body more than they have to, which is the reason why they wear gloves and carry sticks."

"That's all well and good," said Abel, "but *you* must remember that those who die of the pestilence have experienced a dreadful final few hours. That's if they're lucky. If they're not lucky then it will have been a dreadful final few *days*. Your expression must suggest all of that."

"It will."

"For added realism you might piss yourself where you lie."

"Fear will probably do that trick. But if I'm correct, Abel, then these gentlemen will be much more concerned about snaffling up some of the goods in this room than examining me too closely. There's a nice little tapestry over there, for instance. Or what about that silver perfuming-pan?"

"It is a dangerous course, Nick."

"It is for all of us."

"What's that?"

There was the scraping sound of a key turning in the front door. My bowels turned to water. Abel froze, still holding the make-up pot. Then we breathed again to hear Jack Wilson's voice.

Swiftly he entered his mistress's house and came through

the lobby into the ground-floor chamber where Abel had been giving me the plague. Jack said, "My God," when he saw me, and I was pleased because he was taken in. Then in a breathless whisper he told us how he'd primed Kit Kite, as planned. He'd mentioned to the Golden Cross ostler the rumour of a plague-struck house in Grove Street. The rest of the occupants had run away, he'd heard, after one of them fell sick. (That they should run away was plausible enough since anyone discovered in a plaguey dwelling could find himself interned there for forty days.) The implication was that the house stood undefended.

"You did it casual, Jack? He didn't suspect?"

"I did it as well as you would have done, Nick, and all with acting. I asked him whether the story was true, as if I was the ignorant one. I think he took the bait."

"We'll see. How long till dark?"

"A couple of hours or less. It is a dull March day outside."

"If Kite and his accomplice are going to rob this house they will get here as soon as they safely can, for fear that some of the other bearers will beat them to it."

"But none of the other body-carriers in Oxford know about this house," said Abel.

"Kite doesn't know that they don't know," said Jack. "That is, he doesn't if he believed my rumour."

"So the pair of them may get here straight after nightfall – or even earlier. The two of you should hide yourself in the back quarters of this fine place."

"How shall we know when they've come?" said Abel.

"Don't worry, I'll cry out for help – or you'll probably hear them anyway. They've not got much cause to be quiet since they are on official body-fetching business, or pretending to be."

"Will you be safe? Are you armed?" said Abel.

"I have a knife," I said, touched by his concern. (But my knife, tucked in my doublet, was a little object better suited to nail-paring than anything more desperate.)

"So have I," said Abel. "Though I do not believe in violence for I have been a soldier."

"While I have the foil which I employed as Tybalt," said Jack. "I have taken off the tip which blunted it. See."

"Ah, this is the foil which attracted Mistress Maria," said Abel.

"Not the foil alone but my prowess with it," said Jack, enacting his favourite *Romeo and Juliet* lunge. "*Alla stocatta!*"

With that and a few more pleasantries, mostly uttered to steady our nerves, Abel and Jack made themselves scarce in the back passages of the house, leaving me to play dead on the couch. But before he went Abel took a candle and set fire to some small tablet which he'd deposited in the fireplace. All at once a sharp, foul reek filled the chamber.

"Jesus, what are you doing?"

"You're dying of plague, Nick. You will not smell pleasant. Your last hours will stink out the room."

"Our friends can't smell much. They wear those hoods."

"They'll get a taste of it, even so."

"What is it?"

"Another trade secret."

"Well, if I don't die of your face-painting then I most likely will from that stench."

But I grew accustomed to the smell after a time. The room was dark enough – the dead don't require candles. I almost fell asleep. I sensed rather than saw the light dying by slow inches beyond the curtained window.

Sleep and death are like brothers, they say. It was odd to feel sleepy in this hour of danger but I did.

Perhaps there was something soporific in the stinky air which filled the room. Perhaps I was genuinely succumbing to the . . . fever.

Random thoughts floated through my brain. I tried to recall the names of the poison plants from Flower's *Herbal*. How did they go? Belladonna, beautiful lady, devil's herb and dwale (which sounded like a cross between dole and bale and so was highly appropriate) – these were the guises of the deadly nightshade. While monkshood was wolf's bane and friar's cap, as well as Cupid's car.

I reached up to feel the bumps on my face. The dabs of ointment had grown hard as calluses. I reflected that I was imitating the manner of death which my poor parents had endured in reality. Well, that was fitting enough. I was only an imitator. A poor player. I let my hand drop down, fingers clenched in the death agony. I positioned my other hand over my chest, clutching my doublet. I practised my final grin, teeth bared for ever.

Then I must have fallen into a doze or a daze. The couch was surprisingly comfortable, just what I might have chosen for my own death-bed.

In this strange, half-dazed state, a parade of figures passed in front of my mind's eye, figures going two by two, as flat as images in a painting. They were all somehow connected with this peculiar business in Oxford even if I could not see the links at present.

Two by two.

There was the late Doctor Hugh Fern walking abroad, quite unconscious of the fact that he was a ghost, and chatting with his man Pearman, putting a friendly hand on the servant's shoulder.

Then there were the cousins Sarah and Susan Constant, the one pretty and delicate and nervous like a bird, the other reserved and serious but handsome nonetheless. She was trying to persuade her cousin to drink from a leather flask which she carried, but Sarah waved it away using the back of her hand.

Then Jack and Jane Davenant strolled by. To my surprise the landlord and landlady appeared relatively friendly towards each other. In my mind's eye, they vanished behind a clump of willows like those which fringed the river in Christ Church meadows. After a while Mrs Davenant emerged from the trees without her husband but accompanied by William Shakespeare. As usual, it was difficult to read the expression on the playwright's face. She was gesticulating in her gypsy-ish way but I couldn't tell whether it was with excitement or anger or some other emotion altogether.

The couple vanished, to be replaced by Will Sadler. He was talking animatedly to a man whom at first I couldn't identify because he was standing on the far side of the student in what seemed to be a dimly lit room. Then Will moved slightly and I recognized the bullish outline of Doctor Ralph Bodkin. Well, there was nothing out-of-the-way about this, since Bodkin had once been tutor to Sadler and the two of them continued to keep company together.

Next came an odd couple. I'd glimpsed them only once in conjunction together, and it wasn't a happy occasion. Now I saw Angelica Root together again with the carter called . . . what was it? . . . Hobby . . . no, Hoby. John Hoby. The one who'd had the temerity to run her down on Headington Hill and whom she had cursed with a thousand plagues. But for the present they were both dead, surely? I had discovered Mistress Root myself as she was lying on her bed in Cats Street, eyes like currants popping out of a cake. While as for Hoby, he had been drowned in the Isis. If they were both dead, then I could guarantee that their enmity was persisting into the afterlife, for here was Nurse Root still berating the unfortunate carter. At any moment I expected her to retrieve a stockfish from under her voluminous skirts and start bashing him about the bonce. Meantime he stood with shrunken posture and drooping head, the whole effect rendered grotesque by the great wen which hung from his neck.

Then this scene too dissolved before my eyes to be replaced by a more sinister tableau.

I was once again in the passage between high college walls. Two bird-monk figures seemed to float past me like witches, their capes flapping around their ankles. One of them had his hood off, and I understood that I was correct in my suspicions. It was Kit Kite. He saw me looking at him, paused, giggled and tapped himself on the head as if to say, "Yes, it's me." But the other figure remained hidden under the face mask. I had previously thought of this unknown individual as Kite's confederate but it was the other way about. The masked person was the leader and Kite merely an accomplice, I realized. Then the two shapes floated out of my mind's eye.

All at once, I woke up. Or rather, my real eyes suddenly took in my real surroundings. A ground-floor chamber in a fine house in Grove Street in the city of Oxford. Surely I was still in a dream though, for by the light of a hovering lantern I could make out the same two figures, no longer floating through the air but walking on the solid floor. Both were garbed in their protective gear, with their beaked hoods, cloaks and pale wands. One of them was holding up the lantern whose rays through my half-closed eyelids appeared like golden threads.

"Here it is."

It was Kite's voice, muffled up but still recognizable.

The figures advanced towards the couch where I was lying. My head was half angled in their direction, my teeth were bared and my eyes unwaveringly fixed on an imagined point in the gloom surrounding the light. The two halted, as if there were an invisible wall surrounding me.

"He has the tokens," said the other.

"See his hand," said Kite.

"Wait . . . do not go too near."

This voice was more distorted by the headgear than Kite's but even so there was a touch of something familiar in it.

One of them – Kite, I think – put down the lantern and extended the pale wand which he was carrying and poked me in the side with it. It was a tentative poke, almost a respectful one. Thank God, I have some experience of playing dead. Once – having been run through at the beginning of a

233

battle scene – I had to lie at the exposed edge of the Globe stage for what felt like hours while the rain was pissing down, and all without showing any greater facial discomfort than the average endured by a man who's died violently in the field. The trick is to go limp, breath shallow and take your mind off to somewhere else more pleasant. Which I attempted to do now as I lay on the couch and received a couple of more forceful pokes in the side and flank. Then the second voice said simply, "Enough."

Thank God also that they didn't get too close. Circumstances favoured Abel's cosmetic ingenuity and made them trust my corpse. The thin wand allowed the person wielding it to keep his distance from the infection so that Kite must have been standing almost a whole body's length away. In addition, the light was coming up from floor level and the false body-bearers were wearing the hoods which limited their vision. The thick eyepieces glittered. Later I thought that this was how the dying lamb must feel on the upland as it lies surrounded by monstrous carrion birds, by great black crows and ravens.

Playing dead is not so hard when it's a matter just of play. Playing dead is more difficult when it's literally a matter of life and death. It was like being in the middle of a nightmare, powerless to move, powerless to make a sound. Except in a nightmare, in the end, you wake up. I was already awake; awake but turned to stone. Perhaps it was this petrified state which saved me. For if they had discovered that I was pretending now . . .

They didn't discover it, apparently. As I'd predicted to Abel they were more interested in the plentiful contents of this room, in making a hurried survey of what they could seize and carrying it off. Probably they were fearful that a bunch of rival body-bearers would turn up on the doorstep at any moment and steal their thunder. The lantern was retrieved from the floor and the two figures shifted their attention to the more profitable areas of the chamber. I was merely the pretext for their presence, a dead body worth less than a brass pin. I breathed again slow and shallow, only now conscious that I'd been holding my breath all this time.

This was the moment when I should have called out for Jack and Abel but something prevented me. While it had been easy enough to talk about crying for help, it was very hard to actually do it. I don't know why. Perhaps it was because, by calling out, I would throw off the pretence of death which had preserved me up to now.

Instead here I was waiting for my friends to burst through the door and rescue me. Surely they must have heard the intruders when they broke into the house. But I hadn't heard them, had I? The first time I'd been aware of their presence was when the pair were already standing inside this very chamber. Maybe they hadn't even broken into the house but had obtained a key by some roundabout method, like Jack Wilson. Or perhaps Jack had failed to secure the front door properly. What did it matter? They were inside, and where were my friends?

The couple were being quiet as they moved through the shadowy chamber. I prayed for one of them to drop a silver candlestick with a great clatter or to stumble over in the shadows. They didn't. Rather they shifted about the room in a practised way, whispering sometimes when the lantern light was brought to bear on particular objects. These, as far as I could judge from the corner of my eye, were then being deposited in one place.

After a few minutes of this – although it seemed like hours – I realized that I was going to have to do something. Abel and Jack were not going to burst into the room and effect a rescue. I was on my own. My best hope was to act at once. To leap up in a shocking recovery, to shout and scream, to catch them off their guard. The main door to the house was probably unfastened, for I supposed that this pair of thieves planned to make a quick escape once they'd loaded up the cart. I did not wish to be part of their load. If I took them by

Philip Gooden

surprise, I could probably break out into the street and yell
for assistance.

I moved my head very slightly. The light was stationary
on the far side of the room on top of a sideboard. Beside it
were several objects which glinted. I felt a spasm of
indignation on behalf of Edmund Cope, miles away in
Peterborough. This was all his property! Even while I was
watching, a hooded figure brought across a great bowl or
ewer cradled in his arms to add to the hoard. It was Kit Kite.
I was beginning to be able to distinguish between the two of
them. I wondered that they hadn't removed their headpieces
then recalled that, as far as these thieves were concerned, they
were working in an infectious place. I wondered where the
other one was. I could not find out without sitting up and
looking about.

No more thinking, no more wondering.

If I didn't move now I was done for.

I rose up swiftly from my death-bed.

The figure standing by the sideboard turned at once. He
must have seen the movement from the corner of his eyepiece.
To him, I was a dead man resurrected. He said something –
an oath, an exclamation – and let fall the great ewer. It hit the
bare boards and rang like a clear bell. I was already half-way
towards the door.

Then I was through the door and into the lobby.

There was no light out here but by instinct I found the
door to the street. It was closed of course. I fumbled frantically for the handle, with one ear cocked for the sounds of
pursuit from behind. At some level I registered that there
was no sound. Perhaps Kite had dropped dead from terror.
Where was that other hooded figure?

Thankfully the door wasn't locked. It swung inwards.

I almost fell through it and out into Grove Street.

The first surprise was that it was still light, half light. There
were people about. The false bearers had lost no time in
hastening to Cope's house, relying on their dark garments

for pretext. Their cart stood near the door. Between the shafts a piebald nag wearily waited.

I blinked like a man emerging from a cave.

Three or four passers-by watched me while I considered what to do next.

"Help me," I said stretching out my hand.

It was hardly a shout to my mind, more of a reasoned statement.

Then why were they looking so startled, why were they backing away, why were they taking to their heels and disappearing round the corner?

Because, an inner voice said, what they see is a man emerging from a house where the windows are curtained or shuttered. The man looks wild and desperate. He is covered with the tokens of pestilence, those silvery-black swellings are all over his face and hands.

"Wait!" I shouted. "I'm not – "

No good, said the inner voice, they'll never believe you. They've gone now, anyway. You are a marked man. You are a dead man.

Then my inner voice said no more, for I received a great blow to the back of my head. I staggered and swung round to see a hooded figure. Then I lost my footing and the black cloak slid past me until I fell to the cobbled ground on a level with the figure's feet. Then the ground seemed to heave before opening up to let me in.

Cupid's Car

*You kneel beside him in the street after he has tumbled down.
He has cracked his head on the cobbles and blood is seeping
across his face. You suspected a trick once you recognized him
indoors, inside a house that does not belong to him. Now, by
the fading light of day outside, you examine the supposed
marks of the pestilence. You know that he is a resourceful
individual who uses imposture to make his living and therefore you doubt that the marks are genuine.*

*Well, Revill may have eluded you in the house of Mistress
Root but now he has put himself right into the mouth of
danger. If he is not yet dead – and he isn't, you can see his
chest rise and fall – he soon will be. And if he wanted to play
at death he will soon discover that the game has turned
earnest.*

*There is no one in Grove Street. Any passer-by would be
terrified by what they could see: a hooded body-carrier
bending over the corpse of a plague victim.*

Now Kite emerges from the house in a great state.

"We are discovered!"

He looks at the body on the ground.

"Revill?"

"Yes."

"He was the dead man?"

"Not quite dead. Help me put him in the cart."

"He came horribly to life."

238

"He never died."

"There are others still inside," says Kite. Even through the hood you can hear the quivering confusion in his voice.

"How many inside?"

"I don't know. They were shouting. I turned the key on the door to the back quarters of the house."

"Good."

You are surprised that Kite had sufficient presence of mind for this. But any calmness has now deserted him. The frightened ostler flaps about Revill's body like a giant bird.

"Good! How can you say good! We are discovered, I tell you!"

"Put him in the cart," you say. "What will people think?"

Together you hoist up the actor's body and throw it in the back. You make to return indoors but Kite grabs your arm.

"We must fly."

Shaking off his arm, you step into the dark house. Swiftly you make your way to the chamber off the lobby and scoop up as much as you can carry from the sideboard. Distantly you hear shouts and thumps coming from the back of the house. Revill's friends, doubtless. So it was a trick, a trap. You wrap the goods up in a carpet which was covering a table, and carry the load out into the street. Kite is still flapping about, a crow at dusk.

Calmly you instruct him to get on to the driver's perch.

He does so but looks round at Revill's slumped body and the little pile of silverware which peeps out from the folds of the carpet. You can read his mind although his face is shrouded. He is afraid of being stopped and questioned even though it is nearly dark by this stage.

"Contaminated goods," you say simply. "No one will question us."

No one is even going to stop you. Hasn't the little ostler realized by now that the best disguise lies in boldness? The pair of you are performing a service for this fair city. You are clearing victims from houses afflicted by plague ... or by poison. If they were left to rot, the bodies would spread their diseases far and wide as the noxious fumes seeped out of them and through cracked windows and flawed walls. You are taking the bodies to a place where they can do no further harm, to a place where – from one aspect – they may even do some good. Indeed you should be rewarded for your services. You are quite entitled to whatever small pickings you manage to collect on the way.

No one is going to stop you. You glide along at dusk or dawn, two hooded shapes, like licensed angels of death. You feel invulnerable. You think of how many corpses have been borne to their destination in the rear of this battered cart in the space of a few days. Men, women and children. Husbands and wives. Lovers thrown together in a last embrace. Why, the wagon has been a regular Cupid's car. It is nearly finished now. Time for you to quit the town.

You may feel invulnerable but Master Christopher Kite, ostler of the Golden Cross Inn, does not. While you are sitting beside him, he steers the horse and cart through the streets without a word. You can feel his body shaking, a constant shivery motion which is independent of the bumpy progress of the cart. Suddenly he removes his hood and flings it into the back.

"I thought you were afraid of being seen?" you say.

"I am tired of this," he says.

Then he falls quiet again. The only sound is the creaking of the cartwheels. You could remove your headpiece too but somehow it feels more . . . natural . . . to wear it at the moment. It is like a second skin.

"What happened to Hoby?" says Kite eventually.

You glance up at the sky. There is a streak of light to the west but, even as you watch through your eyepieces, the light goes out. The moon is rising in another quarter of the sky, deathly pale.

"Hoby drowned, and bequeathed us his horse and cart."

You turn to look at Kite, and wonder how you must appear

to him. A monstrous bird on its perch, slowly angling its monstrous head in the dark. You can scarcely see him but you sense his fear. Odd how as he grows more fearful, you become calmer.

"Drowned? Hoby's wife says different," says Kite, but he doesn't find it easy to get the words out since he understands the implication of what he's saying.

"Does she now?" you say.

Perhaps there are one or two further small tasks to perform before you will be able to quit Oxford.

"There's drowning and drowning," says Kite.

"It was good riddance to Hoby," you say. "He was taking our goods and selling them on his own account."

"I am tired of all this," Kite says again.

You are passing St Ebbe's. The bells are tolling dully. The horse knows the way. You reach behind you and grasp the stick which you seized from the lobby of the house in Grove Street. The stick which you used to strike down Nicholas Revill. More of a club than a stick, perhaps stored in the lobby so that the servant who kept the front door had something with which to threaten unwelcome callers. It was conveniently to hand when the player blundered past you and out into the street.

Your fingers close round the haft of the club.

Kit Kite reins in the horse as the cart reaches its destination. The ostler turns to jump down from the cart. As he does so you catch him a strong blow on the side of the head. The club jars in your hand. What a solid little nut the ostler has! Kite falls on to the ground and you remove your hood, get down from your side and walk round to where he lies. He is not stirring but you give him another blow to make sure. Then you tug Revill's body from the back of the cart and place it beside Kite's. You think to give Revill another blow too, but your arm is suddenly weary from all this striking. Leave him to the hands of another. He will not last long inside.

Then you go to rap on the door.

I woke up in hell.

I did not realize it straightaway. I was lying on my side on a hard, cold surface. Something was gumming up my eyelids and I raised my hand to my face. There was a clotty substance spread all over it which I realized soon enough was blood. My head throbbed and an exploratory touch established both that it was likely to be my blood and that it had come from a tender, embossed area on my forehead.

Still alive then. Thank God, I suppose.

I moistened the fingers of one hand and wiped at my eyes, clearing away the muck which was deposited there. I tentatively opened one eye then both, but was none the wiser. I was in a dark place.

I lay on the hard surface, considering how I had arrived here. I tried to piece together the last few minutes – no, the last few hours – but they were like scraps of paper covered with scrawled words which I couldn't read. Finally I got a sort of order out of them. I'd spent a period in a house somewhere, followed by the appearance of masked figures and a frantic attempt to escape into the open air. Something had happened in the open. What was it? I had held out my hand to strangers in the street but they fled from me. Time passed. I saw a vision of a cloaked figure and a view of his feet and a cobbled roadway. Then nothing but blackness and a jolting, jagged movement.

I moved my limbs where I lay, moved them singly then together. They were delicate but serviceable so far as I could tell. I made to sit up and immediately felt sick and very feeble. My guts heaved and I retched. My mouth gaped like a gargoyle and water sprung from my eyes. The retching left me even weaker, and I lay back down, thinking that if I never had to move again it would be no great sacrifice. But my vision and my head were beginning to clear. That house was in Grove Street, I recalled. It was the property of a merchant called Edmund Cope. My friend Jack Wilson had been briefly attached to the merchant's wife. Lucky Jack. I was there because I and my friends were laying a trap for the counterfeit body-carriers. Ah yes. I reached for my face once more and felt the bumps and pustules of the false plague-sores.

I could smell now and, over and above the disagreeable odour of myself, there was something worse, much worse. And I could see now that I was not lying in absolute darkness. In the distance there was a pale striped square from which a little light was emanating. For a time I hoped that I was back in Cope's place, and that the thieves had simply abandoned me there. In that case where were Abel and Jack?

But I wasn't in the Grove Street house. This chamber was emptier, danker and colder, and terrible in a way that I didn't want to consider yet. The air was thick and unwholesome. As my eyes grew accustomed to the surroundings I realized that the pale square was an opening, set high up in a wall. The unearthly light coming through it was slight enough. It was night-time and the moon was riding high overhead, infiltrating the room.

Very carefully I lifted myself up, at first on all fours then upright. I was shivering like a man with fever but I managed to stand without being sick again, without falling over. Slowly, slowly, I crossed the room, putting one leg in front of the other, skirting various objects on the way. I reached the wall in which the window was set. Perhaps on account of the chill which the wall gave off, I sensed that the room was at least half below ground level. The "window" was an unglazed opening, positioned just above head height. The stripes I'd noticed were iron bars. The night air was chill but clean and fresh, and I drank it down in great gulps. Then, leaning against the roughcast wall, I surveyed the place where I found myself.

Around me were shapes, some of them mercifully shrouded, lying on blocks or tables. I did not have to examine them. They were human bodies. I counted four or five, with others possibly in the far corners. I was in a dead room. My knees gave way and I sank to the floor, my back sliding against the slimy stone of the wall. I would have vomited again but there was nothing more to bring up.

I don't know how long I was huddled into a ball at the base of the wall, trying to squeeze myself into nothingness, so terrible was this place. There is a kind of pity in consciousness perhaps which takes us away from the continued contemplation of horror. I went numb and retreated into some distant inner region where, if you had enquired after my name or trade, I most likely couldn't have answered.

The next thing I was aware of was a growing light in the room. Of course it was spring-time in the world beyond this room, and morning comes early in the spring. I was rolled up against the wall, stiff and aching. The dawn light showed off the bodies lying flat on their backs atop primitive tables. Next to some of the shapes were cutting implements and in one place, incongruously, a pair of scales. Without moving from my position I could see that one of the corpses was that of Kit Kite, the ostler. I recognized his sandy head, although like mine it was bloodied. This surprised me for wasn't Kite one of the counterfeit body-carriers? If so, what was he doing in this charnel house, this shambles?

I forced myself to inspect the other corpses by the half-light seeping through the window but backed away when I observed that at least two of them bore the authentic marks of the plague, the swellings and buboes which Abel had so artfully faked for me. One of the others I knew. It was Mistress Angelica Root, her poor face bloated and purplish but still recognizable.

Had I really thanked God for preserving me alive? Well, I would not be alive for much longer, surely, having spent the night shut up in such a foul place, wherever it was. The disease which I had played with as an impostor would seize me after all. I would perish as my mother and father had. Strange to say, this realization did not throw me into a state of terror. Perhaps my reserves of terror were all used up.

There was a door to this chamber or cellar but it was firmly sealed. I beat against it and called out but there was no response. I was almost more afraid of someone coming than of no one coming. I went back to the barred window. By raising myself on tiptoe I could stick a hand through the bars and waggle my fingers. I yelled out but failed to convince even myself of my plight. Also there would be nobody about at this early hour, perhaps five in the morning, and I soon gave up.

Then a great calm came over me, almost a lightness of mind. Maybe it was hunger or tiredness, maybe it was the preliminary to the end, in the same way a drowning man is said to fall into a reverie during his last moments. I went back to my position beneath the window opening. I sat down and stretched out my legs in front of me as easily as if I were reclining on a river bank.

In this dream-like state some association between the dead store-house and Shakespeare's *Romeo and Juliet* came to me. When Juliet swallows the sleeping potion prepared by Friar Laurence she dies to the world and is borne off to the vault of the Capulet family. Here she lies among the corpses for two days, waiting to be awakened by her lover's kiss. When she does wake, though, it is to find Romeo already dead at her feet, a horror surpassing all the other horrors. Despite this Juliet possesses sufficient fortitude to pick up Romeo's dagger and sheathe it in her body. If a young girl could so steel herself then a grown male player should certainly be able to . . .

This was not a play, I told myself, even if there was something unreal about it all.

Who was going to unlock the door of the cellar and enter this charnel house? Not Romeo for sure.

Yet someone would come. (It was what I was afraid of, that someone would come.) We were here for a reason, Revill and the dead.

I thought about the reason. Plague victims are usually buried as rapidly as possible, after being removed from their

dwellings at unobtrusive hours. They are forked unceremoniously into a common pit. Yet there were in this room at
least two apparent victims of King Pest – why were they still
above ground? And how to explain the presence of Kit Kite
and Mistress Root in this dreadful chamber? The one had
been poisoned, I was certain, while the other looked to have
been beaten to death.

Why would anyone want to accumulate corpses, with all
their attendant dangers? They have no value, not even a brass
pin's worth. They cannot be cut up and their remains
interrogated, everyone knows that. The doctor is not
permitted to do this. If a man dies, a man dies. Unless there
are patent marks of violence on him, it is not for us to enquire
into the reasons for his passing. It is God's will. So I've heard.

I pulled my doublet more tightly about me. It was streaked
with blood from my head wound. I must have looked a sight,
bloodied, speckled with plague marks. There was a cold
dankness to this room which seemed to be increasing as it
grew lighter beyond the barred opening. Something rustled
against my chest. I reached in and extracted a sheaf of paper,
still warm from where it had been nestling against my heart.

It was a pamphlet.

Kemp's Nine Days' Wonder, I read.

It meant nothing to me. Who was Kemp?

There was a picture on the cover of a dancing man with a
drummer in the background.

But, of course, Kemp was the melancholy clown whom
Abel Glaze and I had called on during another life. Will
Kemp, once of the Chamberlain's Company and now fading
away in Dow-gate. Abel plied him with sack and a pie while
I, less graciously, agreed to purchase his account of how he'd
jigged and tripped his way from Whitechapel to Norwich.
Well, this pamphlet – for which he'd extorted sixpence if I
remembered rightly – had been sitting snug in my doublet
ever since that day in February when we'd visited the old
fool. It seemed like years ago. Perhaps he was dead by now.

I'd never read it, hadn't even realized that I'd been carrying it about with me these several weeks. Forgetting my immediate predicament, I opened the pamphlet and flicked through its pages, one part of my mind thinking that it might be the last document I'd ever look at. No great poetry, no uplifting words of religious consolation, but the vainglorious account of a superannuated clown's progress across a little quarter of the realm. Yet another part of my mind told me wearily that, whatever Master Kemp's faults, they were very small beer compared with the crimes which were being committed all around me now.

I read about Thomas Slye, who played the tabor and kept time for Kemp, and about William Bee, his industrious servant. (Busy Bee, I thought without humour.) I read about the warm welcome Kemp had received at every stop on his tour, and the woman whose legs he'd tied bells to and the other woman whose skirt he'd oh-so-accidentally torn off in his capering. I heard of his triumphal arrival in Norwich and of how his dancing buskins were still displayed in the Guild Hall at Norwich, nailed one next to the other on the wall. Idly I wondered what he'd worn to travel back to London.

Normally, Will Kemp's rather boastful style would have irritated me but after reading his words I thought warmly of him and hoped that he was well – or as well as could be expected – or, if he was no more, that he had died peacefully. I wished him all the things I would have wished for myself. He was a link to my playing company, to my friends and fellows. I tucked the pamphlet back inside the warmth of my doublet.

I considered Kemp's shoes nailed to the wall in Norwich Guild Hall. Famous footwear for famous feet.

Footwear . . . famous and not so famous.

That single chopin which had fallen from Mistress Root's body as she was being hauled from her bedroom in Cats Street.

There was the sound of a key turning in the cellar door. I didn't look up but continued to think of shoes.

Thought of the strange business of the change in Hugh Fern's footwear during the *Romeo and Juliet* performance. Of how he'd changed – or exchanged? – his expensive, buckled shoes for a plainer pair to wear in his character as Friar Laurence. Of how, when his body was discovered, he'd been wearing the buckled shoes once more.

There was the sound of footsteps treading across the flagged floor. I still didn't look up.

I recalled the excellent boots worn by Doctor Ralph Bodkin when he came to attend to the dead body of his colleague in the yard of the Golden Cross Inn. Fine, supple boots of leather which reached almost to the knee.

Now I looked up from where I was sitting propped against the slimy wall. The same boots, fine, supple and reaching almost to the knee, were standing in front of my gaze.

I got to my feet and looked Ralph Bodkin in the face. He was sweating heavily. The veins on his bullish forehead stood out like cords.

I looked beyond Bodkin to the corpses laid out on the table-tops. One of them, I now saw in the strengthening light, had been slashed across the stomach and something dark and billowing was poking out. The arm of another hung down over the side. The skin had been flayed off. I recalled what Hugh Fern had said to me when he was talking about horoscopes. *Doctors may be worse employed, believe me. Much worse employed.*

"It is not permitted," I said.

"What isn't permitted?"

I waved my arm wildly at the underground room, where the bodies of men and women were indiscriminately mixed.

"This. It is sacrilege to the dead to open them up. It is not allowed."

"Who is to say so?"

"The laws of God – "

"Oh."

" – and man."

"The only laws are the laws of nature," said Bodkin.

"What are you doing?" I said.

"Master . . . Revill? Are you well? You have blood on your face. You carry the marks of plague . . . "

"These are not real. I'm not infected," I said, brushing impatiently at my face and at the same time reflecting that I most likely was infected by now.

"You ask what I am doing," said Bodkin. "You came running up recently and asked me another question concerning plays. You remember that?"

The sweat was dripping down from his brow. A strong, meaty smell came off him, as if he was cooking.

"I asked you whether the plague was caused by plays."

"What did I answer?

"You said it was superstition."

"Well, so too is the prohibition against cutting up the dead. That is superstition, all superstition. We will only discover the secrets of nature by digging into her and opening her up. It is hard to do that with living subjects – and I would not wish to – but there is no harm in anatomizing the dead."

"No harm! What of their souls?"

"A fiction. I have not found the soul yet."

"But people have died in this town so that you can lay them open."

"People are dying every day, all around us. I look closely at them when they are brought here in order to discover the secrets of their deaths and their lives. What I do is for our good."

"Our?"

"The good of humankind."

"It's wrong," I said. My mouth was full of a vile taste.

Bodkin swayed slightly on his feet. He reached into a pocket and retrieved the fine octagonal watch which I'd first glimpsed in the Golden Cross yard as he stood over Fern's body.

"You see this," he said, thrusting it towards me. "If I were a watchmaker now and this machine fell ill – that is to say, if it stopped or went slow – I could open it up and poke about among its innards and perhaps restore it to full health. What would you say to that?"

He was a fearsome man but somehow not frightening to me, not now. Maybe I was beyond fear by this point, standing in a plaguey charnel house with a mad physician.

"You are not a watchmaker," I said. "And we are not watches."

"Our hearts tick like clocks," said Bodkin. "We move round in our little circles. We tell time until we run down. We have parts that should work together in harmony – but when something goes wrong we are as helpless as an ape would be confronted by this tiny engine."

He brandished the watch before replacing it in his pocket.

"Did you kill Hugh Fern?" I said.

Bodkin looked surprised. He blinked and swayed again.

"Kill Fern? No, he killed himself. Killed himself by accident. Hugh Fern was a good enough man – I do not mean that he was a good physician, for he relied too much on horoscopes and such, and had no great ambition – but he was a good enough man. Speaking for myself, I am not interested in the living but the dead. Only the dead can utter their secrets."

I recalled Bodkin in the inn yard, standing with a bloody knife over the corpse of his fellow doctor like a conspirator. From somewhere outside this place an early morning church bell began to toll, the universal sound these days.

"You know what would happen to you if the people of the town discovered this?"

"I have faced them down before," said Ralph Bodkin.

"They would tear you to pieces, as you have done these corpses. Then they would set fire to this place."

"I do not tear corpses, Master Revill. I dissect in order to penetrate the great mysteries of life and death."

"You murder to dissect."

"I have committed no murder. Look, you are still alive."

"Your agents have. Like that man over there. Christopher Kite, ostler at the Golden Cross."

Bodkin's face took on a peculiar sheen. His great, meaty countenance looked like a boiled ham.

"It is immaterial now who has done what. I am sick. I above all men can recognize the signs."

"You have caught the infection?"

But I already knew the answer. Instinctively I pressed myself into the wall at my back, as if to distance myself from the Doctor. As if that would be of any use.

"I have very little time," he said.

"What will you do in the interim?"

"I shall make myself secure here, and continue with my work as long as I can."

He moved away from me and went towards the table on which lay the corpse with the gaping innards.

"It is wicked work."

"One day it will be seen differently."

"What should I do?"

"If I were you, Revill, I would leave this place. Look, the door is open. Go now and tell the common townspeople what you wish."

I glanced across towards the door of the cellar. It was half open.

"What if I am infected as well?"

"You are young. Your vital spirits may be strong enough. But stay if you prefer."

I was already on my way towards the door. Before I stepped out of this charnel house and abandoned Ralph Bodkin to his wicked work I turned round.

"Tell me one thing, sir. What have you discovered? Have you penetrated the mysteries?"

"Oh no, Master Revill. Others will do that. I am like the ape holding the watch. But I am a cleverer ape than when I started."

He picked up a long thin knife and bent over the body. I

walked from the room, half expecting to be summoned back. A flight of stone steps led upwards. I emerged into a hallway. There was a door ahead of me. It was bolted but not locked. I slid back the bolts and stepped into the street. I closed the door carefully and quietly behind me. The bell continued to toll close by.

There was scarcely anyone about yet. It was a fine spring morning. The sun was shredding a few early clouds and, although it gave off no heat, the blaze of light was welcome. Blinking after the dimness of the cellar, I half walked, half ran across this suburb of the town. The tolling was coming from St Ebbe's. I passed the western approach to the church and saw the devil faces clustered round the arch of the door. With their pitted beaks and goggling eyes and bat-like ears, they were carved there so as to scare off the real thing. I could have whispered a tale or two in those bat-ears.

I almost ran towards the river. At the water's edge I slid down the muddy bank and plunged my hands into the fast-flowing stream. I wiped at my face repeatedly with handfuls of freezing water, cleaning off the blood which streaked it and picking at the scab-like counterfeit sores.

Then, feeling as if I had wandered in from another world, I made my way in the direction of the town centre. It was a chill morning but the air was like a purge. A few citizens were going about their business by now. Among them were my friends Abel Glaze and Jack Wilson.

"My God, Nick! What happened? We've been looking for you all night," said Jack.

"I see you've recovered from the plague, but that lump is new," said Abel, indicating my swollen forehead.

"First, what happened to *you*? You were supposed to prevent me being carried off."

Their side of the story was easily told. My two friends had made themselves comfortable in the back quarters of Edmund Cope's house, waiting for the signal from me or for some sound which would indicate that the false body-carriers had entered the premises. No sound or signal came. Abel confessed that, waiting in the dark, they might have been less than attentive. (I took this to mean that they'd probably fallen asleep, as I'd done.) The first they knew of anything untoward was a great clatter and a sort of suppressed shriek. That would have been Master Kite dropping the silver bowl when I rose up from the dead on my couch. By the time Abel and Jack had gathered themselves and blundered about in the darkness they found the way out locked or blocked. They shouted and beat on the door but to no avail. And by the time they'd climbed through a window in the rear of the property and made their way back into Grove Street, it was night and the area was quite empty.

They plied me with questions. By now we'd returned to the Golden Cross and I was satisfying my hunger and thirst with some bread and ale. Strange, but despite everything my appetite was good. I sketched out what had happened at Bodkin's house, hardly believing my own ears, so far-fetched did the story seem. After what they'd gone through themselves, though, Abel and Jack were ready enough to accept it.

However, when I reached that point in my narrative where I described how I'd spent the night with corpses, some of which were quite plaguey, my friends shifted uncomfortably on their seats and made to move a little distance away.

"Aren't you worried for yourself, Nick?" said Abel.

"Yes," I said. "But I thought I was facing even more imminent dangers. And I have a little protection."

I unbuttoned my doublet and shirt to display the leather pouch which I'd purchased for sixpence from the bookseller Nathaniel Thornton, at the same time as I obtained Shakespeare's *Lucrece* and Flower's *Herbal*. The pouch contained arsenic. If there was something a little odd at first in walking about with an ounce of poison, I soon forgot about it. So far it seemed to have stood me in good stead.

As if this was a cue, my friends also unfastened shirt buttons to reveal their own personal charms or amulets. Jack was sporting a golden chain from which hung a blue stone. This he referred to as an "Eastern Hyacinth"; it provided infallible protection, he assured me. Abel tapped a glass phial which he claimed to have paid a great deal for, since it contained horn of unicorn, ground to powder. I could have told him a tale or two about that but kept silent, reflecting that nobody can be taken in like a confidence-trickster. Anyway as long as we earnestly believe in our charms and amulets, whether true or fraudulent, who is to say that they will not work for us? We were all alive, so far.

After this diversion I continued with my story. When I'd finished, there was a long silence.

"We should report this dreadful doctor to the authorities," said Abel.

"He *is* one of those authorities," I said. "All in good time. This isn't quite over. Kite is dead. I saw him with my own eyes. But there is another individual in this business. Not Bodkin but someone else."

"Whoever he is, he is a wicked individual," said Jack.

"Why do you say *he*?" I said.

"Is Susan Constant involved?" said Abel suddenly.

"I don't know. Why?"

Jack Wilson laughed out loud.

"Because our friend here has been talking to her. He has a soft spot for her."

"Have you, Abel?"

"She is a lady," he said simply.

"And you are a player. To say nothing of your former trade."

"Which trade was that, Abel?"

"It doesn't matter, Jack. I'd swear my life on it that she is innocent . . . "

"Innocent of what?"

"Of any accusations."

"Who's accused her?"

"You have, Nick, in your mind. You are casting round for people to suspect."

"They are mostly dead or dying," I said, thinking of Ralph Bodkin cutting up corpses in his cellar.

There was another silence.

"I have made a small discovery though I don't know whether it amounts to much," said Abel. "The house which we were spying on in Shoe Lane, the place near the bawdy-house where we saw – "

"Yes, I remember."

"It is occupied by Mrs Hoby and her brood. She is the widow, the new widow, of that carter who drowned in the river after he'd knocked over Mistress Root."

"That makes sense. The woman referred to the place as a house of mourning," I said.

"Coincidence, eh?" said Jack.

"Not coincidence," I said. "John Hoby the carter. He was involved in this as well. He may be dead now but it was his horse standing outside Mr Cope's house in Grove Street. The horse was a clapped-out piebald. And the cart was the same one that rolled up outside Mistress Root's, I'd swear, from its sound."

In some dark recess of my head I remembered the creaking wheels which I'd heard, lapsing in and out of awareness, on my involuntary ride last night.

My thoughts turned to the house in Shoe Lane behind the Golden Cross, the house where the widow dwelt with her brood, the house that had evidently been some kind of meeting place for these thieves and false body-carriers. There were three of them: there was John Hoby (deceased), there was Kit Kite (also deceased), and then there was the other.

Shoe Lane.

Where had Hugh Fern obtained those shoes to play the part of Friar Laurence? Why had he changed back into that fine, silver-buckled pair before his death? Or had it happened *after* his death?

Suddenly I stood up, in my haste knocking over the stool I'd been sitting on.

"What is it, Nick?"

"Jack, your Tybalt sword. The one you had last night. You have it still?"

Jack pulled back his cloak to reveal one of our stage foils. The tip might have been removed so that it was no longer blunt but it remained a pretty paltry weapon.

"Give it me!"

I almost snatched it from his hands and, before my friends could stop me or ask questions, I was out of the door, through the yard and into Cornmarket. I paused to tuck the foil into my belt. I was not permitted to carry such a weapon, the foil being reserved for gentlemen, but these were strange and disordered times. I would not be stopped. No one was going to stop me.

I raced through the maze of alleys and narrow streets that lay on the eastern side of Cornmarket until I reached Shoe Lane. Tucked into a crowded corner was a familiar sight: a piebald horse hitched to a cart whose wheels would surely be creaking if it was on the move. If I wasn't mistaken my ride the previous evening had been courtesy of this conveyance. And here was the Hobys' dwelling – a pinched place maybe but even so, for a mere carter and his family, it represented a considerable stake in the world.

The front door was open. I had already that morning walked away from danger. Now I was preparing to put myself in it once more.

I grasped Jack's foil and pushed the door further open. There was a figure on the other side of the tiny, unfurnished lobby. It was wearing the cloak and bird-like hood with which I was, by now, quite familiar. My heart was beating fast from my run, from fear and excitement.

"There's nobody here," said the figure. "No widow, no children. They have taken the stuff."

I swallowed and said, "They must have known you were coming."

"Close the door – God's bones, it's cold enough."

The figure seemed to shiver in front of my eyes.

"Perhaps you are sick," I said. "Like Doctor Bodkin."

"Close the door."

"If you take off your hood."

With one hand he pulled off the hood. The other hand was clutching the thin, whip-like cane with which the dead had been prodded and poked.

I pushed the door shut. There was very little light in the lobby, only what seeped through from a room to one side of it. I didn't need much illumination, however, to identify Andrew Pearman, the apprentice to Doctor Fern. His face, now it was unmasked, had not changed. It still had that scraped, raw quality.

"I trusted Doctor Bodkin to deal with you," said Pearman.

"He had other things on his mind. Besides, he told me that he was no murderer."

"I should have finished the job myself."

"Why did you change Doctor Fern's shoes after the play performance?" I said. I looked down at Pearman's feet. He was wearing the plain shoes which I'd last seen on Hugh Fern's feet when the Doctor climbed on to the stage as Friar Laurence.

Pearman was quick. He didn't pretend ignorance of who or what I was talking about. He must have realized that either he or I (or both of us) had nearly reached the end-point.

"Because he was wearing mine. We were of a size. He took them because they were more appropriate for the – what part was he playing?"

"A friar. I made some remark about his footwear, never expecting him to act on it. But why did you change the shoes back again after your master was dead?"

"Because they were my shoes, I say. A mere apprentice is not supposed to wear fine shoes with silver buckles."

"True," I said. "Just as a player is not supposed to carry a sword."

I had noticed that Pearman was wearing his master's shoes while he stood, in a distracted state, outside the locked room off the inn yard. Had noticed it but not really taken it in. The next time I glimpsed that fine pair they were once more back on the Doctor's feet.

"It is no crime to take a dead man's shoes," said Pearman, "particularly if they belong to you."

"No crime at all, but it shouldn't have crossed your mind to do it."

"Why not?" said Pearman.

"You were distraught. So distraught with grief that it could not have occurred to you to change shoes with a dead man, whoever they belonged to. Why, I heard you groaning and calling out the Doctor's name."

"He wasn't dead then," said Pearman. "That was why I was calling out, to cover his noise."

I waited for more, holding my breath.

"He should have been dead, but he wasn't."

"What did you do to him?"

"I stabbed him while you were off fetching help."

"I don't understand," I said, scratching my head in a puzzlement that was part genuine, part feigned. If I could keep this man talking now . . .

"It's very simple, Revill. My master was close to uncovering my secret labours, my work harvesting bodies for Doctor Bodkin – "

"And your work for yourself."

"I am entitled to my small pickings."

"Leave that to one side," I said. "Tell me why Hugh Fern had to die."

"We were in conversation before your play started. He assured me that he was very near uncovering a dreadful conspiracy, a sacrilegious business involving Ralph Bodkin. He believed that the other doctor was cutting up corpses. We were all in danger. I had to act straightaway. I do not believe Doctor Fern altogether suspected me – although there was a certain look in his eye. That made it easier for me to do what I had to do."

I remembered the close conversation between Fern and Pearman which I'd observed in the inn yard. I recalled the clouded expression on that normally cheerful man's face and, once again, those words of his: *Doctors may be worse employed, believe me. Much worse employed.*

"What did you do?"

"I was already inside that little room. I called him in as if I had some secret to impart, I shut the door and offered him drink."

"Offered?"

"Pinched his nostrils until his mouth gaped open then poured the potion down. My grip was stronger than his. Held him until his struggling ceased then released him so that he fell to the floor. Went out, locking the door behind me."

"I was there, sitting on the bench with my injured foot. I didn't see you."

"You were dozing. But I saw you, Master Revill. And seeing you gave me an idea."

"You wanted me there when you discovered that he was dead – inside a locked room. In that way there could be no doubt that Doctor Fern had killed himself and been alone at the time."

"Not killed himself," said the doctor's apprentice, "but died a natural death. The poison wouldn't have shown."

"Of course," I said. "Who is to say how a man dies? There is no digging about inside bodies, no dissection. It is not permitted by the laws of God or man."

Pearman grinned humourlessly.

"Nevertheless, you still required a witness even of this 'natural' death. So you – let me see now . . . "

My mind raced.

"You came back all distracted, wanting to know the whereabouts of your master. That was well acted. You should have been on stage."

"Acting is a low trade," said Pearman.

"Then we both went through that mime-show outside the locked room, with you pretending to see something inside and being sweaty and urgent. You convinced me that something was wrong. Then you broke through the panelling on the door – and . . . "

I saw it clearly now.

"The key," I said. "There was no key already in the lock on the other side of the door. It was in your own hand all the time. When I reached through to get it, because you'd claimed your own reach wasn't long enough, the key was slippery to my touch. The metal was warm too. Not surprising since you'd been clutching it in your sweaty palm moments before."

"Yes, I put it there myself," said Pearman, half proud, half reluctant, like a conjuror explaining a trick. "When I reached inside with my hand I replaced the key in the lock."

"It was a sleight of hand. A mere trick."

I felt obscurely disappointed. Absurd, given my present position, but it was so.

"A trick – but it worked," said Pearman.

"Not entirely though, because you discovered that your master was still alive when he should have been dead. That was the reason you looked so shocked. You weren't distracted with grief but you were terrified – terrified of being found out. I knew that wasn't acting, it couldn't have been counterfeited."

"I came back too soon," said Pearman. "The potion would have taken effect eventually. I know my potions. I was a doctor's apprentice."

"But you couldn't wait for it to take effect by that point. You'd brought this disaster on yourself. In a few moments a whole crowd would be gathering outside that little room, and Doctor Fern was still breathing, still groaning, even while you were crouching over him."

"God knows what he might have said."

"He could have accused his apprentice with his dying breath."

"So I stabbed him through the heart. Then everybody came crowding round."

We paused here, as if to take breath.

"And Angelica Root? What had she done to deserve to die? How had she offended you? Did you get a good haul from Cats Quean?"

Pearman said nothing.

"You are a common thief, Pearman," I said.

He lifted his cane and I raised Jack's foil. We stood like that for a time. Then, as if by mutual consent, we lowered our weapons.

"I am no thief. I merely take my dues for harvesting the dead."

"Dues?"

"From Ralph Bodkin at so much per corpse, provided they went unreported . . . while if I take the property of others who is there to protest? Anyway, it is all gone from this house. I should have known better than to trust it to Hoby's wife. Her husband was a thief."

"A thief," I repeated (and remembered the occasion on which I'd seen John Hoby outside the Tavern, being berated by Jane Davenant. I'd wondered what was in the box he'd unloaded, or rather dropped. Goods looted from a plague house, most likely, and sold to a ready customer.).

"Yes, Hoby was a thief and his widow is no better. She has run off with her brats and my profit."

"Why did Mistress Root have to die though?" I persisted. "She didn't die just for a salt cellar surely?"

"Like you, she had started to suspect me."

"I did not suspect you."

This was true; I hadn't.

"You were accustomed to look at me . . . in a certain way."

"Like Doctor Fern looked at you?"

"I can tell from the eyes. Not that you can do me great harm for I am invulnerable like this."

He indicated his costume.

"So I wrote a note to test you, to see whether you'd visit Mistress Root for information. But you were too cunning to keep the appointment, and stayed out of my reach."

I said nothing about the fact that I'd been in the house, hidden under the dead woman's bed. The murderer's words confirmed, however, that the letter from the old nurse was a forgery. Pearman sounded calm, almost resigned, yet he must have been half out of his wits if he took murderous action because he believed men and women were looking at him in a certain way. Why then, on the basis of a glance or two, he might believe the whole world to be against him. (Yet, in a sense, he would have been right to believe this.)

"Mistress Root?" I prompted the cloaked man.

"She roused my suspicions by asking me if I had a plentiful supply of figures. So she too had to drink my potion."

"Figures?"

"The clay images which Doctor Fern used. He would apply a salve to a figure to effect a cure over a distance. Say that a sailor's wife came to him, having heard that her husband was sick overseas. Or a merchant looking to make his wife pregnant."

"At least Doctor Fern tried to heal men and women," I said. "While you merely stuck pins into their images to cause harm."

"I was curious to see whether it worked."

"Sarah Constant fell ill because of such a figure."

"I know nothing about that."

"But you left one of them outside the door of her house."

"I scattered them here and there throughout the town. Simple stuff, early days."

"Her cousin believed that she was being poisoned."

"Then her cousin will have to explain it."

"How many have died through your labours, Master Pearman?"

"Not so many. I started with one of the Ferns' dogs and I moved on to an old woman who beat me once for stealing apples. I took in a carter, and a physician, and an old nurse, with others along the way."

"Not so many, you say!"

"How can one man compete with the pestilence?"

It was the kind of remark Ralph Bodkin might have made. High-handed, almost unhuman. I wondered whether the doctor had infected the apprentice with his diseased outlook, or whether Pearman had started out so cold and arrogant. They were not dissimilar.

"Look around you, Master Revill. See how many perish daily in this city, in this kingdom. Tell me, whose hand is that?"

"That is God's will," I said.

"And all this work was mine," said Andrew Pearman, making to put his billed mask back on. By doing so, he transformed himself from a man into something monstrous.

I raised my foil to strike at him but he was too quick for me. He lashed out with his cane and caught me on the upper part of my sword arm. The force of the blow brought tears to my eyes and I almost dropped my weapon. Instinctively I stepped back and saved myself from another swingeing blow, this time directed at the region of my eyes.

Pearman said, his voice coming clear now through the hood, "I have beaten a man to death with this."

I didn't doubt it and so didn't reply. Instead I saved my breath and crouched with my back against the door. As I've said, the lobby was tiny – if we'd stepped forward a full pace each, we'd have collided – and here I was trapped with a murderous madman. I might have escaped through the door which led into what must have been an equally tiny front room, but the only way to get there was to go past Pearman. I might have unfastened the front door and fled into the street but this would have necessitated fumbling with the handle behind my back and then moving towards my opponent (since the door opened inwards). This would take two or three seconds and during that brief space of time Pearman could disable me with his cane, lash me about the head or neck, get me on the floor, and deal with me at leisure . . .

My only chance was to keep him at a distance with my playhouse sword. I'm no swordsman, as you're aware, despite Jack Wilson's best efforts at tuition. Anyway there's a world of difference between capering about on the stage, flashing your foil, knowing that when you fall down you'll rise again to general applause, a world of difference between that and fighting for your life in a little room. Like Mercutio, I was more for show than use.

I kept my blade up, darting it rapidly from side to side to impede the jabs and swings of Pearman's cane. I tried to recall the strokes and lunges which I'd been taught – all those *stocattas* and *imbrocattas*, those *voltes* and *punta riversas* – but my body had no instinctive knowledge of the moves while my head stayed empty.

Or not quite empty since what ran through it was a single word: "Help!"

Meantime Andrew Pearman loomed up on the other side of the lobby, like a great beetle with a flexible, stinging horn. Although he might have restricted his vision slightly by donning his hood, he was used to wearing it and it gave him extra protection against my blade if, by some accident, I'd succeeded in striking home. And his black cloak was nearly as good as armour.

The wound I'd received the night before began to flow with blood once again, and I wiped frantically to clear my eyes. The dark figure with the pale wand would not stay still but rattled about in this confined area, looking for a gap in my guard. He would find it sooner rather than later. He ducked down and weaved about with his cane as if to cut me off at the legs, then reared up and swung at my exposed face, which was already trickling with blood. Each time I succeeded in avoiding his stroke or warding it off with my foil but I was thoroughly on the defensive.

A wave of dizziness swept over me. I suppose it was the

Plan appears.

effect of the last few hours. Pearman landed a second blow on my sword arm and, although I managed to hang on to my blade, I felt that another hit would cause me to let go. I seemed to see myself from a distance, and Mercutio's words about "worm's meat" flew into my head. Incongruous and unwelcome words – but I'd played the character several times, and knew his dying moments better than anyone.

Then, suddenly, Pearman lost his footing. He crashed into the back of the lobby and slid down the wall, his arms spread wide to prevent his fall, his elongated head wagging from side to side. For a second he couldn't defend himself. I had a single chance. If I didn't take it now ... I darted forward with my foil. He saw me coming and, off balance as he was, threw himself to one side. My blade penetrated the soft plaster of the wall (no oak panelling here in Shoe Lane) and then it struck something solid, probably part of the timber frame. The blade bowed – and snapped.

The useless tip was quivering in the wall while I was left holding a jagged stump. Well, it was only a stage sword and not a proper foil tempered in Toledo. It would do for a Tybalt or a Mercutio, it was not meant for the cut-and-thrust of real life.

Pearman regained his balance. The snout of his hood came up. I wiped at my bloody eyes. He raised the cane. I now clutched a few inches of ragged metal while he wielded an implement several times as long. I threw up one arm – the one holding the remains of the foil – to protect my face while, with the other hand, I fumbled at the door handle behind my back.

Now it was my turn to lose my balance. As I was grappling with the handle, my foot slid on something puddled and my legs shot out in front of me. I made a fall which, on stage, would have been executed only by the clown. That is, I landed with an unheroical thump on my bum. My back and head crashed against the door which I'd been struggling to unfasten. Idly I observed that I'd slipped in my own blood, which was now dripping copiously down my face.

Andrew Pearman, the monstrous insect, came forward. It only took him two strides. He straddled me and looked down, what little light there was glinting off his eyepieces. He lifted up his cane. I knew his purpose. He had said, *"I have beaten a man to death with this."*

There was a thunderous sound and voices calling outside.

"Open up!"

"Nick, are you there?"

Fists beat at the door. My friends shouted out for me. Pearman looked up, or rather he raised his beaked head. I sensed his hesitation, a moment's hesitation. The thundering of fists on wood redoubled.

"Revill! Answer if you're inside."

"Open the door!"

I still held the ragged stump of foil in my right hand. While Pearman was preoccupied with the noise outside, I drove the jagged end into his ankle where he was unprotected, judging the point to a nicety (even if I say it myself) behind the bone. He twisted away to the back of the lobby, tearing out the blade as he did so and leaving it in my hand. He may have cried out or screamed. I don't know. The battering at the door continued and there was a roaring in my ears, as if the blood was coursing through my head in full spate.

I scrambled on to all fours, scuttled forward and stabbed downwards with my broken foil. The blow was random and I missed. The second wasn't so random, and I was lucky. With this second stab I ran him through the foot. I felt the stump of the blade go right through and strike the ground underneath. Pearman was still wearing those plain, simple shoes which – as he'd indicated – were fitting for an apprentice. They did not offer much protection against the jagged edge. And I put more force into the second stroke than I had ever put into anything in my life. It was as if the whole world depended on that blow. And yet, when it came to it, the foil-stump went into his foot as easily as a knife into soft butter.

And then, still on all fours, I swung round and unfastened the door. Abel and Jack tumbled into the lobby. Andrew Pearman, making incomprehensible noises, reached down to remove the end of the foil from his foot. But he was distracted and needed both hands to do it, for in my desperation I had forced the broken end down so hard that it had stuck in the boarded floor. And in order to unpin his foot Pearman had to lay down the white cane which he had used to such deadly effect.

Grunting all the while, Pearman jerked at the handle of the foil and it came free – what it cost him in terms of pain I don't know, but most likely he didn't feel anything. I have heard that men may be oblivious of their wounds in the heat of battle. Meantime Jack and Abel stood open-mouthed at the sight. A monstrous black-clad insect clawing at its feet.

Then just as Pearman freed his foot and picked up his cane, Jack and Abel moved forward. Pearman flung away the gory stump of the foil – the lobby was so small that I retrieved it almost immediately – and tried to stagger upright to face these fresh enemies. But there was scarcely room for four men to stand quiet and still in this place, let alone engage in a mortal combat.

Pearman was at a disadvantage now. Three against one. He was wounded in both feet. I had stabbed him in the ankle of one foot and (by good fortune) run him through in the other, and he seemed distracted. His great beaked head waved up and down, the evil circles which were his eyepieces catching the light which came through the half-open door.

Jack had obtained another sword from somewhere. Abel produced a small knife. I had got back my broken foil. Without a word, I closed the front door while Jack shifted round to prevent Pearman's moving into the little room which lay off the lobby. We were so close that we might have been participating in some intimate dance for a foursome. So close that the masked killer found it impossible to lift his cane to achieve a clear, swinging stroke with it. So close that we were like the tightening knot on a noose.

Without a word being spoken we encircled this man, this wicked man who had murdered Angelica Root and Hugh Fern and (I suspected) his two accomplices, as well as many others whose names I would never know. The noose tightened. I could hear the panting breath of my friends. Blood was still dripping into my eyes.

We raised our various weapons . . .

. . . and then we closed in on him.

Pearman shrank into himself, his back to the wall. All at once he slipped for a second time. He was very unsteady on his poor feet. His arms flailed and Jack leapt in and seized the cane, wresting it from his grasp. Our enemy was now defenceless. I don't know what we would have done next – and even at a little distance in time I don't care to consider the bloody course we might have pursued – but no action was necessary.

Suddenly the great beaked head arched backwards and from the base of the hood emerged a thin spike. A dreadful gurgling sound came from under the shrouded head and then blood poured out from the gap between hood and cloak. Pearman had fallen on to the sword tip which had broken off in my hand and which was still stuck fast in the lobby wall. It had run him through. Only a play foil but even in its ragged, jagged state it was capable of inflicting a mortal wound when it struck a vulnerable point in the neck.

Abel, Jack and I instinctively stood as far back as the confined area would allow, and watched as the black shape wriggled and shook itself into stillness. I put my hands over my ears to silence the terrible wheezing sounds which emerged from this monstrous, dying insect. Eventually a ringing silence fell on the little room.

We were silent ourselves for a long while after that.

Pearman was dead. A dreadful end, maybe, but it was hard to see it as anything but just.

If we'd captured him alive we might, I suppose, have taken

him into custody, a wounded and limping prisoner. Then, after due process of a few weeks, Andrew Pearman would have met his end on the gallows. That is, if there had been a judge and jury to try him, gaolers to imprison him, and a hangman to string him up, for the plague was making inroads through all levels of Oxford society. So it's possible also that Pearman himself might not have lived to see his lawful demise but have fallen victim to the pestilence which he had exploited for his own profit and power.

We debated for some time what to do with the body. If we hadn't gone to the authorities before this point, we certainly couldn't go to them now. Who would believe our account of what was, essentially, an accidental death? Eventually we searched around the little house and found some rags and scraps of cloth which allowed us to handle the corpse without getting ourselves more bloody than we were already. We took down the warm body and prised the gory tip of the foil out of the wall.

I volunteered to drive the body in the back of the cart in which I myself had so recently been a "passenger" to Doctor Bodkin's house near St Ebbe's. The others offered to accompany me but I insisted on doing this alone. We were not interrupted while we removed the body, swaddled in rags, from the Shoe Lane house. This was a dubious area of the town and these were dubious times. Presumably, if we were seen, it was assumed that we were removing a plague victim.

So I too became, for a half-hour or so, a body-carrier, and a counterfeit one at that. We arrived safely – Revill, Pearman and the horse (I never discovered its name). I may not be much good on horseback but even I can control a worn-out nag meandering its way through known streets. Bodkin's house was as I'd left it early that morning, quiet as the grave. I tugged the body from the back of the cart and abandoned it in the lobby, rather as Hamlet leaves Polonius in a lobby at Elsinore. I listened long and hard for signs of life from the steps that led down to the cellar but none came. I wondered if the clever Doctor was already free of this life. As for John Hoby's horse and cart, we left them in the care of one of the other ostlers at the Golden Cross.

Later, I left an unsigned note outside the Guild Hall indicating an outbreak of pestilence at Bodkin's house. I don't suppose anonymous notifications of the plague were very unusual at this time. And the town authorities should be familiar with Bodkin. The Doctor had been one of the most important citizens of Oxford after all. Let them deal with one of their own and all his doings. There would be an anomaly among the corpses discovered in the house, for the authorities would discover one of them to have died by violence (apart from the violence committed by Ralph Bodkin on those who were already corpses, that is). We might not have got away with this in normal circumstances. But then they, Bodkin and Pearman and Kite and the carter Hoby, would not have got away with it either.

Then I tried to wash my hands of the business. But my hands refused to come clean so easily. I could not forget that terrible cellar in Bodkin's house nor my mortal combat with Pearman nor the final stage of the struggle as Pearman wriggled to death on the end of the Tybalt foil.

Later too, for the benefit of Jack and Abel, I outlined the story as far as I could piece it together now that all the participants were dead or dying. I told them that Andrew Pearman had somehow come to an understanding or conspiracy with Ralph Bodkin to supply him with bodies during a time when no very close watch could be kept on the disposal of corpses – in fact, no real watch at all. I wasn't sure how far Bodkin had been complicit in the murder. His words to me – *I have done no murder* – suggested not so much that he didn't know what was going on but that he was prepared, in the interests of his grisly investigations, to turn a blind eye to the provenance of the bodies that were regularly delivered to his doorstep. And, I suppose, from his point of view, the more various the victims and their causes of death, the better. After all he believed that he was working for humankind.

Andrew Pearman, though, was working for no one but himself. His murderous career most likely predated the outbreak of plague in Oxford but he could sniff the air, smell the way things were going. Could see that there would soon be many opportunities for a man of his bent. Where those opportunities did not exist, then he might create them by the application of potions and poisons. These poisons he had learned about during his period as Fern's apprentice and he had probably stolen the ingredients from his master too. He also stole Fern's clay figurines and used them to try to cast spells since, as everyone knows, there is a magic in medicine, good and bad.

This conspiracy, once established, brought benefits to both Pearman and Bodkin. Bodkin gained the bodies which he could cut up and investigate. Jack and Abel were similar to me in that – even when they'd laid aside their abhorrence of such a practice – they could see little point in such investigations.

Meantime Pearman and his confederates were paid twice over – by the Doctor for the bodies they produced and by the profit they could turn on the disposal of goods looted from plague-houses (for the sake of the recipients I hoped they'd been fumigated). There was more to it than this, however. Pearman enjoyed what he'd called his "secret labours". Dressing up in a costume protected him from the pestilence, but it gave him a necessary disguise and, I suspected, fed his vanity or arrogance. "*I am invulnerable*," he'd said to me. But he was only invulnerable through killing off anybody who suspected him or might have harmed him. In the end he turned on his confederates.

Abel asked me once more whether Susan Constant was involved in this dreadful affair and I said no, I didn't think so. I didn't mention my private speculation that she had been animated by dislike and envy of her cousin, who was to marry the man she was herself in love with. Glimpsing on a couple of occasions the figure of Andrew Pearman, out and about at dawn and dressed in his outlandish costume, she had concocted a poison plot against Sarah (perhaps because that was what some small, dark part of her wanted too). Even a clay figure left outside the Constant door became, in Susan's eyes, an attempt to cast a spell on Sarah. Then the upright, respectable part of Susan came to me and outlined the same plot, requesting that I should investigate the matter. Later, perhaps coming to her senses and seeing that the Sadler-Constant marriage was going ahead anyway, she'd asked me to forget the whole business.

(William Sadler and Sarah Constant did marry, I heard a while later. Whether they're happy or not, I don't know. Will was a casual fellow and Sarah was a delicate thing. But at least one couple was able to drive away from this wreckage in what you might call Cupid's car – as opposed to the plague cart. And it may be that Hugh Fern's wish to have a private staging of *Romeo and Juliet* bore fruit in this way.)

It was true that Abel Glaze did have a soft spot for Susan Constant but we were not staying long enough in Oxford for him to pursue matters, even if she, a "lady", would have considered a connection with a mere player. In fact, after what had happened in Shoe Lane it seemed safest for us to beat a fairly hasty retreat from this university town. Almost all of our fellows, including the seniors, had left by now and there was a general eagerness to get back to London, however difficult the situation might be there.

First we had a couple of small tasks to perform. I returned Flower's *Herbal*, the book which I had borrowed from Nathaniel Thornton. The dusty old bookseller with the white beard was still sitting behind his desk as if he hadn't stirred since my last visit. He accepted the heavy volume without surprise.

"Are you still carrying the ratsbane?" he asked.

"Yes," I said.

(In fact, I'd almost forgotten that I was wearing the little leather pouch about my neck.)

"And I can see you are still alive. Though you have that great swelling on your head."

"More or less alive."

"I told you ratsbane was the thing," he said.

"So far I've seen off the rats," I said.

I also took back, with the help of the others, the plate and carpet and other goods which Andrew Pearman and Christopher Kite had stolen from the house in Grove Street. Jack was particularly keen we should do this since he felt that the theft of items from his mistress's house was partly his responsibility. I said that, if it was anyone's, it was mine since I had come up with the scheme to lure the thieves with a pretended outbreak of the pestilence.

Although the widow of John Hoby had decamped from Oxford with her children and with most of the booty from the gang's robberies – going God knows where, but obviously well stocked to begin a new life and getting some recompense for the apparently accidental death of her husband – she must have quit the city *before* that final theft. So when the three of us looked round the pinched house in Shoe Lane once Pearman had been . . . dealt with, we discovered the Grove Street takings still wrapped up in the carpet in the single downstairs room. Pearman must have deposited them there that night, after leaving me and Kite at Bodkin's. There was nothing else. Whether it was then or later he'd discovered that Mrs Hoby had run away with the takings, I don't know. And don't much care. I've explained enough, haven't I?

Queen Mother

Our return to London was subdued. Yet the days were growing clear and warm, even if the nights were still cold or wet. The early flowers had come and gone, but the banks were bright with daffodils and the hedges were more than speckled with fresh green. The three of us followed in reverse the route we had traced out as a Company only a few weeks before, stopping at the same inns overnight and often halting to refresh ourselves at the same wayside spots during the day.

For the most part we walked along without talking. When we shared food at meal-times or a bed for the night there was an absence of the usual jokes and players' banter. One night we had a halting discussion about which was the worse: Ralph Bodkin or Andrew Pearman. The one had (at the least) connived at death and murder in pursuit of some grisly project of discovering what lies under our skins, and then claimed he was doing it for the best. The other, Pearman, had killed simply for power and profit. This was a more human, though still terrible, motive. We came to no conclusion, and the discussion petered out.

It was not surprising that Jack, Abel and I were subdued. We had been present at a man's violent death – even if the death was in a sense self-inflicted – and we seemed to be bound together by bloody strings. This couldn't but cast a pall over our spirits, although as we approached London we grew less oppressed by ourselves.

Of the three of us Abel ought to have been the most accustomed to blood since he had been a soldier, albeit in his youth. But, like some other military veterans, he now eschewed violence. As for Jack Wilson, he'd been involved in some strong affrays in his younger, wilder days, even ending up in the Clink on one occasion. And as for myself, although I'd been caught up in three or four similar homicidal adventures before, my nights were troubled by dreams of shadowy figures tussling together in a sealed room from which they would never be freed. I couldn't avoid the thought either that, just as in WS's *Romeo and Juliet*, the sword used by Tybalt (or Jack) had been responsible for an accidental, mortal stabbing.

Strangely it was also in my dreams that I obtained a kind of absolution when the image of Hugh Fern came to me with a reassuring expression on his face. The Doctor clasped me by the shoulder, and I distinctly heard him say, "Do not be too hard on yourself," the very words which he had spoken to me in the yard of the Golden Cross Inn shortly before he was murdered by the treacherous Pearman. Although that comment had been in relation to some trivial matter – my stupidity in falling off a stage, I think – I chose to apply it to the events in Shoe Lane and elsewhere.

From time to time – just for sake of a diversion, as it were – it was fear rather than guilt which bobbed around in my head. Maybe the fear was a counterweight to the guilt, maybe it was an outgrowth of the guilt. This was the fear that I must have been infected with the pestilence because I had passed a night in Bodkin's charnel house and then been close to the man himself in his last hours. Also I had pretended to have the infection, after being made up by Abel with the false tokens and so on. Was this to tempt fate, or to avert it?

Yet at the same time I did not *really* believe I was contaminated, perhaps because any alternative to that belief would have been so troubling. Instead I trusted to my ratsbane, rather as Jack trusted to his hyacinth-stone and Abel his powdered unicorn-horn. So far we had been preserved. And there's another thing. The more you are surrounded by such forceful reminders of mortality, the more you come to accept that profound philosophy which applies to the pestilence and many other undesirable things besides. Which is: if you're going to catch it, then you're going to catch it. And if not, not. It's in the stars.

Well, we arrived back in London some five days after we'd set out from Oxford. My landlord Samuel Benwell was surprised to see me back so soon. I was surprised to be back so soon. My room, which I had retained in my absence at the rate of sixpence a week, was still empty. That it hadn't been let out to anyone else wasn't honesty or scruple on Benwell's part, I think, but rather that London was in the grip of plague-panic and its citizens leaving in large numbers. There was no great call for accommodation.

Yet this was not the worst or the greatest news in town.

The worst and greatest news was that Queen Elizabeth was dead.

She was seventy years old at her death, and had reigned for more than half her life. She had reigned for all of my life and of Abel's life and Jack's life, and indeed of the lives of the greater part of the population of this island. Some of the seniors in the Chamberlain's had dim recollections of the days of Bloody Mary when they'd been little children. Sam, the old gatherer or money-taker at the Globe playhouse, even claimed to have memories of Mary and Elizabeth's father, the great Henry. All this is to say that, when the Queen died, it was comparable to the removal from the landscape of some natural object, such as a great mountain or a mighty river, which we had long taken for granted and had thought (if we thought about it at all) would never change. A mountain or a river can protect those who lie on the right side of it. Elizabeth was the Queen of England, yet she was also the mother to the nation, nurturing us and watching over us to see that we came to no great harm. And we had not come to any great harm while she reigned over us. In truth, she had left us better than she found us, and of how many rulers can you say that?

I met her once. She questioned me on my knowledge of Latin, for she was a great linguist, and imparted to me the secret of her reign, or one of those secrets at least. She had even thanked me for some small service which I'd performed for the state. Yet she was a very formidable woman, and I was tongue-tied most of the time in her presence and then deeply relieved to be dismissed from it.

She had a comfortable end, they say, after a long period of refusing to lie down but rather sitting or even standing up for days on end. She went mildly like a lamb, they say, she parted this life as easily as the ripe apple comes loose from the tree. They say this – and I hope for her sake it was so.

Her death shook the town, more than the plague was capable of doing. There was talk of insurrection, although by whom or against whom was never entirely clear. Men looked to their property more closely. Landlord Benwell went around proclaiming his favourite proverb, "fast bind fast find", with a smug air. There was an abrupt falling-away of business south of the river in Southwark. I don't mean in the playhouses, which were closed anyway on account of the plague and of the lenten season, but in the brothels and the dives where gambling flourished. The river boatmen modified their swearing for a day at least. The coney-catchers and confidence-tricksters suspended their operations (not that there were many victims about) for a brief time. The drinking in the taverns was moderate, conversation was modest. Such a lurch into respectability could only have been provoked by a very great and shocking event. Thank God it would not last for ever.

The effect on us Chamberlain's could not be assessed yet. Who knew the views of Elizabeth's successor towards the drama? Who, apart from the playing companies, would have cared very much about those views in any case? And who, indeed, knew more about this successor, this royal gentleman, than that his name was James, that he was the sixth king of that name in Scotland, and that he was probably saddling up in Edinburgh at this very moment?

While the fact of the Queen's death sank in, so too did the plague continue in its scuttling progress across the city. You have had enough of this, I dare say, and I will not weary you with yet more descriptions of the inroads made by King Pest. Enough to say that later during that year of 1603 I witnessed scenes like those foreseen by Lucy Milford when she was in her Cassandra mood and had glimpsed an empty street with grass growing in it and a riderless horse, its nostrils stuffed with rue. Witnessed similar things and many more terrible ones over the next several months. Just as Abel and I had been present during the early stages of the infection outside that mean house in Kentish Street – where Alderman Farnaby had issued such precise instructions for the painting of a cross (*It is to be the prescribed fourteen inches in length. You will do it in oil so that it may not be easily rubbed off.*) and condemned the occupants to their forty days in isolation – so it seemed that Abel and I were destined to be in on the end of this *thing*.

Or this thing would be in on the end of us.

I could have left town for a space since there was no immediate prospect of playing, given the uncertainties of the time. But I had nowhere to go and besides I had the feeling that, even if I'd found a bolt-hole, the pestilence would creep in after me. You recognize my philosophy: if you're going to catch it . . .

So far, so sound, however.

Perhaps it's the ratsbane.

Naturally I lost little time in going round to Lucy Milford's house in Thames Street, hoping to renew our amour, hoping for a little love and comfort. I was even prepared to talk a bit about the Oxford mysteries. But Lucy Milford, like so many of our fellow citizens, had departed. A neighbour informed me that she'd gone to an uncle in Bromsgrove – or was it a cousin in Middlesex? I'd thought it was the other way about as far as those uncles and cousins and places were concerned, but my memory may have been at fault. I was glad that Lucy was out of harm's way, though. Quite glad, even if I would have been pleased to see her still in town.

I heard that Will Kemp the clown was clinging to life in Dow-gate even while so many of the younger and fitter were dying around him. Perhaps I should visit and tell him that I'd eventually read his *Nine Days' Wonder* under somewhat strange circumstances and that I'd gained from it a valuable hint concerning shoes. But of course I haven't gone to see him, and the next news I expect to hear will be of his death.

So that was that.

Except for a little chat I had with William Shakespeare by way of rounding things off.

I might have wanted to tell him that his friend Hugh Fern had not killed himself or even, in the coroner's charitable version, fallen accidentally on his knife. Rather Doctor Fern had been cunningly murdered by his wicked servant-apprentice, Andrew Pearman. I might have wanted to tell WS about the events in Oxford and the way in which I and my friends went about unmasking a horrid conspiracy involving the dissection of corpses and the robbing of the dead.

But I could say nothing. Jack and Abel and I had come to an agreement, almost without using words, to keep quiet about what had occurred in the little house in Shoe Lane. And if we kept quiet about that, then we had to keep quiet about everything else. What would be the point of bringing the story into the open anyway? Justice – justice of the roughest, readiest kind – had been done, or mostly done.

So I said nothing of all this but instead asked the playwright if he had heard recently how matters stood in the city of Oxford.

"They stand well enough, Nick, all things considered. Unlike this place, the plague seems to be levelling off in Oxford, as I hear in a letter from my friend Davenant."

"From Mistress Jane Davenant?"

"Why no, from her husband John. He subscribes greetings and good wishes to the members of the Company."

"I thought he had no great love for plays."

"Why should you think so?"

"Oh, only the things he said. The looks he gave."

"Don't believe all you see and hear."

(So we were back to that again. Sensing that WS didn't wish to say more about the Davenants, I switched subjects.)

"Do you believe you can truly know another person?" I said.

"Certainly, in their outward manifestations."

"But inwardly?"

"We hardly know ourselves, Nick. How can we know another? Why do you ask?"

"A little time ago I thought to take note of some – features – of someone else's life. With a view to writing about this person."

Shakespeare didn't ask to whom I was referring (perhaps he guessed) but said, "You have made progress?"

"No progress at all," I said. "I have abandoned the project. I can get no agreement about even a couple of simple stories."

"Then make it up," said WS promptly.

"What about accuracy? What about posterity?"

"Oh, a posterior for posterity," said the playwright. "Let them sort it out after we are all dead."

"And what will happen to us before we die, Will? Under the new dispensation, the new King."

The King. How strange it was to be uttering those two simple words!

"The King has not yet reached London. Until he arrives, who can tell? Be content, Nick. I expect we shall be all right. Players are like corks. Lightweight perhaps but almost unsinkable."

"And sometimes bottling up good stuff."

"Why yes," said WS, smiling with mild indulgence at my comment. Then more seriously, "We can't tell the future, we cannot predict the ending."

"Except when it comes to writing plays. There we already know the finish," I said, thinking of that alternative conclusion to *Romeo and Juliet*, the unwritten one where the hero survives to go off and marry the fair Rosaline.

"But even in plays it's not so straightforward, let me tell you."

"Yes?" I said, all ears.

"Endings now," said William Shakespeare, "endings can be the very devil."

I'm very grateful to Bruna Gushurst-Moore, friend and herbal practitioner, for help and advice on herbs, preparations and poisons, as they might have been applied in the Shakespearean period of *Mask of Night*. It's a wide topic. Poison was a relatively more common method of murder than it is now. The details are mostly accurate (including the poison titles or folk-names given to each section) . . . but the uses to which the poisons are put are entirely my own.

PCG